Scion of Ikshvaku

Amish is a 1974-born, IIM (Kolkata)-educated, boring banker turned happy author. The success of his debut book, *The Immortals of Meluha* (Book 1 of the Shiva Trilogy), encouraged him to give up a fourteen-year-old career in financial services to focus on writing. He is passionate about history, mythology and philosophy, finding beauty and meaning in all world religions. Amish's books have sold more than 4 million copies and have been translated into over 19 languages.

Amish lives in Mumbai with his wife Preeti and son Neel.

www.authoramish.com
www.facebook.com/authoramish
www.twitter.com/authoramish

Shiva Trilogy

The Immortals of Meluha (Book 1 of the Shiva Trilogy)

1900 BC. The inhabitants of that period know the land of Meluha as a near perfect empire created many centuries earlier by Lord Ram, one of the greatest monarchs that ever lived. Now their primary river Saraswati is drying, and they face terrorist attacks from their enemies from the east.
Will their legendary hero, the Neelkanth, emerge to destroy evil?

The Secret of the Nagas (Book 2 of the Shiva Trilogy)

The sinister Naga warrior has killed Brahaspati and now stalks Sati. Shiva, the prophesied destroyer of evil, will not rest till he finds his demonic adversary. Fierce battles will be fought and unbelievable secrets revealed in this second book of the Shiva Trilogy.

The Oath of the Vayuputras (Book 3 of the Shiva Trilogy)

Shiva is gathering his forces. He reaches the Naga capital, Panchavati, and Evil is finally revealed. The Neelkanth prepares for a holy war against his true enemy. Will he succeed? Discover the answer to these mysteries in this concluding part of the bestselling Shiva Trilogy.

Ram Chandra Series

Sita—Warrior of Mithila (Book 2 of the Series)

3400 BCE. India
An abandoned baby is found in a field. Protected by a vulture from a pack of murderous wolves. She is adopted by the ruler of Mithila, a powerless kingdom, ignored by all. Nobody believes this child will amount to much. But they are wrong.
For she is no ordinary girl. She is Sita.
Continue the epic journey with the second book of the Ram Chandra Series: A thrilling adventure that chronicles the rise of an adopted child, who became the prime minister. And then, a Goddess.

'I wish many more would be inspired by Amish Tripathi …'
*– **Amitabh Bachchan***
(Actor & Living Legend)

'Amish is India's first literary popstar.'
*– **Shekhar Kapur***
(Award-Winning Film Director)

'Amish's books, archetypal and stirring, unfold the deepest recesses of the soul as well as our collective consciousness.'
*– **Deepak Chopra***
(Spiritual Guru & Author)

'Amish has a fine eye for detail and a compelling narrative style.'
*– **Dr. Shashi Tharoor***
(Member of Parliament & Author)

'{Amish is} one of the most original thinkers of his generation.'
*– **Arnab Goswami***
(Senior Journalist & MD, Republic TV)

'{Amish is} a deeply thoughtful mind with an unusual, original, and fascinating view of the past.'

– *Shekhar Gupta*
(Senior Journalist & Columnist)

'To understand the New India, you need to read Amish.'

– *Swapan Dasgupta*
(Member of Parliament & Senior Journalist)

'One of India's best storytellers.'

– *Vir Sanghvi*
(Senior Journalist & Columnist)

'Through all of Amish's books flows a current of liberal progressive ideology: about gender, about caste, about discrimination of any kind... He is the only Indian bestselling writer with true philosophical depth – his books are all backed by tremendous research and deep thought.'

– *Sandipan Deb*
(Senior Journalist & Editorial Director, Swarajya Magazine)

'Amish's influence goes beyond his books, his books go beyond literature, his literature is steeped in philosophy, which is anchored in *bhakti*, which powers his love for India.'

– *Gautam Chikermane*
(Senior Journalist & Author)

'Amish is a literary phenomenon.'

– *Anil Dharker*
(Senior Journalist & Author)

Scion of Ikshvaku

Book 1
of the
Ram Chandra Series

Amish

www.authoramish.com

westland publications ltd

61, II Floor, Silverline Building, Alapakkam Main Road, Maduravoyal, Chennai 600095

93, I Floor, Sham Lal Road, Daryaganj, New Delhi 110002

www. westlandbooks.in

Published by westland ltd 2015

Amish Tripathi asserts the moral right to be identified as the author of this work.

This is a work of fiction. Names, characters, places and incidents are either the product of the author's imagination or are used fictitiously and any resemblance to any actual person living or dead, events and locales is entirely coincidental.

ISBN: 978-93-85152-14-6

Cover Design by Think WhyNot

Inside book formatting and typesetting by PrePSol Enterprises Pvt. Ltd.

www.authoramish.com

To my father, Vinay Kumar Tripathi,
and my mother, Usha Tripathi

Khalil Gibran said that parents are like a bow,
And children like arrows.
The more the bow bends and stretches, the farther the arrow flies.
I fly, not because I am special, but because they stretched for me.

Om Namah Shivāya
The universe bows to Lord Shiva.
I bow to Lord Shiva.

Rāmarājyavāsī tvam, procchrayasva te śiram
Nyāyārtham yudhyasva, sarveṣu samam cara
Paripālaya durbalam, viddhi dharmam varam
Procchrayasva te śiram,
Rāmarājyavāsī tvam.

You live in Ram's kingdom, hold your head high.
Fight for justice. Treat all as equal.
Protect the weak. Know that dharma is above all.
Hold your head high,
You live in the kingdom of Ram.

List of Characters and Important Tribes
(In Alphabetical Order)

Arishtanemi: Military chief of the Malayaputras; right-hand man of Vishwamitra

Ashwapati: King of the north-western kingdom of Kekaya; a loyal ally of Dashrath; father of Kaikeyi

Bharat: Ram's half-brother; son of Dashrath and Kaikeyi

Dashrath: The Chakravarti king of Kosala and emperor of Sapt Sindhu; husband of Kaushalya, Kaikeyi and Sumitra; father of Ram, Bharat, Lakshman, and Shatrughan

Janak: King of Mithila; father of Sita and Urmila

Jatayu: A captain of the Malayaputra tribe; a Naga friend of Sita and Ram

Kaikeyi: Daughter of King Ashwapati of Kekaya; second and the favourite wife of Dashrath; mother of Bharat

Kaushalya: Daughter of King Bhanuman of South Kosala and his wife Maheshwari; the eldest queen of Dashrath; mother of Ram

Kubaer: Trader and ruler of Lanka before Raavan

Kumbhakarna: Raavan's brother; he is also a Naga (a human being born with deformities)

Kushadhwaj: King of Sankashya; younger brother of Janak

Lakshman: One of the twin sons of Dashrath; born to Sumitra; faithful to Ram; later married to Urmila

Malayaputras: The tribe left behind by Lord Parshu Ram, the sixth Vishnu

Manthara: The richest merchant of Sapt Sindhu; an ally of Kaikeyi

Mrigasya: General of Dashrath's army; one of the nobles of Ayodhya

Nagas: A feared race of human beings born with deformities

Nilanjana: Lady doctor attending to members of the royal family of Ayodhya, she hails from South Kosala

Raavan: King of Lanka; brother of Vibhishan, Shurpanakha and Kumbhakarna

Ram: Eldest of four brothers, son of Emperor Dashrath of Ayodhya (the capital city of Kosala kingdom) and his eldest wife Kaushalya; later married to Sita

Roshni: Daughter of Manthara; a committed doctor and *rakhi*-sister to the four sons of Dashrath

Samichi: Police and protocol chief of Mithila

Shatrughan: Twin brother of Lakshman; son of Dashrath and Sumitra

Shurpanakha: Half-sister of Raavan

Sita: Adopted daughter of King Janak of Mithila; also the prime minister of Mithila; later married to Ram

Sumitra: Daughter of the king of Kashi; the third wife of Dashrath; mother of the twins Lakshman and Shatrughan

Vashishta: Raj guru, the royal priest of Ayodhya; teacher of the four princes

Vayuputras: The tribe left behind by Lord Rudra, the previous Mahadev

Vibhishan: Half-brother of Raavan

Vishwamitra: Chief of the Malayaputras, the tribe left behind by Lord Parshu Ram, the sixth Vishnu; also temporary guru of Ram and Lakshman

Urmila: Younger sister of Sita; the blood-daughter of Janak; she is later married to Lakshman

Refer to inside back cover for map of India in 3400 BCE

Note on the Narrative Structure

Thank you for picking up this book and giving me the most important thing you can share: your time. The Ram Chandra Series, of which ***Ram – Scion of Ikshvaku*** is the first book, has an intricate narrative structure. This note is my attempt to explain it.

I have been inspired by a storytelling technique called hyperlink, which some call the multilinear narrative. In such a narrative, there are many characters; and a connection brings them all together. The three main characters in the Ram Chandra Series are Ram, Sita, and Raavan. Each character has life experiences which mould who they are and their stories converge with the kidnapping of Sita. And each has their own adventure and riveting back-story.

So, while the first book explores the tale of Ram, the second and third will offer a glimpse into the adventures of Sita and then Raavan respectively, before all three stories merge from the fourth book onwards into a single story.

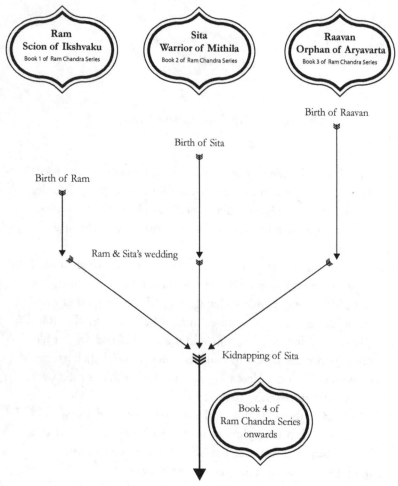

I knew it would be a complicated and time consuming affair, but I must confess, it was thoroughly exciting. I hope this will be as rewarding and thrilling an experience for you as it was for me. Understanding Ram, Sita and Raavan as characters helped me inhabit their worlds and explore the maze of plots and stories that make this epic come alive. I feel truly blessed for this.

There are clues in this book (***Ram – Scion of Ikshvaku***) which will tie up with the stories in the second and third books. Needless to say, there are surprises and twists in store for you in all the books of the series!

I hope you like reading ***Ram – Scion of Ikshvaku***. Do tell me what you think of it, by sending me messages on my Facebook or Twitter accounts listed below.

Love,
Amish

www.facebook.com/authoramish
www.twitter.com/authoramish

Acknowledgements

I don't agree with everything that John Donne wrote, but he was right on one count: 'No man is an island'. I am lucky to be connected to many others who keep me from being 'rifted'. For creativity has no greater sustenance than the love and support of others. I'd like to acknowledge some of them.

Lord Shiva, my God, for blessing me with this life and all there is in it. Also, for bringing Lord Ram (who my grandfather, Pandit Babulal Tripathi, was a great devotee of) back into my life.

Neel, my son, my blessing, my pride, my joy. He gives me happiness by simply being who he is.

Preeti, my wife; Bhavna, my sister; Himanshu, my brother-in-law; Anish and Ashish, my brothers, for all their inputs to the story. My sister Bhavna deserves special mention for her dedication and the time she gave while advising me on the philosophies in the book. My wife Preeti deserves my eternal gratefulness, as always, for her brilliant marketing advice.

My family: Usha, Vinay, Meeta, Donetta, Shernaz, Smita, Anuj, Ruta. For their consistent faith and love.

Sharvani, my editor. We have a strange relationship. Fun and laughter in normal times; we fight with each other passionately when we edit. It's a match made in heaven!

Gautam, Krishnakumar, Preeti, Deepthi, Satish, Varsha, Jayanthi, Vipin, Senthil, Shatrughan, Sarita, Avani, Sanyog,

Naveen, Jaisankar, Gururaj, Sateesh and the fantastic team at Westland, my publishers. They have been partners from the beginning.

Anuj, my agent. Big man with an even bigger heart! The best friend an author could have.

Sangram, Shalini, Parag, Shaista, Rekha, Hrishikesh, Richa, Prasad and the team at Think WhyNot, the advertising agency for the book. They made the cover, which I think is fantastic! They also made most of the marketing material for the book, including the trailer. They are among the best ad agencies in the country.

Hemal, Neha and the Oktobuzz team, the social media agency for the book. Hardworking, super smart and intensely committed. They are an asset to any team.

Jaaved, Parthasarthy, Rohit and the rest of the production team of the trailer film. Brilliant guys. Trust me, the world will soon be their oyster.

Mohan, a friend, whose advice on communication matters is something I always treasure.

Vinod, Toral, Nimisha and the great team at Clea PR for the work that they did on the PR efforts for the book.

Mrunalini, a Sanskrit scholar, who works with me. My discussions with her are stimulating and enlightening. I learn a lot from her.

Nitin, Vishal, Avani and Mayuri for their hospitality in Nashik where I wrote parts of this book.

And last, but certainly not the least, you, the reader. Thank you from the depths of my being for the support you've given to the Shiva Trilogy. I hope I don't disappoint you with this book, the first in a new series. Har Har Mahadev!

Chapter 1

3400 BCE, somewhere near the Godavari River, India

Ram crouched low as he bent his tall, lean and muscular frame. He rested his weight on his right knee as he held the bow steady. The arrow was fixed in place, but he knew that the bowstring should not be pulled too early. He didn't want his muscles to tire out. He had to wait for the perfect moment. *It must be a clean strike.*

'It's moving, *Dada*,' whispered Lakshman to his *elder brother.*

Ram didn't reply. His eyes were fixed on the target. A light breeze played with the few strands of hair that had escaped the practical bun atop his head. His shaggy, unkempt beard and his white *dhoti* gently fluttered in the breeze. Ram corrected his angle as he factored in the strength and direction of the wind. He quietly cast his white *angvastram* aside to reveal a battle-scarred, dark-skinned torso. *The cloth should not interfere with the release of the arrow.*

The deer suddenly came to a standstill as it looked up; perhaps instinct had kicked in with some warning signals. Ram could hear its low snort as it stomped its feet uneasily. Within a few seconds it went back to chewing leaves as silence prevailed. The rest of the herd was a short distance away, hidden from view by the dense foliage of the forest.

'By the great Lord Parshu Ram, it ignored its instincts,' said Lakshman softly. 'Thank the Lord. We need some real food.'

'Quiet…'

Lakshman fell silent. Ram knew they needed this kill. Lakshman and he, accompanied by his wife Sita, had been on the run for the last thirty days. A few members of the *Malayaputra* tribe, the *sons of Malaya*, led by their captain, Jatayu, were also with them.

Jatayu had urged flight well before the inevitable retaliation came. The botched meeting with Shurpanakha and Vibhishan would certainly have consequences. They were, after all, the siblings of Raavan, the wrathful demon-king of Lanka. Raavan was sure to seek vengeance. Lankan royal blood had been shed.

Racing east through the *Dandakaranya*, the dense *forest of Dandak*, they had travelled a reasonable distance parallel to the Godavari. They were fairly reassured now that they wouldn't be easily spotted or tracked. Straying too far from the tributary rivers or other water bodies would mean losing out on the best chance of hunting animals. Ram and Lakshman were princes of Ayodhya, inheritors of the proud Kshatriya tradition of the *Raghukul*, the *descendants of Raghu*. They would not survive on a diet of herbs, fruit and leaves alone.

The deer remained stationary, lost in the pleasure of grazing on tender shoots. Ram knew this was the moment. He held the composite bow steady in his left hand as he pulled the string back with his right, till it almost touched his lips. His elbow was held high, almost perfectly parallel to the ground, exactly the way his guru, Maharishi Vashishta, had taught him.

The elbow is weak. Hold it high. Let the effort come from the back muscles. The back is strong.

Ram pulled the string a notch further and then released the arrow. The missile whizzed past the trees and slammed into the deer's neck. It collapsed immediately, unable to even utter a bleat as blood flooded its lungs. Despite his muscular bulk, Lakshman rushed forward stealthily. Even as he moved, he pulled out a knife from the horizontal scabbard tied to the small of his back. Within moments he reached the deer and quickly plunged the blade deep in between the animal's ribs, right through to its heart.

'Forgive me for killing you, O noble beast,' he whispered the ancient apology that all hunters offered, as he gently touched the deer's head. 'May your soul find purpose again, while your body sustains my soul.'

Ram caught up with Lakshman as his brother pulled the arrow out, wiped it clean and returned it to its rightful owner. 'Still usable,' he murmured.

Ram slipped the arrow back into his quiver as he looked up at the sky. Birds chirped playfully and the deer's own herd displayed no alarm. They had not sensed the killing of one of their own. Ram whispered a short prayer to Lord Rudra, thanking him for what had been a perfect hunt. The last thing they needed was for their position to be given away.

—— 人 ● ☼ ——

Ram and Lakshman made their way through the dense jungle. Ram walked in front, carrying one end of a long staff on his shoulder, while Lakshman walked behind, holding up the other end. The deer's carcass dangled in the middle, its feet having been secured to the staff with a sturdy rope.

'Aah, a decent meal after so many days,' said Lakshman.

Ram's face broke into a hint of a smile, but he remained silent.

'We can't cook this properly though, right *Dada*?'

'No, we can't. The continuous line of smoke will give our position away.'

'Do we really need to be so careful? There have been no attacks. Maybe they have lost track of us. We haven't encountered any assassins, have we? How would they know where we are? The forests of Dandak are impenetrable.'

'Maybe you're right, but I'm not taking any chances. I'd rather be safe.'

Lakshman held his peace even as his shoulders drooped.

'It's better than eating leaves and herbs,' said Ram, without turning to look at his brother.

'That it certainly is,' agreed Lakshman.

The brothers walked on in silence.

'There is some conspiracy afoot, *Dada*. I'm unable to pin down what it is. But there's something going on. Perhaps Bharat *Dada*…'

'Lakshman!' rebuked Ram sternly.

Bharat was the second oldest after Ram, and had been anointed crown prince of Ayodhya by their father Dashrath following Ram's banishment. The youngest, Shatrughan and Lakshman, were twins separated by differing loyalties. While Shatrughan remained in Ayodhya with Bharat, Lakshman unhesitatingly chose a life of hardship with Ram. The impulsive Lakshman was sceptical of Ram's blind trust in Bharat. He considered it his duty to warn his excessively ethical eldest brother about what appeared to him as Bharat's underhand dealings.

'I know you don't like hearing this, *Dada*,' Lakshman persisted. 'But I'm certain that he's hatched a plot against—'

'We'll get to the bottom of it,' reassured Ram, interrupting Lakshman. 'But we first need allies. Jatayu is right. We need to find the local Malayaputra camp. At least they can be trusted to help us.'

'I don't know whom to trust anymore, *Dada*. Maybe the vulture-man is helping our enemies.'

Jatayu was a Naga, a class of people born with deformities. Ram had come around to trusting Jatayu despite the fact that the Nagas were a hated, feared and ostracised people in the *Sapt Sindhu, the Land of the Seven Rivers,* which lay north of the Narmada River.

Jatayu, like all Nagas, had been born with inevitable deformities. He had a hard and bony mouth that extended out of his face in a beak-like protrusion. His head was bare, but his face was covered with fine, downy hair. Although he was human, his appearance was like that of a vulture.

'Sita trusts Jatayu,' said Ram, as though that explained it all. 'I trust Jatayu. And so will you.'

Lakshman fell silent. And the brothers walked on.

'But why do you think it's irrational to think Bharat *Dada* could—'

'Shhh,' said Ram, holding his hand up to silence Lakshman. 'Listen.'

Lakshman strained his ears. A chill ran down his spine. Ram turned towards Lakshman with terror writ large on his face. They had both heard it. *A forceful scream!* It was Sita. The distance made faint her frantic struggle. But it was clearly Sita. She was calling out to her husband.

Ram and Lakshman dropped the deer and dashed forward desperately. They were still some distance away from their temporary camp.

Sita's voice could be heard above the din of the disturbed birds.

'... Raaam!'

They were close enough now to hear the sounds of battle as metal clashed with metal.

Ram screamed as he ran frantically through the forest. 'Sitaaaa!'

Lakshman drew his sword, ready for battle.

'... Raaaam!'

'Leave her alone!' shouted Ram, cutting through the dense foliage, racing ahead.

'... Raaam!'

Ram gripped his bow tight. They were just a few minutes from their camp. 'Sitaaa!'

'... Raa...'

Sita's voice stopped mid-syllable. Trying not to imagine the worst, Ram kept running, his heart pounding desperately, his mind clouded with worry.

They heard the loud whump, whump of rotor blades. It was a sound he clearly remembered from an earlier occasion. This was Raavan's legendary *Pushpak Vimaan*, his *flying vehicle*.

'Nooo!' screamed Ram, wrenching his bow forward as he ran. Tears were streaming down his face.

The brothers broke through to the clearing that was their temporary camp. It stood completely destroyed. There was blood everywhere.

'Sitaaa!'

Ram looked up and shot an arrow at the *Pushpak Vimaan,* which was rapidly ascending into the sky. It was a shot of impotent rage, for the flying vehicle was already soaring high above.

'Sitaaa!'

Lakshman frantically searched the camp. Bodies of dead soldiers were strewn all over. But there was no Sita.

'Pri… nce… Ram…'

Ram recognised that feeble voice. He rushed forward to find the bloodied and mutilated body of the Naga.

'Jatayu!'

The badly wounded Jatayu struggled to speak. 'He's…'

'What?'

'Raavan's… kidnapped… her.'

Ram looked up enraged at the speck moving rapidly away from them. He screamed in anger, 'SITAAAA!'

Chapter 2

Thirty-three years earlier, Port of Karachapa, Western Sea, India

'Lord Parshu Ram, be merciful,' whispered Dashrath, the forty-year-old king of Kosala, the overlord kingdom of the Sapt Sindhu.

The emperor of the Sapt Sindhu had marched right across his sprawling empire from Ayodhya, its capital, to finally arrive at the western coast. Some rebellious traders sorely needed a lesson in royal justice. The combative Dashrath had built on the powerful empire he had inherited from his father Aja. Rulers from various parts of India had either been deposed or made to pay tribute and accept his suzerainty, thus making Dashrath the *Chakravarti Samrat*, or the *Universal Emperor*.

'Yes, My Lord,' said Mrigasya, the general of Dashrath's army. 'This is not the only village that has been laid to waste. The enemy has destroyed all the villages in a fifty-kilometre radius from where we stand. The wells have been poisoned with the carcasses of dead animals. Crops have been burned down ruthlessly. The entire countryside has been ravaged.'

'Scorched earth policy…' said Ashwapati, the king of Kekaya, a loyal ally of Dashrath, and the father of the emperor's second and favourite wife, Kaikeyi.

'Yes,' said another king. 'We cannot feed our army of five hundred thousand soldiers here. Our supply lines are already stretched.'

'How the hell did that barbarian trader Kubaer acquire the intellect for military strategy?' asked Dashrath.

Dashrath could scarcely conceal his Kshatriyan disdain for the trading class, the Vaishyas. For the Sapt Sindhu royalty, wealth was the conqueror's right when acquired as the spoils of war, but inappropriate when earned through mere profiteering. The Vaishyas' 'lack of class' invited scorn. They were subjected to heavy regulation and a draconian system of licences and controls. The children of the Sapt Sindhu aristocracy were encouraged to become warriors or intellectuals, not traders. Resultantly, the trading class in these kingdoms was depleted over the years. With not enough money pouring in from wars, the royal coffers quickly emptied.

Ever sensing an opportunity to profit, Kubaer, the trader king of the island of Lanka, offered his services and expertise to carry out trading activities for all the Sapt Sindhu kingdoms. The then king of Ayodhya, Aja, granted the monopoly to Kubaer in return for a huge annual compensation, which was then distributed to each subordinate kingdom within the Sapt Sindhu Empire. Ayodhya's power soared for it became the source of funds for other kingdoms within the empire. And yet, they could continue to hold on to their old contempt towards trade. Recently, however, Kubaer had unilaterally reduced the commissions that Dashrath rightfully believed were Ayodhya's due. This impertinence of a mere trader certainly deserved punishment. Dashrath directed his vassal kings to merge their troops with his own, and led them to Karachapa to remind Kubaer of his place in the power hierarchy.

'Apparently, My Lord,' said Mrigasya, 'it is not Kubaer who is calling the shots.'

'Then who is?' asked Dashrath.

'We do not know much about him. I have heard that he is no more than thirty years of age. He joined Kubaer some years ago as the head of his trading security force. Over time, he recruited more people and transformed the unit into a proper army. I believe he is the one who convinced Kubaer to rebel against us.'

'I'm not surprised,' said Ashwapati. 'I can't imagine that obese and indolent Kubaer having the nerve to challenge the power of the Sapt Sindhu!'

'Who is this man?' asked Dashrath. 'Where is he from?'

'We really don't know much about him, My Lord,' said Mrigasya.

'Do you at least know his name?'

'Yes, we do. His name is Raavan.'

—— 从 🐚 ☼ ——

Nilanjana, the royal physician, rushed down the hallway of the palace of Ayodhya. She had received an urgent summons late in the evening from the personal staff of Queen Kaushalya, the first wife of King Dashrath.

The gentle and restrained Kaushalya, the daughter of the king of South Kosala, had been married to Dashrath for more than fifteen years now. Her inability to provide the emperor with an heir had been a source of constant dismay to her. Frustrated by the absence of a successor, Dashrath had finally married Kaikeyi, the tall, fair and statuesque princess of the powerful western Indian kingdom of Kekaya, which was ruled by his close ally Ashwapati. That too was of no avail. He finally married Sumitra, the steely but unobtrusive princess of the holy city of Kashi, the city that housed the spirit of Lord Rudra and was famous for non-violence. Even so, the great Emperor Dashrath remained without an heir.

No wonder then that when Kaushalya finally became pregnant, it was an occasion marked by both joy and trepidation. The queen was understandably desperate to ensure that the child was delivered safely. Her entire staff, most of whom were loyal retainers from her father's household, understood the political implications of the birth of an heir. Abundant caution was the norm. This was not the first time that Nilanjana had been summoned, many a times over frivolous reasons and false alarms. However, since the doctor too was from Queen Kaushalya's parental home, her loyalty forbade any overt signs of irritability.

This time, though, it appeared to be the real thing. The queen had gone into labour.

Even as she ran, Nilanjana's lips fervently appealed to Lord Parshu Ram for a smooth delivery, and yes, a male child.

— 𝍐 ▮ ☀ —

'I order you to restore our commission to the very fair nine-tenths of your profits and, in return, I assure you I will let you live,' growled Dashrath.

In keeping with the rules of engagement, Dashrath had sent a messenger in advance to Kubaer for a negotiated settlement as a last resort. The adversaries had decided to meet in person on neutral ground. The chosen site was a beach midway between Dashrath's military camp and the Karachapa fort. Dashrath was accompanied by Ashwapati, Mrigasya, and a bodyguard platoon of twenty soldiers.

Kubaer had arrived along with his army's general, Raavan, and twenty bodyguards.

The Sapt Sindhu warriors could scarcely conceal their contempt as the obese Kubaer had waddled laboriously into the tent. A round, cherubic face with thinning hair was balanced on the humongous body of the seventy-year-old fabulously wealthy trader from Lanka. His smooth complexion and fair skin belied his age. He wore a bright green *dhoti* and pink *angvastram* and was bedecked with extravagant jewellery. A life of excess which, when added to his girth and effeminate manner, summed up in the mind of Dashrath what Kubaer was: the classic effete Vaishya.

Dashrath restrained his thoughts as they struggled to escape through words. *Does this ridiculous peacock actually think he can take me on?!*

'Your Highness…' said Kubaer nervously, 'I think it might be a little difficult to keep the commissions fixed at that level. Our costs have gone up and the trading margins are not what they—'

'Don't try your disgusting negotiating tactics with me!' barked Dashrath as he banged his hand on the table for effect. 'I am not a trader! I am an emperor! Civilised people understand the difference.'

It had not escaped Dashrath's notice that Kubaer seemed ill at ease. Perhaps the trader had not intended for events to reach this stage. The massive troop movement to Karachapa had evidently unnerved him. Dashrath presumed that a few harsh words would effectively dissuade Kubaer from persisting with his foolhardy quest. After which, to be fair, he had decided that he would let Kubaer keep an extra two percent. Dashrath understood that, sometimes, a little magnanimity quelled discontent.

Dashrath leaned forward as he lowered his voice to a menacing whisper. 'I can be merciful. I can forgive mistakes. But you really need to stop this nonsense and do as I say.'

With a nervous gulp, Kubaer glanced at the impassive Raavan who sat to his right. Even sitting, Raavan's great height and rippling musculature was intimidating. His battle-worn, swarthy skin was pock-marked, probably by a childhood disease. A thick beard valiantly attempted to cover his ugly marks while a handlebar moustache set off his menacing features. His attire was unremarkable though, consisting of a white *dhoti* and a cream *angvastram*. His headgear was singular, with two threatening six-inch-long horns reaching out from the top on either side.

Kubaer helplessly turned back to Dashrath as his general remained deathly still. 'But Your Highness, we are facing many problems and our invested capital is—'

'You are trying my patience now, Kubaer!' growled Dashrath as he ignored Raavan and focused his attention on the chief trader. 'You are irritating the emperor of the Sapt Sindhu!'

'But My Lord…'

'Look, if you do not continue to pay our rightful commissions, believe me you will all be dead by this time tomorrow. I will first defeat your miserable army, then travel all the way to that cursed island of yours and burn your city to the ground.'

'But there are problems with our ships and labour costs have—'

'I don't care about your problems!' shouted Dashrath, his legendary temper at boiling point now.

'You will, after tomorrow,' said Raavan softly.

Dashrath swung sharply towards Raavan, riled that Kubaer's deputy had had the audacity to interrupt the conversation.

'How dare you speak out of—'

'How dare *you*, Dashrath?' asked Raavan, an octave higher this time.

Dashrath, Ashwapati and Mrigasya sat in stunned silence, shocked that the mere head of a protection force had had the temerity to address the emperor of the Sapt Sindhu by his name.

'How dare you imagine that you can even come close to defeating an army that I lead?' asked Raavan with an eerie sense of calm.

Dashrath stood up angrily and his chair went flying back with a loud clutter. He thrust his finger in Raavan's direction. 'I'll be looking for you on the battlefield tomorrow, you upstart!'

Slowly and menacingly, Raavan rose from his chair, all the while his closed right fist covering a pendant that hung from a gold chain around his neck. As Raavan's fist unclenched, Dashrath was horrified by what he saw. The pendant was actually the bones of two human fingers — the phalanges of which were carefully fastened with gold links. Clenching this macabre souvenir again, Raavan appeared to derive enormous power from it.

Dashrath stared in disbelief. He had heard of demons that drank blood and wine from the skulls of their enemies and even kept their body parts as trophies. But here was a warrior who wore the relics of his enemy! *Who is this monster?*

'I assure you, I'll be waiting,' said Raavan, with a hint of wry humour lacing his voice, as he watched Dashrath gape at him with horror. 'I look forward to drinking your blood.'

Raavan turned around and strode out of the tent. Kubaer hurriedly wobbled out behind him, followed by the Lankan bodyguards.

Dashrath's anger bubbled over. 'Tomorrow we annihilate these scum. But no one will touch that man,' he growled pointing towards the retreating figure of Raavan. 'He will be killed by me! Only me!'

Dashrath was bristling with fury even as the day drew to a close. 'I will personally chop up his body and throw it to the dogs!' he shouted.

Kaikeyi sat impassively as her seething husband paced up and down the royal tent of the Ayodhya camp. She always accompanied him on his military campaigns.

'How dare he speak to me like that?'

Kaikeyi scrutinised Dashrath languidly. He was tall, dark and handsome, the quintessential Kshatriya. A well-manicured moustache only added to his attractiveness. Though muscular and strong, age had begun to take its toll on his well-built physique. Stray streaks of white in his hair were accompanied by a faint hint of a sag in the muscles. Even the Somras, the mysterious anti-ageing drink reserved for the royals by their sages, had not been able to adequately counter a lifetime of ceaseless warring and hard drinking.

'I am the emperor of the Sapt Sindhu!' shouted Dashrath, striking his chest with unconcealed rage. 'How dare he?'

Even though alone with her husband, Kaikeyi maintained the demure demeanour normally reserved for her public interactions with him. She had never seen him so angry.

'My love,' said Kaikeyi, 'save the anger for tomorrow. Have your dinner. You will need your strength for the battle that lies ahead.'

'Does that outcaste mercenary even have a clue as to who he has challenged? I have never lost a battle in my life!' Dashrath continued as though Kaikeyi hadn't spoken.

'And you will win tomorrow as well.'

Dashrath turned towards Kaikeyi. 'Yes, I will win tomorrow. Then I will cut him to pieces and feed his corpse to mongrel dogs and gutter pigs!'

'Of course you will, my love. You have determined that already.'

Dashrath snorted angrily and turned around, ready to storm out of the tent. But Kaikeyi could no longer contain herself.

'Dashrath!' she said harshly.

Dashrath stopped in his tracks. His favourite wife used that tone with him only when necessary. Kaikeyi walked up to him, held his hand and led him to the dinner table. She held his shoulders and roughly pushed him into the chair. Then she tore a piece of the *roti*, scooped up some vegetables and meat with it, and offered it to him. 'You cannot defeat that demon tomorrow if you don't eat and sleep tonight,' she barely whispered.

Dashrath opened his mouth. Kaikeyi stuffed the morsel of food into it.

Chapter 3

Lying in her bed, Queen Kaushalya of Ayodhya appeared frail and worn. All of forty, her prematurely grey hair seemed incongruous against her dark, still gleaming skin. Though short in stature, she'd once been strong. In a culture that valued women for their ability to produce heirs, being childless had broken her spirit. Despite being the senior-most wife, King Dashrath acknowledged her only on ceremonial occasions. At most other times, she was relegated to obscurity, a fact that ate away at her. All she desired was a fraction of the time and attention that Dashrath lavished on his favourite wife, Kaikeyi.

She was keenly aware that giving birth to an heir, hopefully Dashrath's first son, had the potential to dramatically alter her status. No wonder then that today her spirit was all fired up, even though her body was weak. She had been in labour for more than sixteen hours but she barely felt the pain. She soldiered on determinedly, refusing the doctor her permission to perform a surgical procedure to extract her baby from her womb.

'My son will be born naturally,' announced Kaushalya firmly.

A natural birth was considered more auspicious. She had no intention of putting the future prospects of her child at risk.

'He will be king one day,' continued Kaushalya. 'He will be born with good fortune.'

Nilanjana sighed. She wasn't even sure if the child would be a boy. But she wouldn't risk the merest flagging of her mistress' spirits. She administered some herbal pain relievers to the queen and bided her time. Ideally, the doctor wanted the birth to take place before midday. The royal astrologer had warned her that if the child was born later, he would suffer great hardships throughout his life. On the other hand, if the child was born before the sun reached its zenith, he would be remembered as one of the greatest among men and would be celebrated for millennia.

Nilanjana cast a quick glance at the *prahar* lamp, which measured time in six-hour intervals. The sun had already risen and it was the third hour of the second *prahar*. In another three hours it would be midday. Nilanjana had decided to wait till a half hour before noon and, if the baby was still not born, she would go ahead with the surgery.

Kaushalya was stricken with another bout of dilatory pain. She pursed her lips together and began chanting in her mind the name she had chosen for her child. This gave her strength for it wasn't an ordinary name. The name she had picked was that of the sixth Vishnu.

'Vishnu' was a title given to the greatest of leaders who were remembered as the Propagators of Good. The sixth man to have achieved this title was Lord Parshu Ram. That is how he was remembered by the common folk. *Parshu* means *axe*, and the word had been added to the name of the sixth Vishnu because the mighty battle axe had been his favourite weapon. His birth name was Ram. That was the name that reverberated in Kaushalya's mind.

Ram… Ram… Ram… Ram…

The fourth hour of the second *prahar* saw Dashrath battle-ready. He had hardly slept the previous night, his self-righteous rage having refused to dissipate. He had never lost a battle in his life, but this time it was not mere victory that he sought. Redemption now lay in his vanquishing that mercenary trader and squeezing the life out of him.

The Ayodhyan emperor had arranged his army in a *suchi vyuha*, the *needle formation*. This was because Kubaer's hordes had planted dense thorny bushes all around the Karachapa fort. It was almost impossible to charge from the landward side of the port city. Dashrath's army could have cleared the bushes and created a path to charge the fort, but that would have taken weeks. Kubaer's army had scorched the earth around Karachapa, and the absence of local food and water ensured that Dashrath's army did not possess the luxury of time. They had to attack before they ran out of rations.

More importantly, Dashrath was too angry to be patient. Therefore he had decided to launch his attack from the only strip of open land that had access to the fort of Karachapa: its beach.

The beach was broad by usual standards, but not enough for a large army. Hence, Dashrath's tactical decision to form a *suchi vyuha*. The best troops, along with the emperor, would man the front of the formation, while the rest of the army would fall in a long column behind. They intended a rolling charge, where the first lines would strike the Lankan ranks, and after twenty minutes of battle slip back, allowing the next line of warriors to charge in. It would be an unrelenting surge of brave Sapt Sindhu soldiers aiming to scatter and decimate the enemy troops of Kubaer.

Ashwapati nudged his horse a few steps ahead and halted next to Dashrath.

'Your Highness,' he said, 'are you sure about this tactic?'

'Don't tell me you're having second thoughts, King Ashwapati!' remarked Dashrath, surprised by the words of caution from his normally aggressive father-in-law. He had been a worthy ally in most of Dashrath's conquering expeditions throughout the realms of India.

'I was just thinking we will not be using our numerical superiority in full strength. The bulk of our soldiers will be behind the ones charging upfront. They will not be fighting at the same time. Is that wise?'

'It is the only way, believe me,' asserted Dashrath confidently. 'Even if our first charge is unsuccessful, the soldiers at the back will keep coming in waves. We can sustain our onslaught on Kubaer's eunuch forces till they all die to the last man. I do not see it coming to that though. I will annihilate them with our first charge!'

Ashwapati looked to his left where Kubaer's ships lay at anchor more than two kilometres into the sea. There was something strange about their structure. The front section, the bow, was unusually broad. 'What role will those ships play in the battle?'

'Nothing!' dismissed Dashrath, smiling fondly at his father-in-law; while Dashrath had had experience of a few naval battles, Ashwapati hadn't. 'Those fools haven't even lowered their row-boats from the vessels. Even if they have a reserve force on those ships, they cannot be brought into battle quickly enough. It will take them at least a few hours to lower their row-boats, load their soldiers, and then ferry them to the beach to join the battle. By then, we would've wiped out the soldiers who are inside the fort.'

'Outside the fort,' corrected Ashwapati, pointing towards Karachapa.

Raavan had, strangely, abandoned the immense advantage of being safe within the walls of the well-designed fort. Instead of lining them up along the ramparts, he had chosen to arrange his army of probably fifty thousand soldiers in a standard formation *outside* the city, on the beach.

'It is the strangest tactic I have ever seen,' said Ashwapati warily. 'Why is he giving up his strategic advantage? With the fort walls being right behind his army, he does not even have room to retreat. Why has Raavan done this?'

Dashrath sniggered. 'Because he is a reactionary idiot. He wants to prove a point to me. Well, I will make the final point when I dig my sword into his heart.'

Ashwapati turned his head towards the fort walls again as he surveyed Raavan's soldiers. Even from this distance he could see Raavan, wearing his hideous horned helmet, leading his troops from the front.

Ashwapati cast a look at his own army. The soldiers were roaring loudly, hurling obscenities at their enemy, as warriors are wont to do before the commencement of war. He turned his gaze to Raavan's army once again. In sharp contrast, they emanated no sound. There was no movement either. They stood quietly in rigid formation, a brilliant tribute to soldierly discipline.

A shiver ran down Ashwapati's spine.

He couldn't get it out of his mind that those soldiers were bait that Dashrath had chosen to take.

If you are a fish charging at bait, then it usually doesn't end well.

Ashwapati turned towards Dashrath to voice his fears, but the emperor of the Sapt Sindhu had already ridden away.

—— 𝝽 ◉ ☼ ——

Dashrath was on horseback at the head of his troops. He ran his eyes over his men confidently. They were a rowdy, raucous bunch with swords drawn, eager for battle. The horses, too, seemed to have succumbed to the excitement of the moment, for the soldiers were pulling hard at their reins, holding them in check. Dashrath and his army could almost smell the blood that would soon be shed; the magnificent killings! They believed, as usual, that the Goddess of Victory was poised to bless them. *Let the war drums roll!*

Dashrath squinted his eyes as he observed the Lankans and their commander Raavan up ahead in the distance. Molten rage was coursing through him. He drew his sword and held it aloft, and then bellowed the unmistakable war cry of his kingdom, Kosala and its capital city, Ayodhya. *'Ayodhyatah Vijetaarah!'*

The conquerors from the unconquerable city!

Not all in his army were citizens of Ayodhya, and yet they were proud to fight under the great Kosala banner. They echoed the war cry, *'Ayodhyatah Vijetaarah!'*

Dashrath roared as he brought his sword down and spurred his horse. 'Kill them all! No mercy!'

'No mercy!' shouted the riders of the first charge, kicking their horses and taking off behind their fearless lord.

But then it all began to unravel.

Dashrath and his finest warriors comprised the sturdy tip of the Sapt Sindhu needle formation. As they charged down the beach towards the Lankans, Raavan's troops remained stationary. When the enemy cavalry was just a few hundred metres away, Raavan unexpectedly turned his horse around and retreated from the front lines, even as his soldiers held firm. This further infuriated Dashrath. He screamed loudly as he kicked his horse to gather speed, intending to mow down the Lankan front line and quickly reach Raavan.

This was exactly what Raavan had envisaged. The Lankan front line roared stridently as the soldiers suddenly dropped their swords, bent, and picked up unnaturally long spears, almost twenty feet in length, that had been hitherto lying at their feet. Made of wood and metal, the spears were so heavy that it took two soldiers to pick each one up. The soldiers pointed these spears, tipped with sharp copper heads, directly at Dashrath's oncoming cavalry. The pointed heads tore into the unprepared horses and their mounted soldiers. Even as the charge of Dashrath's cavalry was halted in its tracks and the mounted soldiers thrown forward as their horses suddenly collapsed under them, Lankan archers emerged, high on the walls of the Karachapa fort. They shot a continuous stream of arrows in a long arc from the fort ramparts, right into the dense formation of Dashrath's troops at the back, ripping through the Sapt Sindhu lines.

Many of Dashrath's warriors, who had been flung off their impaled horses, broke into a fierce hand-to-hand battle with their enemies. Their liege Dashrath led the way as he swung his sword ferociously, killing all who dared to come in his path. But the Ayodhyan king was alive to the devastation being wrought upon his fellow soldiers who rapidly fell under the barrage of Lankan arrows and superbly-trained swordsmen. Dashrath ordered his flag bearer, who was beside him, to raise the flag as a signal for the Sapt Sindhu soldiers at the back to also break into a charge immediately and support the first line.

But things continued to deteriorate.

The troops on the Lankan ships in the distance abruptly weighed anchor, extended the oars, and began to row rapidly to the beach, with their sails up at full mast to help them catch the wind. Within moments, arrows were being fired from the ships into the densely packed forces under Dashrath's command. The Lankan archers on the ships tore through the ranks of the Sapt Sindhus.

No brigadier in Dashrath's army had factored in the possibility of the enemy ships beaching; it would have cracked their hulls. Unbeknownst to them, though, these were amphibious crafts, built by Kubaer's ingenious ship-designers, with specially constructed hulls that could absorb the shock of landing. Even as these landing crafts stormed onto the beach with tremendous force, the broad bows of the hulls rolled out from the top. These were no ordinary bows of a standard hull. They were attached to the bottom of the hull by huge hinges which simply rolled out onto the sand like a landing ramp. This opened a gangway straight onto the beach, disgorging cavalrymen of the Lankan army mounted on disproportionately large horses imported from the west. The cavalry rode out of the ships and straight onto the beach, mercilessly slicing into all who lay in their path.

Even as he watched the destruction unleashed upon his forces near the fort, Dashrath's instincts warned him that something terrible was ensuing at the rear guard. As the emperor stretched to gaze beyond the sea of frenzied battling humanity, he detected a quick movement to his left and raised his shield in time to block a vicious blow from a Lankan soldier. Screaming ferociously, the king of Ayodhya brutally swung low at his attacker, his sword slicing through a chink in the armour. The Lankan fell back as his abdomen ripped open with a massive spurt of blood, accompanied by slick pink intestines that tumbled out in a rush. Dashrath knew no mercy as he turned away from the poor sod even as he bled to his miserable end.

'NO!' he yelled. What he saw was enough to break his mighty warrior's heart.

Caught between the vicious pincer attack of the brutal Lankan archers and infantry at the Karachapa walls from the front, and the fierce Lankan cavalry at the back, the spirit of his all-conquering army had all but collapsed. Dashrath stared at a scene he'd never imagined he would as the supreme commander of his glorious army. His men had broken rank and were in retreat.

'NO!' thundered Dashrath. 'FIGHT! FIGHT! WE ARE AYODHYA! THE UNCONQUERABLES!'

Dashrath swung hard and decapitated a giant Lankan in one mighty blow. As he turned to face another of the seemingly never-ending waves of Raavan's hordes, his gaze fell upon the monster who was the mastermind of this devastation. Raavan, on horseback, was leading his cavalry down the beach on the left, skirting the sea. It was the only flank of the Lankans that was open to counter-attack from the Ayodhya infantry. Accompanied by his well-trained cavalry, Raavan was shrieking maniacally and hacking his way brutally through the Ayodhya outer infantry lines before they could regroup. This was not a war anymore. It was a massacre.

Dashrath knew that he'd lost the battle. He also knew that he'd rather die than face defeat. But he had one last wish. Redemption lay in his spitting on the decapitated head of that ogre from Lanka.

'YAAAAAHH!' screamed Dashrath, as he hacked at the arm of a Lankan who jumped at him, severing the limb cleanly just above the wrist. Pushing his enemy out of the way, Dashrath lunged forward as he desperately tried to reach Raavan. He felt a shield crash into his calf and heard the crack of a bone above the din.

The mighty emperor of the Sapt Sindhu screamed as he spun around and swung his sword at the Lankan who had broken the rules of combat, decapitating him cleanly. He felt a hard knock on his back. He turned right back with a parry, but his broken leg gave way. As he fell forward, he felt a sharp thrust into his chest. *Someone had stabbed him.* He didn't feel the blade go in too deep. *Or had it gone in deeper than he thought? Maybe his body was shutting the pain out...* Dashrath felt darkness enveloping him. His fall was cushioned by another soldier from among the heaving mass of warriors battling in close combat. As his eyes slowly closed, he whispered his last prayers within the confines of his mind; to the God he revered the most: the sustainer of the world, the mighty Sun God Surya himself.

Don't let me live to bear this, Lord Surya. Let me die. Let me die...

—— |ﾊ| ⬤ ☼ ——

This is a disaster!

A panic-stricken Ashwapati rounded up his bravest mounted soldiers and raced across the battlefield on horseback. He negotiated his way through the clutter of bodies to quickly reach the kill zone right outside Karachapa fort, where Dashrath lay, probably seriously injured, if not dead.

Ashwapati knew the war had been lost. Vast numbers of the Sapt Sindhu soldiers were being massacred before his very eyes. All he wanted now was to save Emperor Dashrath, who was also his son-in-law. His Kaikeyi would not be widowed.

They rode hard through the battle zone, even as they held their shields high to protect themselves from the unrelenting barrage of arrows raining down from the Karachapa walls.

'There!' screamed a soldier.

Ashwapati saw Dashrath's motionless form wedged between the corpses of two soldiers. His son-in-law lay there firmly clutching his sword. The king of Kekaya leapt off his horse even as two soldiers rushed forward to offer him protection. Ashwapati dragged Dashrath towards his own horse, lifted him, and laid the emperor's severely injured body across the saddle. He then jumped astride and rode off towards the field of thorny bushes even as his soldiers struggled to keep up with him.

Kaikeyi stood resolute in her chariot near the clearing along the line of bushes, her demeanour admirably calm. As her father's horse drew near, she reached across and dragged Dashrath's prone body into the chariot. She didn't turn to look at her father, who had also been pierced by many arrows. She picked up the reins and whipped the four horses tethered to her chariot.

'Hyaah!' screamed Kaikeyi, as she charged into the bushes. Thorns tore mercilessly into the sides of the horses, ripping skin and even some flesh off the hapless animals. But Kaikeyi only kept whipping them harder and harder. Bloodied and tired, the horses soon broke through to the other side, onto clear land.

Kaikeyi finally pulled the reins and looked back. Riding furiously on the other side of the field of thorns, her father and his bodyguards were being chased by a group of mounted soldiers from Raavan's army. Kaikeyi understood immediately what her father was trying to do. He was leading Raavan's soldiers away from her.

The sun had nearly reached its zenith now. It was close to midday.

Kaikeyi cursed. *Damn you, Lord Surya! How could you allow this to happen to your most fervent devotee?*

She kneeled beside her unconscious husband, ripped off a large piece of her *angvastram,* and tied it firmly around a deep wound on his chest, which was losing blood at an alarming rate. Having staunched the blood flow somewhat, she stood and picked up the reins. She desperately wanted to cry but this was not the time. She had to save her husband first. She needed her wits about her.

She looked at the horses. Blood was pouring down their sides in torrents, and specks of flesh hung limply where the skin had been ripped off. They were panting frantically, exhausted by the effort of having pulled the chariot through the dense field of thorns. But she couldn't allow them any respite. Not yet.

'Forgive me,' whispered Kaikeyi, as she raised her whip.

The leather hummed through the air and lashed the horses cruelly. Neighing for mercy, they refused to move. Kaikeyi cracked her whip again and the horses edged forward.

'MOVE!' screamed Kaikeyi as she whipped the horses ruthlessly, again and again, forcing them to pick up a desperate but fearsome momentum.

She had to save her husband.

Suddenly an arrow whizzed past her and crashed into the front board of the chariot with frightening intensity. Kaikeyi spun around in alarm. One of Raavan's cavalrymen had broken off from his group and was in pursuit.

Kaikeyi turned back and whipped her horses harder. 'FASTER! FASTER!'

Even as she whipped her horses into delirious frenzy, Kaikeyi had the presence of mind to shift slightly and use her body to shield her husband.

Even Raavan's demons would be chivalrous enough not to attack an unarmed woman.

She was wrong.

She heard the arrow's threatening hum before it slammed into her back with vicious force. Its shock was so massive that it threw her forward as her head flung back. Her eyes beheld the sky as Kaikeyi screamed in agony. But she recovered immediately, the adrenaline pumping furiously through her body, compelling her to focus.

'FASTER!' she screamed, as she whipped the horses ferociously.

Another arrow whizzed by her ears, missing the back of her head by a tiny whisker. Kaikeyi cast a quick look at her husband's immobile body bouncing furiously as the chariot tore through the uneven countryside.

'FASTER!'

She heard another arrow approach, and within a flash it slammed into her right hand, slicing through the forefinger cleanly; it bounced away like a pebble thrown to the side. The whip fell from her suddenly-loosened grip. Her mind was ready for further injuries now, her body equipped for pain. She didn't scream. She didn't cry.

She bent quickly and picked up the whip with her left hand, transferring the reins to her bloodied right hand. She resumed the whipping with mechanical precision.

'MOVE! YOUR EMPEROR'S LIFE IS AT STAKE!'

She heard the dreaded whizz of another arrow. She steeled herself for another hit; instead, she now heard a scream of agony from behind her. A quick side glance revealed her injured foe; the arrow had buried itself deep into his right eye. What she also perceived was a band of horsemen moving in; her father and his faithful bodyguards. A flurry of arrows ensured that the Lankan attacker toppled off his animal, even as his leg got entangled in the stirrup. Raavan's soldier was dragged for many metres by his still galloping horse, his head smashing repeatedly against the rocks strewn on the path.

Kaikeyi looked ahead once again. She did not have the time to savour the brutal death of the man who'd injured her. *Dashrath must be saved.*

The rhythmic whipping continued ceaselessly.

'FASTER! FASTER!'

— 시 🐟 ☼ —

Nilanjana was patting the baby's back insistently. He still wasn't breathing.

'Come on! Breathe!'

Kaushalya watched anxiously as she lay exhausted from the abnormally long labour. She tried to prop herself up on her elbows. 'What's wrong? What's the matter with my boy?'

'Get the queen to rest, will you?' Nilanjana admonished the attendant who was peering over her shoulder.

Rushing over, the attendant put her hand on the queen's shoulder and attempted to coax her to lie down. A severely weakened Kaushalya, however, refused to submit. 'Give him to me!'

'Your Highness…' whispered Nilanjana as tears welled up in her eyes.

'Give him to me!'

'I don't think that…'

'GIVE HIM TO ME!'

Nilanjana hurried over to her side and placed the lifeless baby next to Kaushalya. The queen held her motionless son close to her bosom. Almost instantly the baby moved and intuitively gripped Kaushalya's long hair.

'Ram!' said Kaushalya loudly.

With a loud and vigorous cry, Ram sucked in his first breath in this, his current worldly life.

'Ram!' cried Kaushalya once again, as tears streamed down her cheeks.

Ram continued to bawl with robust gusto, holding on to his mother's hair as firmly as his tiny hands would permit. He opened his mouth and suckled reflexively.

Nilanjana felt as if a dam had burst and began to bawl like a child. Her mistress had given birth to a beautiful baby boy. The prince had been born!

Despite her evident delirium, Nilanjana did not forget her training. She looked to the far corner of the room at the *prahar* lamp to record the exact time of birth. She knew that the royal astrologer would need that information.

She held her breath as she noticed the time.

Lord Rudra, be merciful!

It was exactly midday.

—— |大| 🐚 ☼ ——

'What does this mean?' asked Nilanjana.

The astrologer sat still.

The sun was poised to sink into the horizon and both Kaushalya and Ram were sound asleep. Nilanjana had finally walked into the chamber of the royal astrologer to discuss Ram's future.

'You'd said that if he was born before midday then history would remember him as one of the greatest,' said Nilanjana. 'And that if he was born after midday, he'd suffer misfortune and not know personal happiness.'

'Are you sure he was born exactly at midday?' asked the astrologer. 'Not before? Not after?'

'Of course I'm sure! Exactly at noon.'

The astrologer inhaled deeply and became contemplative once again.

'What does this mean?' asked Nilanjana. 'What will his future be like? Will he be great or will he suffer misfortune?'

'I don't know.'

'What do you mean you don't know?'

'I mean I don't know!' said the astrologer, unable to contain his irritation.

Nilanjana looked out of the window, towards the exquisite royal gardens that rolled endlessly over many acres. The palace was perched atop a hill which also was the highest point in Ayodhya. As she gazed vacantly at the waters beyond the city walls, she knew what needed to be done. It was really up to her to record the time of birth, and she didn't *have* to record it as midday. How would anyone be any the wiser? She'd made her decision: Ram was born a minute *before* midday.

She turned to the astrologer. 'You will remain quiet about the actual time of birth.'

She needn't have exercised any caution. The astrologer, who also belonged to Kaushalya's parental kingdom, didn't need any convincing. His loyalties were as clear as Nilanjana's.

'Of course.'

Chapter 4

Maharishi Vashishta approached the fort gates of Ayodhya, followed by his bodyguards at a respectful distance. As the guards on duty sprang to attention, they wondered where the great *raj guru*, the *royal sage* of Ayodhya, was headed early in the morning.

The chief of the guards bowed low, folded his hands into a namaste and addressed the *great man of knowledge* respectfully, '*Maharishiji.*'

Vashishta did not break a step as he nodded in acknowledgement with a polite namaste.

He was thin to a fault and towering in height, despite which his gait was composed and self-assured. His *dhoti* and *angvastram* were white, the colour of purity. His head was shaven bare, but for a knotted tuft of hair at the top of his head which announced his Brahmin status. A flowing, snowy beard, calm, gentle eyes, and a wizened face conveyed the impression of a soul at peace with itself.

Yet, Vashishta was brooding as he walked slowly towards the massive Grand Canal that encircled the ramparts of *Ayodhya,* the *impregnable city.* His thoughts were consumed by what he knew he must do.

Six years ago, Raavan's barbaric hordes had decimated the Sapt Sindhu army. Though its prestige had depleted, Ayodhya's suzerainty had not thus far been challenged by other kingdoms of North India, for every subordinate kingdom of the empire had bled heavily on that fateful day. Wounded themselves, none had the strength to confront even a weakened Ayodhya. Dashrath remained the emperor of the Sapt Sindhu, albeit a poorer and less powerful one.

The pitiless Raavan had extracted his pound of flesh from Ayodhya. Trade commissions paid by Lanka were unilaterally reduced to a tenth of what they had been before the humiliating defeat. In addition, the purchase of goods from the Sapt Sindhu was now at a reduced price. Inevitably, even as Lanka's wealth soared, Ayodhya and the other kingdoms of North India slipped into penury. Why, rumours even abounded that the streets of the demon city were paved with gold!

Vashishta raised his hand to signal his bodyguards to fall behind. He walked up to the shaded terrace that overlooked the Grand Canal. He raised his eyes towards the exquisite ceiling that ran along the canal's entire length. He then ran his gaze along the almost limitless expanse of water that lay ahead. It had once symbolised Ayodhya's immense wealth but had begun to exhibit signs of decay and poverty.

The canal had been built a few centuries ago, during the reign of Emperor Ayutayus, by drawing in the waters of the feisty Sarayu River. Its dimensions were almost celestial. It stretched for over fifty kilometres as it circumnavigated the third and outermost wall of the city of Ayodhya. It was enormous in breadth as well, extending to about two-and-a-half kilometres across the banks. Its storage capacity was so massive that for the first few years of its construction, many of the kingdoms downriver had complained of water shortages. Their objections had been crushed by the brute force of the powerful Ayodhyan warriors.

One of the main purposes of this canal was militaristic. It was, in a sense, a moat. To be fair, it could be called the Moat of Moats, protecting the city from all sides. Prospective attackers would have to row across a moat that had river-like dimensions. The adventurous fools would be out in the open, vulnerable to an unending barrage of missiles from the high walls of the unconquerable city. Four bridges spanned the canal in the four cardinal directions. The roads that emerged from these bridges led into the city through four massive gates in the outermost wall: the North Gate, East Gate, South Gate and West Gate. Each bridge was divided into two sections. Each section had its own tower and drawbridge, thus offering two levels of defence at the canal itself.

Even so, to consider this Grand Canal a mere defensive structure was to do it a disservice. The Ayodhyans also looked upon the canal as a religious symbol. To them, the massive canal, with its dark, impenetrable and eerily calm waters, was reminiscent of the sea; similar to the mythic, primeval ocean of nothingness that was the source of creation. It was believed that at the centre of this primeval ocean, billions of years ago, the universe was born when *The One*, *Ekam*, split into many in a great big bang, thus activating the cycle of creation.

The impenetrable city, Ayodhya, viewed itself as a representative on earth of that most supreme of Gods, the *One God*, the formless *Ekam*, popularly known in modern times as the *Brahman* or *Parmatma*. It was believed that the *Parmatma* inhabited every single being, animate and inanimate. Some men and women were able to awaken the *Parmatma* within, and thus become Gods. These Gods among men had been immortalised in great temples across Ayodhya. Small islands had been constructed within the Grand Canal as well, on which temples had been built in honour of these Gods.

Vashishta, however, knew that despite all the symbolism and romance, the canal had, in fact, been built for more prosaic purposes. It worked as an effective flood-control mechanism, as water from the tempestuous Sarayu could be led in through control-gates. Floods were a recurrent problem in North India.

Furthermore, its placid surface made drawing water relatively easy, as compared to taking it directly from the Sarayu. Smaller canals radiated out of the Grand Canal into the hinterland of Ayodhya, increasing the productivity of farming dramatically. The increase in agricultural yield allowed many farmers to free themselves from the toil of tilling the land. Only a few were enough to feed the massive population of the entire kingdom of Kosala. This surplus labour transformed into a large army, trained by talented generals into a brilliant fighting unit. The army conquered more and more of the surrounding lands, till the great Lord Raghu, the grandfather of the present Emperor Dashrath, finally subjugated the entire Sapt Sindhu, thus becoming the *Chakravarti Samrat.*

Wealth pouring into Kosala sparked a construction spree: massive temples, palaces, public baths, theatres and market places were built. Sheer poetry in stone, these buildings were a testament to the power and glory of Ayodhya. One among them was the grand terrace that overhung the inner banks of the Grand Canal. It was a continuous colonnaded structure built of red sandstone mined from beyond the river Ganga; the terrace was entirely covered by a majestic vaulted ceiling, providing shade to the constant stream of visitors.

Every square inch of the ceiling had been painted in vivid colours, chronicling the stories of ancient Gods such as Indra, and the ancestors of kings who ruled Ayodhya, all the way up to the first, the noble Ikshvaku. The ceiling was divided into separate sections and, at the centre of each was a massive sun, with its rays streaming boldly out in all directions. This was significant, for the kings of Ayodhya were Suryavanshis, the descendants of the Sun God, and just like the sun, their power boldly extended out in all directions. Or so it had been before the demon from Lanka destroyed their prestige in one fell swoop.

Vashishta looked into the distance at one of the numerous artificial islands that dotted the canal. This island, unlike the others, did not have a temple but three gigantic statues, placed back to back, facing different directions. One was of Lord Brahma, the Creator, one of the greatest scientists ever. He was credited with many inventions upon which the Vedic way of life had been built. His disciples lived by the code he'd established: relentless pursuit of knowledge and selfless service to society. They had, over the years, evolved into the tribe of Brahma, or Brahmins.

To its right was the statue of Lord Parshu Ram, worshipped as the sixth Vishnu. Periodically, when a way of life became inefficient, corrupt or fanatical, a new leader emerged, who guided his people to an improved social order. Vishnu was an ancient title accorded to the greatest of leaders, idolised as the Propagators of Good. The Vishnus were worshipped like Gods. Lord Parshu Ram, the previous Vishnu, had many centuries ago guided India out of its Age of Kshatriya, which had degenerated into vicious violence. He'd ushered in the Age of Brahmin, an age of knowledge.

Next to Lord Parshu Ram, and to the left of Lord Brahma, completing the circle of trinity was the statue of Lord Rudra, the previous Mahadev. This was an ancient title accorded to those who were the Destroyers of Evil. The Mahadev's was not the task to guide humanity to a new way of life;

this was reserved for the Vishnu. His task was restricted to finding and destroying Evil. Once Evil had been destroyed, Good would burst through with renewed vigour. Unlike the Vishnu, the Mahadev could not be a native of India, for that would predispose him towards one or the other side within this great land. He had to be an outsider to enable him to clearly see Evil for what it was, when it arose. Lord Rudra belonged to a land beyond the western borders of India: Pariha.

Vashishta went down on his knees and touched the ground with his forehead, in reverence to the glorious trinity who were the bedrock of the present Vedic way of life. He raised his head and folded his hands in a namaste.

'Guide me, O Holy Trinity,' whispered Vashishta. 'For I intend to rebel.'

A sudden gust of wind echoed around his ears as he gazed at the triumvirate. The marble was not what it used to be. The Ayodhya royalty wasn't able to maintain the outer surface anymore. The gold leafing on the crowns of Lords Brahma, Parshu Ram and Rudra had begun to peel off. The ceiling of the terrace had paint flaking off its beautiful images, and the sandstone floor was chipped in many places. The Grand Canal itself had begun to silt and dry up, with no repairs undertaken; the Ayodhya royal administration was probably unable to budget for such tasks.

However, it was clear to Vashishta that not only was the administration short of funds for adequate governance, it had also lost the will for it. As the canal water receded, the exposed dry land had been encroached upon with impunity. The Ayodhyan population had grown till the city almost seemed to burst at its seams. Even a few years ago it would have been unthinkable that the canal would be defiled thus;

that new housing would not be constructed for the poor. But, alas, many improbables had now become habitual.

We need a new way of life, Lord Parshu Ram. My great country must be rejuvenated with the blood and sweat of patriots. What I want is revolutionary, and patriots are often called traitors by the very people they choose to serve, till history passes the final judgement.

Vashishta scooped some mud from the canal that was deposited on the steps of the terrace, and used his thumb to apply it on his forehead in a vertical line.

This soil is worth more than my life to me. I love my country. I love my India. I swear I will do what must be done. Give me courage, My Lord.

The soft rhythm of liturgical chanting wafted through the breeze, making him turn to his right. A small group of people walked solemnly in the distance, wearing robes of blue, the holy colour of the divine. It was an unusual sight these days. Along with wealth and power, the citizens of the Sapt Sindhu had also lost their spiritual ardour. Many believed their Gods had abandoned them. Why else would they suffer so?

The worshippers chanted the name of the sixth Vishnu, Lord Parshu Ram.

'Ram, Ram, Ram bolo; Ram, Ram, Ram. Ram, Ram, Ram bolo; Ram, Ram, Ram.'

It was a simple chant: 'Speak the name of Ram.'

Vashishta smiled; to him, this was a sign.

Thank you, Lord Parshu Ram. Thank you for your blessings.

Vashishta had pinned his hopes on the namesake of the sixth Vishnu: the six-year-old eldest prince of Ayodhya, Ram. The sage had insisted that Queen Kaushalya's chosen name, Ram, be expanded to Ram Chandra. Kaushalya's father, King Bhanuman of South Kosala, and mother, Queen Maheshwari of the Kurus, were *Chandravanshis,* the *descendants of the moon.* Vashishta thought it would be wise to show fealty towards

Ram's maternal home as well. Furthermore, Ram Chandra meant 'pleasant face of the moon', and it was well known that the moon shone with the reflected light of the sun. Poetically, the sun was the face and the moon its reflection; who, then, was responsible for the pleasant face of the moon? *The sun!* It was appropriate thus: Ram Chandra was also a Suryavanshi name, for Dashrath, his father, was a Suryavanshi.

That names guided destiny was an ancient belief. Parents chose the names of their children with care. A name, in a sense, became an aspiration, *swadharma, individual dharma,* for the child. Having been named after the sixth Vishnu himself, the aspirations for this child could not have been set higher!

There was another name that Vashishta had placed his hopes on: Bharat, Ram's brother, younger to him by seven months. His mother, Kaikeyi, did not know at the time of the great battle with Raavan that she was carrying Dashrath's child in her womb. Vashishta was aware that Kaikeyi was a passionate, wilful woman. She was ambitious for herself and those she viewed as her own. She had not settled for the eldest queen, Kaushalya, being one up on her by choosing a great name for her son. Her son, then, was the namesake of the legendary Chandravanshi emperor, Bharat, who had ruled millennia ago.

The ancient Emperor Bharat had united the warring Suryavanshis and Chandravanshis under one banner. Notwithstanding the occasional skirmishes, they had learnt to live in relative peace; a peace that held. It was exemplified today by the Emperor Dashrath, a Suryavanshi, having two queens who traced their lineage to Chandravanshi royalty, Kaushalya and Kaikeyi. Ashwapati, the father of Kaikeyi and the Chandravanshi king of Kekaya, was in fact the emperor's closest advisor.

One of the two names will surely serve my purpose.

He looked at Lord Parshu Ram again, drawing strength from the image.

I know they will think I'm wrong. They may even curse my soul. But you were the one who had said, My Lord, that a leader must love his country more than he loves his own soul.

Vashishta reached for his scabbard, hidden within the folds of his *angvastram*. He pulled out the knife and beheld the name that had been inscribed on the hilt in an ancient script: Parshu Ram.

Inhaling deeply, he shifted the knife to his left hand and pricked his forefinger, puncturing deep to draw out blood. He pressed the finger with his thumb, just under the drop of blood, and let some droplets drip into the canal.

By this blood oath, I swear on all my knowledge, I will make my rebellion succeed, or I will die trying.

Vashishta took one last look at Lord Parshu Ram, bowed his head as he brought his hands together in a respectful namaste, and softly whispered the cry of the followers of the great Vishnu. *'Jai Parshu Ram!'*

Glory to Parshu Ram!

Chapter 5

Kaushalya, the queen, was happy; Kaushalya, the mother, was not. She understood that Ram should leave the Ayodhya palace. Emperor Dashrath had blamed him for the horrific defeat he'd suffered at the hands of Raavan, on the day that Ram was born. Till that fateful day, he had never lost a battle; in fact, he'd been the only unbeaten ruler in all of India. Dashrath was convinced that Ram was born with bad karma and his birth was the undoing of the noble lineage of Raghu. There was little the powerless Kaushalya could do to change this.

Kaikeyi had always been the favourite wife, and saving the emperor's life in the Battle of Karachapa had only made her hold over Dashrath absolute. Kaikeyi and her coterie had speedily let it be known that Dashrath believed Ram's birth was inauspicious. Soon the city of Ayodhya shared its emperor's belief. It was widely held that all the good deeds of Ram's life would not succeed in washing away the 'taint of 7,032', the year that, according to the calendar of Lord Manu, Dashrath was defeated and Ram was born.

It would be best if Ram left the palace with Raj Guru Vashishta, Kaushalya knew. He would be away from the Ayodhya nobility, which had never accepted him anyway. Furthermore, he would stand to gain from the education he'd receive at Vashishta's *gurukul. Gurukul* meant the *guru's family,* but in practice it was the *residential school* of gurus. He would learn philosophy, science, mathematics, ethics, warfare and the arts. He would return, years later, a man in charge of his destiny.

The queen understood this, but the doting mother was unable to let go. She held on to her child and wept. Ram stood stoic as he held his mother, who hugged and smothered him with kisses; even at this tender age, he was an unusually calm boy.

Bharat, unlike Ram, was crying hysterically, refusing to let his mother go. Kaikeyi glared at her son with exasperation. 'You are my son! Don't be such a sissy! Behave like the king you will be one day! Go, make your mother proud!'

Vashishta watched the proceedings and smiled.

Passionate children have strong emotions that insist on finding expression. They laugh loudly. They cry even more loudly.

He observed the brothers as he wondered whether his goal would be met through stoic duty or passionate feeling. The twins, Lakshman and Shatrughan, the youngest of the four sons of Dashrath, stood at the back with their mother, Sumitra. The poor three-year-olds seemed lost, not quite understanding what was going on. Vashishta knew it was too soon for them, but he couldn't leave them behind. Ram and Bharat's training would take a long time, maybe even a decade, if not more. He could not risk the twins being in the palace during this period, for the political intrigue among the nobility would lead to the younger princes being co-opted into camps. This malicious nobility was already bleeding Ayodhya dry with its scheming and plotting to enrich itself; the emperor was weak and distracted.

The princes would return home for two *nine-day* holidays, twice a year, during the summer and winter solstices. The ancient *navratra* festival, which commemorated the six-monthly change in the direction of the Sun God's north-south journey across the horizon, was celebrated with great vigour. Vashishta believed those eighteen days would suffice to console the bereft mothers and sons. The autumn and spring *navratras*, aligned with the two equinoxes, would be commemorated at the *gurukul*.

The raj guru turned his attention to Dashrath.

The last six years had taken their toll on the emperor. Parchment-like skin stretched thinly over a face that was worn out by grief, his eyes sunken, his hair grey. The grievous battle wound on his leg had long since turned into a permanent deformity, depriving him of the hunting and exercising that he so loved. Seeking refuge in drink, his bent body gave little indication of the strong and handsome warrior he'd once been. Raavan had not just defeated him on that terrible day. He continued to defeat him every single day.

'Your Highness,' said Vashishta, loudly. 'With your permission.'

A distracted Dashrath waved his hand, confirming his order.

——— 从 ⚱ ☼ ———

It was a day after the winter solstice and the princes were in Ayodhya on their half-yearly holiday. It had been three years since they first left for the *gurukul*. *Uttaraayan*, the northward movement of the sun across the horizon, had begun. Six months later, in peak summer, Lord Surya would reverse his direction and *Dakshinaayan*, the southward movement of the sun, would begin.

Ram spent most of his time, even on holiday, with Guru Vashishta, who had moved back to the palace with the boys;

Kaushalya could not do much besides complain. Bharat, on the other hand, was strictly confined to Kaikeyi's chambers, subjected to incessant tutoring and interrogation by his forceful mother. Lakshman had already started riding small ponies, and he loved it. Shatrughan … just read books!

Lakshman was rushing to his mother Sumitra after one such riding lesson when he stopped short, hearing voices outside her chamber. He peeped in from behind the curtains.

'You must understand, Shatrughan, that your brother Bharat may make fun of you, but he loves you the most. You should always stay by his side.'

Shatrughan was holding a palm-leaf booklet in his hand, desperately trying to read as he pretended to pay attention to his mother.

'Are you listening to me, Shatrughan?' asked Sumitra, sharply.

'Yes Mother,' Shatrughan said, looking up, sincerity dripping from his voice.

'I don't think so.'

Shatrughan repeated his mother's last sentence. His diction was remarkably clear and crisp for his age. Sumitra knew that her son hadn't been paying attention, and yet she couldn't do anything about the fact that he'd not been genuinely listening to her at all!

Lakshman smiled as he ran up to his mother, yelping with delight as he leapt onto her lap.

'I will li*th*en to you, *Maa*!' he said with his childish lisp.

Sumitra smiled as she wrapped her arms around Lakshman. 'Yes, I know you will always listen to me. You are my good son!'

Shatrughan glanced briefly at his mother before going back to his palm-leaf booklet.

'I will do whatever you tell me to do,' said Lakshman, his earnest eyes filled with love. 'Alway*th*.'

'Then listen to me,' said Sumitra, leaning in with a clownish, conspiratorial expression, the kind she knew Lakshman loved. 'Your elder brother Ram needs you.' Her expression changed to compassionate wistfulness as she continued. 'He is a simple and innocent soul. He needs someone who can be his eyes and ears. No one really likes him.' She focused on Lakshman once again and murmured, 'You have to protect him from harm. People always say mean things about him behind his back, but he sees the best in them. He has too many enemies. His life may depend on you…'

'Really?' asked Lakshman, his eyes widening with barely-understood dread.

'Yes! And believe me, I can only count on you to protect him. Ram has a good heart, but he's too trusting of others.'

'Don't worry, *Maa*,' said Lakshman, stiffening his back and pursing his lips, his eyes gleaming like a soldier honoured with a most important undertaking. 'I will alway*th* take care of Ram *Dada*.'

Sumitra hugged Lakshman again and smiled fondly. 'I know you will.'

— 𝍢 ⬮ ☼ —

'*Dada*!' shouted Lakshman, banging his little heels against the pony's sides, willing it to run faster. But the pony, specially trained for children, refused to oblige.

Nine-year-old Ram rode ahead of Lakshman on a taller, faster pony. True to his training, he rose gracefully in his saddle at every alternate step of the canter, in perfect unison with the animal. On this vacant afternoon, they'd decided to practise by themselves the art of horsemanship, at the royal Ayodhya riding grounds.

'*Dada*! *Th*op!' screamed Lakshman desperately, having abandoned by now any pretence at following vaguely-learnt instructions. He kicked and whipped his pony to the best of his ability.

Ram looked back at the enthusiastic Lakshman and smiled as he cautioned his little brother, 'Lakshman, slow down. Ride properly.'

'*Th*op!' yelled Lakshman.

Ram immediately understood Lakshman's frantic cry and pulled his reins as Lakshman caught up and dismounted rapidly. '*Dada*, get off!'

'What?'

'Get off!' shouted an agitated Lakshman as he grabbed Ram's hand, trying to drag him down.

Ram frowned as he got off the horse. 'What is it, Lakshman?'

'Look!' Lakshman exclaimed, as he pointed at the billet strap that went through the buckle on the girth strap; the girth, in turn, kept the saddle in place. The buckle had almost come undone.

'By the great Lord Rudra!' whispered Ram. Had the buckle released while he was riding, he would have been thrown off the dislodged saddle, resulting in serious injury. Lakshman had saved him from a terrible accident.

Lakshman looked around furtively, his mother's words echoing in his brain. '*Th*omeone tried to kill you, *Dada*.'

Ram carefully examined the girth strap and the attached buckle. It simply looked worn out; there were no signs of tampering. Lakshman had certainly saved him from an injury, though, and possibly even death.

Ram embraced Lakshman gently. 'Thank you, my brother.'

'Don't worry about any con*th*pira*th*ie*th*,' said Lakshman, wearing a solemn expression. He was now certain about his mother's warnings. 'I will protect you, *Dada*. Alway*th*.'

Ram tried hard to prevent himself from smiling. 'Conspiracies, huh? Who taught you such a big word?'

'*Th*atrughan,' said Lakshman, looking around again, scanning the area for threats.

'Shatrughan, *hmm*?'

'Ye*th*. Don't worry, *Dada*. Lakh*th*man will protect you.'

Ram kissed his brother's forehead and reassured his little protector. 'I feel safe already.'

—— |人| 🐟 ☼ ——

The brothers were all set to go back to the *gurukul* two days after the horse saddle incident. Ram visited the royal stable the night before their departure to groom his horse; both of them had a long day ahead. There were stable hands, of course, but Ram enjoyed this work; it soothed him. The animals were among the handful in Ayodhya who did not judge him. He liked to spend time with them occasionally. He looked back at the sound of the clip-clop of hooves.

'Lakshman!' cried Ram in alarm, as little Lakshman trooped in atop his pony, obviously injured. Ram rushed forward and helped him dismount. Lakshman's chin had split open, deep enough to urgently need stitches. His face was covered with blood, but with typical bravado, he did not flinch at all when Ram examined his wound.

'You are not supposed to go horseback riding in the night, you know that, don't you?' Ram admonished him gently.

Lakshman shrugged. '*Th*orry... The hor*the* *th*uddenly...'

'Don't talk,' interrupted Ram, as the blood flow increased.

'Come with me.'

— |大| 🐟 ☼ —

Ram hastily sped towards Nilanjana's chambers along with his injured brother. En route, they were accosted by Sumitra and her maids who had been frantically searching for her missing son.

'What happened?' shouted Sumitra, as her eyes fell upon the profusely bleeding Lakshman.

Lakshman stood stoic and tight-lipped. He knew he was in for trouble as his *dada* never lied; there was no scope for creative storytelling. He would have to confess, and then come up with strategies to escape the inevitable punishment.

'It's nothing serious, *Chhoti Maa*,' said Ram to his *younger stepmother*, Sumitra. 'But we should get him to Nilanjana*ji* immediately.'

'What happened?' Sumitra persisted.

Ram instinctively felt compelled to protect Lakshman from his mother's wrath. After all, Lakshman had saved his life just the other day. He did what his conscience demanded at the time; shift the blame on himself. '*Chhoti Maa*, it's my fault. I'd gone to the stable with Lakshman to groom my horse. It's a little high-spirited and suddenly reared and kicked Lakshman. I should have ensured that Lakshman stood behind me.'

Sumitra immediately stepped aside. 'Quickly, take him to Nilanjana.'

She knows Ram Dada *never lies,* Lakshman thought, filled with guilt.

Ram and Lakshman rushed off, as a maid attempted to follow them. Sumitra raised her hand to stop her as she watched the boys moving down the corridor. Ram held his brother's hand firmly. She smiled with satisfaction.

Lakshman brought Ram's hand to his heart, and whispered, 'Together alway*th*, *Dada*. Alway*th*.'

'Don't talk, Lakshman. The blood will…'

—— 材 🐟 ☼ ——

The Ayodhyan princes had been in the *gurukul* for five years now. Vashishta watched with pride as the eleven-year-old Ram practised with his full-grown opponent. Combat training had commenced for Ram and Bharat this year; Lakshman and Shatrughan would have to wait for two more years. For now, they had to remain content with lessons in philosophy, mathematics and science.

'Come on, *Dada*!' shouted Lakshman. 'Move in and hit him!'

Vashishta observed Lakshman with an indulgent smile. He sometimes missed the cute lisp that Lakshman had now lost; but the eight-year-old had not lost his headstrong spirit. He also remained immensely loyal to Ram, whom he loved dearly. Perhaps Ram would eventually be able to channel Lakshman's wild streak.

The soft-spoken and intellect-oriented Shatrughan sat beside Lakshman, reading a palm-leaf manuscript of the *Isha Vasya Upanishad*. He read a Sanskrit verse.

'Pushannekarshe yama surya praajaapatya vyuha rashmeen samuha tejah;

Yatte roopam kalyaanatamam tatte pashyaami yo'saavasau purushah so'hamasmi.'

O Lord Surya, nurturing Son of Prajapati, solitary Traveller, celestial Controller; Diffuse Your rays, Diminish your light;

Let me see your gracious Self beyond the luminosity; And realise that the God in You is Me.

Shatrughan smiled to himself, lost in the philosophical beauty of the words. Bharat, who sat behind him, bent over and tapped Shatrughan on his head, then pointed at Ram. Shatrughan looked at Bharat, protest writ large in his eyes. Bharat glared at his younger brother. Shatrughan put his manuscript aside and looked at Ram.

The opposing swordsman Vashishta had selected for Ram belonged to the forest people who lived close to Vashishta's *gurukul*. It had been built deep in the untamed forests far south of the river Ganga, close to the western-most point of the course of the river Shon. The river took a sharp eastward turn thereafter, and flowed north-east to merge with the Ganga. This area had been used by many gurus for thousands of years. The forest people maintained the premises and gave it on rent to gurus.

The solitary approach to the *gurukul* was camouflaged first by dense foliage and then by the overhanging roots of a giant banyan. A small glade lay beyond, at the centre of which descending steps had been carved out of the earth, leading to a long, deep trench covered by vegetation. The trench then became a tunnel as it made its way under a steep hill. Light flooded the other end of this tunnel as it emerged at the banks of a stream which was spanned by a wooden bridge. Across lay the *gurukul*, a simple monolithic structure hewn into a rocky hillside.

The hill face had been neatly cut as though a huge, cube-shaped block of stone had been removed. Twenty small temples carved into the surface faced the entrance to the structure, some with deities in them, others empty. Six of these were adorned with an idol each of the previous Vishnus, one housed Lord Rudra, the previous Mahadev, and in yet another sat Lord Brahma, the brilliant scientist. The king of the *Devas*, the *Gods*, Lord Indra, who was also the God of Thunder and the Sky, occupied his rightful place in the central temple, surrounded by the other Gods. Of the two rock surfaces that faced each other, one had been cut to comprise the kitchen and store rooms, and the other, alcove-like sleeping quarters for the guru and his students.

Within the *ashram*, the princes of Ayodhya lived not as nobility, but as children of working-class parents; their royal background, in fact, was not public knowledge at the *gurukul*. In keeping with tradition, the princes had been accorded *gurukul* names: Ram was called Sudas, Bharat became Vasu, Lakshman was Paurav, and Shatrughan, Nalatardak. All reminders of their royal lineage were proscribed. Over and above their academic pursuits, they cleaned the *gurukul*, cooked food and served the guru. Scholastic mastery would help them achieve their life goals; the other activities would ingrain humility, with which they'd choose the *right* life goals.

'Looks like you're warmed up, Sudas,' Vashishta addressed Ram, one of his two star pupils. The guru then turned to the chief of the tribe, who sat beside him. 'Chief Varun, time to see some combat?'

The local people, besides being good hosts, were also brilliant warriors. Vashishta had hired their services to help train his wards in the fine art of warfare. They also served as combat opponents during examination, like right now.

Varun addressed the tribal warrior who had been practising with Ram. 'Matsya…'

Matsya and Ram immediately turned to the spectator stand and bowed to Vashishta and Varun. They walked over to the edge of the platform, picked up a paintbrush broom each, dipped it in a paint can filled with red dye, and painted the sides and tips of their wooden practice swords. It would leave marks on the body when struck, thus indicating how lethal the strike was.

Ram stepped on the platform and moved to the centre, followed by Matsya. Face-to-face, they bowed low with respect for their opponent.

'Truth. Duty. Honour,' said Ram, repeating a slogan he'd heard from his guru, Vashishta, which had made a deep impact on him.

Matsya, almost a foot taller than the boy, smiled. 'Victory at all costs.'

Ram took position: his back erect, his body turned sideways, his eyes looking over his right shoulder, just as Guru Vashishta had trained him to do. This position exposed the least amount of his body surface to his opponent. His breathing was steady and relaxed, just as he had been taught. His left hand held firmly by his side, extended a little away from the body to maintain balance. His sword hand was extended out, a few degrees above the horizontal position, bended slightly at the elbow. He adjusted his arm position till the weight of the sword was borne by his trapezius and triceps muscles. His knees were bent and his weight was on the ball of his feet, affording quick movement in any direction. Matsya was impressed. This young boy followed every rule to perfection.

The remarkable feature in the young boy was his eyes. With steely focus, they were fixed on those of his opponent, Matsya. *Guru Vashishta has taught the boy well. The eye moves before the hand does.*

Matsya's eyes fractionally widened. Ram knew an attack was imminent. Matsya lunged forward and thrust his sword at

Ram's chest, using his superior reach. It could have been a kill-wound, but Ram shifted swiftly to his right, avoiding the blow as he flicked his right hand forward, nicking Matsya's neck.

Matsya stepped back immediately.

'Why didn't you slash hard, *Dada*!' screamed Lakshman. 'That should have been a kill-wound!'

Matsya smiled appreciatively. He understood what Lakshman hadn't. Ram was probing him. Being a cautious fighter, he would move into kill strikes only after he knew his opponent's psyche. Ram didn't respond to Matsya's smile of approval. His eyes remained focused, his breathing normal. He had to discern his opponent's weaknesses. Waiting for the kill.

Matsya charged at him aggressively, bringing in his sword with force from the right. Ram stepped back and fended off the blow with as much strength as his smaller frame could muster. Matsya bent towards the right and brought in his sword from Ram's left now, belligerently swinging in close to the boy's head. Ram stepped back again, raising his sword up to block. Matsya kept moving forward, striking repeatedly, hoping to pin Ram against the wall and then deliver a kill-wound. Ram kept retreating as he fended off the blows. Suddenly he jumped to the right, avoiding Matsya's slash and in the same smooth movement, swung hard, hitting Matsya on the arm, leaving a splash of red paint. It was a 'wound' again, but not the one that would finally stop the duel.

Matsya stepped back without losing eye contact with Ram. *Perhaps he's too cautious.*

'Don't you have the guts to charge?'

Ram didn't respond. He took position once again, bending his knees a little, keeping his left hand lightly on his hips with the right hand extended out, his sword held steady.

'You cannot win the game if you don't play the game,' teased Matsya. 'Are you simply trying to avoid losing or do you actually want to win?'

Ram remained calm, focused and steady. Silent. He was conserving his energy.

This kid is unflappable, Matsya mused. He charged once again, repeatedly striking from above, using his height to try and knock Ram down. Ram bent sideways as he parried, stepping backwards steadily.

Vashishta smiled for he knew what Ram was attempting.

Matsya did not notice the small rocky outcrop that Ram smoothly sidestepped as he slowly moved backwards. Within moments, Matsya stumbled and lost his balance. Not wasting a moment, Ram went down on one knee and struck hard, right across the groin of the tribal warrior. A kill-wound!

Matsya looked down at the red paint smeared across his groin. The wooden sword had not drawn blood but had caused tremendous pain; he was too proud to let it show.

Impressed by the young student, Matsya stepped forward and patted Ram on his shoulder. 'One must check the layout of the battlefield before a fight; know every nook and cranny. You remembered this basic rule. I didn't. Well done, my boy.'

Ram put the sword down, clasped his right elbow with his left hand and touched his forehead with the clenched right fist, in the traditional salute typical of the tribe of Matsya, showing respect to the *noble* forest-dweller. 'It was an honour to battle with you, great *Arya.*'

Matsya smiled and folded his hands into a namaste. 'No, young man, the honour was mine. I look forward to seeing what you do with your life.'

Varun turned to Vashishta. 'You have a good student here, Guru*ji*. Not only is he a fine swordsman, he is also noble in his conduct. Who is he?'

Vashishta smiled. 'You know I'm not going to reveal that, Chief.'

Meanwhile, Matsya and Ram had walked to the edge of the platform. They chucked their swords into a water tank, allowing the paint to wash off. The swords would then be dried, oiled and hammered, ready to be used again.

Varun turned to another warrior of his tribe. 'Gouda, you are next.'

Vashishta signalled Bharat, addressing him by his *gurukul* name. 'Vasu!'

Gouda touched the ground with reverence, seeking its blessings before stepping onto the platform. Bharat did no such thing. He simply sprang up and sprinted towards the box that contained the swords. He'd marked a sword for himself already; the longest. It negated the advantage of reach that his opponent, a fully grown man, had.

Gouda smiled indulgently; his opponent was a child after all. The warrior picked up a wooden sword and marched to the centre, surprised to not find Bharat there. The intrepid child was already at the far end of the platform where the red dye and paintbrush brooms were stored. He was painting the edges and point of his sword.

'No practice?' asked a surprised Gouda.

Bharat turned around. 'Let's not waste time.'

Gouda raised his eyebrows in amusement; he walked up and painted his sword edges as well.

The combatants walked to the centre of the platform. Keeping with tradition, they bowed to each other. Gouda waited for Bharat to state his personal credo, expecting a repeat of that of his elder brother's.

'Live free or die,' said Bharat, thumping his chest with gusto.

Gouda couldn't contain himself now, and burst into laughter. 'Live free or die? *That* is your slogan?'

Bharat glared at him with unvarnished hostility. Still smiling broadly, the tribal warrior bowed his head and announced his credo. 'Victory at all costs.'

Gouda was again taken aback, now by Bharat's stance. Unlike his brother, he faced his enemy boldly, offering his entire body as target. His sword arm remained casually by his side, his weapon held loose. He wore a look of utter defiance.

'Aren't you going to take position?' asked Gouda, worried now that he might actually injure this reckless boy.

'I am always battle ready,' whispered Bharat, smiling with nonchalance.

Gouda shrugged and got into position.

Bharat waited for Gouda to make the first move as he observed the tribal warrior lazily.

Gouda suddenly lunged forward and thrust his sword into Bharat's abdomen. Bharat smoothly twirled around and brought his sword in from a height, landing a sharp blow at Gouda's right shoulder. Gouda smiled and retreated, careful not to reveal any pain.

'I could have disembowelled you,' said Gouda, drawing the boy's attention to the red mark smeared across his abdomen.

'Your arm would be lying on the floor before that,' said Bharat, pointing at the red mark his wooden sword had made on Gouda's shoulder.

Gouda laughed and charged in again. To his surprise, Bharat suddenly leapt high to his right, bringing his sword down from a height once again. It was an exquisite manoeuvre. Gouda could not have parried that strike from such height, especially since the attack was not on the side of the sword-arm. It could only have been blocked by a shield. However, Bharat was not tall enough to successfully pull off this ingenious manoeuvre. Gouda leaned back and struck hard, using his superior reach.

Gouda's sword brutally hit the airborne Bharat's chest, throwing him backwards. Bharat fell on his back, a kill-wound clearly marking his chest, right where his heart lay encased within.

Bharat immediately got back on his feet. The blood capillaries below the skin had burst, forming a red blotch on his bare chest. Even with a wooden sword, the blow must have hurt. To Gouda's admiration, Bharat disregarded the pain. He stood his ground, staring defiantly at his opponent.

'That was a good move,' said Gouda. 'I haven't seen it before. But you need to be taller to pull it off.'

Bharat glared at Gouda, his eyes flashing with anger. 'I will be taller one day. We will fight again.'

Gouda smiled. 'We certainly will, boy. I look forward to it.'

Varun turned to Vashishta. 'Guru*ji*, both are talented. I can't wait for them to grow up.'

Vashishta smiled with satisfaction. 'Neither can I.'

— |剂| ▮ ☼ —

Dusk had fallen as a contemplative Ram sat by the stream, which flowed a little away from the *ashram*. Spotting him from a distance as he set out for his evening walk, the guru walked up to his student.

Hearing the quick footsteps of his guru, Ram rose immediately with a namaste. 'Guru*ji*.'

'Sit, sit,' said Vashishta, and then lowered himself beside Ram. 'What are you thinking about?'

'I was wondering why you did not reveal our identity to Chief Varun,' said Ram. 'He seems like a good man. Why do we withhold the truth from him? Why do we lie?'

'Withholding the truth is different from lying!' Vashishta remarked with a twinkle in his eye.

'Not revealing the truth is lying, isn't it, Guru*ji*?'

'No, it isn't. Sometimes, truth causes pain and suffering. At such times, silence is preferred. In fact, there may be times when a white lie, or even an outright lie, could actually lead to a good outcome.'

'But lying has consequences, Guru*ji*. It's bad karma.'

'Sometimes, the truth may also have consequences that are bad. Lying may save someone's life. Lying may bring one into a position of authority, which in turn may result in an opportunity to do good. Would you still advocate not lying? It may well be said that a true leader loves his people more than he loves his own soul. There would be no doubt in the mind of such a leader. He would lie for the good of his people.'

Ram frowned. 'But Guru*ji*, people who compel their leaders to lie aren't worth fighting for...'

'That's simplistic, Ram. You lied for Lakshman once, didn't you?'

'It was instinct. I felt I had to protect him. But I've always felt uneasy about it. That's the reason why I needed to talk to you about it, Guru*ji*.'

'And, I am repeating what I said then. You needn't feel guilty. Wisdom lies in moderation, in balance. If you lie to save an innocent person from some bandits, is that wrong?'

'One odd example, out of context, doesn't justify lying, Guru*ji*,' Ram wouldn't give up. 'Mother lied once to save me from Father's anger; Father soon discovered the truth. There was a time when he would visit my mother regularly. But after that incident, he stopped seeing her completely. He cut her off.'

The guru observed his student with sadness. *Truth be told, Emperor Dashrath blamed Ram for his defeat at the hands of Raavan. He would have found some excuse or the other to stop visiting Kaushalya, regardless of the incident.*

Vashishta measured his words carefully. 'I am not suggesting that lying is good. But sometimes, just like a tiny dose of a poison can prove medicinal, a small lie may actually help. Your habit of speaking the truth is good. But what is your reason for it? Is it because you believe it's the lawful thing to do? Or, is it because this incident has made you fear lying?'

Ram remained silent, almost thoughtful.

'Now, I am sure you are wondering what this has to do with Chief Varun.'

'Yes, Guru*ji*.'

'Do you remember our visit to the chief's village?'

'Of course, I do.'

The boys had once accompanied their guru to Varun's village. With a population of fifty thousand, it was practically a small town. The princes were enchanted by what they saw. Streets were laid out in a semi-urban, well-organised living area in the form of a square grid. The houses were made of bamboo, but were strong and sturdy; they were exactly the same, from the chief's to the ordinary villager's. Houses were without doors, each with an open entrance, simply because there was no crime. The children were raised communally by the elders, not just by their own parents.

During their visit, the princes had had a most interesting conversation with an assistant to the chief. They had wanted to know who the houses belonged to: the individual living in that unit, or to the chief, or to the community as a whole. The assistant had answered with the most quizzical response: *'How can the land belong to any of us? We belong to the land!'*

'What did you think about the village?' asked Vashishta, bringing Ram back to the present.

'What a wonderful way to live. They lead a more civilised life than we city-dwellers do. We could learn so much from them.'

'Hmm, and what do you think is the foundation of their way of life? Why is Chief Varun's village so idyllic? Why have they not changed for centuries?'

'They live selflessly for each other, Guru*ji*. They don't have a grain of selfishness in them.'

Vashishta shook his head. 'No, Sudas, it is because at the heart of their society are simple laws. These laws can never be broken, and must be followed, come what may.'

Ram's eyes opened wide, like he had discovered the secret to life. 'Laws…'

'Yes, Ram. Laws! Laws are the foundation on which a fulfilling life is built for a community. Laws are the answer.'

'Laws…'

'One might believe that there's no harm in occasionally breaking a minor law, right? Especially if it's for the Greater Good? Truth be told, I too have occasionally broken some rules for a laudable purpose. But Chief Varun thinks differently. Their commitment to the law is not based on traditions alone. Or the conviction that it is the right thing to do. It's based on one of the most powerful impressions in a human being: the childhood memory of guilt. The first time a child breaks a law in their society, however minor and inconsequential it may be, he's made to suffer; every child. Any recurrent breach of the law results in further shaming. Just like you find it difficult to lie even when it benefits someone because of what your mother suffered, Varun finds it impossible to do the same.'

'So, not revealing our identity is in some way linked to their laws? Will knowing who we are mean that they're breaking their laws?'

'Yes!'

'What law?'

'Their law prevents them from coming to the aid of the Ayodhya royalty. I don't know why. I'm not sure if even they know why. But this law has held for centuries. It serves no purpose now but they follow it strictly. They don't know where I'm from; I sometimes think they do not want to know. All they know is that my name is Vashishta.'

Ram seemed troubled. 'Are we safe here?'

'They are duty-bound to protect those who are accepted into this *gurukul*. That is also their law. Now that they've accepted us, they cannot harm us. However, they might expel us if they discover who the four of you are. We're safe here, though, from other more powerful enemies who are a threat to our cause.'

Ram fell into deep contemplation.

'So, I haven't lied, Sudas. I've just not revealed the truth. There's a difference.'

Chapter 6

Dawn broke over the *gurukul* at the fifth hour of the first *prahar*, to the chirping of birds. Even as the nocturnal forest creatures returned to their daytime shelters, others emerged to face the rigours of another day. The four Ayodhyan princes though, had been up and about for a while. Having swept the *gurukul*, they had bathed, cooked and completed their morning prayers. Hands folded in respect, they sat composed and cross-legged in a semi-circle around Guru Vashishta. The teacher himself sat in *padmaasan*, the *lotus position*, on a raised platform under a large banyan tree.

In keeping with tradition, they were reciting the *Guru Stotram*, the *hymn in praise of the teacher,* before the class commenced.

As the hymn ended, the students rose and ceremoniously touched the feet of their guru, Vashishta. He gave them all the same blessing: 'May my knowledge grow within you, and may you, one day, become my teacher.'

Ram, Bharat, Lakshman and Shatrughan took their allotted seats. Thirteen years had passed since the terrible battle with Raavan. Ram was thirteen years old, and both Bharat and he were showing signs of adolescence. Their voices had begun to break and drop in pitch. Faint signs of moustaches had made an appearance on their upper lips. They'd suddenly shot up in height, even as their boyish bodies had begun to develop lean muscle.

Lakshman and Shatrughan had now begun combat practice, though their pre-adolescent bodies made fighting a little difficult for them. They'd all learnt the basics of philosophy, science and mathematics. They had mastered the divine language, Sanskrit. The ground work had been done. The guru knew it was time to sow the seed.

'Do you know the origins of our civilisation?' asked Vashishta.

Lakshman, always eager to answer but not well read, raised his hand and began to speak. 'The universe itself began with—'

'No, Paurav,' said Vashishta, using Lakshman's *gurukul* name. 'My question was not about the universe but about us, the Vedic people of this *yug*.'

Ram and Bharat turned to Shatrughan in unison.

'Guru*ji*,' began Shatrughan, 'it goes back to Lord Manu, a prince of the Pandya dynasty, thousands of years ago.'

'Teacher's pet,' whispered Bharat, indulgently. While he teased Shatrughan mercilessly for his bookish ways, he appreciated the fearsome intellect of his youngest brother.

Vashishta looked at Bharat. 'Do you have something to add?'

'No, Guru*ji*,' said Bharat, immediately contrite.

'Yes, Nalatardak,' said Vashishta, turning his attention back to Shatrughan and using his *gurukul* name. 'Please continue.'

'It is believed that thousands of years ago, swathes of land were covered in great sheets of ice. Since large quantities of water were frozen in solid form, sea levels were a lot lower than they are today.'

'You are correct,' said Vashishta, 'except for one point. It is not a belief, Nalatardak. The "Ice Age" is not a theory. It is fact.'

'Yes, Guru*ji*,' said Shatrughan. 'Since sea levels were a lot lower, the Indian landmass extended a lot farther into the sea. The island of Lanka, the demon-king Raavan's kingdom, was joined to the Indian landmass. Gujarat and Konkan also reached out into the sea.'

'And?'

'And, I believe, there were—'

Shatrughan stopped short as Vashishta cast him a stern look. He smiled and folded his hands into a namaste. 'My apologies, Guru*ji*. Not belief, but fact.'

Vashishta smiled.

'Two great civilisations existed in India during the Ice Age. One in south-eastern India called the Sangamtamil, which included a small portion of the Lankan landmass, along with large tracts of land that are now underwater. The course of the river Kaveri was much broader and longer at the time. This rich and powerful empire was ruled by the Pandya dynasty.'

'And?'

'The other civilisation, Dwarka, spread across large parts of the landmass, off the coast of modern Gujarat and Konkan. It now lies submerged. It was ruled by the Yadav dynasty, the descendants of Yadu.'

'Carry on.'

'Sea levels rose dramatically at the end of the Ice Age. The Sangamtamil and Dwarka civilisations were destroyed, their heartland now lying under the sea. The survivors, led by Lord Manu, the father of our nation, escaped up north and began life once again. They called themselves the people of *vidya*, *knowledge*; the Vedic people. We are their proud descendants.'

'Very good, Nalatardak,' said Vashishta. 'Just one more point. The Ice Age came to an abrupt end in the time-scale that Mother Earth operates in. But in human terms, it wasn't abrupt at all. We had decades, even centuries, of warning. And yet, we did nothing.'

The children listened with rapt attention.

'Why did the Sangamtamil and Dwarka, clearly very advanced civilisations, not take timely corrective actions? Evidence suggests that they were aware of the impending calamity. Mother Earth had given them enough warning signs. They were intelligent enough to either possess or invent the technology required to save themselves. And yet, they did nothing. Only a few survived, under the able leadership of Lord Manu. Why?'

'They were lazy,' said Lakshman, as usual jumping to conclusions.

Vashishta sighed. 'Paurav, if only you'd think before answering.'

A chagrined Lakshman fell silent.

'You have the ability to think, Paurav,' said Vashishta, 'but you're always in a hurry. Remember, it's more important to be right than to be first.'

'Yes, Guru*ji*,' said Lakshman, his eyes downcast. But he raised his hand again. 'Were the people debauched and careless?'

'Now you're guessing, Paurav. Don't try to pry open the door with your fingernails. Use the key.'

Lakshman seemed nonplussed.

'Do not rush to the "right answer",' clarified Vashishta. 'The key, always, is to ask the "right question".'

'Guru*ji*,' said Ram. 'May I ask a question?'

'Of course, Sudas,' said Vashishta.

'You said earlier that they had decades, even centuries of warning. I assume their scientists had decoded these warnings?'

'Yes, they had.'

'And had they communicated these warnings to everyone,

including the royalty?'

'Yes, they had.'

'Was Lord Manu the Pandyan king or a prince, at the time? I have heard conflicting accounts.'

Vashishta smiled approvingly. 'Lord Manu was one of the younger princes.'

'And yet, it was he and not the king who saved his people.'

'Yes.'

'If anyone other than the king was required to lead the people to safety, then the answer is obvious. The king wasn't doing his job. Bad leadership, then, was responsible for the downfall of Sangamtamil and Dwarka.'

'Do you think a bad king is also a bad man?' asked Vashishta.

'No,' said Bharat. 'Even honourable men sometimes prove to be terrible leaders. Conversely, men of questionable character can occasionally be exactly what a nation requires.'

'Absolutely! A king need be judged solely on the basis of what he achieves for his people. His personal life is of no consequence. His public life, though, has one singular purpose: to provide for his people and improve their lives.'

'True,' said Bharat.

Vashishta took a deep breath. The time was ripe. 'So, does that make Raavan a good king for his people?'

There was stunned silence.

Ram wouldn't answer. He hated Raavan viscerally. Not only had the Lankan devastated Ayodhya, he had also ruined Ram's future. His birth was permanently associated with the 'taint' of Raavan's victory. No matter what he did, Ram would always remain inauspicious for his father and the people of Ayodhya.

Bharat finally spoke. 'We may not want to admit it, but Raavan is a good king, loved by his people. He is an able administrator who has brought prosperity through maritime trade, and he even runs the seaports under his control efficiently. It is fabled that the streets of his capital are paved with gold, thus earning his kingdom the name "Golden Lanka". Yes, he is a good king.'

'And what would you say about a very good man, a king, who has fallen into depression? He has converted his personal loss to that of his people. They suffer because he does. Is he, then, a good king?'

It was obvious whom Vashishta was referring to. The students were quiet for a long time, afraid to answer.

It had to be Bharat who raised his hand. 'No, he is not a good king.'

Vashishta nodded. *Trust the boldness of a born rebel.*

'That's it for today,' Vashishta brought the class to an abrupt end, leaving a lot unsaid. 'As always, your homework is to mull over our discussion.'

— 𝌆 ▮ ☼ —

'My turn, *Dada*,' whispered Bharat as he softly tapped Ram's shoulder.

Ram immediately tied his pouch to his waistband. 'Sorry.'

Bharat turned to the injured rabbit lying on the ground. He first anesthetised the animal and then quickly pulled out the splinter of wood buried in its paw. The wound was almost septic, but the medicine he applied would prevent further infection. The animal would awaken a few minutes later, on the road to recovery, if not immediately ready to face the world.

As Bharat cleaned his hands with medicinal herbs, Ram gently picked up the rabbit and wedged it into a nook in a tree to keep it away from predators. He glanced at Bharat. 'It will wake up soon. It'll live.'

Bharat smiled. 'By the grace of Lord Rudra.'

Ram, Bharat, Lakshman and Shatrughan were on one of their fortnightly expeditions into the jungle, where they tended to injured animals. They did not interfere in a predator's hunt; it was only its natural behaviour. But, if they came upon an injured animal, they assisted it to the best of their abilities.

'*Dada*,' said Shatrughan, standing at a distance, watching his elder brothers with keen concentration.

Ram and Bharat turned around. A dishevelled Lakshman was even farther away, behind Shatrughan. He was distractedly throwing stones at a tree.

'Lakshman, don't linger at the back,' said Ram. 'We are not in the *ashram*. This is the jungle. There is danger in being alone.'

Lakshman sighed in irritation and walked up to the group.

'Yes, what is it, Shatrughan?' asked Ram, turning to his youngest brother.

'Bharat *Dada* put *jatyadi tel* on the rabbit's wound. Unless you cover it with neem leaves, the medicine will not be effective.'

'Of course,' exclaimed Ram, tapping his forehead. 'You're right, Shatrughan.'

Ram picked up the rabbit as Bharat pulled out some neem leaves from his leather pouch.

Bharat looked at Shatrughan, grinning broadly. 'Is there anything in the world that you do not know, Shatrughan?'

Shatrughan smiled. 'Not much.'

Bharat applied the neem leaves on the rabbit's wound, tied the bandage again, and placed him back in the nook.

Ram said, 'I wonder if we actually help these animals on our bi-weekly medical tour or are we just assuaging our conscience?'

'We are assuaging our conscience,' said Bharat, with a wry smile. 'Nothing more, but at least we aren't ignoring our conscience.'

Ram shook his head. 'Why are you so cynical?'

'Why are you not cynical at all?'

Ram raised his eyebrows resignedly and began to walk. Bharat caught up with him. Lakshman and Shatrughan fell in line, a few steps behind.

'Knowing the human race, how can you not be cynical?' Bharat asked.

'Come on,' said Ram. 'We're capable of greatness, Bharat. All we need is an inspirational leader.'

'*Dada*,' said Bharat, 'I'm not suggesting that there is no goodness in human beings. There is, and it is worth fighting for. But there is also so much viciousness that sometimes I think it would have been better for the planet if the human species simply did not exist.'

'That's too much! We're not so bad.'

Bharat laughed softly. 'All I'm suggesting is that greatness and goodness is a potential in a majority of humans, not a reality.'

'What do you mean?'

'Expecting people to follow rules just because they should is being too hopeful. Rules must be designed to dovetail with selfish interest because people are primarily driven by it. They need to be shepherded into good behaviour through this proclivity.'

'People also respond to calls for greatness.'

'No, they don't, *Dada*. There may be a few who will answer that call. Most won't.'

'Lord Rudra led people selflessly, didn't he?'

'Yes,' said Bharat. 'But many who followed him had their own selfish interests in mind. That is a fact.'

Ram shook his head. 'We'll never agree on this.'

Bharat smiled. 'Yes, we won't. But I still love you!'

Ram smiled as well, changing the topic. 'How was your holiday? I never get to speak with you when we are there…'

'You know why,' muttered Bharat. 'But I must admit it was not too bad this time.'

Bharat loved to have his maternal relatives visit Ayodhya. It was an opportunity for him to escape his stern mother. Kaikeyi did not like his spending too much time with his brothers. In fact, if she could have her way, she would keep him to herself exclusively during the times when they were home. To make matters worse, she would insist on endless conversations about the need for him to be great and fulfil his mother's destiny. The only people Kaikeyi did not mind sharing her son with were her own blood-family. The presence of his maternal grandparents and uncle on this holiday ensured that Bharat was free of his mother. He had spent practically the entire vacation in their indulgent company.

Ram punched Bharat playfully in his stomach. 'She's your mother, Bharat. She only wants what is best for you.'

'I could do with some love instead, *Dada*. You know, I remember when I was three, I once dropped a glass of milk and she slapped me! She slapped me so hard, in the presence of her maids.'

'You remember stuff from when you were three? I thought I was the only one who did.'

'How can I forget? I was a little boy. The glass was too big for my hands. It was heavy; it slipped! That's it! Why did she have to slap me?'

Ram understood his stepmother, Kaikeyi. She had her share of frustrations. She'd been the brightest child in her family. Unfortunately, her brilliance did not make her father proud. Quite the contrary, Ashwapati was unhappy that Kaikeyi outshone his son, Yudhaajit. It appalled Ram that society did not value capable women. And now, the intelligent yet frustrated Kaikeyi sought vicarious recognition through Bharat, her son. She aimed to realise her ambitions through him.

Ram held his counsel though.

Bharat continued, wistfully, 'If only I had a mother like yours. She would have loved me unconditionally and not chewed my brains.'

Ram did not respond, but he got the feeling that something was playing on Bharat's mind.

'What is it, Bharat?' asked Ram, without turning to look at his younger brother.

Bharat lowered his voice so that Lakshman and Shatrughan wouldn't overhear. 'Ram *Dada*, have you thought about what Guru*ji* said today?'

Ram held his breath.

'*Dada?*' asked Bharat.

Ram stiffened. 'This is treason. I refuse to entertain such thoughts.'

'Treason? To think about the good of your country?'

'He is our father! There are duties that we have—'

'Do you think he's a good king?' Bharat interrupted.

'There's a law in the *Manu Smriti* that clearly states a son must—'

'Don't tell me what the law says, *Dada*,' said Bharat, dismissing with a wave of his hand the laws recorded in the *Book of Manu*. 'I have read the *Manu Smriti* too. I want to know what *you* think.'

'I think the law must be obeyed.'

'Really? Is that all you have to say?'

'I can add to that.'

'Please do!'

'The law must *always* be obeyed.'

Bharat rolled his eyes in exasperation.

'I understand that this might not work under a few exceptional circumstances,' said Ram. 'But if the law is obeyed diligently, come what may, then over a period of time a better society *has* to emerge.'

'Nobody in Ayodhya gives two hoots about the law, *Dada*! We are a civilisation in an advanced state of decay. We're the most hypocritical people on earth. We criticise corruption in others, but are blind to our own dishonesty. We hate others who do wrong and commit crimes, blithely ignoring our own misdeeds, big and small. We vehemently blame Raavan for all our ills, refusing to acknowledge that we created the mess we find ourselves in.'

'And how will this change?'

'This attitude is basic human nature. We'd rather look outward and blame others for the ills that befall us than point the finger at ourselves. I've said it before and I'll say it again. We need a king who can create systems with which one can harness even selfish human nature for the betterment of society.'

'*Nonsense*. We need a great leader, one who will lead by example. A leader who will inspire his people to discover their godhood within! We don't need a leader who will leave his people free to do whatever they desire.'

'No, *Dada*. Freedom is an ally, if used with wisdom.'

'Freedom is never the ally of the law. You can have freedom to choose whether you want to join or leave a society based on the rule of law. But so long as you live in such a society, you must obey the law.'

'The law is and always will be an ass. It's a tool, a means to an end,' said Bharat.

Ram brought the exchange to an end with a convivial laugh. Bharat grinned and patted his brother on his back.

'So, all these things you say about a great leader being inspirational and enabling the discovery of the God within and other such noble things…' said Bharat. 'You think Father lives up to that ideal?'

Ram cast a reproachful look at his brother, refusing to rise to the bait.

Bharat grinned, playfully boxing Ram on his shoulder. 'Let it be, *Dada*. Let it be.'

Ram was genuinely conflicted. But, as a dutiful son, he would not allow himself, even in his own mind, to entertain rebellious thoughts against his father.

Lakshman, walking a few steps behind, was engrossed in the frenetic activities of the jungle.

Shatrughan, however, was listening in on the conversation with keen interest. *Ram* Dada *is too idealistic. Bharat* Dada *is practical and real.*

Chapter 7

Another one? Ram refrained from voicing his thoughts, trying to control his surprise. *This is his fifth girlfriend.*

Seventeen years had gone by since Dashrath lost the Battle of Karachapa. At the age of sixteen, Bharat had discovered the pleasures of love. Charismatic and flamboyant as he was, girls liked Bharat as much as he liked them. Tribal traditions being liberal, the empowered women of the tribe of Chief Varun, the local hosts of the *gurukul*, were free to form relationships with whomever they pleased. And Bharat was especially popular.

He walked up to Ram now, holding hands with an ethereally beautiful maiden who was clearly older than him, perhaps twenty years of age.

'How are you, Bharat?'

'Never been better, *Dada*,' grinned Bharat. 'Any better and it would be downright sinful.'

Ram smiled politely and turned to the girl with grace.

'*Dada*,' said Bharat, 'allow me to introduce Radhika, the daughter of Chief Varun.'

'Honoured to make your acquaintance,' said Ram, formally bringing his hands together in a polite namaste and bowing his head.

Radhika raised her eyebrows, amused. 'Bharat was right. You are ridiculously formal.'

Ram's eyes widened at her forthrightness.

'I did not use the word "ridiculous",' protested Bharat, as he let her hand go. 'How can I use a word like that for *Dada*?'

Radhika ruffled Bharat's hair affectionately. 'All right, "ridiculous" was my own addition. But I find your formality charming. So does Bharat, actually. But I'm sure you know that already.'

'Thank you,' said Ram, straightening his *angvastram* stiffly.

Radhika giggled at Ram's obvious discomfort. Even Ram, relatively immune to feminine wiles, was forced to acknowledge that her laughter had a pleasing lilt, like that of the *apsaras, celestial nymphs*.

Ram said to Bharat, careful to speak in old Sanskrit so that Radhika wouldn't understand, '*Saa Vartate Lavanyavati.*'

Though Bharat's understanding of archaic Sanskrit was not as good as Ram's, he understood the simple compliment. Ram had said, '*She is exquisitely beautiful.*'

Before Bharat could respond, Radhika spoke. '*Aham Jaanaami.*'

'*I know.*'

An embarrassed Ram retorted, 'By the great Lord Brahma! Your old Sanskrit is perfect.'

Radhika smiled. 'We may speak new Sanskrit these days, but the ancient scriptures can only be understood in the old language.'

Bharat felt the need to cut in. 'Don't be fooled by her intelligence, *Dada*. She is also very beautiful!'

Ram smiled and brought his hands together once again, in a respectful namaste. 'My apologies if I offended you in any way, Radhika.'

Radhika smiled, shaking her head. 'No, you didn't. Why would a girl not enjoy an elegant compliment to her beauty?'

'My little brother is lucky.'

'I'm not so unlucky myself,' assured Radhika, ruffling Bharat's hair once again.

Ram could see that his brother was besotted. Clearly, this time it was different; Radhika meant a lot more to him than his previous girlfriends. But he was also aware of the traditions of the forest people. Their girls, no doubt, were liberated, but they did not marry outside their community. Their law simply forbade it. Ram did not understand the reason for this. It could be an effort to retain the sense of purity of the forest people, or it might even be that they considered city dwellers inferior for having moved away from Mother Nature. He hoped his brother's heart would not be broken in the process.

—— 𝕏 ▮ ☼ ——

'How much butter will you eat?!' Ram could never quite understand Bharat's addiction.

Evening time, the last hour of the third *prahar,* found Ram and Bharat relaxing under a tree at the *gurukul.* Lakshman and Shatrughan were using their free time for some riding practice; in fact, they were competing fiercely in the open ground. Lakshman, by far the best rider among the four, was beating Shatrughan hollow.

'I like it, *Dada,*' shrugged Bharat, butter smeared around his mouth.

'But it's unhealthy. It's fattening!'

Bharat flexed his biceps as he sucked in his breath and puffed up his chest, displaying his muscular and well-toned physique. 'Do I look fat to you?'

Ram smiled. 'Girls certainly do not find you unappealing. So my opinion really is of no consequence.'

'Exactly!' Bharat chuckled, digging his hand into the clay pot and spooning some more butter into his mouth.

Ram gently put his hand on Bharat's shoulder. Bharat stopped eating as he read the concerned look on his brother's face.

Ram spoke softly. 'Bharat, you do know—'

Bharat interrupted him immediately. 'It won't happen, *Dada*.'

'But Bharat…'

'*Dada*, trust me. I know girls better than you do.'

'You're aware that Chief Varun's people do not…'

'*Dada*, she loves me as much as I love her. Radhika will break the law for me. She will not leave me. Trust me.'

'How can you be so sure?'

'*I am!*'

'But Bharat…'

'*Dada*, stop worrying about me. Just be happy for me.'

Ram gave up and patted him on his shoulder. 'Well then, congratulations!'

Bharat bowed his head theatrically, 'Thank you, kind sir!'

Ram's face broke into a broad smile.

'When will I get the opportunity to congratulate *you*, *Dada*?' asked Bharat.

Ram looked at Bharat and frowned.

'Aren't you attracted to any girl? Here or in Ayodhya? We have met so many on our annual holidays…'

'Nobody is worth it.'

'Nobody?'

'No.'

'What are you looking for?'

Ram looked into the distance at the forest line. 'I want a woman, not a girl.'

'Aha! I always knew there was a naughty devil behind that serious exterior!'

Ram rolled his eyes and punched Bharat playfully on his abdomen. 'That's not what I meant. You know that.'

'Then what did you mean?'

'I don't want an immature girl. Love is secondary. It's not important. I want someone whom I can respect.'

'Respect?' frowned Bharat. 'Sounds boring.'

'A relationship is not just for fun, it is also about trust and the knowledge that you can depend on your partner. Relationships based on passion and excitement do not last.'

'Really?'

Ram quickly corrected himself. 'Of course, Radhika and you will be different.'

'Of course,' grinned Bharat.

'I guess what I'm trying to say is that I want a woman who is better than I am; a woman who will compel me to bow my head in admiration.'

'You bow to elders and parents, *Dada*. A wife is the one you share your life and passions with,' said Bharat, a crooked grin on his face, brows arched suggestively. 'By the great Lord Brahma, I pity the woman you will marry. Your relationship will go down in history as the most boring of them all!'

Ram laughed aloud as he pushed Bharat playfully. Bharat dropped the pot and pushed Ram back, then sprang to his feet and sprinted away from Ram.

'You can't outrun me, Bharat!' laughed Ram, quickly rising to his feet and taking off after his brother.

— 大 🐟 ☼ —

'Whom do you favour?' asked the visitor.

A mysterious stranger had made a quiet entry into the *gurukul*. In keeping with Vashishta's desire to maintain the secrecy of this visit, he'd arrived late in the night. As luck would have it, the intrepid Lakshman was out riding at the same time, having broken the rule of being in the sleeping quarters at this time of the night. As he traced his way back, he came upon an unknown horse tied discreetly to a tree far from the *ashram* premises.

He led his own animal quietly back into the stable. The Ayodhyan prince then decided to inform his guru of a possible intruder. On finding Vashishta's room empty, Lakshman grew suspicious. Unable to contain himself, he decided to investigate the goings-on. He finally spotted the sage under the bridge, conversing softly with the mysterious visitor. Lakshman crept close, hid behind the bushes, and eavesdropped on the conversation. 'I haven't made up my mind as yet,' answered Vashishta.

'You need to decide quickly, Guru*ji*.'

'Why?'

Though unable to see the visitor clearly, Lakshman was barely able to contain the panic rising within him. Even the failing light couldn't conceal the stranger's unnaturally fair skin, giant size and rippling musculature. His body was covered with fur-like hair, and a peculiar outgrowth emerged from his lower back. Clearly he was a dangerous Naga, the mysterious race of the deformed, which was feared in all of the Sapt Sindhu. He made no attempt to conceal his identity, like most Nagas did, with a face mask or a hooded robe. Notably, his lower body was draped in a *dhoti*, in keeping with traditional Indian custom.

'Because *they* are on to you,' said the Naga, with a meaningful look.

'So?'

'Are you not afraid?'

Vashishta shrugged. 'Why should I be?'

The Naga laughed softly. 'There's a thin line that separates courage from stupidity.'

'And that line is only visible in retrospect, my friend. If I'm successful, people will call me brave. If I fail, I will be called foolish. Let me do what I think is right. I'll leave the verdict to the future.'

The Naga thrust his chin forward in a show of disagreement, but gave up the argument. 'What would you have me do?'

'Nothing for now. Just wait,' answered Vashishta.

'Are you aware that Raavan is—'

'Yes, I know.'

'And you still choose to remain here and not do anything?'

'Raavan…' murmured Vashishta, choosing his words carefully, 'well, he has his uses.'

Lakshman could barely control his shock. Yet, the teenager had the presence of mind to stay silent.

'There are some who are convinced you are preparing for a rebellion against Emperor Dashrath,' said the Naga, his tone clearly indicating his disbelief.

Vashishta laughed softly. 'There is no need to rebel against him. The kingdom is practically out of his hands anyway. He's a good man, but he has sunk into the depths of depression and defeatism. My goal is bigger.'

'Our goal,' corrected the Naga.

'Of course,' smiled Vashishta, patting him on his shoulder. 'Forgive me. It is our collective goal. But if people insist on thinking that our ambitions are limited to Ayodhya, I suggest we let them be.'

'Yes, that's true.'

'Come with me,' said Vashishta. 'I have something to show you.'

Lakshman let out a deep breath as the two men walked away. His heart was pounding desperately.

What is Guruji up to? Are we safe here?

Checking carefully that the coast was clear, Lakshman slipped away and rushed to Ram's quarters.

'Lakshman, go back to sleep,' admonished an irritated Ram. He had been woken up by a hysterical Lakshman. He'd heard the panic-stricken report, and groggily decided that his brother was once again indulging his love for conspiracy.

'*Dada*, I'm telling you, there's something going on. It concerns Ayodhya, and Guru*ji* is involved,' insisted Lakshman.

'Have you told Bharat?'

'Of course not! He could be in on it too.'

Ram glared at Lakshman. 'He too is your *dada*, Lakshman!'

'*Dada*, you are too simple. You refuse to see the den of conspiracies that Ayodhya is. Guru*ji* is in on it. Others could be too. I trust only you. You are supposed to protect us all. I have done my duty by letting you know. Now, it is up to you to investigate this.'

'There is nothing to investigate, Lakshman. Go back to your room and sleep.'

'*Dada*…'

'Back to your room, Lakshman! Now!'

Chapter 8

'What is the ideal way of life?' asked Vashishta.

In the early hours of the morning, the four Ayodhyan princes sat facing their guru, having just completed the *Guru Stotram*.

'Well?' prompted Vashishta, having been met with silence.

He looked at Lakshman, expecting him to take the first shot. However, to Vashishta's surprise, the boy sat tense, barely able to conceal his hostility.

'Is there a problem, Paurav?' enquired Vashishta.

Lakshman cast an accusatory glance at Ram, then stared at the ground. 'No, Guru*ji*. There is no problem.'

'Do you want to attempt an answer?'

'I don't know the answer, Guru*ji*.'

Vashishta frowned. Ignorance had never deterred Lakshman from attempting a response before. He spoke to Bharat. 'Vasu, can you try and answer?'

'An ideal way of life, Guru*ji*,' said Bharat, 'is one where everyone is healthy, wealthy, happy, and working in consonance with his purpose in life.'

'And, how does a society achieve this?'

'It's probably impossible! But if it were possible at all, it would only be through freedom. Allow people the freedom to forge their own path. They will find their way.'

'But will freedom help each person realise his dreams? What if one person's dream is in conflict with that of another's?'

Bharat gave that question some careful thought before replying. 'You are right. A strong man's effort will always overwhelm that of a weak man.'

'So?'

'So the government has to ensure that it protects the weak. We cannot allow the strong to keep winning. It would create discontent among the masses.'

'Why, *Dada*?' asked Shatrughan. 'I would say, allow the strong to win. Will that not be better for the society as a whole?'

'But isn't that the law of the jungle?' asked Vashishta. 'The weak would die out.'

'If you call it the law of the jungle, then I say that this is the law of nature, Guru*ji*,' said Shatrughan. 'Who are we to judge nature? If the weakest deer are not killed by tigers, the population of deer will explode. They will eat prodigious amounts of greens and the jungle itself may die out, in the long run. It is better for the jungle if only the strong survive — it is nature's way of maintaining balance. The government should not interfere with this natural process. It should merely establish systems that ensure the protection of the weak, giving them a fair chance at survival. Beyond that, it must get out of the way and let society find its own path. It's not the government's job to ensure that all achieve their dreams.'

'Then why even bother with a government?'

'It's needed for a few essentials that individuals cannot provide: an army to protect the borders from external attack, a system of basic education for all. One of the things that differentiates us from animals is that we do not kill our weak. But if the government interferes to such an extent that the weak thrive and the strong are oppressed, society itself will collapse over time. A society should not forget that it thrives on the ideas and performance of the talented among its citizens. If you compromise the prospects of the strong, and lean too much towards the interests of the weak, then your society itself goes into decline.'

Vashishta smiled. 'You have carefully studied the reasons for the decline of India under the successors of Emperor Bharat, haven't you?'

Shatrughan nodded. Bharat was a legendary Chandravanshi emperor who lived thousands of years ago. He was one of the greatest rulers since the great Indra of the Devas. He brought all of India under his rule and his government had been the most compassionate and nurturing of all times.

'Why, then, did Bharat's successors not change their ways when they could see that it wasn't working anymore?' asked Vashishta.

'I don't know,' said Shatrughan.

'It was because the philosophy that guided Emperor Bharat's empire was itself a reaction to an equally successful, but radically different one which determined how society was organised earlier. Emperor Bharat's empire could be described as the apogee of the feminine way of life — of freedom, passion and beauty. At its best, it is compassionate, creative and especially nurturing towards the weak. But as feminine civilisations decline, they tend to become corrupt, irresponsible and decadent.'

'Guru*ji*,' said Ram, 'are you saying there is another way of life? The masculine way?'

'Yes. The masculine way of life is defined by truth, duty and honour. At its peak, masculine civilisations are efficient, just and egalitarian. But as they decline, they become fanatical, rigid and especially harsh towards the weak.'

'So when feminine civilisations decline, the masculine way is the answer,' said Ram. 'And, as masculine civilisations decline, the feminine way should take over.'

'Yes,' said the teacher. 'Life is cyclical.'

'Can it be safely said that today's India is a feminine nation in decline?' asked Bharat.

Vashishta looked at Bharat. 'Actually, India is a confused nation today. It does not understand its nature, which seems to be a hotchpotch of the masculine and feminine way. But if you force me to choose, then I would state that, at this point in time, we're a feminine culture in decline.'

'Then the question is: is it time to move towards a masculine way of life or a revived feminine culture?' argued Bharat. 'I'm not sure India can live without freedom. We're a nation of rebels. We argue and fight about everything. We can only succeed by walking down the path of femininity, of freedom. The masculine way may work for a short span of time, but it cannot last. We are simply not obedient enough to follow the masculine way for too long.'

'So it seems today,' said Vashishta. 'But it wasn't always so. There was a time when the masculine way of life characterised India.'

Bharat was silenced into contemplation.

But Ram was intrigued. 'Guru*ji*, you said that the feminine way of life established by Emperor Bharat was unable to change even when it needed to, because it was a reaction to the ills that an earlier masculine culture had degenerated into. Possibly, to them, the earlier way of life was stamped as evil.'

'You're right, Sudas,' said Vashishta, using Ram's *gurukul* name.

'Can you tell us about this earlier masculine way of life? What was this empire like?' asked Ram. 'Could we find answers in it, to our present-day ills?'

'It was an empire that arose many millennia ago, and conquered practically all of India with stunning swiftness. It had a radically different way of life and, at its peak, it scaled the heights of greatness.'

'Who were these people?'

'Their foundations were laid right here, where we are. It was so long ago that most have forgotten the significance of this *ashram.*'

'Here?'

'Yes. It was here that the progenitors of that empire received their education from their great guru. He taught them the essentials of an enlightened masculine way of life. This was his *ashram.*'

'Who was this great sage?' asked Ram in awe.

Vashishta took a deep breath. He knew that the answer would evoke shock. The name of that ancient *great rishi* was feared today; so much so that it was not even uttered aloud, ever. Keeping his eyes fixed on Ram, he answered, *'Maharishi* Shukracharya.'

Bharat, Lakshman and Shatrughan froze. Shukracharya was the guru of the Asuras, and the Asuras were demonic fanatics who had controlled almost the entire Indian landmass thousands of years ago. They were finally defeated by the *Devas*, respected today as *Gods*, in brutal battles fought over a protracted period of time. Although the Asura Empire was eventually destroyed, the wars took a heavy toll on India. Millions died, and rebuilding civilisation took a very long time. Indra, the leader of the Devas, ensured the expulsion of the Asuras from India. Shukracharya's name was reduced to mud, his memory violated by righteous indignation and irrational fear.

The students were too stunned to react. Ram's eyes, though, conveyed curiosity, unlike the others.

— |大| 🐟 ☼ —

Vashishta stepped out late in the night, expecting a tumult among his students; the conversation about Guru Shukracharya had been meant to provoke. Lakshman and Shatrughan were sound asleep in their rooms, but Ram and Bharat were missing. Vashishta decided to walk around the premises in search of them, the moonlight providing adequate illumination. Hearing soft voices ahead, he soon came upon the silhouette of an animated Bharat in the company of a girl.

Bharat seemed to be pleading. 'But why…'

'I'm sorry, Bharat,' the girl said calmly. 'I will not break the laws of my people.'

'But I love you, Radhika … I know you love me… Why should we care about what others think?'

Vashishta quickly turned around and began to walk in the other direction. It was inappropriate to intrude on a private and painful moment.

Where is Ram?

On a whim, he changed course once again and walked up the stone pathway that led to the small temples built into the central facade of the rock face. He entered the temple of Lord Indra, the king of the Devas; the one who defeated the Asuras. The symbolism of Indra's temple being in the centre was powerful, for Indra had led the army that obliterated Shukracharya's legacy.

Vashishta heard a soft sound from behind the massive idol, and instinctively moved towards it. The space at the back was large enough to comfortably accommodate four or five people. The shadows of Vashishta and the idol seemed to dance on the floor as flames leapt from a torch on the wall.

As his gaze travelled beyond the idol, he could vaguely make out the figure of Ram on his knees, prising open with a metal bar a heavy stone that covered an ancient inscription on the floor. Just as he succeeded, Ram sensed Vashishta's presence.

'Guru*ji*,' said Ram, as he dropped the tool and stood up immediately.

Vashishta walked up to him, put his arm around his shoulder and gently sat him down again as he bent down to examine the inscription that Ram had uncovered.

'Can you read what it says?' asked Vashishta.

It was an ancient, long-forgotten script.

'I have not seen this script before,' said Ram.

'It is particularly ancient, banned in India because the Asuras used it.'

'The Asuras were the great masculine empire you mentioned today, isn't it?'

'That's obvious!'

Ram gestured towards the inscription. 'What does it say, Guru*ji*?'

Vashishta ran his forefinger along the words of the inscription. '"How can the universe speak the name of Shukracharya? For the universe is so small. And Shukracharya is so big."'

Ram touched the inscription lightly.

'Legend holds that this was his *aasan*, the *seat* that he sat upon as he taught,' said Vashishta.

Ram looked up at Vashishta. 'Tell me about him, Guru*ji*.'

'A very small minority still maintains that he probably was one of the greatest Indians that trod the earth. I don't know much about his childhood; apocryphal accounts suggest that he was born to a slave family in Egypt that abandoned him when he was but an infant. He was then adopted by a visiting Asura princess, who raised him as her own, in India. However, records of his works were deliberately obliterated and the ones that remained were heavily doctored by the powerful and wealthy elite of that time. He was a brilliant, charismatic soul who transformed marginalised Indian royals into the greatest conquering force of his time.'

'Marginalised *Indian* royals? But the Asuras were foreigners, weren't they?'

'Nonsense. This is propaganda spread by those with an agenda. Most Asuras were actually related to the Devas. In fact, the Devas and Asuras descended from common ancestors, known as the Manaskul. But the Asuras were the poorer, weaker cousins, scorned and half-forgotten members of an extended family. Shukracharya remoulded them with a powerful philosophy of hard work, discipline, unity and fierce loyalty for fellow Asuras.'

'But that would not add up to a recipe for victory and dominance. So how did they succeed so spectacularly?'

'The ones who hate them say they succeeded because they were barbaric warriors.'

'But you obviously disagree with them.'

'Well, the Devas weren't cowards either. It was the Age of Kshatriya, warrior-like qualities were highly sought after. They were probably as good as the Asuras in the art of warfare, if not better. The Asuras succeeded because they were united by a common purpose, unlike the Devas who had too many divisions.'

'Then why did the Asuras eventually decline? Did they become soft? How were the Devas able to defeat them?'

'As it often happens, the very reason for your success, over a prolonged period of time, can lead to your downfall. Shukracharya united the Asuras with the concept of the *Ekam*, the *One God*. All who worshipped the One God were equal in His eyes.'

Ram frowned. 'But that was hardly a new idea! Even the *Rig Veda* refers to *Ekam*, the *One Absolute*. To this day we call him the *Sum of all Souls*, the *Parmatma*. Even the followers of the feminine principle, like the Devas, believed in the *Ekam*.'

'There is a nuance that you're missing, Sudas. The *Rig Veda* states clearly that while the *Ekam* is the One God, He comes to us in many forms, as many Gods, to help us grow spiritually, in the hope that we will eventually understand Him in His original form. After all, variety is what surrounds us in nature; it is what we relate to. Shukracharya was different. He said that all other manifestations of the *Ekam* were false, leading us into *maya*, the *illusion*. The *Ekam* was the only True God, the only Reality, so to speak. It was a radical thought for that period. Suddenly, there was no hierarchy in the spiritual journey of both, the one who knew no scripture, as well as the one who was an expert on them, simply because they both believed in the *Ekam*.'

'This would make all human beings equal.'

'True. And, it worked well for some time for it obliterated all divisions within the Asuras. Furthermore, the dispossessed and oppressed among other groups like the Devas began to join the Asuras; it suddenly raised their social status. But like I've said many times, every idea has a positive and a negative. The Asuras thought that everyone who believed in their *Ekam* was equal. And what did they think of those who did not believe in their *Ekam*?'

'That they were not equal to them?' asked Ram, tentatively.

'Yes. All efforts to impose the concept of the One God upon minds that do not respect diversity will only result in intolerance. The *Upanishads* contain this warning.'

'Yes, I remember the hymn. Especially this couplet: *Giving a sharp sword to a child is not an act of generosity, but irresponsibility.* Is that what happened with the Asuras?'

'Yes. Shukracharya's immediate students, having been chosen by him, were intellectually and spiritually equipped to understand the seemingly radical concept of the *Ekam*. But the Asura Empire inevitably expanded, including within its folds increasing multitudes of people. As time went by, these believers held on to their faith in the *Ekam* but became exclusionist, demanding undivided devotion; their God was true, the other Gods were false. They grew to hate those who didn't believe in their One God, and ultimately began to kill them.'

'What?' Ram asked flabbergasted. 'That's preposterous! Doesn't the hymn on the *Ekam* also state that the only marker as to whether one truly understands the One God is that it becomes impossible to hate anyone? The *Ekam* exists in everybody and everything; if you feel any hatred at all towards anything or anyone, then you hate the *Ekam* Himself!'

'Yes, that's true. Unfortunately, the Asuras genuinely believed they were doing the right thing. As their numbers grew, their storm troopers let loose a reign of terror, tearing down temples, smashing idols and shrines, slaughtering those who persisted with the practice of worshipping other Gods.'

Ram shook his head. 'They must have turned everyone against them.'

'Exactly! And when circumstances changed, as they invariably do, the Asuras had no allies. The Devas, on the other hand, were always divided and hence did not attempt to force their ways on others. How could they? They could not even agree among themselves on what their own way of life was! Fortuitously then, they were spoilt for choice when it came to allies. All the non-Asuras were tired of the constant provocation and violence from the Asuras. They joined forces with their enemies, the Devas. Ironically, many Asuras themselves had begun to question this over-reliance on violence. They too changed allegiance and moved over to the other side. Is it any surprise that the Asuras lost?'

Ram shook his head. 'That is a major risk with the masculine way, isn't it? Exclusivist thought can easily lapse into intolerance and rigidity, especially in times of trouble. The feminine way will not face this problem.'

'Yes, rigid intolerance creates mortal enemies with whom negotiation is impossible. But the feminine way has other problems; most importantly, of how to unite their own behind a larger cause. The followers of the feminine way are usually so divided that it takes a miracle for them to come together for any one purpose, under a single banner.'

Ram, who had seen the worst of the divisions and inefficiencies of the feminine way of life in the India of today, appeared genuinely curious about the masculine order. 'The masculine way needs to be revived. The way of the Asuras is a possible answer to India's current problems. But the Asura way cannot and should not be replicated. Some improvements and adjustments are necessary. Questioning must be encouraged. And, it has to be tailored to suit our current circumstances.'

'Why not the feminine way?' asked the guru.

'I believe leaders of the feminine way tend to shirk responsibilities. Their message to their followers is: "It's your decision". When things go wrong, there's no one who can be held accountable. In the masculine way, the leader has to assume all the responsibility. And only when leaders assume responsibility can society actually function. There is clear direction and purpose for society as a whole. Otherwise, there is endless debate, analysis and paralysis.'

Vashishta smiled. 'You are oversimplifying things. But I will not deny that if you want quick improvements, the masculine way works better. The feminine route takes time, but in the long run, it can be more stable and durable.'

'The masculine way can also prove to be stable, if we learn lessons from the past.'

'Are you willing to forge such a new path?'

'I will certainly try,' said Ram with disarming honesty. 'It is my duty to my motherland; to this great country of ours.'

'Well, you are welcome to revive the masculine way. But I suggest you don't name it Asura. It is such a reviled name today that your ideas will be doomed from the very beginning.'

'Then what do you suggest?'

'Names don't matter. What matters is the philosophy underlying them. There was a time when the Asuras represented the masculine way and the Devas, the feminine. Then, the Asuras were destroyed and only the Devas survived. The Suryavanshis and Chandravanshis are descendants of the Devas; both representatives of the feminine. But, for all you know, if you achieve what I think you can, the Suryavanshis could end up representing the masculine way of life and the Chandravanshis could carry forward the legacy of their ancestors, the Devas. Like I said, names don't matter.'

Ram looked down again at the inscription as he pondered over the unknown person who had carved this message long ago. It seemed like an act of impotent rebellion. Shukracharya's name had been banned across the land. His loyal followers were not even allowed to speak his name. Perhaps this was their way of applying a salve to their conscience at not being able to publicly honour their guru.

Vashishta put his hand on Ram's shoulder. 'I will tell you more about Shukracharya, his life and his philosophy. He was a genius. You can learn from him and create a great empire. But you must remember that while you can certainly learn from the successes of great men, you can learn even more from their failures and mistakes.'

'Yes, Guru*ji*.'

Chapter 9

'We will not be meeting for a long time after this, Guru*ji*,' said the Naga.

A few months had elapsed since Ram and Vashishta's conversation on Shukracharya in the temple of Lord Indra. The formal education of the princes in the *gurukul* was complete, and the boys would be returning home for good the following day. Lakshman had decided to go riding one last time, late in the night. While trying to return undetected, he came upon a replay of the meeting between his guru and the suspicious Naga.

They had met under the bridge, once again.

'Yes, it will be difficult,' agreed Vashishta. 'People in Ayodhya do not know about my other life. But I will find ways to communicate.'

The outgrowth from his lower back flicked like a tail as the Naga spoke. 'I have heard that your former friend's alliance with Raavan grows stronger.'

Vashishta closed his eyes and took a deep breath before speaking softly. 'He will always remain my friend. He helped me when I was alone.'

The Naga narrowed his eyes, his interest piqued. 'You have to tell me this story sometime, Guru*ji*. What happened?'

Vashishta gave the hint of a wry smile. 'Some stories are best left untold.'

The Naga realised he had ventured into painful territory and decided not to pry any further.

'But I know what you've come for,' said Vashishta, changing the topic.

The Naga smiled. 'I have to know…'

'Ram,' said Vashishta, simply.

The Naga seemed surprised. 'I thought it would be Prince Bharat…'

'No. It's Ram. It has to be.'

The Naga nodded. 'Then, Prince Ram it is. You know you can count on our support.'

'Yes, I know.'

Lakshman felt his heartbeat quicken as he continued to listen, soundlessly.

— 𑀑 🐟 ☼ —

'*Dada*, you really do not understand the world,' cried Lakshman.

'In the name of Lord Ikshvaku, just go back to sleep,' mumbled an exasperated Ram. 'You see conspiracies everywhere.'

'But…'

'Lakshman!'

'They have decided to kill you, *Dada*! I know it.'

'When will you believe that nobody is trying to kill me? Why would Guru*ji* want me dead? Why would *anyone* want me dead, for crying out loud?!' exclaimed Ram. 'Nobody was trying to kill me then, when we were out riding. And, nobody is trying to kill me now. I am not so important, you know. Now go to sleep!'

'*Dada*, you're just so clueless! At this rate, I don't know how I'm supposed to protect you.'

'You will protect me forever, somehow,' said Ram, softening and smiling indulgently as he pulled his brother's cheek. 'Go back to sleep now.'

'*Dada*...'

'Lakshman!'

—— 𐰴 ♦ ☼ ——

'Welcome home, my son,' cried Kaushalya.

Unable to suppress her tears of joy, the queen looked proudly at her son as he held her awkwardly, slightly embarrassed by her open display of emotion. Like his mother, the eighteen-year-old eldest prince of the Raghu clan of Ayodhya had a dark, flawless complexion, which perfectly set off his sober white *dhoti* and *angvastram*. His broad shoulders, lean body and powerful back were a testimony to his archery skills. Long hair tied neatly in an unassuming bun, he wore simple ear studs and a string of Rudraaksh beads around his neck. The studs were shaped like the sun with streaming rays, which was symbolic of the Suryavanshi rulers, descendants of the sun. The Rudraaksh, brown, elliptical beads derived from the tree of the same name, represented Lord Rudra, who had saved India from Evil some millennia ago.

He stepped away from his mother as she finally stopped crying. He went down on one knee, bowing his head with respect towards his father. A hushed silence descended on the court, in full attendance during this ceremonial occasion. The impressive Great Hall of the Unconquerable hadn't seen a gathering like this in nearly two decades. This royal court hall, along with the palace, had been built by the charismatic warrior-king Raghu, the great-grandfather of Ram. He had famously restored the power of the Ayodhya royalty through stunning conquests, so much so that the title of the House of Ayodhya had been changed from the 'Clan of Ikshvaku', to the 'Clan of Raghu'. Ram did not approve of this change, for to him it was a betrayal of his lineage. Howsoever great one's achievements were, they could not overshadow those of one's ancestors. He would have preferred the use of 'Clan of Ikshvaku' for his family; after all, Ikshvaku was the founder of the dynasty. But few were interested in Ram's opinions.

Ram continued to kneel, but the official acknowledgment was not forthcoming. Vashishta, the raj guru, sat to the right of the emperor, looking at him with silent disapproval.

Dashrath seemed lost in thought as he stared blankly into space. His hands rested on golden armrests shaped like lions. A gold-coloured canopy, embedded with priceless jewels, was suspended over the throne. The magnificent court hall and the throne were symbolic of the power and might of the Ayodhyans; or at least, they had been so, once upon a time. Peeling paint and fraying edges spoke volumes of the decline of this once-great kingdom. Precious stones from the throne had been pulled out, probably to pay the bills. The thousand-pillared hall still appeared grand, but an old eye would know that it had seen better days in years past, when vibrant silk pennants hung from the walls, separating engraved figures of ancient *rishis* — *seers* and *men of knowledge*. The figures could have certainly done with a thorough cleaning.

Palpable embarrassment spread in the hall as Ram waited. A murmur among the courtiers reaffirmed what was well known: Ram was not the favoured son.

The son remained still and unmoved. Truth be told, he was not the least bit surprised. Used to disdain and calumny, he had learnt to ignore it. Every trip back home from the *gurukul* had been torture. Almost by design, most people found some way to constantly remind him of the misfortune of his birth. The 'taint of 7,032', the year of his birth according to the calendar of Manu, would not be forgotten. It had troubled him in his childhood, but he found himself wryly recalling what the man he admired as a father, Guru Vashishta, had said to him once.

Kimapi Nu Janaahaa Vadishyanti. Tadeva Kaaryam Janaanaam.
People will talk nonsense. It is, after all, their job.

Kaikeyi walked up to her husband, went down on her knees and placed Dashrath's partially paralysed right leg on the foot stand. Carefully displaying the dutiful and submissive gesture for public consumption, she brought her aggression into full play in private, as she hissed her command. 'Acknowledge Ram. Remember, descendant, not protector.'

A flicker of life flashed across the emperor's face. He raised his chin imperiously as he spoke. 'Rise, Ram Chandra, descendant of the Raghu clan.'

Vashishta narrowed his eyes with disapproval and cast a glance at Ram.

Adorned in rich finery and heavy gold ornaments, prominent among the first row of nobility, was a fair-skinned woman with a bent back. Her face was scarred by an old disease, and along with the hunched back, she had a menacing presence. Turning slightly to the man standing beside her, she whispered, 'Hmm, did you understand, Druhyu? Descendant, not protector.'

Druhyu bowed his head in deference as he addressed the wealthiest and most powerful merchant of the Sapt Sindhu, 'Yes, Manthara*ji*.'

That Dashrath had avoided the word 'protector' was a clear indication to all who were present that Ram would not be accorded what was the birthright of the first-born. Ram did not show disappointment as he rose to his feet with stoic decorum. Folding his hands together in a namaste, he bowed his head and spoke with crisp solemnity, 'May all the Gods of our great land continue to protect you, my father.' He then stepped back to take his position in single file along with his brothers.

Standing beside Ram, Bharat, though shorter, was heavier in build. Years of hard work showed in his musculature, while the scars he bore gave him a fearsome yet attractive look. He'd inherited his mother's fair complexion and had set it off with a bright blue *dhoti* and *angvastram*. The headband that held his long hair in place was embellished with an intricate, embroidered golden peacock feather. His charisma, though, lay in his eyes and face; a sharp nose, strong chin and eyes that danced with mischief. At this moment though, they displayed sadness. He cast a concerned look at his brother Ram before turning to Dashrath, visibly angry.

Bharat marched forward with studied nonchalance and went down on one knee. Shockingly for the assemblage, he refused to bow his head. He stared at his father with open hostility.

Kaikeyi had remained standing next to Dashrath. She glared at her son, willing him into submission. But Bharat was too old for such efforts at intimidation. Imperceptibly, unnoticed by anyone, Kaikeyi bowed her head and whispered to her husband. Dashrath repeated what was told to him.

'Rise, Bharat, descendant of the Raghu clan.'

Bharat smiled delightedly at not being accorded the title of the 'protector' either. He stood up and spoke with casual aplomb, 'May Lord Indra and Lord Varun grant you wisdom, my father.'

He winked at Ram as he quickly walked back to where his brothers stood. Ram was impassive.

It was then Lakshman's turn. As he stepped forward, those assembled were struck by his gigantic frame and towering height. Though usually dishevelled, his mother Sumitra had ensured that the fair-complexioned Lakshman had turned up dressed neatly for the ceremony. Much like his beloved brother Ram, Lakshman too avoided wearing jewellery, save for the ear studs and the threaded Rudraaksh beads around his neck. His ceremony was completed without fuss, and he was soon followed by Shatrughan. The diminutive youngest prince was meticulously attired as always, his hair precisely tied, his *dhoti* and *angvastram* neatly pressed, his jewellery sober and minimal. The completion of his ceremony marked his acknowledgement, too, as a descendant of Raghu.

The court crier brought the proceedings of the court to an end. Kaikeyi stepped up to assist Dashrath, signalling an aide who stood next to the emperor. Dashrath placed his hand on the attendant's shoulder as his eyes fell on Vashishta, who had also risen from his seat. Dashrath folded his hands together into a namaste. 'Guru*ji*.'

Vashishta raised his right hand and blessed the king. 'May Lord Indra bless you with a long life, Your Majesty.'

Dashrath nodded and cast a cursory look towards his sons, standing firmly together. His eyes rested on Ram; he coughed irritably, turned and hobbled away with assistance. Kaikeyi followed Dashrath out of the court.

The crier then announced that the emperor had left the court and the courtiers immediately began filing out of the hall.

Manthara remained rooted to her spot, staring intently at the four princes in the distance.

'What is it, My Lady?' whispered Druhyu.

The man's submissive demeanour was a clear indication of the dread he felt for the lady. It was rumoured that Manthara was even wealthier than the emperor. Added to this, she was believed to be a close confidante of the most powerful person in the empire, Queen Kaikeyi. The mischievous even suggested that the demon-king Raavan of Lanka was an ally; the reasonable, however, dismissed the last as fanciful.

'The brothers are close to each other,' whispered Manthara.

'Yes, they appear to be…'

'Interesting… Unexpected, but interesting…'

Druhyu cast a furtive glance over his shoulder, and then murmured. 'What are you thinking, My Lady?'

'I have been thinking about this for some time. I'm not sure we can write Ram off. If, after all the hatred and vilification that he has been subjected to for eighteen years, he is still standing strong, we must assume that he is made of sterner stuff. And Bharat, very obviously, is spirited and devoted to his brother.'

'So, what should we do?'

'They are both worthy. It's difficult to decide which one to bet on.'

'But Bharat is Queen Kaikeyi's—'

'I think,' said Manthara, cutting off her aide mid-sentence, 'I will find some way to make Roshni increase her interaction with them. I need to know more about the character of these princes.'

Druhyu was taken aback. 'My Lady, please accept my sincere apologies, but your daughter is very innocent, almost like *Kanyakumari*, the *Virgin Goddess*. She may not be able to—'

'Her innocence is exactly what we need, you fool. Nothing disarms strong men like a genuinely innocent and decent woman. It's the fascination that all strong men have for the Virgin Goddess, who must always be honoured and protected.'

Chapter 10

'Thank you,' smiled Bharat, as he held up his right hand and admired the exquisite golden-thread *rakhi* tied around his wrist. A petite young woman stood by his side; she answered to the name of Roshni.

A few weeks had lapsed since the recognition ceremony of the Ayodhya princes. Lakshman and Shatrughan already wore the *rakhi* thread, signifying a promise of protection made by a brother to his sister. In a break from tradition, Roshni had chosen to tie the *rakhi* threads first to the youngest and then move on, age-wise, towards the eldest. They sat together in the magnificent royal garden of the main Ayodhya palace. Situated high on a hill, the palace afforded a breathtaking view of the city, its walls and the Grand Canal beyond. The garden had been laid out in the style of a botanical reserve, filled with flowering trees from not only the Sapt Sindhu but other great empires around the world as well. Its splendid diversity was also the source of its beauty, reflecting the composite character of the people of the Sapt Sindhu. Winding paths bordered what should have been a carefully laid out lush carpet of dense grass in geometric symmetry. Alas, the depleting resources of Ayodhya had taken a toll on the maintenance of the garden, and ugly bald patches dotted the expanse.

Roshni applied the ceremonial sandalwood paste on Bharat's forehead. Manthara's daughter had inherited her mother's fair complexion, but in all other ways the dissimilarity could not be more obvious. Dainty and small-boned, she was soft-spoken, gentle and childlike. The simplicity of her attire was a subtle rejection of the opulence afforded by her family's wealth: a white upper garment coupled with a cream-coloured *dhoti*. Tiny studs and a bracelet made from Rudraaksh beads gave a hint of festive gaiety to a solemn face framed by long, wavy hair that was tied, as usual, in a neat ponytail. Her most magical attribute, though, was her eyes: overflowing with innocent tenderness and the unconditional, compassionate love of a true *yogini; one who had discovered union with God.*

Bharat pulled out a pouch full of gold coins from his waistband and held it out to Roshni. 'Here you go, my sister.'

Roshni gave the slightest of frowns. It had become fashionable of late for brothers to offer money or a gift to sisters during the *rakhi* ceremony. Women like Roshni did not approve of this trend. They believed that they were capable of doing the work of Brahmins, Vaishyas and Shudras: disseminating knowledge, trading or performing physical labour. The only task that sometimes proved challenging for them was that of a Kshatriya. They simply did not possess the physical strength and proclivity for violence. Nature had blessed them with other attributes. They believed that accepting anything besides the promise of physical protection during the *rakhi* ceremony was an admission of the inferiority of women. Equally, though, Roshni didn't want to be rude.

'Bharat, I'm elder to you,' smiled Roshni. 'I don't think it's appropriate for you to give me money. But I most willingly accept your promise of protection.'

'Of course,' said Bharat, quickly tucking the pouch back into his waistband. 'You are Mantharaji's daughter. Why would you need any money?'

Roshni immediately fell silent. Ram could see that she was hurt. He knew she was uncomfortable about the fabulous wealth that her mother possessed. It pained her that many in her country were mired in poverty. Roshni was known to avoid, if possible, the legendary parties that her mother frequently threw. Nor did she move around with an escort. She gave money and time to many charitable causes, especially the education and health of children, considered the worthiest of all by the great law book, *Maitreyi Smriti*. She also frequently used her medical skills as a doctor to help the needy.

'It's a wonder Bharat *Dada* allowed you to tie a *rakhi*, Roshni *Didi*,' Shatrughan broke the awkward silence even as he teased his elder brother.

'Yes,' said Lakshman. 'Our dear *dada* certainly loves women, but not necessarily as a brother.'

'And, from what I have heard, women love him in return,' said Roshni, as she gazed fondly at Bharat. 'Haven't you come across any dream lover yet, someone who will sweep you off your feet and make you want to settle down?'

'I do have a dream lover,' quipped Bharat. 'The problem is, she disappears when I wake up.'

Shatrughan, Lakshman and Roshni laughed heartily, but Ram could not bring himself to join in. He knew Bharat was assiduously hiding the pain in his heart with his jest. He had still not gotten over Radhika. Ram hoped his sensitive brother would not pine for her forever.

'My turn now,' said Ram, as he stepped forward and held out his right hand.

Lakshman spotted Vashishta walking by in the distance. He immediately scanned the area for possible threats, as he had not completely set aside his suspicions regarding their guru.

'I promise to protect you forever, my sister,' said Ram, looking solemnly at the golden *rakhi* tied to his wrist, and then equally, at Roshni.

Roshni smiled and applied some sandalwood paste on Ram's forehead. She turned around and walked towards a bench to put away the *aarti thali*.

'*DADA!*' screamed Lakshman, as he lunged forward and pushed Ram aside.

Lakshman's tremendous strength threw Ram back. In the same instant, a heavy branch landed with a loud thud at the very spot that Ram had been standing a moment ago. It had first smashed into Lakshman's shoulder, cracking his collar bone in two. Shards of bone jut out as blood gushed in a horrifying flow.

'Lakshman!' screamed his brothers as they rushed towards him.

— 𝙭 🐚 ☼ —

'He'll be all right,' said Roshni, as she stepped out of the operation theatre. Vashishta, Ram, Bharat and Shatrughan stood anxiously in the lobby of the *ayuralay*. Sumitra sat still on a chair against the wall of the *hospital*, her eyes clouded with tears. She immediately rose and embraced Roshni.

'There will be no permanent damage, Your Highness,' assured Roshni. 'His bone has been set. Your son will recover fully. We are very lucky that the branch missed his head.'

'We're also lucky that Lakshman is built like a bull,' said Vashishta. 'A lesser man would not have survived that hit.'

Lakshman opened his eyes in a large room, meant for nobility. His bed was big but not too soft, providing the support needed for his injured shoulder. He couldn't see too well in the dark but he detected a soft sound. Within moments, he found a red-eyed Ram standing by his bedside.

I woke Dada *up,* thought Lakshman.

Three nurses rushed towards the bed. Lakshman shook his head slowly and they stepped back.

Ram touched Lakshman's head gently. 'My brother…'

'*Dada*… the tree…'

'The branch was rotten, Lakshman. That's why it fell. It was bad luck. You saved my life once again…'

'*Dada*… Guru*ji*…'

'You took the hit for me, my brother… You took the hit that fate had meant for me…' said Ram, as he bent over and ran his hand over Lakshman's forehead.

Lakshman felt a tear fall on his face. '*Dada*…'

'Don't talk. Try to sleep. Relax,' said Ram, turning his face away.

Roshni entered the *ayuralay* room with some medicines for the prince. A week had elapsed since the accident. Lakshman was stronger now, and restless.

'Where is everyone?'

'The nurses are still here,' said Roshni with a smile, mixing the medicines into a paste in a bowl and handing it over to Lakshman. 'Your brothers have gone to the palace to bathe and change into fresh clothes. They'll be back soon.'

Lakshman's face contorted involuntarily as he ingested the medicine. 'Yuck!'

'The yuckier it is, the more effective the medicine!'

'Why do you doctors torture patients like this?'

'Thank you,' Roshni smiled as she handed the bowl to a nurse. Turning her attention back to Lakshman, she asked, 'How are you feeling now?'

'There is still a lot of numbness in my left shoulder.'

'That's because of the pain-killers.'

'I don't need them.'

'I know you can tolerate any amount of pain. But, for as long as you are my patient, you won't.'

Lakshman smiled. 'Spoken like an older sister.'

'Spoken like a doctor,' scolded Roshni, as her kindly gaze fell upon the golden *rakhi* still tied around Lakshman's right wrist. She turned to leave and then stopped.

'What is it?' asked Lakshman.

Roshni requested the nurses to leave. She then walked back to his bedside. 'Your brothers were here for most of the time. Your mother too was here; so were your stepmothers. They came to see you every day, remained here for most of the time and only went back to the palace to sleep. I'd expected that. But you must know that Ram refused to leave for one full week. He slept here in this room. He did a lot of the work that our nurses should have rightfully done.'

'I know. He's my *dada*…'

Roshni smiled. 'I came in late one night to check on you and I heard him talking in his sleep: "Don't punish my brother for my sins; punish me, punish me".'

'He blames himself for everything,' said Lakshman. 'Everyone has made his life a living hell.'

Roshni knew what Lakshman was talking about.

'How can anyone blame *Dada* for our defeat? *Dada* was just born on that day. We lost to Lanka because they fought better than us.'

'Lakshman, you don't have to…'

'Inauspicious! Cursed! Unholy! Is there any insult that has not been heaped upon him? And yet, he stands strong and steadfast. He doesn't hate, or even resent, anyone. He could have spent a lifetime being angry with the entire world. But he chooses to live a life of honour. He never lies. Did you know that? He never lies!' Lakshman was crying now. 'And yet, he lied once, just for me! I was out riding in the night, despite knowing that it wasn't allowed. I fell and hurt myself pretty badly. My mother was so angry. But *Dada* lied to save me. He said I was in the stable with him and that the horse kicked me. My mother instantly believed him, for *Dada* never lies. In his mind, he tainted his soul, but he did it to save me from my mother's wrath. And yet, people call him…'

Roshni stepped forward and gently touched Lakshman's face, wiping away some of his tears.

He continued with fervent vigour, tears streaming down his cheeks, 'There will come a time when the world will know what a great man he is. Dark clouds cannot hide the sun forever. One day, they will clear and true light will shine through. Everyone will know then, how great my *dada* is.'

'I already know that,' said Roshni, softly.

Manthara stood by the window in her office room, built at the far end of the official wing of her palatial residence. The exquisitely symmetrical garden, along with the estate, was appropriately smaller when compared to the emperor's; a conscious choice. It was also perched on a hill, though lower than the one on which the royal palace stood. Her residence adequately reflected her social status.

She was a brilliant businesswoman, no doubt, and she was no fool. The anti-mercantile atmosphere of the Sapt Sindhu accorded her a low stature, notwithstanding her wealth. None had the courage to say it to her face, but she knew what she was called: a 'profiteering lackey of the foreign-demon Raavan'. Truth was, all businessmen had no choice but to trade with Raavan's Lankan traders as the demon-king held a monopoly over external trade with the Sapt Sindhu. This was not a treaty signed by the Sapt Sindhu traders but their kings. Yet, it was the traders who were reviled for playing by the rules of this agreement. Being the most successful businesswoman, Manthara was the prime recipient of the anti-trader prejudice.

But she had suffered enough abuse in her childhood to inure her from bigotry for many a lifetime. Born into a poor family, she was afflicted with smallpox when young, leaving her pallid face scarred for life. As if that wasn't enough, she contracted polio at the age of eleven. The symptoms gradually abated but her right foot remained partially paralysed, giving her an odd limp. At age twenty, owing to her awkward gait, she slipped from the balcony at a friend's house, leaving her back hideously disfigured. She was teased wretchedly when young, and looked at with disdain even today, except that nobody dared to say anything to her face. Her wealth could have easily financed the entire royal expenditure of Kosala, along with a few other kingdoms, without even having to draw on her credit. Needless to say, it brought her immense power and influence.

'My Lady, what did you want to talk about?' asked Druhyu, standing deferentially a few feet away from her.

Manthara limped to her desk and sat on the specially designed padded chair. Druhyu stood at the other end of the desk.

She crooked her finger and he immediately shuffled around the desk, going down on his knees as he reached her. They were alone in the office, and no one would have heard a word of what was exchanged between them. The assistants were on the ground floor in the secretarial annexe. But he understood her silences. And, he didn't dare argue. So he waited.

'I know all there is to know,' declared Manthara. 'My sweet Roshni has unwittingly revealed the character of the princes to me. I've thought hard about this and I've made up my mind. Bharat will be in charge of diplomatic affairs and Ram will look after the city police.'

Druhyu was surprised. 'I thought you had begun to like Prince Ram, My Lady.'

Diplomatic affairs were a perfect opportunity for an Ayodhyan prince to build relations with other kingdoms; and thus, build his base for a future strong empire. Although Ayodhya was still the overlord of the Sapt Sindhu confederacy, it was nowhere near as powerful as it had once been. Building relations with other kings would prove to be advantageous.

The role of the city police chief, on the other hand, would not serve as a suitable training ground for a prince. Crime rates were high, law and order was abysmal, and most rich people maintained their own personal security set-up. The poor suffered terribly as a result. Simplistic explanations would not do justice to the complex picture, though. The people were, to a fairly large extent, themselves responsible for the chaotic state of affairs. Guru Vashishta had once remarked that it was possible for the system to maintain order if a small percentage of the people disobeyed the law, but no system could prevent upheaval and disruption if practically all the citizens had no respect for the law. And Ayodhyans broke every law with impunity.

If Bharat managed diplomatic relations well, he would be in a strong position to succeed Dashrath eventually, whereas Ram would be left with a thankless job. If he was tough and managed to control crime, people would resent him for his ruthlessness. If he was kind, crime rates would continue to soar and he would be blamed for it. Even if, by some miracle, he managed to control crime and be popular at the same time, then too it would not prove beneficial for him, for the opinion of the people did not matter in the selection of the next king.

'Oh, I like Ram,' said Manthara dismissively. 'I just like profits more. It'll be good for business if we back the right horse. This is not about choosing between Ram and Bharat, but Kaushalya and Kaikeyi. And, rest assured, Kaikeyi will win. That is a certainty. Ram may well be capable, but he does not have the ability to take on Kaikeyi.'

'Yes, My Lady.'

'Also, don't forget, the nobility hates Ram. They blame him for the defeat at the Battle of Karachapa. So it would cost us more in bribes to secure a good position for Ram. We won't have to pay that much to the nobility to get them to accept Bharat as the chief of diplomatic affairs.'

'Our costs go down as well,' said Druhyu, smiling.

'Yes. That too is good for business.'

'And, I think, Queen Kaikeyi will be grateful.'

'Which will not hurt us either.'

'I will take care of it, My Lady. Raj Guru Vashishta is away from Ayodhya, and that will make our task easier. He has been a strong supporter of Prince Ram.'

Druhyu regretted mentioning the raj guru as soon as the words escaped his lips.

'You still haven't discovered where Guru*ji* is, have you?' asked an irritated Manthara. 'Where has he gone for such a long period? When is he returning? You know nothing!'

'No, My Lady,' said Druhyu, keeping his head bowed. 'I'm sorry.'

'Sometimes I wonder why I pay you so much.'

Druhyu remained still, afraid of uttering another sound. Manthara dismissed him from her presence with a wave of the hand.

Chapter 11

'You will make an excellent chief of police,' said Roshni, her eyes glittering with childlike excitement. 'Crime will decrease and that will be good for our beleaguered people.'

Roshni sat in the palace garden with a restrained but disappointed Ram, who'd been hoping for a greater responsibility, like the deputy chief of the army. But he wasn't about to reveal this to her.

'I'm not sure if I'll be able to handle it,' said Ram. 'A good chief of police needs the support of the people.'

'And, you imagine that you don't have it?'

Ram smiled wanly. 'Roshni, I know you don't lie; do you really think the people will support me? Everyone blames me for the defeat at the hands of Lanka. I am tainted by 7,032.'

Roshni leaned forward and spoke earnestly. 'You have only interacted with the elite, the ones who were "born-right", people like us. Yes, they do not like you. But there is another Ayodhya, Ram, where people who were "not born-right" exist. There's no love lost between them and the elite. And remember, they will be sympathetic towards anyone the elite ostracise, even one from the nobility itself. The common folk will like you simply because the elite don't like you. They might even follow you for the same reason.'

Ram had lived in the bubble of the royal experience. He was intrigued by this possibility.

'People like us don't step out into the real world. We don't know what's going on out there. I have interacted with the common people and I think I understand them to some extent. The elite have done you a favour by hating you. They have made it possible for you to endear yourself to the common man. I'm sure you can make them listen to you. I know you can bring crime under control in this city; dramatically so. You can do a lot of good. Believe in yourself as much as I believe in you, my brother.'

— 𑀫 𑀛 ☀ —

Within a year the reforms that Ram instituted began to have a visible effect. He tackled the main problem head on: most people were unaware of the laws. Some did not even know the names of the law books, called *Smritis*. This was because there were too many of them, containing contradictory laws that had accumulated over centuries. The *Manu Smriti* was well known, but most people were unaware that there were versions of it as well, for instance the *BrihadManu Smriti*. There were other popular ones too — the *Yajnavalkya Smriti, Narad Smriti, Aapastamb Smriti, Atri Smriti, Yam Smriti* and *Vyas Smriti,* to name a few. The police applied sections from the law that they were familiar with, in an ad hoc fashion. The court judges were sometimes aware of other *Smritis*, depending on the communities they were born into. Confusion was exacerbated when the police would arrest under a law of one *Smriti*, while the judge would base his judgement on a law from another *Smriti*. The result was almighty chaos. The guilty would escape by exploiting the loopholes and contradictions among the *Smritis*. Many innocents, however, languished in prisons due to ignorance, leading to horrific overcrowding.

Ram understood that he had to simplify and unify the law. He studied the *Smritis* and carefully selected laws that he felt were fair, coherent, simple and relevant to the times. Henceforth, this law code would govern Ayodhya; all the other *Smritis* would be rendered obsolete. The laws were inscribed on stone tablets and put up at all the temples in Ayodhya; the most important among them being engraved at the end: Ignorance of the law is not a legitimate excuse. Town criers were assigned the task of reading the code aloud every morning. It was only a matter of time before the laws were known to all.

Ram was soon given a respectful title by the common people: Ram, the Law Giver.

His second reform was even more revolutionary. He gave the police force the power to implement the law without any fear or favour. Ram understood a simple fact: policemen desired respect from society. They hadn't been given the opportunity to earn it earlier. If they unhesitatingly took action against any law-breaker, high and mighty though he may be, they would be feared and respected. Ram himself repeatedly demonstrated that the law applied equally to him.

In an oft-quoted incident, Ram returned to the city after dusk, when the fort gates had been shut. The gatekeeper opened the gates for the prince. Ram upbraided him for breaking the law: the gates were not to be opened for anyone at night time. Ram slept outside the city walls that night and entered the city the next morning. The ordinary people of Ayodhya talked about it for months, though it was studiously ignored by the nobles.

What did get the elite into a tizzy was Ram's intervention in cases where members of the nobility attempted to browbeat the police when the law caught up with them. They were aghast that they were being brought to book, but soon understood there would be no leniency. Their hatred of Ram increased manifold; they began to call him dictatorial and dangerous. But the people loved him more, this eldest prince of Ayodhya. Crime rates collapsed as criminals were either thrown in jail or speedily executed. Innocents were increasingly spared in a city that steadily became safer. Women began to venture out alone at night. Ram was rightfully credited with this dramatic improvement in their lives.

It would be decades before the name of Ram would transform into a splendid legend. But the journey had begun, for among the common folk, a star was slowly sputtering to life.

'You are making too many enemies, my son,' said Kaushalya. 'You should not be so rigid about enforcing the law.'

Kaushalya had finally summoned Ram to her private chamber, having received too many complaints from nobles. She was worried that, in his zeal, her son was losing the few allies he still had in court.

'The rule of law cannot be selective, *Maa*,' said Ram. 'The same law has to apply to everyone. If the nobles don't like it, they should not break the law.'

'I'm not discussing the law, Ram. If you think that penalising one of General Mrigasya's key aides will please your father, you're wrong. He's completely under Kaikeyi's spell.'

Mrigasya, the army chief, had become increasingly powerful as Dashrath sank into depression. He was the magnet around whom all those who opposed the powerful Queen Kaikeyi had coalesced. His reputation of fiercely defending his loyalists, even if they committed crimes or were thoroughly incompetent, ensured ferocious allegiance. Kaikeyi intensely disliked him for his wilful disregard of her wishes, which influenced Dashrath's attitude towards the general.

Recently, Ram had used the law to recover land that one of Mrigasya's aides had illegally appropriated from poor villagers. Ram had even had the temerity to enforce a penalty on the aide, something nobody had dared to do with the men who surrounded the powerful general.

'General Mrigasya and Kaikeyi *Maa*'s politics do not interest me. His aide broke the law. That's all there is to it.'

'The nobility will do as they please, Ram.'

'Not if I can help it!'

'Ram…'

'Nobility is about being *noble*, *Maa*. It's about the way of the *Arya*. It's not about your birth, but how you conduct yourself. Being a noble is a great responsibility, not a birthright.'

'Ram, why don't you understand?! General Mrigasya is our only ally. All the other powerful nobles are in Kaikeyi's camp. He's the only one who can stand up to her. We are safe for as long as we have Mrigasya and his coterie on our side.'

'What does this have to do with the law?'

Kaushalya consciously made an effort to contain her irritation. 'Do you know how difficult it is for me to build support for you? Everyone blames you for Lanka.'

When her comment was met with a stony silence, Kaushalya turned placatory. 'I'm not suggesting that it was your fault, my child. But this is the reality. We must be pragmatic. Do you want to be king or not?'

'I want to be a good king. Or else, believe me, I'd rather not be one.'

Kaushalya closed her eyes in exasperation. 'Ram, you seem to live in your own theoretical world. You have to learn to be practical. Know that I love you and I'm only trying to help you.'

'If you love me, *Maa*, then understand what I'm made of.' Ram spoke calmly but there was steely determination in his eyes. 'This is my *janmabhoomi*, my *land of birth*. I have to serve it by leaving it better than I found it. I can fulfil my karma as a king, a police chief or even a simple villager.'

'Ram, you don't—'

Kaushalya was interrupted by a loud announcement. 'Her Highness Kaikeyi, queen of Ayodhya!'

Ram immediately got to his feet, as did Kaushalya. He discreetly glanced at his mother, noting the impotent anger in her eyes. Kaikeyi approached her with a smile on her lips, her hands folded in a namaste. 'Namaste, *Didi*. Please accept my sincere apologies for disturbing you during your private time with your son.'

'That's quite all right, Kaikeyi,' remarked Kaushalya with studied affability. 'I'm sure it's something important.'

'Yes, it is, actually,' said Kaikeyi, turning to Ram. 'Your father has decided to go on a hunting trip, Ram.'

'A hunting trip?' asked a surprised Ram.

Dashrath had not gone big game hunting in Ram's living memory. His battle injury had precluded even such simple pleasures from the life of the once great hunter.

'Yes. I would have sent Bharat along with him. I could do with some of my favourite deer meat. But as you know, Bharat is in Branga on a diplomatic mission. I was wondering if I could lay this onerous responsibility on your able shoulders.'

Ram smiled slightly. He knew Kaikeyi wanted him to accompany Dashrath in order to protect him, and not for any choice meats. But Kaikeyi never said anything derogatory about Dashrath in public; and the royal family was 'public' for her. Ram folded his hands into a namaste. 'It will be my honour to serve you, *Chhoti Maa*.'

Kaikeyi smiled. 'Thank you.'

Kaushalya looked at Ram quietly, her face inscrutable.

'What is she doing here?' asked Dashrath gruffly.

Kaushalya had just been announced by the doorman in Kaikeyi's wing of the royal palace. Dashrath and Kaikeyi lay in bed. She reached out and tucked Dashrath's long hair behind his ear. 'Just finish whatever it is and come back quickly.'

'You will also have to get up, my love,' said Dashrath.

Kaikeyi sighed in irritation and rolled off the bed. She quickly picked up her *angvastram* and placed it across her shoulder, rolling the other end around her right wrist. She walked over to Dashrath and helped him off the bed. She went down on her knees and straightened his *dhoti*. Finally, she picked up Dashrath's *angvastram* and placed it across his shoulder. She then helped him walk into the reception room and bade him wait.

'Let Her Majesty in,' ordered Kaikeyi.

Kaushalya entered the room with two attendants in tow. One of them carried a large golden plate on which was placed Dashrath's battle sword. The other attendant carried a small *puja thali*. Kaikeyi straightened up in surprise. Dashrath seemed lost as usual.

'*Didi*,' said Kaikeyi, folding her hands together in a namaste. 'What a pleasure to see you twice in the same day.'

'The pleasure is all mine, Kaikeyi,' replied Kaushalya. 'You mentioned that His Majesty is going on a hunt. I thought I should perform the proper ceremony.'

The ritual of the chief wife of a warrior ceremonially handing the sword to her departing husband had come down through the ancient times.

'Things have not gone too well whenever I have not presented His Majesty with the sword,' said Kaushalya.

Dashrath's vacant expression changed suddenly. He frowned, as if he was struck by the enormity of the not-so-subtle implication. Kaushalya had not handed him the sword when he had set out for Karachapa, and that had been his first defeat. He slowly took a step towards his first wife.

Kaushalya took the small *puja thali* from her attendant and looped it in small circles around Dashrath's face seven times. Then she took a pinch of vermillion from the plate and smeared it across Dashrath's forehead in a vertical *tilak*. 'Come back victorious…'

Kaikeyi sniggered, interrupting the ceremony. 'He's not going to war, *Didi*.'

Dashrath ignored Kaikeyi. 'Complete the line, Kaushalya.'

Kaushalya swallowed nervously, half convinced now that this was a big mistake; that she should not have listened to Sumitra. But she completed the ritual statement. 'Come back victorious, or do not come back at all.'

Kaushalya thought she detected a flicker of fire in her husband's eyes, reminiscent of the young Dashrath, who lived for thrill and glory. 'Where's my sword?' Dashrath demanded, as he extended his arms solemnly.

Kaushalya immediately turned and handed the *puja thali* back to her attendant. She then picked up the sword with both her hands, faced her husband, bowed ceremonially and handed him the sword. Dashrath held it firmly, as if drawing energy from it.

Kaikeyi looked at Dashrath and then at Kaushalya as she narrowed her eyes, deep in thought.

This must be Sumitra's doing. Kaushalya couldn't have planned this by herself. Perhaps I've made a mistake in asking Ram to accompany Dashrath.

—— 𝗜𝗻 🐟 ☼ ——

Royal hunts were grand affairs that lasted many weeks. A large entourage accompanied the emperor on the expedition, moving the headquarters of the court to a hunting lodge built deep in the great forest to the far north of Ayodhya.

Action commenced on the day after their arrival. The technique involved numerous soldiers spreading out in a giant circle, circumscribing almost fifty kilometres sometimes. They beat loud drums ceaselessly as they slowly moved to the centre, steadily drawing the animals into an increasingly restricted area, at times a watering hole. The animals would then be attacked in the kill-zone, where the emperor and his hunting party would indulge in this royal sport.

Dashrath stood on a howdah atop the royal elephant. Ram and Lakshman were seated behind him. The emperor thought he heard the soft chuff of an unsuspecting tiger; he ordered the mahout to charge forward. Within no time, Dashrath's elephant had separated from the rest of the hunting party. He was alone with his sons.

They were surrounded on all sides by dense vegetation. Many trees were so tall that they towered over the elephant, blocking out much of the sunlight. It was almost impossible to see beyond the first few lines of trees into the impenetrable darkness.

Lakshman leaned in and whispered to Ram, '*Dada*, I don't think there is any tiger here.'

Ram gestured for Lakshman to remain quiet as he observed his father, standing in front. Dashrath was barely able to contain his enthusiasm. His body weight was on his strong left foot. His inert right foot was stabilised with an innovative mechanism built into the howdah platform: a swivelling circular base with a sturdy column fixed in the centre. Boot straps attached to the base secured his foot as it leaned on the column, the leather support extending all the way to his knee. The circular base allowed him swift movement for shooting his arrows in all directions. Nevertheless, his back showed signs of visible strain as he held the bow aloft with the arrow nocked on the bowstring.

Ram would have preferred it if his father did not exert his weakened body so. But he also admired the spirit that drove him to push his corporeal frame beyond its natural limits.

'There's nothing there, I tell you,' whispered Lakshman.

'Shh,' said Ram.

Lakshman fell silent. Suddenly, Dashrath flexed his right shoulder and pulled the bowstring back. Ram winced as he watched the technique. Dashrath's elbow was not in line with the arrow, which would put greater pressure on his shoulder and triceps. Sweat beads formed on the emperor's forehead, but he held position. A moment later he released the arrow, and a loud roar confirmed that it had found its mark. Ram revelled in the spirit of the all-conquering hero that his father had once been.

Dashrath swivelled awkwardly on the howdah and looked at Lakshman with a sneer. 'Don't underestimate me, young man.'

Lakshman immediately bowed his head. 'I'm sorry, Father. I didn't mean to…'

'Order some soldiers to fetch the carcass of that tiger. They will find it with an arrow pierced through its eye and buried in its brain.'

'Yes, Father, I'll—'

'Father!' screamed Ram as he lunged forward, drawing a knife quickly from the scabbard tied around his waist.

There was a loud rustle of leaves as a leopard emerged on a branch overhanging the howdah. The sly beast had planned its attack meticulously. Dashrath was distracted as the leopard leapt from the branch. Ram's timing, however, was perfect. He jumped up and plunged his knife into the airborne animal's chest. But the suddenness of the charge made Ram miss his mark. The knife didn't find the leopard's heart. The beast was injured, but not dead. It roared in fury and slashed with its claws. Ram wrestled with the leopard as he tried to pull the knife out so he could take another stab; but it was stuck. The animal pulled back and sank his teeth into the prince's left triceps. Ram yelled in pain as he attempted to push the animal out of the howdah. The leopard pulled back its head, ripping out flesh and drawing large spurts of blood. It instinctively struggled to move to Ram's neck, to asphyxiate the prince. Ram pulled back his right fist and hit the leopard hard across its head.

Lakshman, in the meantime, was desperately trying to reach Ram even as Dashrath blocked his way, tied as he was to the stationary column. Lakshman jumped high, caught an overhanging branch and swung out of the howdah in an arc. He propelled himself forward and landed in front of the howdah, right behind the leopard. He drew his knife as the leopard pulled back again to bite into Ram. Lakshman thrust brutally and, by good fortune, the blade sank into the leopard's eye. The animal howled in pain as a shower of blood sprang out of its shattered eye-socket. Lakshman strained his mighty shoulder and jammed hard, pushing the knife deep into the animal's brain. The beast struggled for a brief moment and then fell, lifeless.

Lakshman picked up the leopard's body with his bare hands, and threw it to the ground. Ram had collapsed in a pool of blood.

'Ram!' screamed Dashrath, twisting desperately as his right leg remained fixed to the column.

Lakshman turned to the mahout. 'Back to the camp!'

The mahout sat paralysed, shaken by the sudden turn of events. Dashrath bellowed his imperial command. 'Back to the camp! Now!'

—— |大| 🐟 ☼ ——

Torches were lit across a hunting camp seized with frenetic activity late into the night. The injured prince of Ayodhya lay in the massive and luxurious tent of the emperor. He should have been in the medical tent, but Dashrath had insisted that his son be tended to in the comfort of the emperor's living quarters. Ram's pallid body was covered in bandages, weak from tremendous loss of blood.

'Prince Ram,' whispered the doctor as he touched the prince gently.

'Do you *have* to wake him up?' demanded Dashrath, sitting on a comfortable chair placed to the left of the bed.

'Yes, Your Majesty,' said the doctor. 'He must take this medicine now.'

As the doctor repeated Ram's name, the prince opened his eyes, blinking slowly to adjust to the light. He saw the doctor holding the bowl of medicine. He opened his mouth and swallowed the paste, wincing at the bitter taste. The doctor turned, bowed towards the emperor and left the room. Ram was about to slip back into sleep when he noticed the ceremonial gold umbrella on top of the bed. At its centre was a massive sun in intricate embroidery, with rays streaming boldly out in all directions; the Suryavanshi symbol. Ram's eyes flew open as he struggled to get up. He wasn't supposed to be sleeping on the emperor's bed.

'Lie down,' commanded Dashrath, raising his hand.

Lakshman rushed over to the bed and gently tried to calm his brother down.

'In the name of Lord Surya, lie down, Ram!' said Dashrath.

Ram fell back on the bed as he looked towards Dashrath. 'Father, I'm sorry. I shouldn't be on your—'

Dashrath cut him off mid-sentence with a wave of his hand. Ram couldn't help but notice a subtle change in his father's appearance. A spark in the eyes, steel in the voice, and an alertness that brought back stories his mother would constantly repeat, about the kind of man Dashrath had once been. Here sat a powerful man who wouldn't take kindly to his orders being disregarded. Ram had never seen him like this.

Dashrath turned to his attendants. 'Leave us.'

Lakshman rose to join the attendants.

'Not you, Lakshman,' said Dashrath.

Lakshman stopped in his tracks and waited for further orders. Dashrath stared at the tiger and leopard skins spread out in the corner of the tent; trophies of the animals he and his sons had hunted.

'Why?' asked Dashrath.

'Father?' asked Ram, confused.

'Why did you risk your life for me?'

Ram did not utter a word.

Dashrath continued, 'I blamed you for my defeat. My entire kingdom blamed you; cursed you. You've suffered all your life, and yet you never rebelled. I thought it was because you were weak. But weak people celebrate when twists of fate hurt their tormentors. And yet, you risked your life trying to protect me. Why?'

Ram answered with one simple statement. 'Because that is my *dharma*, Father.'

Dashrath looked quizzically at Ram. This was the first real conversation he was having with his eldest son. 'Is that the only reason?'

'What other reason can there be?'

'Oh, I don't know,' said Dashrath, snorting with disbelief. 'How about angling for the position of crown prince?'

Ram couldn't help smiling at the irony. 'The nobility will never accept me, Father, even if I'm able to convince you. It is not in my scheme of things. What I did today, is what I must always do: be true to my *dharma*. Nothing is more important than *dharma*.'

'So, you don't believe that you are to blame for my defeat at the hands of Raavan, is it?'

'It doesn't matter what I think, Father.'

'You didn't answer my question.'

Ram remained silent.

Dashrath leaned forward. 'Answer me, prince.'

'I don't understand how the universe keeps track of our karma across many births, Father. I know I could not have done anything in this birth to make you lose the battle. Maybe it was something to do with my previous birth?'

Dashrath laughed softly, amazed at his son's equanimity.

'Do you know whom I blame?' asked Dashrath. 'If I were truly honest, if I had had the courage to look deep into my heart, the answer would have been obvious. It was my fault; only my fault. I was reckless and foolhardy. I attacked without a plan, driven only by anger. I paid the price, didn't I? My first defeat ever... And, my last battle, forever.'

'Father, there are many—'

'Do not interrupt me, Ram. I'm not finished.' Ram fell silent and Dashrath continued. 'It was my fault. And I blamed the infant that you were. It was so easy. I just had to say it, and everyone agreed with me. I made your life hell from the day you were born. You should hate me. You should hate Ayodhya.'

'I don't hate anyone, Father.'

Dashrath stared hard at his son. After what seemed like eternity, his face broke into a peculiar smile. 'I don't know whether you've suppressed your true feelings completely or you genuinely don't care about the ignominy that people have heaped on you. Whatever be the truth, you have held strong. The entire universe conspired to break you, and here you are, still unbowed. What metal have you been forged in, my son?'

Ram's eyes moistened as emotion welled within him. He could handle disdain and apathy from his father; he was used to it. Respect was difficult to deal with. 'I was forged from your metal, my father.'

Dashrath laughed softly. He was discovering his son.

'What are your differences with Mrigasya?' asked Dashrath.

Ram was surprised to discover that his father kept track of court matters. 'None at all, Father.'

'Then why did you penalise one of his men?'

'He broke the law.'

'Don't you know how powerful Mrigasya is? Aren't you afraid of him?'

'Nobody is above the law, Father. None can be more powerful than *dharma*.'

Dashrath laughed. 'Not even me?'

'A great emperor said something beautiful once: *Dharma* is above all, even the king. *Dharma* is above the Gods themselves.'

Dashrath frowned. 'Who said this?'

'You did, Father, when you took your oath at your coronation, decades ago. I was told that you had paraphrased our great ancestor Lord Ikshvaku himself.'

Dashrath stared at Ram as he jogged his memory to remember the powerful man he had once been.

'Go to sleep, my son,' said Dashrath. 'You need the rest.'

Chapter 12

Ram was awakened by the doctor at the beginning of the second *prahar* for his next dose of medicine. As he looked around the room, his eyes fell on a visibly delighted Lakshman, standing by his bedside bedecked in a formal *dhoti* and *angvastram*. The saffron *angvastram* had a Suryavanshi sun emblazoned across its length.

'Son?'

Ram turned his head to the left and saw his father attired in regal finery. The emperor sat on his travel-throne; the Suryavanshi crown was placed on his head.

'Father,' said Ram. 'Good morning.'

Dashrath nodded crisply. 'It will be a fine morning, no doubt.'

The emperor turned towards the entrance of his tent. 'Is anyone there?'

A guard pulled the curtain aside and rushed in, saluting rapidly.

'Let the nobles in.'

The guard saluted once again and retraced his steps. Within minutes, the nobles entered the tent in single file. They gathered in a semicircle around the emperor, waiting with a solemn air of ceremony.

'Let me see my son,' said Dashrath.

The nobles parted immediately, surprised at the voice of authority emerging from their emperor.

Dashrath looked directly at Ram. 'Rise.'

Lakshman rushed over to help Ram, but Dashrath raised his hand firmly to stop him from doing so. The assemblage stood rooted as it watched a severely weakened Ram struggle to raise himself, stand on his feet and hobble towards his father. He saluted slowly once he reached the emperor.

Dashrath locked eyes with his son, inhaled deeply and spoke clearly, 'Kneel.'

Ram was unable to move, overwhelmed by a sense of shocked disbelief. Tears welled up in his eyes, despite his willing them not to do so.

Dashrath's voice softened slightly. 'Kneel, my son.'

Ram struggled with emotions as he sought the support of a table close at hand. Laboriously, he went down on one knee, bowed his head and awaited the call of destiny.

Dashrath spoke evenly, his voice reverberating even outside the royal tent. 'Rise, Ram Chandra, *protector* of the Raghu clan.'

A collective gasp resounded through the tent.

Dashrath raised his head and the courtiers fell into a taut silence.

Ram still had his head bowed, lest his enemies see the tears in his eyes. He stared at the floor till he regained absolute control. Then he looked up at his father and spoke in a calm voice. 'May all the Gods of our great land continue to protect you, my father.'

Dashrath's eyes seemed to penetrate the soul of his eldest son. A hint of a smile appeared on his face as he looked towards his nobles. 'Leave us.'

General Mrigasya attempted to say something. 'Your Majesty, but—'

Dashrath interrupted him with a glare. 'What part of "leave us" did you not understand, Mrigasya?'

'My apologies, Your Majesty,' said Mrigasya, as he saluted and led the nobles out.

Dashrath, Ram and Lakshman were soon alone in the tent. Dashrath leaned heavily to his left as he made an effort to get up, resisting Lakshman's offer of help with a brusque grunt. Once on his feet, he beckoned Lakshman, placed his hand on his son's massive shoulders and hobbled over to Ram. Ram, too, had risen slowly to his feet and stood erect. His face was inscrutable, his eyes awash with emotion, though coupled with surprising tranquillity.

Dashrath placed his hands on Ram's shoulders. 'Become the man that I could have become; the man that I did not become.'

Ram whispered softly, his vision clouded, 'Father…'

'Make me proud,' said Dashrath, with tears finally welling up in his eyes.

'Father…'

'Make me proud, my son.'

——— 𑀚 𑀤 ☼ ———

All doubts about the tectonic shifts that had taken place in the royal family were laid to rest when Dashrath moved out of Kaikeyi's wing of the Ayodhya palace. He had been unable to convincingly answer Kaikeyi's repeated and forceful questions as to why he had suddenly made Ram the crown prince. Dashrath moved in, along with his personal staff, to Kaushalya's wing. The bewildered chief queen of Ayodhya had suddenly regained her status. But the timid Kaushalya was careful with her new-found elevation. No changes were attempted, though it was difficult to say whether this was because of her diffidence or fear that the good fortune might not last.

Ram's brothers were delighted. Bharat and Shatrughan had rushed to his chambers on their return from Branga, word having reached them even as they travelled back home. Roshni had decided to join them.

'Congratulations, *Dada*!' said Bharat, embracing his elder brother with obvious delight.

'You deserve it,' said Shatrughan.

'He surely does,' said Roshni, her face suffused with joy. 'I ran into Guru Vashishta on my way here. He mentioned that the reduction in the crime rate in Ayodhya is only a tiny example of what Ram can truly achieve.'

'You bet!' said Lakshman, enthusiastically.

'All right, all right,' said Ram, 'you're embarrassing me now!'

'Aaah,' grinned Bharat, 'that's the point of it all, *Dada*!'

'As far as I know, speaking the truth has not been banned in any scripture,' said Shatrughan.

'And we'd better believe him, *Dada*,' said Lakshman, laughing heartily. 'Shatrughan is the only man I know who can recite every single *Veda, Upanishad, Brahmana, Aranyaka, Vedanga, Smriti,* and everything else communicated or known to man!'

'The weight of his formidable brain pressed so hard upon his body that it arrested his vertical growth!' Bharat joined in.

Shatrughan boxed Lakshman playfully on his well-toned abdomen, chuckling along good-naturedly.

Lakshman laughed boisterously. 'Do you really think I can feel your feeble hits, Shatrughan? You may have got all the brain cells created in *Maa's* womb, but I got all the brawn!'

The brothers laughed even louder. Roshni was happy that, despite all the political intrigue in the Ayodhyan court, the princes shared a healthy camaraderie with each other. Clearly the Gods were looking out for the future of the kingdom.

She patted Ram on his shoulder. 'I have to go.'

'Go where?' asked Ram.

'Saraiya. You're aware that I hold a medical camp in our surrounding villages once a month, right? It's Saraiya's turn this month.'

Ram looked a little worried. 'I will send some bodyguards with you. The villages around Saraiya are not safe.'

Roshni smiled. 'Thanks to you, criminal activity is at an all-time low. Your law enforcement has ensured that. There is nothing to worry about.'

'I have not been able to achieve that completely, and you know it. Look, there's no harm in being safe.'

Roshni noticed that Ram was still wearing the *rakhi* she had tied on his wrist a long time ago. She smiled. 'Don't worry, Ram. It's a day trip, I'll be back before nightfall. And I will not be alone. My assistants will be accompanying me. We will give the villagers free medicines and treatment, if required. Nobody will hurt me. Why would they want to?'

Bharat, who had been listening in on the conversation, stepped up and put his arm around Roshni's shoulder. 'You are a good woman, Roshni.'

Roshni smiled in a childlike manner. 'That I am.'

—— 以 ● ☼ ——

The blazing afternoon sun did not deter Lakshman, Ayodhya's finest rider, from honing his skills. He knew that the ability of horse and horseman to come to a sudden halt was of critical advantage in battle. To practise this art he chose a spot some distance away from the city, where sheer cliffs descended into the rapids of the Sarayu deep below.

'Come on!' shouted Lakshman, spurring his horse on as it galloped towards the cliff edge.

As his horse thundered dangerously near the edge of the precipice, Lakshman waited till the last moment, leaned forward in his saddle, and wrapped his left arm around the horse's neck even as he pulled the reins hard with his right. The magnificent beast responded instantly by rearing up on its hind legs. The rear hooves left a mark on the ground as the horse stopped a few feet away from certain death. Gracefully dismounting, Lakshman stroked its mane in appreciation.

'Well done ... well done.'

The horse's tail swished in acknowledgment of the praise.

'Once again?'

The animal had had enough and snorted its refusal with a vigorous shake of its head. Lakshman laughed softly as he patted the horse, remounted and steered the reins in the opposite direction. 'All right. Let's go home.'

As he rode through the woods, a meeting was in progress a short distance away; one he may have liked to eavesdrop on, had he been aware of it. Guru Vashishta was engrossed in deep discussion with the same mysterious Naga.

'That said, I'm sorry you...'

'...failed?' Vashishta completed his sentence. The guru had returned to Ayodhya after a long and unexplained absence.

'That is not the word I would have used, Guru*ji*.'

'It's appropriate, though. But it's not just our failure. It's a failure of—'

Vashishta stopped mid-sentence as he thought he heard a sound.

'What is it?' asked the Naga.

'Did you hear something?' asked Vashishta.

The Naga looked around, listened carefully for a few seconds, and then shook his head.

'What about Prince Ram?' asked the Naga, resuming the conversation. 'Are you aware that your friend is on his way here, seeking him?'

'I know that.'

'What do you intend to do?'

'What can I do?' asked Vashishta, raising his hands helplessly. 'Ram will have to handle this himself.'

They heard the unmistakable sound of a twig snapping. Perhaps it was an animal. The Naga murmured cautiously, 'I had better go.'

'Yes,' agreed Vashishta.

He quickly mounted his horse and looked at Vashishta. 'With your permission.'

Vashishta smiled and folded his hands into a namaste. 'Go with Lord Rudra, my friend.'

The Naga returned his namaste. 'Have faith in Lord Rudra, Guru*ji*.'

The Naga gently tapped his horse into motion and rode away.

—— 𝍏 ⦿ ☼ ——

'It's only a sprain,' Roshni reassured the child as she wrapped a bandage around his ankle. 'It will heal in a day or two.'

'Are you sure?' asked the worried mother.

Numerous villagers from the surrounding settlements had gathered at the Saraiya village square. Roshni had patiently attended to them all. This was the last patient.

'Yes,' said Roshni, as she patted the child on his head. 'Now, listen to me,' she cupped the child's face with her hands. 'No climbing trees or running around for the next few days. You have to take it easy till your ankle heals.'

The mother cut in. 'I will ensure that he stays at home.'

'Good,' said Roshni.

'Hey, Roshni *Didi!*' said the child, pouting with pretend annoyance. 'Where is my sweet?'

Roshni laughed as she beckoned one of her assistants. She pulled out a sweet from his bag and handed it to the delighted child. She ruffled his hair and then rose from her stool. Stretching her back, she turned to the village chief. 'If you will excuse me, I should be leaving now.'

'Are you sure, My Lady?' asked the chief. 'It's late and you may not be able to reach Ayodhya before nightfall. The city gates will be shut.'

'No, I think I'll make it in time,' said a determined Roshni. 'I have to. My mother wants me back in Ayodhya tonight. She has planned a celebration and I need to be there for it.'

'All right, My Lady, as you wish,' said the chief. 'Thank you so much, once again. I don't know what we would do without you.'

'The one you must truly thank is Lord Brahma, for he has given me the skills to be of use to you.'

The chief, as always, bent down respectfully to touch her feet. Roshni, as always, stepped back. 'Please, don't embarrass me by touching my feet. I am younger than you.'

The chief folded his hands together in a namaste. 'May Lord Rudra bless you, My Lady.'

'May he bless us all!' said Roshni. She walked up to her horse and mounted swiftly. Her assistants had already gathered all their medical material and had mounted their horses. At a signal from Roshni, the trio rode out of the village.

Moments later, eight horse-mounted men appeared at the chief's front door. They were from a nearby village called Isla, and had taken some medicines from Roshni earlier in the day. Their village had been struck by an epidemic of viral fever. One of the riders was an adolescent called Dhenuka, the son of the Isla village chief.

'Brothers,' said the chief. 'Have you got everything you need?'

'Yes,' said Dhenuka. 'But where is Lady Roshni? I wanted to thank her.'

The village chief was surprised. Dhenuka was famous for his rude, uncouth behaviour. But then he had met Roshni for the first time today. She must have impressed even this rowdy youth with her decency and goodness. 'She has ridden out already. She needed to get to Ayodhya before nightfall.'

'Right,' said Dhenuka, scanning the road leading out of the village. He smiled and spurred his horse into action.

— 𑀓 ♠ ☼ —

'Can I help you, My Lady?' asked Dhenuka.

Roshni turned around, surprised at the intrusion. They had made good time and she had stopped for some rest near the banks of the Sarayu River. They were an hour's ride from Ayodhya.

At first she didn't recognise him, but soon smiled in acknowledgment.

'That's all right, Dhenuka,' said Roshni. 'Our horses needed some rest. I hope one of my assistants explained how the medicine should be administered to your people.'

'Yes, they have,' said Dhenuka, smiling strangely.

Roshni suddenly felt uneasy. Her gut instinct told her that she must leave. 'Well, I hope everyone in your village gets better soon.'

She walked up to her horse and reached for the reins. Dhenuka immediately jumped off his horse and held Roshni's hand, pulling her back. 'What's the rush, My Lady?'

Roshni shoved him back and retreated slowly. The other members of Dhenuka's gang had dismounted by then. Three of them moved towards her assistants.

A terrifying chill went up Roshni's spine. 'I... I helped your people...'

Dhenuka grinned ominously. 'Oh, I know. I'm hoping you can help me too...'

Roshni suddenly turned around and ran. Three men took off after her and caught up in no time. One of them slapped her hard. As blood burst forth from Roshni's injured lips, the second man twisted her hand brutally behind her back.

Dhenuka ambled up slowly, reached out and caressed her face. 'A noble woman... Mmm... This is going to be fun.'

His gang burst out laughing.

'*Dada*!' screamed Lakshman as he rushed into Ram's office.

Ram did not raise his eyes as he continued to pore over the documents on his desk. It was the first hour of the second *prahar* and he had expected some peace and quiet.

Ram spoke with casual detachment, continuing to read the document in his hand, 'What's the matter now, Lakshman?'

'*Dada*...' Lakshman was choked with emotion.

'Laksh...' Ram stopped mid-sentence as he looked up and saw the tears streaming down Lakshman's face. 'What happened?'

'*Dada...* Roshni *Didi...*'

Ram immediately stood up, and his chair hurtled back. 'What happened to Roshni?'

'*Dada...*'

'Where is she?'

Chapter 13

A stunned Bharat stood immobile. Lakshman and Shatrughan were bent over, crying inconsolably. Manthara held her daughter's head in her lap, looking into the distance with a vacant expression, her eyes swollen but dry. She was drained of tears. Roshni's body was covered with a white cloth. She had been found lying next to the Sarayu River by Manthara's men, violated and bare. The corpse of one of her assistants lay a short distance away. He had been brutally bludgeoned to death. The other assistant was found by the side of the road, severely injured but still alive. Doctors tended to him as Ram stood by their side; his face was impassive but his hands shook with fury. He had questions for Roshni's assistant.

When Roshni had not returned by the next morning, Manthara had sent out her men to Saraiya to find and bring back her daughter. They had ridden out at dawn as soon as the city gates were unlocked. An hour's ride away from the city, they had chanced upon Roshni's body. She had been brutally gang-raped. Her head had been banged repeatedly against a flat surface. The marks on her wrist and her back suggested that she had been tied to a tree. Her body was covered with bruises and vicious bite marks. The monsters had ripped off some of her skin with their teeth, around her abdomen and bare arms. She had been beaten with a blunt object all over her body, probably in a sick, sadistic ritual. Her face was torn on one side, from her mouth to the cheekbone, the injuries and blood clots in her mouth suggesting that she was probably alive through this torture. There were semen stains all over her body. She had died in a most gruesome manner, as one of the assailants had poured acid down her throat.

The assistant opened his eyes painfully. Ram bent over him and growled. 'Who were they?'

'I don't think he can speak, My Lord,' said the doctor.

Ram ignored the man as he knelt next to the injured assistant. 'Who were they?' he repeated.

Roshni's assistant barely found the strength to whisper a name before he passed out once again.

—— |夼| 🐟 ☼ ——

Roshni was a rare figure who was popular among the masses as well as the classes. She had devoted her life to charity. She was a woman of impeccable character, a picture of grace and dignity. Many compared her to the fabled *Kanyakumari*, the *Virgin Goddess*. The rage that this brutal crime generated was unprecedented. The city demanded retribution.

The criminals were rounded up quickly from Isla village just as they were planning to escape. The chief of Isla was beaten black and blue by the women of his village when he made vain attempts to protect his son. They had suffered Dhenuka's bestiality in silence for too long. Even by the standards of Ram's vastly improved police force, the investigations were completed, the case presented in front of judges, and sentences delivered in record time. Within a week, preparations were on to mete out punishment to the perpetrators. They had all been sentenced to death; all except one; all except Dhenuka.

Ram was devastated that Dhenuka, the main perpetrator of the heinous gang rape and murder, had been exempted from maximum punishment on a legal technicality: he was underage. But the law could not be broken. Not on Ram's watch. Ram, the Law Giver, had to do what he had to do. But Ram, the *rakhi*-brother of Roshni, was drowning in guilt, for he was unable to avenge the horrifying death of his sister. He had to punish himself. And he was doing so by inflicting pain on himself.

He sat alone on a chair in the balcony of his private study, gazing out towards the garden where Roshni had tied a *rakhi* on his wrist. He looked down at the golden thread, eyes brimming with tears. The heat of the mid-day sun bore down mercilessly on his bare torso. He shaded his eyes as he looked up at the sun, and inhaled deeply before turning his attention back to his injured right hand. He picked up the wedge of wood placed on the table by his side. Its tip was smouldering.

He looked up at the sky and whispered, 'I'm sorry, Roshni.'

He pressed the burning wood on the inner side of his right arm, the one that still had the sacred thread which represented his solemn promise to protect his sister. He didn't make a sound, his eyes did not flicker. The acrid smell of burning flesh spread through the air.

'I'm sorry…'

Ram closed his eyes as tears flowed freely down his face.

—— |ㄒ| 🐟 ☼ ——

Hours later, Ram sat in his office with a vacant air of misery. His injured arm was covered by his archer's arm band.

'This is wrong, *Dada*!'

Lakshman entered Ram's office, visibly seething with fury. Ram looked up from his desk, the grief in his eyes concealing the rage within.

'It is the law, Lakshman,' said Ram calmly. 'The law cannot be broken. It is supreme, more important than you or me. Even more important than…'

Ram choked on his words as he could not bring himself to take her name.

'Complete your sentence, *Dada*!' Bharat lashed out harshly from near the door.

Ram looked up. He raised his hand towards Bharat, wincing in pain. 'Bharat…'

Bharat strode into the room, his eyes clouded with sorrow, his body taut, his fingers trembling, yet unable to adequately convey the storm that raged within. 'Finish what you were saying, *Dada*. Say it!'

'Bharat, my brother, listen to me…'

'Let it out! Tell us that your damned law is more important than Roshni!' Fierce tears were flowing in a torrent from Bharat's eyes now. 'Say that it matters more to you than that *rakhi* around your wrist.' He leaned over and grabbed Ram's right arm. Ram did not flinch. 'Say that the law is more important to you than our promise to protect our Roshni forever.'

'Bharat,' said Ram, as he gently freed his arm from his brother's vice-like grip. 'The law is clear: minors cannot be executed. Dhenuka is underage and, according to the law, will not be executed.'

'The hell with the law!' shouted Bharat. 'This is not about the law! This is about justice! Don't you understand the difference, *Dada*? That monster deserves to die!'

'Yes, he does,' said Ram, tormented by the guilt that wracked his soul. 'But a juvenile will not be killed by Ayodhya. That is the law.'

'Dammit, *Dada*!' shouted Bharat, banging his hand on the table.

A loud voice boomed from behind them. 'Bharat!'

The three brothers looked up to find Raj Guru Vashishta standing at the door. Bharat immediately straightened and folded his hands together in a respectful namaste. Lakshman refused to react, his untrammelled anger now focused on his guru.

Vashishta walked in with deliberate, slow-paced footsteps. 'Bharat, Lakshman, your elder brother is right. The law must be respected and obeyed, whatever the circumstances.'

'And what about the promise we made to Roshni, Guru*ji*? Doesn't that count?' asked Bharat. 'We gave our word that we would protect her. We had a duty towards her too, and we failed in that. Now, we must avenge her.'

'Your word is not above the law.'

'Guru*ji*, the descendants of Raghu never break their word,' said Bharat, repeating an ancient family code.

'If your word of honour is in conflict with the law, then you must break your word and take dishonour upon your name,' said Vashishta. 'That is *dharma*.'

'Guru*ji*!' shouted Lakshman, on the brink of losing all semblance of propriety and control.

'Look at this!' said Vashishta, as he walked up to Ram, tore his archer's band off and raised his arm for all to see. Ram tried to pull it away but Vashishta held firm.

Bharat and Lakshman were shocked. Ram's right inner arm was badly burnt. The skin around the wound was charred and discoloured.

'He has been doing this again and again, every single day, ever since the judge announced that Dhenuka will escape death on a legal technicality,' said Vashishta. 'I have been trying to get him to stop. But this is his way of punishing himself for having broken his word to Roshni. However, he will not break the law.'

Ram did not attend the execution of the seven rapists.

The judges, in their anger at not being able to put the main accused to death, had, in an act of judicial overreach, prescribed in detail the manner of punishment to be meted out to the seven other accused. Ram's new law on execution had laid out a quick procedure: to be hanged by the neck till the person is dead. Furthermore, he had decreed that the execution be carried out in a designated area of the prison premises, the clause ending with giving the judge discretion in matters of procedure. Using this clause, the fuming judges had pronounced a detailed, exceptional procedure for the execution: that it would be carried out in public, that they would be made to bleed to death, and that it would be as painful as can be; they justified their impropriety by asserting that it would serve as a lesson for all time to come. In private they argued that this would also allow people to adequately give vent to their righteous rage. The police had no choice but to obey the ruling.

The execution platform was constructed outside the city walls, built to a height of four feet to enable an adequate view from even a distance. Thousands gathered outside the city walls from early morning to witness the spectacle. Many were armed with eggs and rotten fruit, to be used as missiles.

An angry roar erupted from the crowds as the seven convicts were led out of the mobile prison carts that they had been transported in. It was clear from the injuries on their body that they had already been beaten mercilessly in the prison; despite his best efforts, Ram had not been able to control the moral outrage of not only the prison guards, but also the other prisoners. Without exception, they had all been the recipients, in some form or the other, of Roshni's benevolence. The desire for retribution was strong.

The criminals walked up the steps of the platform. They were first led to wooden pillories erected on a post, with holes where the head and hands were inserted, exposed to the people for ritual public abuse. Having secured the prisoners, the guards marched off the platform.

That was the cue for the crowd. Missiles began to fly with unerring accuracy, accompanied by vehement cursing and spitting. At this distance, even eggs and fruit drew blood, causing tremendous pain. The crowd had been strictly forbidden from hurling any sharp objects or big stones. No one wanted the convicts to die too quickly. They had to suffer. They had to pay.

This lasted for almost a half hour. The executioner finally called the mass attack to an end when the people began to slow down, probably with exhaustion. He stepped onto the platform and walked up to the first convict, whose wild eyes were frantic with terror. With the help of two assistants, he stretched the convict's legs to the maximum, making him almost choke on the pillory. Then the executioner picked up a large nail and an ironsmith's hammer from the floor, with slow, deliberate movements. As his assistants held the splayed legs apart, the executioner calmly nailed the foot into the wooden platform, hammering with rhythmic precision. The convict screamed desperately as the crowd roared its approval. The executioner carefully examined his handiwork before giving it a few more hits. He stepped back with satisfaction. The convict had just about stopped shrieking in agony when the executioner walked up to his other leg.

He then repeated the horror, one by one, with each of the six other miserable convicts, nailing their feet to the wooden platform. The crowd was delirious and roared with each desperate cry of pain that the criminals let out. When finally finished, the executioner moved to the edge of the platform and waved at the crowd as it cheered him on.

He walked up to the first convict he had nailed. The criminal had fainted by now. Some medicine was forced down his throat and he was slapped till he was awake once again.

'You need to be awake to enjoy this,' hissed the executioner.

'Kill ... me,' pleaded the convict. 'Please ... mercy...'

The executioner's face turned to stone. Roshni had helped deliver his baby girl four months back; all she had accepted in return was a meal in his humble abode. 'Did you have mercy on Lady Roshni, you son of a rabid dog?'

'Sorry ... sorry ... please ... kill me.' The criminal burst into tears.

The executioner walked away nonchalantly.

After three hours of brutal, public torture, the executioner pulled out a small, sharp knife from a scabbard tied to his waist. He loosened the pillory hold on the first convict's right hand and pulled the arm farther out. He examined the wrist closely; he needed to pick the right artery, one that would not bleed out too quickly. He smiled as he found one.

'Perfect,' said the executioner, as he brought his knife close and cut delicately, letting the blood spurt out in small bursts. The convict groaned in agony. Death was at least a painful couple of hours away. The executioner moved quickly, slitting the same artery on the wrists of the remaining criminals. The crowd roared and hurled obscenities each time the knife cut.

The executioner gestured to the crowd that he was done for the day, before stepping down from the platform. They began hurling missiles again, only to be interrupted periodically by an official who would check on the flow of blood. It took two-and-a half more hours for the last of the criminals to finally die, all having suffered a slow and painful death that would scar their soul for many rebirths.

As the criminals were declared dead, the crowd roared loudly: 'Glory to Lady Roshni!'

Manthara sat hunched on an elevated chair, close to the platform. Her eyes still blazed with hatred and fury. She had no doubt the executioner would have tortured the monsters of his own accord; her Roshni was so well loved. Notwithstanding that, she had paid him handsomely to not hold back on the brutality of the execution. She had barely blinked throughout the long and tortuous proceeding, keenly observing each twitch of pain that they had been made to suffer. It was over now, and yet, there was no sense of release, no satisfaction. Her heart had turned to stone.

She clutched an urn close to her chest as she sat. It contained her Roshni's ashes. She looked down as a tear slipped from one eye. It fell on the urn. 'I promise you my child, even the last one will be made to pay for what he did to you. Dhenuka too will face the wrath of justice.'

Chapter 14

'This is barbaric,' said Ram. 'It is against everything Roshni stood for.'

Ram and Vashishta were in the prince's private office.

'Why is it barbaric?' asked Vashishta. 'Do you think the rapists should not have been killed?'

'They should have been executed. That is the law. But the way it was done … at least judges should not give in to anger. It was savage, violent and inhumane.'

'Really? Is there such a thing as humane killing?'

'Are you justifying this behaviour, Guru*ji*?'

'Tell me, will rapists and murderers be terrified of breaking the law now?'

Ram was forced to concede. 'Yes…'

'Then, the punishment has served its purpose.'

'But Roshni wouldn't have…'

'There is a school of thought which states that brute force can only be met with equal brute force. One fights fire with fire, Ram.'

'But Roshni would have said that an eye for an eye will only make the whole world blind.'

'There is virtue in non-violence, no doubt, but only when you're not living in the Age of Kshatriya, of violence. If in the Age of Kshatriya, you are among the very few who believe that "an eye for an eye makes the whole world blind", while everyone else believes otherwise, then you will be the one who is blinded. Universal principles too need to adjust themselves to a changing universe.'

Ram shook his head. 'Sometimes I wonder if my people are even worth fighting for.'

'A real leader doesn't choose to lead only the deserving. He will, instead, inspire his people into becoming the best that they are capable of. A real leader will not defend a monster, but convert that demon into a God; tap into the God that dwells within even him. He takes upon himself the burden of *dharma sankat*, but he ensures that his people become better human beings.'

'You are contradicting yourself, Guru*ji*. Was this brutal punishment justified, in that case?'

'According to me, no. But society is not made up of people like you and me. There are all kinds of people with all shades of opinion. A good ruler must prod his people gently in the direction of *dharma*, which lies in the centre, in balance. If there is too much anger in society, leading to chaos and disruptive violence, then the leader needs to move it towards stability and calm. If, on the other hand, a society is passive and uncomplaining, then the leader needs to incite active participation and outrage, even anger, among the people. Every emotion in the universe exists for a purpose; nothing is superfluous in nature's design. Every emotion also has an opposite: like anger and calm. Society ultimately needs balance. But is this display of anger towards Roshni's rapists and murderers the answer to injustice? Maybe, maybe not. We will know for sure in a few decades. For now, it serves as a pressure-release mechanism.'

Ram looked out of the window, deeply unsettled.

Vashishta knew he couldn't afford any further delay. He didn't have much time on his hands. 'Ram, listen to me.'

'Yes, Guru*ji*,' said Ram.

'Someone is on his way here, he's coming for you. He's a great man, and he's going to take you away. I cannot stop it. It is beyond me.'

'Who is this—'

Vashishta cut in. 'I assure you, you will not be in danger. But you may be told things about me. I want you to remember that you are like my son. I want to see you fulfil your *swadharma*, your *true purpose*. My actions have been defined by that goal.'

'Guru*ji*, I don't understand what…'

'Do not believe what you hear about me. You are like my son. That is all I will say for now.'

A confused Ram folded his hands together into a namaste. 'Yes, Guru*ji*.'

—— 人 🐟 ☼ ——

'Manthara, please understand, I can do nothing,' said Kaikeyi. 'It is the law.'

Manthara had not wasted any time in seeking an audience with Ayodhya's second queen. Kaikeyi had a determined visitor early the next morning. The queen continued with her breakfast, Manthara having refused the repast; all she sought was her personal brand of justice. But Kaikeyi would never admit to anyone that she had little influence over Dashrath now, much less on Ram. She resorted to blaming the law. To the proud, the pretence of noble compliance is better than admittance of failure.

But Manthara would not be denied. She was aware that Dhenuka was incarcerated in a high-security prison within the city. She also knew that only a member of the royal family could pull off what she had in mind. 'My Lady, I have enough money to buy every nobleman in the kingdom. You know that. It will all be put at your disposal. I promise.'

Kaikeyi's heart skipped a beat. She knew that with Manthara's immense resources on her side, she might even be able to force Bharat onto the throne. She was careful to remain non-committal. 'Thank you for the promise. But it is a promise for tomorrow. And, who has seen tomorrow?'

Manthara reached into the folds of her *angvastram* and pulled out a *hundi*, a *document bearing her official seal*. It promised to honour the debt of a stated sum of money. Kaikeyi was keenly aware that what she was receiving was, for all practical purposes, cash. Anyone in the Sapt Sindhu would give her money against a *hundi* signed by Manthara; her reputation in such matters was unquestionable. Kaikeyi accepted the *hundi* and scanned it quickly as she did so. The queen was shocked. The staggering amount that was neatly inscribed in the document was the equivalent of more than ten years of Ayodhya's royal revenue. In a flash, she had made Kaikeyi richer than the king! The extent of this woman's fabulous wealth was beyond even the queen's imagination.

'I understand that encashing a *hundi* of this large an amount of money might prove difficult for most merchants, My Lady,' said Manthara. 'Whenever you need the money, I will reimburse this *hundi* myself and pay the amount in gold coins.'

Kaikeyi was well aware of another exemplary law: refusal to honour a *hundi* led to many years of imprisonment in a debtor's prison.

Manthara drove her advantage home. 'I have a lot more where this came from. It is all at your disposal.'

Kaikeyi held the *hundi* tight. She knew that it was her ticket to realising all her dreams for her son; ones that had started looking distant due to recent events.

Manthara struggled out of her chair, hobbled to Kaikeyi, and leaned over as she hissed, 'I want him to suffer. I want him to suffer as much as he made my daughter suffer. I am not interested in a speedy death.'

Kaikeyi gripped Manthara's hands firmly. 'I swear by the great Lord Indra, that monster shall know what justice means.'

Manthara stared at the queen in stony silence. Her body quivered with cold rage.

'He will suffer,' promised Kaikeyi. 'Roshni will be avenged. That is the word of the queen of Ayodhya.'

— 𝍢 🐟 ☼ —

'*Maa*, believe me, I would love to kill that monster with my bare hands,' said Bharat, earnestly. 'I know I would be serving the cause of justice if I were to do so. But Ram *Dada's* new law forbids it.'

Kaikeyi had left for Bharat's quarters as soon as Manthara exited the palace. She knew exactly what she had to do, and how to go about it. Appealing to her son's ambition would be a waste of time; he was more loyal to his half-brother than he was to his own mother. She had to appeal to his sense of justice, his righteous anger, his love for Roshni.

'I fail to understand this new law, Bharat. What kind of justice did it serve?' asked Kaikeyi passionately. 'Doesn't the *Manu Smriti* clearly state that the Gods abandon the land where women are not respected?'

'Yes, *Maa*, but this is the law! Minors cannot be given the death sentence.'

'Do you know that Dhenuka is not even underage anymore? He was a minor only when the crime was committed.'

'I'm aware of that, *Maa*. I've had a massive fight with *Dada* over it. I agree with you, justice is far more important than the technicalities of a law. But *Dada* doesn't understand that.'

'Yes, he doesn't,' fumed Kaikeyi.

'*Dada* lives in a world that should be, not the world as it is. He wants to enforce the values of an ideal society, but he forgets that Ayodhya is not an ideal society. We are very far from it. And monsters like Dhenuka will always exploit the loopholes in the law and escape. Others will learn from him. A leader has to first make the society worthy of enlightened laws before implementing them.'

'Then, why don't you...'

'I can't. If I break, or even question *Dada*'s law, I will hurt his credibility. Why will anyone else take him seriously if his own brother doesn't?'

'You are missing the point. Criminals who were afraid of Ram's laws thus far, will now know that there are ways to exploit and work around them. Juveniles will be made to commit crimes planned by adults. There are enough poor, frustrated, underage youths who can easily be influenced into a life of crime for a handful of coins.'

'It's possible.'

'An example must be made of Dhenuka. That will serve as a lesson to others.'

Bharat looked at Kaikeyi quizzically. 'Why are you so interested in this, *Maa*?'

'I just want justice for our Roshni.'

'Really?'

'She was a noblewoman, Bharat. Your *rakhi*-sister was raped by a bloody villager,' Kaikeyi drove the point home.

'I'm curious; would you be thinking differently had it been the other way round? Had a nobleman raped a village woman, would you still be clamouring for justice?'

Kaikeyi remained silent. She knew that if she said yes, Bharat would not believe her.

'I would want a rapist-murderer from the nobility to be killed as well,' growled Bharat. 'Just like I want Dhenuka to be killed. That is true justice.'

'Then why is Dhenuka still alive?'

'The other rapists *have* been punished.'

'This is a first! Partial justice! Disingenuous, isn't it? There is no such thing as partial justice, son! You either get justice or you don't!'

'*Maa…*'

'The most brutal among them is still alive! What's more, he's a guest of Ayodhya! His board and lodging are being financed by the royal treasury; from your coffers. You are personally feeding the man who brutalised your *rakhi*-sister.'

Bharat remained quiet.

'Maybe Ram did not love Roshni enough,' ventured Kaikeyi.

'In the name of Lord Rudra, how can you say that, *Maa*? Ram *Dada* has been punishing himself because…'

'How does that make any sense?! How does that get her justice?'

Bharat fell silent.

'You have Kekaya blood in you. You have the blood of Ashwapati coursing through your veins. Have you forgotten our ancient motto? "Blood shall always be answered with blood!" Only then do others learn to be afraid of you.'

'Of course, I remember that, *Maa!* But I will not hurt Ram *Dada's* credibility.'

'I know a way…'

Bharat looked at Kaikeyi, puzzled.

'You should leave Ayodhya on a diplomatic visit. I will publicise your absence. Double back to Ayodhya incognito; get some of your trusted men to break into prison and escape with Dhenuka. You know what you have to do with him. Resume your foreign visit after the deed is done. Nobody will be any the wiser. Practically the whole city will come under suspicion for the killing, for there is no one in Ayodhya who doesn't want Dhenuka dead. It will be impossible for Ram to discover who did it. Ram will escape the stigma of being seen as shielding his brother, for no one will connect you to it. It will just be seen as the one time that Ram was unable to catch the so-called killer. Most importantly, justice will be served.'

'You have really thought this through,' said Bharat. 'And, how do I leave the city without a diplomatic invitation? If I ask for royal permission to leave without one, it will raise suspicion.'

'There is already an invitation for you from Kekaya for a diplomatic visit.'

'No, there isn't.'

'Yes, there is,' said Kaikeyi. 'It did not come to anyone's notice in the chaos and confusion following Roshni's death.' What she did not reveal to Bharat was that she had used some of her newly-acquired wealth to get a back-dated invitation from Kekaya inserted into the Ayodhya diplomatic files. 'Accept the invitation. And then get justice for your sister's soul.'

Bharat sat still, cold as ice, as he contemplated what his mother had just said.

'Bharat?'

He looked at his mother, as if startled by her presence.

'Will you or won't you?'

Bharat murmured, almost to himself, 'Sometimes you have to break the law to do justice.'

Kaikeyi pulled out a piece of bloodied white cloth from the folds of her *angvastram*; it was from the one that had been used to cover Roshni's brutalised body. 'Help her get justice.'

Bharat took the cloth gently from his mother, gazed at it and then at his *rakhi*. He closed his eyes as a tear slid down his cheek.

Kaikeyi came up to her son and held him tight. 'Shakti *Maa* has her eyes on you, my son. You cannot allow the one who has committed such a heinous crime on a woman to go unpunished. Remember that.'

Shakti Maa, the *Mother Goddess*, was a deity that all Indians looked upon with love. And fear.

Blood shall always be answered with blood.

—— |大| 🐟 ☼ ——

Dhenuka was awoken by the sound of a door creaking open in his solitary cell at the royal prison.

There was no light streaming in, even from the high window on this dark, moonless night. He sensed danger. He turned his body towards the door, pretending to be asleep as he clenched his fists tight, ready for attack. He opened his eyes slightly, but it was impossible to see anything in the dark.

He heard a soft whistle above his head. Dhenuka sprang up as he hit out hard. There was nobody there. But the sound *had* come from above. A confused Dhenuka's eyes darted in all directions, desperately trying to see what was going on. The blow came unexpectedly.

He felt a sharp blow on the back of his head and he was thrown to the front. A hand yanked him by the hair and shoved a wet cloth against his nose. Dhenuka instantly recognised the odour of the sweet-smelling liquid. He himself had used it on his victims on many an occasion. He knew he couldn't fight it. He fell unconscious in a matter of seconds.

Dhenuka awoke to the gentle rolling of wheels on a dirt road. He seemed unhurt, except for the blow to his head, which made it throb unbearably. His kidnappers hadn't injured him. He wondered who they were. Could they be his father's men, helping him escape? Where was he? Now, bumps on the road were making the wheels bounce, and the steady sound of crickets seemed to indicate that they were in a jungle, already outside the city. He tried to raise his head to get a better sense of his whereabouts, but the wet cloth made an appearance again. He fell unconscious.

A splash of water woke Dhenuka up with a start. He shook his head, cursing loudly.

A surprisingly gentle voice was heard. 'Come, now.'

An astonished but wary Dhenuka tried to sit upright. He realised that he was in a covered bullock cart, the kind used to transport hay. He brushed some that was still lying around off his body. He was assisted as he stepped down. It was still pitch dark but some torches had been lit, which allowed him to look around to find his bearings. He still felt groggy and unsteady on his feet; perhaps the after-effects of the sedative that had been administered. He reached out and grabbed the cart to steady himself.

'Drink this,' said a man who silently materialised beside him, holding a cup.

Dhenuka took the cup from his hand but hesitated as he examined the contents warily.

'If I had wanted to kill you, I would have done so already,' said the man. 'This will clear your head. You will need your wits about you for what is to follow.'

Dhenuka drank the contents without a protest. The effect was almost instantaneous. His head cleared and his mind became alert. As his senses stabilised, Dhenuka heard the sound of flowing water.

Perhaps I'm near the river. The moment the sun rises, I will swim across to safety. But where is Father? Only he could have bribed the officials to engineer my escape.

'Thank you,' said Dhenuka, as he returned the cup to the man. 'But where is my father?'

The man silently took the cup and melted into the darkness. Dhenuka was left alone. 'Hey! Where are you going?'

A well-built figure emerged from where the man had disappeared. His fair skin shone in the light of the fire torches, as did his bright green *dhoti* and *angvastram*. He wore a small head band that held his long hair in place; it had an intricately-built, golden peacock feather attached to it. His eyes, normally mischievous, were like shards of ice.

'Prince Bharat!' exclaimed Dhenuka, as he quickly went down on one knee.

Bharat walked up to Dhenuka without replying.

Dhenuka had heard of Bharat's popularity with the women of Kosala. 'I knew you would understand me. I didn't expect any better from your strait-laced elder brother.'

Bharat stood still, breathing evenly.

'I knew you would understand that women have been created for our enjoyment, My Lord. Women are meant to be used by men!' Dhenuka laughed softly, bowed his head, and reached out to hold Bharat's *angvastram* in a gesture of humble gratitude.

Bharat moved suddenly, flung Dhenuka's hand aside, and grabbed his throat, a menacing voice emerging through his gritted teeth. 'Women are not meant to be used. They are meant to be loved.'

Dhenuka's expression changed to one of unadulterated terror. Like a trapped animal, he stood rooted to the spot as twenty powerfully-built men emerged, seemingly from nowhere. He struggled to break free of Bharat as the prince began to slowly squeeze his throat.

'My Lord,' interrupted a man from behind.

Bharat caught his breath and abruptly released Dhenuka. 'You will not die so quickly.'

Dhenuka coughed desperately as he strained to recover his breath. All of a sudden he straightened, whirled around and tried to make a dash for it. Two men grabbed him roughly and dragged him back to the cart, kicking and screaming.

'The law!' screeched Dhenuka. 'The law! I cannot be touched. I was a juvenile!'

A third man stepped forward and punched Dhenuka in the jaw, breaking a tooth and drawing blood. 'You are not a juvenile anymore.'

'But Prince Ram's laws—'

Dhenuka's words were cut short as the man boxed him again in the face, this time breaking his nose. 'Do you see Prince Ram anywhere?'

'Tie him up,' said Bharat.

Some men picked up the torches as two others dragged Dhenuka backwards, to a large tree. They spread his arms wide and tied them around the tree trunk with a rope. They spread his legs apart and repeated the process with his feet. One of them turned around. 'It is done, My Lord.'

Bharat turned to his side. 'I'm saying this for the last time, Shatrughan. Leave. You don't have to be here. Stay away from this…'

Shatrughan cut in. 'I will always be by your side, *Dada*.'

Bharat stared at Shatrughan with expressionless eyes.

Shatrughan continued. 'This may be against the law, but it is just.'

Bharat nodded and began to walk forward. As he approached Dhenuka, he pulled out a piece of bloodied white cloth from under his waistband, touched it to his head reverentially, and tied it around his right wrist, above the *rakhi*.

Dhenuka was as desperate as a tethered goat surrounded by a pride of lions. He bleated, 'My Lord, please, let me go. I swear, I will never touch a woman again.'

Bharat slapped him hard across his face. 'Do you recognise this place?'

Dhenuka looked around and realisation dawned. This was where he and his gang had raped and murdered Roshni.

Bharat held out his hand. One of his soldiers immediately stepped up and handed him a metallic bottle. Bharat opened the lid and held it close to Dhenuka's nose. 'You will soon know what pain really means.'

Dhenuka burst into tears as he recognised the acidic smell. 'My Lord, I'm sorry… I'm so sorry… Forgive me… Let me go… Please…'

'Remember Roshni *Didi's* cries, you filthy dog,' growled Shatrughan.

Dhenuka pleaded desperately, 'Lady Roshni was a good woman, My Lord... I was a monster... I'm sorry... But she wouldn't want you to do this...'

Bharat returned the bottle to the soldier while another soldier handed him a large twisted drill. Bharat placed the sharp end of the drill on Dhenuka's shoulder. 'Maybe you are right. She was so good that she would have forgiven even a monster like you. But I am not as good as she was.'

Dhenuka began wailing in a loud, high-pitched voice as a soldier stepped up and handed Bharat a hammer.

'Scream all you want, you demented bastard,' said the soldier. 'Nobody will hear you.'

'*Nooooo! Please...*'

Bharat raised his arm and held the hammer high. He positioned the twisted drill on Dhenuka's shoulder. He just wanted a hole large enough to pour some acid into. A quick death would end the suffering and pain too soon.

'Blood shall always be answered with blood...' whispered Bharat.

The hammer came down, the drill penetrated perfectly. Desperate screams rang out loud and clear, above the noise of the raging Sarayu.

Chapter 15

As the first rays of the sun hesitantly nudged at the darkness, Kaikeyi set off for a rendezvous with Bharat and Shatrughan across the Sarayu River, beyond the northernmost tip of Ayodhya; it was at least a two-hour ride from the southern side, where Dhenuka's corpse lay.

The brothers had assiduously washed off the blood and other signs of the events of the night before. Their blood-stained clothes had been burnt after they donned fresh garments. Kaikeyi was accompanied by Bharat's bodyguards.

She stepped down from her chariot and embraced the two. 'You have served justice, my boys.'

Bharat and Shatrughan did not say anything, their faces a mask that hid the storm still raging within; anger still coursing through them. Sometimes wrath is required to deliver justice. But the strange thing about anger is that it is like fire; the more you feed it, the more it grows. It takes a lot of wisdom to know when to let anger go. The princes, still young, had not yet mastered this.

'And now, you must leave,' said Kaikeyi.

Bharat held out the piece from the blood-stained cloth that had covered Roshni's body.

'I will return this to Manthara personally,' said Kaikeyi, as she took the cloth from Bharat.

Bharat bent down to touch his mother's feet. 'Bye, *Maa*.'
Shatrughan followed suit wordlessly.

——— |大| 🐟 ☀ ———

Dhenuka's body was found by a group of villagers walking by,
as they heard the cawing of a murder of crows, fighting over
his entrails.

The villagers cut the ropes that still held the body and
laid it on the ground. Numerous holes had been viciously
hammered into him while he was still alive, judging by the clot
formation around the wounds. The burn marks around the
holes indicated that something acidic had been poured into
each of these wounds.

Death had become inevitable once a sword was rammed
into Dhenuka's abdomen, right through to the tree trunk. He
must have slowly bled to death; he was probably still alive
when the crows had swooped down for a feast.

One of the villagers recognised Dhenuka. 'Why don't we
just leave?' he asked.

'No, we'll wait,' said the leader of the group, wiping a tear
from his eye as he asked one of his men to walk to Ayodhya
and convey the news. He too had known Roshni's kindness.
His anger had known no bounds when he had discovered that
Dhenuka would be let off on a legal technicality. He wished
that he'd been the one who killed this monster. He turned to
the Sarayu and thanked the River Goddess, for justice had
been served.

He looked down and spat on the corpse.

——— |大| 🐟 ☀ ———

Manthara rode out of the North Gate on a horse-drawn carriage, accompanied by Druhyu, her man Friday, and some bodyguards. They crossed the Grand Canal, moving steadily till they reached the cremation ground by the river in half an hour. At the far end of the ghats was the temple of the mythical first mortal, Lord Yama. Interestingly, Lord Yama was revered as both the God of Death as well as the God of Dharma. The ancients believed that *dharma* and death were interlinked. In a sense, a tally sheet was drawn at the end of one's mortal life; if there was an imbalance, the soul would have to return to physical form in another mortal body; if the accounts were in balance and karma was in alignment with *dharma*, then the soul would attain ultimate salvation: release from the cycle of rebirth, and reunification with the universal soul, the *Parmatma*, the *Ekam*, the *Brahman*.

Seven pandits conducted the rites in the temple of Lord Yama as Manthara held the urn, within which lay the ashes of her most beauteous creation. In a second urn was the bloodied white cloth that Kaikeyi had handed to her in the morning.

Druhyu sat by the river, quietly contemplating the tumultuous changes that had occurred within a brief span of time. His mistress had changed forever. He had never seen her do the things she had done in the past few days; actions that could directly harm her business and even her personal well-being. She had staked her life's work at the altar of vengeance. Druhyu suspected that his true lord would be incensed by the amount of money that had been thrown away of late. A large portion of it was not Manthara's to do with as she pleased. He was afraid for his own well-being. A movement at the temple door distracted him.

As Manthara walked towards the ghats, her limp seemed more pronounced, her hunched back more bent. Her guards walked silently behind her, followed by the chanting *pandits*. She slowly descended to the river, one step at a time. She sat on the final step, the water from the river edge gently lapping around her feet. She waved the guards away. The *pandits* stood a step above, diligently reciting Sanskrit mantras to help the soul on its journey into the next world, beyond the mythical river Vaitarni. They concluded their prayers by repeating a hymn from the *Isha Vasya Upanishad,* one that had also been recited during the cremation ceremony.

Vayur anilam amritam; Athedam bhasmantam shariram

Let this temporary body be burned to ashes. But the breath of life belongs elsewhere. May it find its way back to the Immortal Breath.

Druhyu observed the proceedings from a distance, his attention focused on the pathetic shadow of the calculating, sharp woman that Manthara had once been. A single thought kept running in his mind, as if on a loop.

The old woman has lost it. She is no longer useful to the true lord. I need to take care of myself now.

Manthara held the urn close to her bosom. Inhaling deeply, she finally mustered the strength to do what had to be done. She opened the lid and turned the urn upside down, allowing her daughter's ashes to drift away in the river waters. She held the bloodied white cloth close to her face and whispered, 'Don't come back to this ugly world, my child; it has not been created for one as pure as you.'

Manthara stared at her daughter's remains moving steadily away from her. She looked up at the sky, her chest bursting with anger.

Ram…

Manthara squeezed her eyes shut, her breath emerging in erratic rasps.

You protected that monster... You protected Dhenuka... I will remember...

'Who's responsible for this?' growled Ram, his body taut with tension. He was surrounded by police officials.

Ram had rushed to the scene of the crime as soon as he received intimation of the grisly murder of Dhenuka. The officers were silent, taken aback by the fury of a man who was defined by his composure.

'This is a travesty of the law, a perversion of justice,' said Ram. 'Who did this?'

'I ... I don't know, My Lord,' said one of the officers nervously.

Ram leaned towards the frightened man, stepping closer. 'Do you really expect me to believe that?'

A loud shout was heard from behind. '*Dada!*'

Ram looked up to see Lakshman galloping furiously towards them.

'*Dada,*' said Lakshman, as he pulled up close. 'You need to come with me right away.'

'Not now, Lakshman,' said Ram, waving his hand in dismissal. 'I'm busy.'

'*Dada,*' said Lakshman, 'Guru Vashishta has asked for you.'

Ram looked at Lakshman with irritation. 'I will be back soon. Please tell Guru*ji* that I have to—'

Lakshman interrupted his elder brother. '*Dada*, Maharishi Vishwamitra is here! He is asking for you; *specifically* for you.'

Ram stared at Lakshman, stunned.

Vishwamitra was the chief of the Malayaputras, the mysterious tribe left behind by the previous Vishnu, Lord Parshu Ram. They represented the sixth Vishnu, tasked with carrying forward his mission on earth. The legendary powers of the Malayaputras instilled a sense of awe among the people of the Sapt Sindhu. This effect was further enhanced by Vishwamitra's fearsome reputation. Born as Kaushik, a Kshatriya, he was the son of the great King Gaadhi. Despite being a brave warrior in his youth, his nature drove him towards becoming a *rishi*. Against all odds, he succeeded. Thereafter, he reached the pinnacle of Brahmin ascension when he became the chief of the Malayaputras. After taking over as the chief, he had changed his name to Vishwamitra. The Malayaputras were tasked with assisting the next Mahadev, when he appeared. They believed their primary reason for existing, however, was to give rise to the next Vishnu when the time came.

Ram looked down at Dhenuka's body and then at his brother, torn between the two calls of duty. Lakshman dismounted and caught him by his elbow.

'*Dada*, you can come back to this,' insisted Lakshman, 'but Maharishi Vishwamitra should not be kept waiting. We have all heard about his legendary temper.'

Ram relented. 'My horse,' he ordered.

One of the officers quickly fetched his horse. Ram mounted and swiftly tapped the animal into action; Lakshman followed him. As the horses galloped towards the city, Ram recalled the odd conversation he had had with Vashishta a few days earlier.

Someone is on his way here… I cannot stop it…

'What can Maharishi Vishwamitra possibly want from me?' whispered Ram to himself.

…you serve a purpose for him too…

Ram brought his attention back to the present and made a clicking noise, urging the horse to move quicker.

'Are you saying no to me, Your Highness?' asked Vishwamitra in a mellifluous voice. But the underlying threat was unmistakable.

As if his position and reputation were not fearsome enough, Maharishi Vishwamitra's towering persona added to his indomitable aura. He was almost seven feet in height, of gigantic proportions, with a large belly offset by a sturdy, muscular chest, shoulders and arms. His flowing white beard, Brahmin knotted tuft of hair on an otherwise shaven head, large limpid eyes and the holy *janau*, *sacred thread*, tied over his shoulder, stood in startling contrast to the numerous battle scars that lined his face and body. His dark complexion was enhanced by his saffron *dhoti* and *angvastram*.

Emperor Dashrath and his three queens had received the maharishi in the king's private office. The maharishi had come straight to the point. One of his *ashrams* was under attack and he needed Ram's help to defend it; that was it. No explanations were offered as to the nature of the attack, and how exactly the young prince would defend the mighty Malayaputras, who were reputed to have one of the most feared militias in India within their ranks. The great chief of the Malayaputras would not be questioned or denied.

Dashrath swallowed nervously. Even at the peak of his powers, he would have been afraid to take on Vishwamitra; he was frankly terrified now, though thoroughly confused. He had grown increasingly fond of Ram over the last few months and he did not want to part with him. 'My Lord, I'm not suggesting that I do not want to send him with you. It's just that, I feel General Mrigasya should be equal to the task. My entire army is at your disposal and…'

'I want Ram,' said Vishwamitra, his eyes boring into Dashrath's, unnerving the emperor of the Sapt Sindhu. 'And, I also want Lakshman.'

Kaushalya did not know what to make of the offer from Vishwamitra. While, on the one hand, she was delighted with the possibility that Ram would have a chance to get closer to the great sage, on the other, she was concerned that Vishwamitra would simply use Ram's martial skills for his own ends and then discard him. Moreover, Kaikeyi could easily grab the opportunity presented by Ram's absence to have Bharat installed as the crown prince. Kaushalya responded the only way she could when faced with such situations: she shed silent tears.

Kaikeyi felt no such conflict. She already found herself regretting having agreed to Manthara's plotting, and wished her son was here. 'Maharishi*ji*,' said Kaikeyi, 'I would be honoured to send Bharat to accompany you. We may just have to—'

'But Bharat is not in Ayodhya,' said Vishwamitra. It seemed that there was nothing he did not know.

'You are right, Maharishi*ji*,' said Kaikeyi. 'That's what I was about to say. We may have to wait for a few weeks. I can send a message immediately to have Bharat recalled.'

Vishwamitra stared into Kaikeyi's eyes. A nervous Kaikeyi looked down, feeling inexplicably as if her secrets had been suddenly exposed. There was an uncomfortable silence. Then Vishwamitra's booming voice filled the room. 'I want Ram, Your Highness; and Lakshman, of course. I don't need anyone else. Now, are you sending them with me or not?'

'Guru*ji*,' said Sumitra, 'I offer my sincere apologies for interrupting the conversation. But I think that there has been a big protocol blunder. You have already been with us for a while, but our venerated raj guru, Maharishi Vashishta, has still not had the pleasure of meeting you. Should we send word to him to grace us with his presence? We will carry on our discussion once he's here.'

Vishwamitra laughed. 'Hmm! What I've heard is true, after all. The third and junior-most queen is the smartest of them all.'

'Of course I'm not the smartest, Maharishi*ji*,' said Sumitra, feeling her face redden with embarrassment. 'I was just suggesting that protocol…'

'Yes. Yes, of course,' said Vishwamitra. 'Follow your protocol. Bring your raj guru. We shall then talk about Ram.'

The king and his wives rushed out of the room, leaving the maharishi alone with some petrified attendants.

Vashishta entered the private royal office alone and dismissed the attendants. No sooner did they leave than Vishwamitra stood up with a sneer, 'So what arguments will you use to keep him away from me, Divodas?'

Vishwamitra had purposely used the *gurukul* name of Vashishta, a name that the sage had had when he was a child in school.

'I am not a child anymore, Maharishi Vishwamitra,' said Vashishta, with deliberate politeness. 'My name is Vashishta. And I would prefer it if you addressed me as Maharishi Vashishta.'

Vishwamitra stepped close. 'Divodas, what are your arguments? Your royal family is a divided house, in any case. Dashrath does not want to part with his sons. Kaushalya is confused, while Kaikeyi definitely wants Bharat to be the one who accompanies me. And Sumitra, smart Sumitra, is happy come what may, for one of her sons will be aligned to whoever wins. You have done quite a job here, haven't you, *Raj Guru*?'

Vashishta ignored the barb. It was clear to him that there was little he could do. Ram and Lakshman would have to go with Vishwamitra, regardless of the arguments he could make.

'Kaushik,' said Vashishta, using Vishwamitra's childhood name, 'it looks like you will force your way once again; no matter how unfair it is.'

Vishwamitra took one more step towards Vashishta, looming large over the raj guru. 'And it looks like you will run away, once again. Still scared of a fight, eh, Divodas?'

Vashishta closed his fist tight, but his face remained deadpan. 'You will never understand why I did what I did. It was for—'

'For the greater good?' sniggered Vishwamitra, stopping him mid-sentence. 'Do you really expect me to believe that? There is nothing more pathetic than people hiding their cowardice behind seemingly noble intentions.'

'You haven't lost any of your haughty Kshatriya ways, have you? It's amazing that you actually have the temerity to imagine that you represent the great Lord Parshu Ram, the one who destroyed Kshatriya arrogance!'

'Everyone is aware of my background, Divodas. At least I don't hide anything.' Vishwamitra glared at the shorter man. 'Should I reveal your true origin to your precious little boy? Tell him what I did to—'

'You didn't do me any favour!' shouted Vashishta, finally losing control.

'I may just do one now,' smiled Vishwamitra.

Vashishta turned around and stormed out of the room. Despite the passage of time, he felt he still owed the arrogant Vishwamitra a modicum of courtesy for the memory of the friendship they once had.

Chapter 16

A week later, Ram and Lakshman stood at the balustrade of the ship of the chief of Malayaputras as it sailed down the Sarayu. They were on their way to one of Vishwamitra's several *ashrams* on the banks of the Ganga River.

'*Dada*, this massive ship belongs to Maharishi Vishwamitra, as do the two that are following us,' whispered Lakshman. 'There are at least three hundred trained and battle-hardened warriors aboard. I have heard stories about thousands more at his secret capital, wherever that is. What in Lord Parshu Ram's name does he need us for?'

'I don't know,' said Ram, as he looked into the dark expanse of water. Everyone aboard kept a safe distance from them. 'This makes no sense. But Father has ordered us to treat Maharishi Vishwamitra as our guru and that is—'

'*Dada*, I don't think Father had a choice.'

'And neither do we.'

— 𑀓 🐟 ☀ —

A few days later, Vishwamitra ordered the ships to drop anchor. Boats were quickly lowered and fifty people rowed across to the shore, Ram and Lakshman included.

As the boats banked, the Malayaputras jumped ashore onto the narrow beach and began to prepare the ground for a *puja*.

'What are we planning to do here, Guru*ji*?' asked Ram politely as he folded his hands into a namaste.

'Hasn't your raj guru taught you anything about this place?' asked Vishwamitra, his eyebrows furrowed together, a sardonic smile on his face.

Ram would not say anything uncomplimentary about his guru, Vashishta. But Lakshman had no such compunctions.

'No Guru*ji*, he hasn't,' said Lakshman, shaking his head vigorously.

'Well, this is where Lord Parshu Ram offered a prayer to the fifth Vishnu, Lord Vaaman, before he set out to battle Kaartaveerya Arjun.'

'Wow,' said Lakshman, as he looked around with newfound respect.

'He also performed the *Bal-Atibal puja* here,' continued Vishwamitra, 'which bestowed upon him health, and freedom from hunger and thirst.'

'May I request you, Guru*ji*,' said Ram, his hands held together in respect before Vishwamitra, 'to teach us as well.'

Lakshman became distinctly uncomfortable. He had no desire to be free of hunger and thirst. He quite liked his food and drink.

'Of course,' said Vishwamitra. 'Both of you can sit beside me as I conduct the *puja*. The effect of the *puja* reduces your hunger and thirst for at least one week. The impact on your health is life-long.'

Within a few weeks, the convoy of ships reached the confluence of the Sarayu and the Ganga, after which they steered westwards up the Ganga. They dropped anchor a few days later and secured the vessels to a makeshift jetty. Leaving a skeletal staff behind, Vishwamitra, Ram and Lakshman set off on foot along with two hundred warriors. The entourage finally reached the local *ashram* of the Malayaputras after a four-hour march in a south-easterly direction.

Ram and Lakshman had been told that they were being brought to the *ashram* to bolster the efforts to protect it from enemy attacks. But what they saw was a complete surprise to the brothers. The *ashram* was not designed for any kind of serious defence. A rudimentary fence of hedge and thorny creepers would probably suffice to keep out some animals, but was certainly not enough to stave off well-armed soldiers. The shallow stream near the *ashram* had not been adequately barricaded to prevent a determined attack on the camp. There was no area cleared, either outside or inside the fence, to afford a line of sight. The mud-walled, thatch-roofed huts in the *ashram* were clustered together; a serious fire hazard. All one needed to do was set fire to a single hut, and the blaze would quickly spread through the *ashram*. Even the animals had been housed in the innermost circle of the camp, instead of near the boundary, from where their instinct would provide a timely warning of an attack.

'Something is not right, *Dada*,' Lakshman spoke under his breath. 'This camp looks like it's a new settlement; recent, in fact. The defences are, quite frankly, useless and...'

Ram signalled him with his eyes to keep quiet. Lakshman stopped talking and turned around to find Vishwamitra walking up to them. The maharishi was slightly taller than even the gigantic Lakshman.

'Have your lunch, princes of Ayodhya,' said Vishwamitra. 'Then we will talk.'

— 八 🐟 ☼ —

The Ayodhyan princes sat by themselves, ignored by the denizens of the camp who scurried about, implementing the instructions of Arishtanemi, the legendary military chief of the Malayaputras and Vishwamitra's right-hand man. Vishwamitra sat in *sukhaasan* under a banyan tree: his legs folded in a simple cross-legged position, with each foot tucked beneath the opposite knee. His hands lay on his knees, palms down; his eyes were closed; the relaxed yogic *aasan* for non-rigorous meditation.

Lakshman observed Arishtanemi speaking to an aide as he pointed towards the princes. Within moments, a woman dressed in a saffron *dhoti* and blouse approached Ram and Lakshman with two plantain leaves. She spread them out in front of the princes and sprinkled ritual water on them. She was followed by a couple of young students bearing food bowls. Food was served under the able supervision of the woman.

She smiled, folded her hands together into a namaste and said, 'Please eat, princes of Ayodhya.'

Lakshman looked suspiciously at the food and then at Vishwamitra in the distance. A banana leaf had been placed in front of the maharishi as well, on which was placed a solitary *jambu* fruit: the fruit that had been consecrated with the ancient name of India, *Jambudweep*.

'I think they are trying to poison us, *Dada*,' said Lakshman. 'As guests we have been served all this food, while Maharishi Vishwamitra is eating just one *jambu* fruit.'

'That fruit is not for eating, Lakshman,' said Ram, as he tore a piece of the *roti* and scooped some vegetables with it.

'*Dada!*' said Lakshman, as he grabbed Ram's hand, preventing him from eating.

Ram smiled. 'If they wanted to kill us, they had better opportunities on the ship. This food is not poisoned. Eat!'

'*Dada*, you trust every—'

'Just eat, Lakshman.'

'This is where they attacked,' said Vishwamitra, pointing to the partially-burnt hedge fencing.

'Here, Guru*ji*?' asked Ram, astonished as he cast a quick look at Lakshman before turning his attention back to Vishwamitra.

'Yes, here,' said Vishwamitra.

Arishtanemi stood behind Vishwamitra in silence.

Ram's incredulity was well founded. It didn't look like much of an attack. A two-metre wide strip of the hedge fencing had been partially burnt. Some miscreants seemed to have poured paraffin and set it on fire; they must not have had sufficient quantities of it, for practically the whole fence was still intact. The vandals must have struck at night time, when dew formation on the hedge had thwarted their amateur attempts at arson.

These were clearly not professionals.

Ram stepped out of the boundary through the small breach in the fencing and picked up a partially burnt piece of cloth.

Lakshman quickly followed his brother, took the cloth from Ram and sniffed it, but detected no flammable substance. 'It's a piece of cloth from an *angvastram*. One of them must have accidentally set his own clothes on fire. Idiot!'

Lakshman's eyes fell on a knife; he examined it closely before handing it to his brother. It was old and rusty, though well sharpened; it clearly did not belong to a professional soldier.

Ram looked at Vishwamitra. 'What are your orders, Guru*ji*?'

'I need you to find these attackers who disrupt our rituals and other *ashram* activities,' said Vishwamitra. 'They must be destroyed.'

An irritated Lakshman butted in. 'But these people are not even…'

Ram signalled for silence. 'I will follow your orders, Guru*ji*, because that is what my father has asked me to do. But you need to be honest with me. Why have you brought us here when you have so many soldiers at your command?'

'Because you have something that my soldiers do not possess,' answered Vishwamitra.

'What is that?'

'Ayodhya blood.'

'What difference does that make?'

'The attackers are the Asuras of the old code.'

'They're Asuras?!' exclaimed Lakshman. 'But there are no more Asuras left in India. Those demons were killed by Lord Rudra a long time ago.'

Vishwamitra looked at Lakshman with exasperation. 'I'm talking to your elder brother.' Turning back to Ram, he said, 'The Asuras of the old code would not dream of attacking an Ayodhyan.'

'Why, Guru*ji*?'

'Have you heard of Shukracharya?'

'Yes, he was the guru of the Asuras. He is, or was, worshipped by the Asuras.'

'And do you know where Shukracharya was from?'

'Egypt.'

Vishwamitra smiled. 'Yes, that is technically true. But India has a big heart. If a foreigner comes here and accepts our land as his motherland, he is a foreigner no more. He becomes Indian. Shukracharya was brought up here. Can you guess which Indian city was his home town?'

Ram's eyes widened with amazement. 'Ayodhya?!'

'Yes, Ayodhya. The Asuras of the old code will not attack any Ayodhyan, for that land is sacred to them.'

Ram, Lakshman and Arishtanemi rode out of the *ashram* the following day, at the first hour of the second *prahar*. Accompanied by fifty soldiers, they moved in a southward direction. The local Asura settlement was believed to be a little more than a day's ride away.

'Tell me about their leaders, Arishtanemi*ji*,' Ram respectfully asked the military chief of the Malayaputras.

Arishtanemi was equal in height to Lakshman, but unlike the young prince, was lean, almost lanky. He wore a saffron *dhoti* with an *angvastram* slung over his right shoulder, one end of which was wrapped around his right arm. He wore a *janau* thread; his shaven head and a knotted tuft of hair at the crown were signs of his Brahmin antecedents. Unlike most Brahmins, though, Arishtanemi's wheat-complexioned body had a profusion of battle scars. It was rumoured that he was more than seventy years of age, although he did not look a day older than twenty. Perhaps Maharishi Vishwamitra had revealed to him the secret of the mysterious Somras, the drink of the Gods. Its anti-ageing properties could keep one healthy till the astounding age of two hundred.

'The Asura horde is led by a woman called Tadaka, the wife of their deceased chieftain, Sumali,' said Arishtanemi. 'Tadaka belongs to a Rakshasa clan.'

Ram frowned. 'I thought the Rakshasas were aligned with the Devas, and by extension, their descendants: us.'

'The Rakshasas are warriors, Prince Ram. Do you know what the word "Rakshasa" means? It's derived from the old Sanskrit word for protection, *Raksha*. It is said that the word Rakshasa emerged from their victims asking to "be protected from them". They were the finest mercenaries of ancient times. Some had allied with the Devas, while others joined the Asuras. Raavan himself is half Rakshasa.'

'Oh!' Ram exclaimed, as his eyebrows rose.

Arishtanemi continued. 'Tadaka maintains a militia of fifteen soldiers, led by her son, Subahu. Along with women, children and the old, the settlement must be made up of not more than fifty people.'

Ram frowned. *Just fifteen soldiers?*

—— |大| 🐟 ☼ ——

Early next morning, the party left the temporary camp they'd set up the previous night.

'The Asura camp is an hour's ride from here,' said Arishtanemi. 'I have asked our soldiers to be on the lookout for scouts and possible traps.'

As they rode on, Ram steered his horse towards Arishtanemi's, clearly intending to impose further conversation on the taciturn soldier. 'Arishtanemi*ji*,' said Ram, 'Maharishi Vishwamitra mentioned the Asuras of the old code. It can't possibly comprise only this band of fifty. Fifty people cannot keep an ancient code alive. Where are the others?'

Arishtanemi smiled but did not proffer a response. *This boy is smart. I should warn Guruji to be careful with his words.*

Ram persisted with his questioning. 'Had they been in India, the Asuras would have launched an attack on us, the descendants of the Devas. This suggests that they must not be here. Where are they?'

Arishtanemi sighed imperceptibly and looked up at the dense canopy of trees preventing light from shining through. He decided to oblige the prince with the truth. 'Have you heard about the Vayuputras?'

'Of course, I have,' said Ram. 'Who hasn't? They are the tribe left behind by the previous Mahadev, Lord Rudra, just as your people are the ones left behind by the previous Vishnu, Lord Parshu Ram. The Vayuputras are tasked with protecting India from Evil whenever it arises. They believe that one among them will rise and become the next Mahadev when the time comes.'

Arishtanemi smiled enigmatically.

'But what does this have to do with the Asuras?' asked Ram.

Arishtanemi's expression did not change.

'By the great Lord Rudra, are the Vayuputras giving shelter to the Asuras, to India's enemies?'

Arishtanemi's smile broadened.

And then, the truth hit Ram. 'The Asuras have joined the Vayuputras...'

'Yes, they have.'

Ram was perplexed. 'But, why? Our ancestors went to great lengths to destroy the Asura Empire in India. They should hate all the Devas and their descendants. And here they are, having joined a group whose sole purpose is to protect India from Evil; why are they protecting the descendants of their mortal enemies?'

'Yes, they are, aren't they?'

Ram was stunned. 'But, why?'

'Because Lord Rudra ordered them to do so.'

This made no sense anymore! Ram was shocked beyond belief, but more importantly, intellectually provoked. He looked towards the sky with a bemused expression. *The people of the masculine are very strange, no doubt; but also magnificent!* He was on his way now to meet some of these quixotic creatures.

But why should they be destroyed? What law have they broken? I'm sure Arishtanemji knows. But he will not tell me. He is loyal to Maharishi Vishwamitra. I need to get some more information about the Asuras, instead of blindly attacking them.

Ram frowned as he suddenly became aware that Arishtanemi was keenly observing him, almost as if he was attempting to read his mind.

—— 肰 ♟ ☼ ——

The mounted platoon had ridden for half an hour when Ram silently signalled for them to halt. Everyone immediately pulled their reins. Lakshman and Arishtanemi steered their horses gently towards Ram.

'Up ahead,' whispered Ram, 'high up that tree.'

Around fifty metres ahead, an enemy soldier sat on a *machan* built on a fig tree, around twenty metres from the ground. Some branches had been pulled in front, in a vain attempt to conceal it.

'The idiot is not even camouflaged properly,' whispered Lakshman with disgust.

The Asura soldier was dressed in a red *dhoti;* if the intention was to serve as a spy or a lookout, the effect was disastrous, for the colour screamed his presence; like a parrot in a parade of crows.

'Red is their holy colour,' said Arishtanemi. 'They wear it whenever they go into battle.'

Lakshman was incredulous. 'But he is supposed to be a spy, not a warrior! Amateurs!'

Ram removed the bow slung over his shoulder and tested the pull of the string. He bent forward and rubbed his horse's neck as he crooned a soft tune; the animal became completely still. Ram pulled an arrow from the quiver tied to his back, nocked it and pulled the string back, aiming quickly. He flicked his releasing thumb and fired the arrow. The missile spun ferociously as it sped to its target, hitting its mark with precision: the thick rope that held the *machan* in place. It immediately gave way and the Asura came crashing down, hitting the branches on his downward journey. This effectively broke his fall and he landed on the ground, reasonably uninjured.

Arishtanemi stared in wonder at Ram's exquisite archery. *This boy is talented.*

'Surrender immediately and you will not be harmed,' Ram reassured. 'We only need some answers from you.'

The Asura quickly rose to his feet. He was, really, a youth, no more than fifteen years of age. His face was twisted with anger and disgust. He spat loudly and tried to draw his sword. Since he had not held the scabbard with his other hand to steady it, he only succeeded in getting the sword stuck. He cursed and yanked hard and the blade finally came free. Arishtanemi jumped off his horse and casually drew his sword.

'We don't want to kill you,' said Ram. 'Please surrender.'

Lakshman noticed that the poor boy's grip on the sword hilt was all wrong; it was vice-like, which would quickly tire him out. Also, the weight of the sword was taken by his forearm, instead of his shoulder and triceps, the way it should be. He held the weapon from the farthest edge of the hilt; it would just get knocked out of his hand!

The Asura spat again, before screaming loudly. 'You excreta of vermin! Do you think you can defeat us? The True Lord is with us. Your false gods cannot protect you! You will all die! Die! Die!'

'Why are we here, hunting these imbeciles?' Lakshman threw up his hands.

Ram ignored Lakshman and spoke to the young warrior again, politely. 'I'm requesting you. Throw down your weapon. We don't want to kill you. Please.'

Arishtanemi began to move forward slowly, intending to intimidate the Asura. The effect, however, was quite the opposite.

The Asura screamed loudly. *'Satyam Ekam!'*

The True One!

He charged at Arishtanemi. It all happened so quickly that Ram had no time to intervene. The Asura tried to strike Arishtanemi with a standard downward slice, in what was intended to be a kill-strike. But he was not close enough to his opponent. The tall Arishtanemi deftly avoided the blow by swaying back.

'Stop!' warned Arishtanemi.

The young soldier, however, screamed loudly, moved his sword arm, and swung from the left. He should have used both his hands for this backhand attempt. Even then, it would have been a mistake against a man of Arishtanemi's strength. The Malayaputra swung hard, his blow so powerful that the Asura's sword flew out of his hand. Without losing momentum, Arishtanemi sliced from a high angle and nicked the Asura's chest. Perhaps hoping to scare him into surrendering.

Arishtanemi stepped back and drove his sword tip into the soft ground in a gesture that conveyed he meant no harm.

He said loudly, 'Just step back. I don't want to kill you. I am a Malayaputra.' Then, under his breath, low enough for only the Asura to hear, Arishtanemi whispered, 'Shukracharya's pig.'

The enraged Asura suddenly pulled out a knife from a scabbard tied to the small of his back and charged forward, screaming, 'Malayaputra dog!'

Arishtanemi instinctively stepped back, bringing his hands up in defence. The sword, held in his right hand, came up horizontal. The Asura simply ran into Arishtanemi's sword, the blade cutting through his abdomen cleanly.

'Dammit!' cursed Arishtanemi as he stepped back and pulled his sword out. He turned towards Ram, eyes filled with remorse.

The stunned Asura dropped his knife and looked down at his abdomen, at the blood that began as a trickle and, within moments, burst forth with steadily increasing intensity. The shock of the trauma had blocked out the pain, and he stared at his body as though it was another's. He collapsed on the ground when it became too much for his brain to handle. He screamed, more with fright than in pain.

Arishtanemi threw his shield to the ground in frustration. 'I told you to stop, Asura!'

Ram held his head. 'Lord Rudra, be merciful…'

The Asura was bawling helplessly. There was no saving him, now. The force of the blood flow was a clear indication that the sword had pierced many vital organs and arteries. It was only a matter of time before he bled to death.

The Malayaputra turned to Ram. 'I warned him… You warned him… He just ran into…'

Ram closed his eyes and shook his head in frustration. 'Put this poor fool out of his misery.'

Arishtanemi looked at the Asura lying prone at his feet. He went down on one knee. He bent close, so that his expression was visible only to the Asura, and sneered slightly before he carried out Ram's order.

Chapter 17

Ram signalled for the party to halt once again.

'These people are beyond all limits of incompetence,' said Lakshman, as he steered his horse close to his brother.

Ram, Lakshman and Arishtanemi looked into the distance, at what appeared to be the Asura camp. They had barricaded themselves for a veritable siege, but it was not exactly a sterling example of military genius. The entire camp was surrounded by high wooden palisade fencing, held together with hemp rope. Whereas this provided an adequate defence against arrows, spears and other missiles, a good fire would wreak havoc with this barricade. A stream flowing by the camp had been left unfenced. It was too deep for warriors to wade through on foot, but mounted soldiers could easily ride across.

'I'm sure they imagine that the unguarded opening at the stream will serve as bait for the unsuspecting,' laughed Arishtanemi.

As if expecting the enemy cavalry to attempt an attack by riding across the shallow stream, the Asuras had dug a small trench on the far side, just short of the bank, which had been crudely camouflaged. Asura archers, hidden within the trench, could rain a shower of arrows on enemy riders once they were mid-stream. In theory, it was an effective military tactic. The execution, however, was shoddy and amateurish.

A dull splash had sounded from the ground nearby alerting Ram to the possibility of the trench. Owing to its proximity to the stream, water had seeped through, making the trench slippery; it had not been adequately waterproofed. A soldier must have slipped.

In what seemed like another stroke of amateur brilliance, the Asuras had built a *machan* atop a tree, seemingly overlooking the trench. The *machan* had been built with the same idea in mind, to man it with archers who would fire at enemy soldiers crossing the stream. However, the *machan* was empty. This gave Ram an easy solution to the matter of the Asura soldiers hidden in the trench.

Ram crooned gently in the horse's ear; as the animal became still, he reached for an arrow, nocked it in one fluid movement and took aim.

'The arrow cannot curve in flight and fall into the trench with force, prince,' objected Arishtanemi. 'They are positioned deep in the ground. You cannot hit them this time.'

As Ram adjusted for the wind, he whispered, 'I'm not aiming for the trench, Arishtanemi*ji*.'

He pulled the string back and released the missile as he flicked the fletching, making the arrow spin furiously as it sped forward. The missile hit the main rope that tethered the *machan,* slashing it cleanly. As the rope snapped, the logs came loose and thundered down, many falling right into the trench.

'Brilliant!' Arishtanemi laughed.

These were logs with which a *machan* had been built: good enough to injure, not to kill. Frantic shouts emanated from the trench.

Lakshman looked at Ram. 'Should we—'

'No,' he interrupted Lakshman. 'We'll wait and watch. I don't want to trigger a battle. I hope to take them alive.'

A faint smile played on Arishtanemi's lips.

Yells of distress and anger continued to emerge from the trench. Perhaps the Asuras were clearing the logs that had landed on them. Soon enough, an Asura popped up, followed by others who dragged themselves out. The tallest, obviously the leader, surveyed his men. He turned around defiantly and stared at his opponents.

'That is Subahu,' offered Arishtanemi. 'Tadaka's son and their military chief.'

Subahu's left arm had been dislocated by a fallen log, but the rest of him appeared unharmed. He pulled out his sword; it took some effort to do so, for his left arm was disabled with the injury, and he was unable to hold his scabbard. He held his sword aloft and roared in defiance. His soldiers followed his cue.

Ram was thoroughly bemused now. He did not know whether to laugh at, or applaud, this foolhardy heroism that bordered on unheard-of stupidity.

'Oh, for Lord Parshu Ram's sake,' groaned Lakshman. 'Are these people mad? Can't they see that we have fifty mounted soldiers on our side?'

'*Satyam Ekam!*' bellowed Subahu.

'*Satyam Ekam!*' shouted the other Asuras.

Ram was astonished that the Asuras still persisted with what seemed like foolishness, despite what Guru Vishwamitra had said. He turned around and was annoyed at what he saw. 'Lakshman, where is the Ayodhya standard? Why haven't you raised it?'

'What?' asked Lakshman. He quickly looked back and realised that the soldiers behind him had raised the banner of the Malayaputras. The mission had been tasked by Vishwamitra, after all.

'Do it now!' shouted Ram, not taking his eyes off the Asuras, who appeared to be preparing to charge.

Lakshman pulled out the flag lying folded in the bag attached to the horse saddle. He unfurled it and held high the standard under which the Ayodhyans marched to battle. It was a white cloth with a red circular sun in the centre, its rays streaming out in all directions. At the bottom of the standard, suffused in the brightness of the rays of the sun, was a magnificent tiger appearing to leap out.

'Charge!' shouted Subahu.

'*Satyam Ekam!*' cried the Asuras as they took off.

Ram raised a balled fist and shouted aloud, '*Ayodhyatah Vijetaarah!*'

It was the war cry of the Ayodhyans. *The conquerors from the unconquerable city!*

Lakshman held the standard high and roared. '*Ayodhyatah Vijetaarah!*'

The Asuras stopped in their tracks as they gaped at the two princes and the Ayodhya flag. They had come to a halt a mere fifty feet from where Ram's horse stood still.

Subahu edged forward slowly, holding his sword low, non-threateningly.

'Are you from Ayodhya?' asked Subahu, as he reached close enough to be heard.

'I am the crown prince of Ayodhya,' said Ram. 'Surrender and I swear by the honour of Ayodhya, you will not be harmed.'

Subahu's sword fell from his suddenly limp hand as he went down on his knees. As did the other Asuras. Some of them were whispering to each other. But it was loud enough to reach Ram's ears.

'Shukracharya...'

'Ayodhya...'

'The voice of *Ekam*...'

— 从 ⚱ ☼ —

Ram, Lakshman and the Malayaputras were ceremoniously led into the Asura camp. The fourteen Asura soldiers were received by Tadaka; the women quickly got down to tending to the injuries of their men, who had been disarmed by the Malayaputras.

The hosts and the guests eventually settled down in the central square. After a quick round of meagre refreshments, Ram addressed the Malayaputra military chief. 'Arishtanemi*ji*, please leave me alone with the Asuras.'

'Why?' asked Arishtanemi.

'I would like to speak with them alone.'

Lakshman objected vehemently. '*Dada*, when I said that we shouldn't attack these people, I didn't mean that they are good and we should talk to them. I just meant that it is beneath us to attack these morons. Now that they have surrendered, we're done with them. Let's leave them to the Malayaputras and return to Ayodhya.'

'Lakshman,' said Ram. 'I said I would like to speak with them.'

'What will you talk about, *Dada*?' persisted Lakshman, beyond caring that he was within earshot of the Asuras. 'These people are savages. They are animals. They are the remnants of those who survived the wrath of Lord Rudra. Don't waste your time on them.'

Ram's breathing slowed down as his body stiffened imperceptibly. His face acquired an expression of forbidding calm. Lakshman immediately recognised it for what it was: a sign of deep anger welling up beneath the still waters of his brother's essentially cool personality. He also knew that this anger was coupled with unrelenting stubbornness. He threw up his hands in a gesture of frustrated surrender.

Arishtanemi shrugged. 'All right, you can talk to them. But it is not advisable that you do it in our absence.'

'I have taken note of your advice. Thank you! But I trust them,' said Ram.

Tadaka and Subahu heard Ram's words. It took them by surprise because they had been considered the enemy for so long.

Arishtanemi gave in. However, he also made sure the Asuras heard him loud and clear. 'Fine, we'll move away. But we will be battle-ready, mounted on horseback. At the slightest sign of trouble, we'll ride in and kill them all.'

As Arishtanemi turned to leave, Ram repeated his directive, this time to his protective brother. 'I would like to speak to them *alone*, Lakshman.'

'I'm not leaving you alone with them, *Dada*.'

'Lakshman…'

'I am not leaving you alone, *Dada*!'

'Listen, brother, I need…'

Lakshman raised his voice. 'I am not leaving you alone, *Dada*!'

'All right,' said Ram, giving in.

— 📿 ☀ —

Arishtanemi and the Malayaputra warriors lined up at the border of the camp with the stream behind them, mounted on horses, ready to ride to Ram and Lakshman's rescue at the first hint of trouble. The brothers were seated on a raised platform in the central square, with the Asuras gathered around them. Subahu wore an arm sling; he sat in front, beside his mother, Tadaka.

'You are committing slow suicide,' said Ram.

'We are only following our law,' said Tadaka.

Ram frowned. 'What do you intend to achieve by continually attacking the Malayaputras?'

'We hope to save them. If they come to our side, reject their false beliefs and listen to the call of the *Ekam*, they will save their own souls.'

'So, you think you are saving them by persistently harassing them, interfering in their rituals, and even trying to kill them.'

'Yes,' said Tadaka, making it obvious that her strange logic was irrefutable to her. 'And, really, it is not we who are trying to save the Malayaputras. It is, in fact, the True One, the *Ekam* himself! We are mere instruments.'

'But if the *Ekam* is on your side, how come the Malayaputras have been thriving for centuries? How do you explain that the people of the Sapt Sindhu, almost all of whom reject your interpretation of the *Ekam*, have been dominant for so long? Why haven't you Asuras conquered India once again? Why isn't the *Ekam* helping you?'

'The Lord is testing us. We haven't been sufficiently true to his path.'

'Testing you?' asked Ram. 'Is the *Ekam* making the Asuras lose every single major battle they have fought for centuries, for millennia actually, just so he can test you?'

Tadaka did not respond.

'Have you considered that he may not be testing you at all?' asked Ram. 'Maybe he is trying to teach you something? Maybe he is trying to tell you that you have to change with the times? Didn't Shukracharya himself say that if a tactic has led to failure, then persisting with it unquestioningly, in the wild hope of a different outcome, is nothing short of insanity?'

'But how can we live by the rules of these disgusting, decadent Devas who worship everything in theory but nothing in practice?' asked Tadaka.

'These "disgusting, decadent Devas" and their descendants have been in power for centuries,' said Lakshman aggressively. 'They have created magnificent cities and a sparkling civilisation, while you have been living in a run-down pathetic camp in the middle of nowhere. Maybe it is you people who need to change your theory *and* practice, whatever it may be!'

'Lakshman...' said Ram, raising a hand to silence him.

'This is nonsense, *Dada*.' Lakshman would not relent. 'How delusional can these people be? Don't they see reality?'

'Their only reality is their law, Lakshman. Change is difficult for the people of the masculine way of life. They are only guided by their law and, if that is out of sync with the times, it is very difficult for them to accept and initiate change; instead, more often than not, they will cling more strongly to the certainties of their law. We don't see the attitude of the feminine civilisations towards change as open-minded and liberal; instead, to us, it appears fickle, corrupt and debauched.'

'*We? Us?*' asked Lakshman, frowning at Ram identifying himself with the masculine way.

Tadaka and Subahu keenly watched the exchange between the brothers. Subahu raised his balled fist to his heart, in an ancient Asura salute.

Ram asked Lakshman. 'Do you think what was done to Dhenuka was wrong?'

'I think the way the Asuras randomly kill people who do not agree with their interpretation of the *Ekam* is even more wrong.'

'On that I agree with you. The Asura actions were not just wrong, they were evil,' said Ram. 'But I was talking about Dhenuka. Do you think what was done to him was wrong?'

Lakshman refused to respond.

'Answer me, my brother,' said Ram. 'Was it wrong?'

'You know I will not oppose you, *Dada*...'

'I'm not asking what you will do. What do you *think*, Lakshman?'

Lakshman remained silent. But his answer was obvious.

'Who is Dhenuka?' asked Subahu.

'A hardened criminal, a blot on society whose soul will atone for his deed for at least a million births,' said Ram. 'But the law did not allow for his execution. Had Shukracharya's law not permitted it, no matter how heinous the crime, should he have been executed?'

Subahu didn't need a moment to think. 'No.'

Ram smiled ever so slightly as he turned to Lakshman. 'The law applies equally to all. No exceptions. And the law cannot be broken. Except when...'

Lakshman turned away from him. He remained convinced that in Dhenuka's case, justice had been served.

Ram turned to address the small band of Asuras. 'Try to understand what I am saying to you. You are law-abiding people; you follow the masculine way. But your laws are not working anymore. They haven't been for centuries, because the world has changed. That is what karma is trying to teach you, again and again. If karma is giving you a negative signal repeatedly, then it is not testing you, it is trying to teach you. You need to tap into the disciple in you and find a new Shukracharya. You need a new masculine way. You need new laws.'

Tadaka spoke up. 'Guru Shukracharya had said that he would reincarnate when the time was ripe, to lead us to a new way...'

There was a long silence in the assemblage.

Tadaka and Subahu suddenly stood up in unison. They brought their balled right fists to their heart, as they bowed low to Ram; the traditional full Asura salute. Their soldiers sprang to their feet and followed suit, as did the women, children and the old.

Ram felt as if a crushing weight was suddenly placed on his chest and the wind knocked out of him. Guru Vashishta's words entered his mind of their own volition. *Your responsibility is great; your mission is all-important. Stay true to it. Stay humble, but not so humble that you don't accept your responsibilities.*

Lakshman glared at the Asuras, and then at Ram, scarcely believing what was going on.

'What would you have us do, My Lord?' asked Tadaka.

'Most Asuras live with the Vayuputras today, far beyond the western borders of India, in a land called Pariha,' said Ram. 'I want you to seek refuge there, with the help of the Malayaputras.'

'But why would the Malayaputras help us?'

'I will request them.'

'What will we do there?'

'Honour the promise that your ancestors made to Lord Rudra. You will work with the Vayuputras to protect India.'

'But protecting India today means protecting the Devas…'

'Yes, it does.'

'Why should we protect them? They are our enemies. They are…'

'You will protect them because that is what Lord Rudra ordered you to do.'

Subahu held his mother's hand to restrain her. 'We will do as you order, My Lord.'

Uncertain, Tadaka yanked her wrist out of her son's grip. 'But this is our holy land. We want to live in India. We cannot be happy outside of its sacred embrace.'

'You will return eventually. But you cannot come back as Asuras. That way of life is over. You will return in a new form. This is my promise to you.'

Chapter 18

Lakshman had expected anger from the volatile Vishwamitra, instead he looked intrigued; even impressed. Lakshman did not know what to make of it.

The maharishi sat in *padmaasan* on the platform built around a banyan tree. His feet were placed on opposite thighs, facing upwards; the knotted tuft of hair at the back of his shaven head fluttered in the strong breeze. His white *angvastram* had been placed on the side.

'Sit,' commanded Vishwamitra. 'This will probably take some time.'

Ram, Lakshman and Arishtanemi took their seats around him. Vishwamitra observed the Asuras standing quietly in the distance. They had not been tied up; Ram had insisted on that, to the consternation of the camp denizens. But it appeared that shackling them was not required, after all. They stood in a disciplined line, not moving from their positions. Arishtanemi had nevertheless kept thirty guards stationed around them, just in case.

Vishwamitra addressed Ram. 'You have surprised me, prince of Ayodhya. Why did you disobey my direct order to kill all the Asuras? And what did you tell them to bring about this dramatic transformation? Is there some secret mantra that can suddenly civilise the uncivilised?'

'I know even you don't believe what you have just said, Guru*ji*,' said Ram in a calm voice. 'You don't really think the Asuras are uncivilised; you cannot, for I have seen you worship Lord Rudra, and I know that the Asuras have joined the Vayuputras, the tribe that he left behind. The Vayuputras are your *partners in deed*, your *karmasaathis*. So, my suspicion is that you were trying to provoke me with what you just said. I find myself wondering, why?'

Vishwamitra's eyes widened fractionally as they focused on Ram, to the exclusion of all others. But he did not give him an answer. 'Do you really think these imbeciles are worth the effort of rescuing?'

'But that question is immaterial, Guru*ji*. The question really is: why should they be wiped out? What law have they broken?'

'They attacked my camp repeatedly.'

'But they didn't kill anyone. All they did the last time was burn a small portion of the hedge fencing. And they broke some of your mining equipment. Do these crimes deserve the death sentence under the laws of any *Smriti*? No. The laws of Ayodhya, which I always obey, clearly state that if the weak have not broken any law, then it is the duty of the strong to protect them.'

'But my orders were explicit.'

'Forgive me for being explicit too, Guru*ji*, but if you genuinely intended to kill these Asuras, then Arishtanemi*ji* would have easily done it for you. Your warriors are trained professionals. These Asuras are amateurs. I believe you brought us here because you knew that they would listen to the princes of Ayodhya, and no one else. You wanted to find a practical, non-confrontational solution to the problem they posed. Not only have I followed the law, but I've also delivered on what you truly wanted. What I fail to understand is why you did not want to reveal your true intentions to me.'

Vishwamitra wore an expression that was rare for this great Brahmin: one of bemused respect. He also felt outfoxed. He smiled. 'Do you always question your guru like this?'

Ram remained silent. The unspoken answer was obvious. Vashishta, not Vishwamitra, was his guru. Ram was merely following the orders of his father in according Vishwamitra that stature.

'You are right,' Vishwamitra continued, ignoring the subtle slight. 'The Asuras are not bad people; they just have an understanding of *dharma* that is not valid for today's world. Sometimes, the followers are good but the leaders let them down. Sending them to Pariha is a good idea. They will find some purpose. We'll arrange for their departure.'

'Thank you, Guru*ji*,' said Ram.

'As for your original question, I'm not going to give you an answer right now. Maybe later.'

—— 展 ● ☼ ——

Within two weeks, a small group of Malayaputras had been readied, along with the Asuras, to undertake the journey to the hidden city of the Vayuputras, beyond the western borders of India. The Asuras had recovered completely from their injuries.

Vishwamitra stood at the gate of the Malayaputra camp, giving last-minute instructions to his men. Arishtanemi, Ram and Lakshman stood beside him. As the Malayaputra group walked away to mount their horses, Tadaka and Subahu approached Vishwamitra.

'Thank you for this,' said Tadaka, bowing her head low and folding her hands together into a namaste.

As Vishwamitra broke into a smile at the surprising display of manners from the Asura woman, Tadaka turned to Ram, her eyes seeking approval. Ram smiled his gentle appreciation.

'Your fellow Asuras live in the west,' said Vishwamitra. 'They will keep you safe. Follow the setting sun and it will guide you home.'

Tadaka stiffened. 'Pariha is not our home. This is our home, right here, in India. We have lived here for as long as the Devas have. We've lived here from the very beginning.'

Ram cut in. 'And you will return when the time is right. For now, follow the path of the sun.'

Vishwamitra looked at Ram with surprise, but remained silent.

— |大| 🐟 ☼ —

'It didn't work out the way we had planned, Guru*ji*,' said Arishtanemi.

Vishwamitra was sitting by a lake, not far from the Malayaputra camp. Arishtanemi, as was his practice whenever he was alone with his master, had kept his sword close at hand, unsheathed and ready. He would need to move fast if anyone dared attack Vishwamitra.

'You don't seem particularly unhappy,' said Vishwamitra.

Arishtanemi looked into the distance, avoiding eye contact with his leader. He was hesitant. 'Honestly, Guru*ji*… I like the boy… I think he has…'

Vishwamitra narrowed his eyes and glared at Arishtanemi. 'Don't forget the one we have committed ourselves to.'

Arishtanemi bowed his head. 'Of course, Guru*ji*. Can I ever go against your wishes?'

There was an uncomfortable silence. Vishwamitra took a deep breath and looked across the vast expanse of water. 'Had the Asuras been killed in their camp by him, it would have proved … useful.'

Arishtanemi, wisely, did not contradict him.

Vishwamitra laughed ruefully, shaking his head. 'Outwitted by a boy who wasn't even trying to outwit me. He was just following his "rules".'

'What do we do?'

'We follow plan B,' said Vishwamitra. 'Obvious, isn't it?'

'I have never been too sure about the other plan, Guru*ji*. It's not like we have complete control over matters of—'

Vishwamitra did not allow him to complete his statement. 'You are wrong.'

Arishtanemi remained silent.

'That traitor Vashishta is Ram's guru. I can never trust Ram as long as he continues to trust Vashishta.'

Arishtanemi had his misgivings, but kept quiet. He knew any discussion on the subject of Vashishta was one that was fraught with danger.

'We will go ahead with the other plan,' said Vishwamitra, with finality.

'But will he do what we expect him to?'

'We will have to use his beloved "rules" on him. Once it is done, I will have complete control over what will follow. The Vayuputras are wrong. I will show them that I am right.'

—— 从 🐟 ☀ ——

Two days after the Asuras left for Pariha, Ram and Lakshman woke up to feverish activity in the camp. Keeping to themselves, they stepped out of their hut and set out for the lake to offer early morning prayers to the Sun God and Lord Rudra.

Arishtanemi fell into step alongside them. 'We'll be leaving soon.'

'Thank you for letting us know, Arishtanemi*ji*,' said Ram.

Ram noticed an unusually large trunk being carried out with great care. It evidently contained something heavy, for it was placed on a metallic palanquin which was being carried on the shoulders of twelve men.

'What is that?' asked Lakshman, frowning and instantly suspicious.

'Something that is both Good and Evil,' said Arishtanemi mysteriously, as he placed his hand on Ram's shoulder. 'Where are you going?'

'For our morning prayers.'

'I'll come with you.'

Arishtanemi normally prayed to Lord Parshu Ram every morning. In the company of Ram and Lakshman, he also decided to pray to the great Mahadev, Lord Rudra. All Gods trace their divinity to the same source, after all.

They sat together on a large boulder on the banks of the lake, once the prayers were done.

'I wonder whether Tadaka and her tribe will be able to cope with Pariha,' said Arishtanemi.

'I'm sure they will,' said Ram. 'They are easy to manage if they see you as one of their own.'

'That appears to be the only way to handle them: keep them among their own. They find it impossible to get along with outsiders.'

'I have been giving their ideas a lot of thought. The problem lies in the way they look upon the *Ekam*.'

'The One God…?'

'Yes,' Ram said. 'We've been told repeatedly that the *Ekam* lives beyond our world of illusion. He is beyond *gunas*, the *characteristics* of created things. For isn't it *gunas* that create this world of illusion, of temporary existence, illusive because no moment in time lasts? Isn't that why he is not only called *niraakaar*, *formless*; but also *nirguna*, *beyond characteristics*?'

'Exactly,' said Arishtanemi.

'And if the *Ekam* is beyond all this, how can He pick a side?' asked Ram. 'If He is beyond *form* then how can He have a preference for any one form? He can, therefore, never belong to any one specific group. He belongs to all, and at the same time, to none. And this is not just applicable to human beings but to every created entity in the universe: animals, plants, water, earth, energy, stars, space, everything. Regardless of what they do or think or believe, all created entities belong to, and are drawn from, the *Ekam*.'

Arishtanemi nodded. 'This fundamental misunderstanding between our world of forms, and the *Ekam's* formless world, makes them believe in the lie that my God is the true God and your God is a false God. Just like a wise human will have no preference for his kidneys over his liver, the One God will not pick one group over another. It's stupid to even think otherwise.'

'*Exactly!*' said Ram. 'If He is *my* God, if He picks my side over someone else's, He is *not* the *One God*. The only true One God is the one who picks no sides, who belongs to everything, who doesn't demand loyalty or fear; in fact, who doesn't demand anything at all. Because the *Ekam* just exists; and His existence allows for the existence of all else.'

Arishtanemi was beginning to respect this wise young prince of Ayodhya. But he was afraid to admit this to Vishwamitra.

Ram continued. 'Shukracharya was right in wanting to create a perfect masculine society. Such a society is efficient, just, and honourable. The mistake he made was that he based it on faith. He should have built it purely on laws, keeping the spiritual separate from the material. When times change, as they inevitably do, one finds it impossible to give up on one's faith; in fact, one clings to it with renewed vigour. Difficult times make men cling to their faith even more strongly. But if you base a masculine way of life on laws, then, possibly, when needed, the laws can be changed. The masculine way of life should be built on laws, not faith.'

'Do you actually believe that it is possible to save the Asuras? There are many of them in India. Hidden in small groups, but they are there.'

'I think they will make disciplined followers. Certainly better than the rebellious, law-breaking people I call my own. The problem with the Asuras is that their laws are obsolete. The people are good; what they need is enlightened and effective leadership.'

'Do you think you can be that leader? Can you create a new way of life for them?'

Ram inhaled deeply. 'I don't know what role fate has in store for me but—'

Lakshman cut in. 'Guru Vashishta believes Ram *Dada* can be the next Vishnu. He will not just provide leadership for the Asuras, but everyone; all of India. I believe that too. There is nobody like Ram *Dada*.'

Ram looked at Lakshman, his face inscrutable.

Arishtanemi leaned back, sucking in a deep breath. 'You are a good man; in fact, a special man. And I can certainly see that you will play an important role in history. Though what exactly, I do not know.'

Ram's face remained expressionless.

'My suggestion to you is to listen to Maharishi Vishwamitra,' said Arishtanemi. 'He is the wisest and most powerful among the *rishis* today, bar none.'

Ram didn't react, though his face hardened imperceptibly.

'Bar none,' repeated Arishtanemi for emphasis, clearly referring to Vashishta.

— 凶 ▮ ☀ —

The group rode unhurriedly through the jungle. Vishwamitra and Arishtanemi rode in front, at the head of the caravan, right behind the cart cradling the heavy trunk. Ram and Lakshman had been asked to ride at the back, with the rest of the Malayaputras marching on foot. It would take a few hours for them to reach the ships anchored on the Ganga.

Vishwamitra beckoned Arishtanemi with a nod. He immediately pulled the reins to the right and drew close.

'So?' asked Vishwamitra.

'He knows,' said Arishtanemi. 'Maharishi Vashishta has told him.'

'Why, that conniving two-faced upstart; that rootless piece of...'

Arishtanemi kept his gaze pinned to the distance as Vishwamitra vented his fury. It was followed by a charged silence. Finally the disciple gathered the courage to ask, 'So, what do we do now, Guru*ji*?'

'We will do what we have to do.'

Chapter 19

Ram and Lakshman stood on the deck of the lead vessel as the three-ship convoy sailed smoothly down the Ganga. Vishwamitra chose to stay ensconced in his cabin for most of the trip. Arishtanemi made the most of this opportunity; the Ayodhya princes aroused inordinate interest in this Malayaputra.

'How are the princes doing today?' asked Arishtanemi, as he approached them.

Ram had washed his long hair and left it loose, struggling to dry it in the sultry air.

'Suffering in this oppressive heat,' said Lakshman.

Arishtanemi smiled. 'It has only just begun. The rains are months away. It'll get worse before it gets better.'

'Which is why we are on the open deck; any draught is a gift from the Gods!' said Lakshman, as he dramatically fanned his face with his hands. Many had gathered on the deck, seeking a brief, post-lunch break before descending to the lower deck and on to their assigned tasks.

Arishtanemi stepped closer to Ram. 'I was surprised by what you said about our ancestors. Are you against the Devas?'

'I was wondering when you were going to bring that up,' said Ram, with a sense of wry inevitability.

'Well, you can stop wondering now.'

Ram laughed. 'I'm not against the Devas. We are their descendants, after all. But I am an admirer of the way of the masculine, a life of laws, obedience, honour and justice. I prefer and advocate it as opposed to a life of freedom without end.'

'There is more to the way of the feminine than just passion and freedom, prince,' Arishtanemi said. 'There is unbridled creativity as well.'

'That, I concede; but when civilisation goes into decline, the people of the feminine are prone to divisiveness and victim-mongering. In the middle ages of the Devas, the caste system, which was originally based on karma and not birth, became rigid, sectarian and politicised. This allowed the Asuras to easily defeat them. When the later Devas reformed and made the caste system flexible again, they regained their strength and defeated the Asuras.'

'Yes, but the masculine way can also become rigid and fanatical when such a society goes into a decline. That the Asuras relentlessly attacked the Devas, just because the Devas had a different interpretation of the *Ekam*, was inexcusable.'

'I agree. But didn't these attacks unite the Devas? Maybe the Devas should acknowledge the few positives that emerged from that horrific violence. They were forced to confront the evil that the caste system had descended into; they needed unity. In my opinion, the most important reform that Lord Indra was able to carry out was making the caste system flexible once again. The united later-age Devas finally defeated the Asuras, who lost because of their fanatical rigidity.'

'Are you suggesting that the Devas should be grateful to the Asuras for all that brutal violence?'

'No, I'm not,' said Ram. 'What I'm suggesting is that some good can emerge from the most horrific of events. There is something positive hidden in every negative, and something negative hidden in every positive. Life is complicated, and a balanced person can see both sides. For instance, can you deny that, with the Asura experience long forgotten, the caste system has become rigid once again? A man's status in society today is determined by his birth and not his karma. Will you deny that this evil is ravaging the vitals of the modern Sapt Sindhu?'

'All right!' said Lakshman. 'Enough of this philosophical stuff; you will make my head explode!'

Arishtanemi laughed uproariously, while Ram gazed indulgently at Lakshman.

'Thankfully, this will all end as soon as we disembark at Ayodhya,' said Lakshman.

'*Uhh*,' said Arishtanemi. 'There may be a little delay, prince.'

'What do you mean?' asked Ram.

'Guru Vishwamitra intends to visit Mithila en route to Ayodhya. He has an important mission there as well.'

'When were you planning to tell us about this?' asked Lakshman, irritated.

'I'm telling you now,' said Arishtanemi.

Signalling Lakshman to be patient, Ram said, 'It's all right, Arishtanemi*ji*. Our father commanded us to remain with Guru Vishwamitra till he sees fit. A delay of a few months will not harm us in any way.'

'Mithila…' groaned Lakshman. 'It's the back of beyond!'

Unlike most big cities of the Sapt Sindhu, *Mithila*, the *city for the sons of the soil* or the *city founded by King Mithi*, was not a river-town; at least not after the Gandaki River had changed course westwards a few decades ago. This altered the fate of Mithila dramatically. From being counted among the great cities of the Sapt Sindhu, it speedily declined. Most trade in India was conducted through riverine ports. With Gandaki turning its face away, Mithila's fortunes collapsed overnight. Raavan's nifty traders withdrew the appointed sub-traders from Mithila; the miniscule volume of trade simply didn't justify their presence anymore.

The city was ruled by King Janak, a devout, decent and spiritual man. He was a classic example of a good man, albeit not for the job at hand. Had Janak chosen to be a spiritual guru, he would have been among the finest in the world. However, fate had decreed that he would be king. Even as a monarch, he assiduously guided the spiritual growth of his people through his *dharma sabhas*, or *spiritual gatherings*. Material growth and security, though, had been severely neglected.

To add to Mithila's woes, power within the royal family had decidedly shifted to Janak's younger brother, Kushadhwaj. The Gandaki River's new course skirted the border of Sankashya, whose ruler was Kushadhwaj. Mithila's loss was Sankashya's gain. Easy availability of water led to a boom in trade as well as a dramatic increase in the population of Sankashya. Armed with the heft of both money and numbers, Kushadhwaj made moves to establish himself as the representative of his royal family within the Sapt Sindhu. Careful to maintain appearances, he remained outwardly deferential towards his saintly elder brother. Despite this, rumours abounded that this was just a charade; that Kushadhwaj plotted to absorb Mithila and bring it under his own rule.

'That's where we're headed, Lakshman, if that is what Guru*ji* wants,' said Ram. 'We will need an escort from Sankashya, right? I have heard that there are no proper roads that lead to Mithila from Sankashya.'

'There used to be one,' said Arishtanemi. 'It was washed away when the river changed course. There were no efforts made to rebuild it. Mithila is … short of funds. But their prime minister has been informed and she has arranged for an escort party.'

'Is it true that King Janak's daughter is his prime minister?' asked Lakshman. 'We found that hard to believe. Is her name Urmila?'

'Why is it hard to believe that a woman could be prime minister, Lakshman?' Ram asked, before Arishtanemi could reply. 'Women are equal to men in mental abilities.'

'I know, *Dada*,' said Lakshman. 'It's unusual, that's all.'

'Lady Mohini was a woman,' continued Ram. 'And she was a Vishnu. Remember that.'

Lakshman fell silent.

Arishtanemi touched Lakshman's shoulder in a kindly way as he said, 'You are right, Prince Lakshman. King Janak's daughter is his prime minister. But it's not Princess Urmila, who incidentally is his biological daughter. It's his adopted daughter who is the prime minister.'

'Adopted daughter?' asked Ram, surprised. Adopted children were rarely given equal rights in India these days. He had it in mind to set this right by changing the law.

'Yes,' said Arishtanemi.

'I wasn't aware of that. What's her name?'

'Her name is Sita.'

'Are we not going to meet the king of Sankashya?' asked Ram.

Vishwamitra's ships had docked at the port of Sankashya, a few kilometres from the city. They were met by officials from Mithila, led by Samichi, the police and protocol chief of the city. Samichi and her team would lead a small band of one hundred Malayaputras to Mithila. The others would remain aboard the anchored ships.

'No,' said Arishtanemi, as he mounted his horse. 'Guru Vishwamitra would prefer to pass this town incognito. In any case, King Kushadhwaj is travelling right now.'

Lakshman surveyed the simple white garments that Ram and he had been asked to wear. Clearly, the princes were supposed to pass off as commoners.

'Incognito?' asked Lakshman, his suspicions immediately aroused as he sceptically gazed upon the Malayaputra party. 'You could have fooled me.'

Arishtanemi smiled and squeezed his knees; his horse began to move. Ram and Lakshman mounted their horses and followed him. Vishwamitra had already left, at the head of the convoy, accompanied by Samichi.

—— 因 ❢ ☼ ——

The pathway through the jungle was so narrow that only three horses could ride abreast. At some spots glimpses of an old cobble-stoned road would emerge where the pathway suddenly got broader. For the most part though, the jungle had aggressively reclaimed the land. Often, the convoy rode single file for long stretches.

'You have not visited Mithila, have you?' asked Arishtanemi.

'There was never any need to go there,' answered Ram.

'Your brother Bharat did visit Sankashya a few months ago.'

'He is in charge of diplomatic relations for Ayodhya. It's natural that he would meet with kings from across the Sapt Sindhu.'

'Oh? I thought he may have visited King Kushadhwaj for a marriage alliance.'

Lakshman frowned. 'Marriage alliance? If Ayodhya wanted a marriage alliance, it would be with one of the more powerful kingdoms. Why ally with Sankashya?'

'Nothing prevents you from forming multiple marriage alliances. After all, some say marriages are a way to build political alliances by strengthening personal ties.'

Lakshman cast a furtive glance at Ram.

'What is it?' asked Arishtanemi, following Lakshman's gaze. 'You disagree?'

Lakshman butted in. 'Ram *Dada* believes marriage is sacred. It should not be treated as a political alliance.'

Arishtanemi raised his eyebrows. 'That was the way it was in the ancient world, yes. Nobody really believes in those values anymore.'

'I'm not a fan of everything that our ancestors did,' said Ram. 'But some practices are worth reviving. One of them is looking upon marriage as a sacred partnership between two souls; not as a political alliance between two power centres.'

'You are, perhaps, among the very few people who think this way.'

'That doesn't mean that I am wrong.'

Lakshman interrupted the conversation again. '*Dada* also believes that a man must marry only one woman. He believes that polygamy is unfair to women and must be banned.'

'That's not exactly what I believe, Lakshman,' said Ram. 'I say that the law must be equal for all. If you allow a man to marry many women, then you should also allow a woman to marry many men if she so chooses. What is wrong is that the current law favours men. Polygamy is allowed but polyandry is not. That is simply wrong. Having said that, my personal preference is for a man to find one woman, and remain loyal to her for the rest of his life.'

'I thank Lord Brahma that your preference doesn't extend to a man being loyal to the same woman for many lifetimes!' Arishtanemi chuckled.

Ram smiled.

'But Prince Ram,' said Arishtanemi, 'I'm sure you must be aware that polygamy as a practice rose a few centuries ago with good reason. We had survived the fifty-year war between the Suryavanshis and the Chandravanshis. Millions of men died. There were simply not enough bridegrooms left, which is why men were encouraged to marry more than one woman. Quite frankly, we also needed to repopulate our country. Thereafter, more and more people began to practice polygamy.'

'Yes, but we don't have that problem now, do we?' asked Ram. 'So why should men continue to be allowed this privilege?'

Arishtanemi fell silent. After a few moments, he asked Ram, 'Do you intend to marry only one woman?'

'Yes. And I will remain loyal to her for the rest of my life. I will not look at another woman.'

'*Dada*,' said Lakshman, grinning slyly, 'how can you avoid looking at other women? They're everywhere! Are you going to shut your eyes every time a woman passes by?'

Ram laughed. 'You know what I mean. I will not look at other women the way I would look at my wife.'

'So, what are you looking for in a woman?' asked Arishtanemi, intrigued.

Ram was about to start speaking when Lakshman promptly jumped in. 'No. No. No. I have to answer this.'

Arishtanemi looked at Lakshman with an amused grin.

'*Dada* had once said,' continued Lakshman, 'that he wants a woman who can make him bow his head in admiration.'

Lakshman smiled proudly as he said this. Proud that he knew something so personal about his elder brother.

Arishtanemi cast a bemused look at Ram and smiled. 'Bow your head in admiration?'

Ram had nothing to say.

Arishtanemi looked ahead. He knew a woman who Ram would almost certainly admire.

Chapter 20

Vishwamitra and his entourage reached Mithila a week later. Being a fertile, marshy plain that received plentiful monsoonal rain, the land around Mithila was productive beyond measure. It was said that all a Mithila farmer needed to do was fling some seeds and return a few months later to harvest the crop. The land of Mithila would do the rest. But since the farmers of Mithila had not cleared too much land or flung too many seeds, the forest had used the bounty of nature and created a dense barrier all around the city. The absence of a major river added to its isolation. Mithila was cut off from most other Indian cities, which were usually accessed by river.

'Why are we so dependent on rivers?' Ram asked. 'Why don't we build roads? A city like Mithila need not be cut off.'

'We did have good roads once upon a time,' said Arishtanemi. 'Maybe you can rebuild them.'

As the convoy broke through the forest line, they came upon what must have served as a defensive moat once, but had now been converted into a lake to draw water from. The lake circumscribed the entire city within itself so effectively that Mithila was like an island. There were no animals, like crocodiles, in the lake, for it no longer served a military purpose. Steps had been built on the banks for easy access to water. Giant wheels drew water from the lake, which was carried into the city through pipes.

'It is incredibly dim-witted to use the moat as your main water supply,' said Lakshman. 'The first thing a besieging army would do is to cut it off. Or worse; they may even poison the water.'

'You are right,' said Arishtanemi. 'The prime minister of Mithila realised this. That is why she had a small, but very deep lake constructed, within the city walls.'

Ram, Lakshman and Arishtanemi dismounted at the outer banks of the lake. They had to cross a pontoon bridge to enter the city. Because a pontoon bridge is essentially a floating platform supported by parallel lines of barges or boats, making the structure shaky and unstable, it was wiser to walk across on foot, leading your horse.

Arishtanemi explained enthusiastically, 'Not only is it cheaper than a conventional bridge, it can also be destroyed easily if the city is attacked. And, of course, be rebuilt just as easily.'

Ram nodded politely, wondering why Arishtanemi felt the need to talk up Mithila. In any case, the city was obviously not wealthy enough to convert the temporary bridge into a more permanent structure.

But then, which kingdom in India, besides Lanka, is wealthy today? The Lankans have taken away all our wealth.

After they crossed over, they came upon the gates of Mithila's fort walls. Interestingly, there were no slogans or military symbols of royal pride emblazoned across the gate. Instead, there was a large image of Lady Saraswati, the Goddess of Knowledge, which had been carved into the top half of the gate. Below it was a simple couplet:

Swagruhe Pujyate Murkhaha; Swagraame Pujyate Prabhuhu

Swadeshe Pujyate Raja; Vidvaansarvatra Pujyate.

A fool is worshipped in his home.

A chief is worshipped in his village.

A king is worshipped in his kingdom.

A knowledgeable person is worshipped everywhere.

Ram smiled. *A city dedicated to knowledge.*

'Shall we enter?' asked Arishtanemi, pulling his horse's lead rope and clicking as he stepped forward.

Ram nodded to Lakshman, and they led their horses behind Arishtanemi as he entered the city. Behind the gates, a simple road led to another fort wall, at a distance of a kilometre from the outer wall. The rest of the area between the two walls was neatly partitioned into plots of agricultural land. Food crops were ready for harvest.

'Smart,' said Ram.

'Yes *Dada*, growing crops within the fort walls secures their food supply,' said Lakshman.

'More importantly, there's no human habitation here. This area would be a killing field for an enemy who manages to breach the outer fort wall. An attacking force will lose too many men in the effort to reach the second wall, without any hope of a quick retreat. It's militarily brilliant — two fort walls with uninhabited land in between. We should replicate this in Ayodhya as well.'

Arishtanemi quickened his footsteps as they approached the inner fort wall.

'Are those windows I see?' asked Lakshman, pointing towards the top section of the inner fort wall.

'Yes,' said Arishtanemi.

'Do people use the fort wall as a part of their accommodation?' asked Lakshman, surprised.

'Yes, they do,' said Arishtanemi.

'Oh,' said Lakshman, shrugging.

Arishtanemi smiled as he looked ahead again.

—— |太| ⬮ ☼ ——

'What the hell!' said Lakshman, stopping short as soon as he passed the gates of the inner city walls of Mithila. He reached for his sword, instinctively. 'We've been led into a trap!'

'Calm down, prince,' said Arishtanemi, with a broad smile. 'This is not a trap. This is just the way Mithila is.'

They had walked into a large, single-walled structure that lay on the other side of the gate; it was a continuous line of homes that shared a huge wall. All the houses were built against each other, like a honeycomb, with absolutely no divisions or space in between. There was a window high on the wall for each individual home, but no doors existed at the street level. It was no surprise that Lakshman thought they had been led into a dead end, a perfect trap or ambush. The fact that most of Vishwamitra's convoy was missing only added to his suspicions.

'Where are the streets?' asked Ram.

Since all the houses were packed against each other in one continuous line, there was no room for streets or even small paths.

'Follow me,' said Arishtanemi, enjoying the obvious befuddlement of his fellow travellers. He led his horse to a stone stairway built into the structure of a house.

'Why on earth are you climbing up to the roof?! And that too, with your horse!' Lakshman exclaimed.

'Just follow me, prince,' said Arishtanemi calmly.

Ram patted Lakshman, as though to soothe him, and started walking up the steps. Lakshman reluctantly followed, leading his horse. They reached the rooftop to confront a scene that was simply unimaginable.

The 'rooftops' of all the houses was in fact a single smooth platform; a 'ground' above the 'ground'. 'Streets' had been demarcated with paint, and they could see people headed in different directions, purposefully or otherwise. Vishwamitra's convoy could be seen far ahead.

'My God! Where are we? And where are those people headed?' asked Lakshman, who had never seen anything like this.

'But how do these people enter their houses?' asked Ram.

As if in answer, a man pulled open a flat door on what evidently was the 'sidewalk' on the roof, and then stepped down, into his house, shutting the door behind him. Ram could now see that, at regular intervals on the sidewalks, where no traffic was allowed, were trapdoors to allow residents access to their homes. Small vertical gaps between some lines of houses exposed grilled windows on the side walls, which allowed sunlight and air into some of the homes.

'What do they do during the monsoon?' asked Lakshman.

'They keep the doors and windows closed when it rains,' said Arishtanemi.

'But what about light, air?'

Arishtanemi pointed to ducts that had been drilled at regular intervals. 'Ducts have been built for a group of four houses each. Windows from inside the houses open up into these ducts to allow in air and light. Rainwater run-off collects in drains below the duct. The drains run under the "Bees Quarter" and lead into either the moat outside the walls, or the lake inside the city. Some of it is used for agriculture.'

'By the great Lord Parshu Ram,' said Lakshman. 'Underground drains. What a brilliant idea! It's the perfect way to control disease.'

But Ram had caught on to something else. 'Bees Quarter? Is that what this area is called?'

'Yes,' answered Arishtanemi.

'Why? Because it is built like a honeycomb?'

'Yes,' smiled Arishtanemi.

'Someone obviously has a sense of humour.'

'I hope you have one as well, because this is where we will be living.'

'What?' asked Lakshman.

'Prince,' said Arishtanemi apologetically, 'the Bees Quarter is where the workers of Mithila live. As we move inwards, beyond the gardens, streets, temples and mercantile areas, we arrive at the abodes and palaces of the rich, including the royalty. But, as you're aware, Guru Vishwamitra wants you to travel incognito.'

'How exactly do we do that if the prime minister knows we are here?' asked Lakshman.

'The prime minister only knows that Guru Vishwamitra has arrived with his companions. She doesn't know about the princes of Ayodhya. At least, not as yet.'

'We're the princes of Ayodhya,' said Lakshman, his fists clenched tight. 'A kingdom that is the overlord of the Sapt Sindhu. Is this how we will be treated here?'

'We're only here for a week,' said Arishtanemi. 'Please…'

'It's all right,' said Ram, cutting in. 'We'll stay here.'

Lakshman turned to Ram. 'But *Dada…*'

'We have stayed in simpler quarters before, Lakshman; it's just for a short while. Then we can go home. We have to honour our father's wishes.'

— |大| 🐟 ☼ —

'I hope you both are comfortable,' said Vishwamitra, as he stepped down into the apartment through the roof door.

In the afternoon, the third hour of the third *prahar*, Vishwamitra had finally visited the Bees Quarter. The brothers had been given accommodation in an apartment at the inner extreme end, beyond which lay a garden; one of the many that proliferated the inner, more upmarket parts of the city. Being at one end of the massive Bees Quarter structure, they were lucky to have a window on the outer wall, which overlooked the garden. Ram and Lakshman had not visited the inner city as yet.

Vishwamitra had been housed in the royal palace, within the heart of the city. It used to be a massive structure once upon a time, but the kindly King Janak had gradually given away parts of the palace to be used as residences and classrooms for *rishis* and their students. The philosopher-king wanted Mithila to serve as a magnet for men of knowledge from across the land. He showered gifts from his meagre treasury upon these great teachers.

'Well, certainly less comfortable than you must be, Guru*ji*,' said Lakshman, a sneer on his face. 'I guess only my brother and I need to remain incognito.'

Vishwamitra ignored Lakshman.

'We are all right, Guru*ji*,' said Ram. 'Perhaps the time has come for you to guide us on the mission we have to complete in Mithila. We are eager to return to Ayodhya.'

'Right,' said Vishwamitra. 'Let me get to the point straight away. The king of Mithila has organised a *swayamvar* for his eldest daughter, Sita.'

A *swayamvar* was an ancient tradition in India. The father of the bride organised a gathering of prospective bridegrooms, from whom his daughter was free to either select her husband, or mandate a competition. The victor would win her hand.

Mithila did not figure in the list of powerful kingdoms of the Sapt Sindhu. The prospect of the overlord kingdom of Ayodhya making a marriage alliance with Mithila was remote at best. Even Ram was at a loss for words. But Lakshman had had enough by now.

'Have we been brought here to provide security for the *swayamvar*?' asked Lakshman. 'This is even more bizarre than making us fight with those imbecile Asuras.'

Vishwamitra turned towards Lakshman and glared, but before he could say anything Ram spoke up.

'Guru*ji*,' said Ram politely, although even his legendary patience was running thin, 'I do not think that Father would want a marriage alliance with Mithila. I, too, have sworn that I will not marry for politics but for—'

Vishwamitra interrupted Ram. 'It may be a little late to refuse participation in the *swayamvar*, prince.'

Ram immediately understood what had been implied. With superhuman effort, he maintained his polite tone. 'How could you have nominated me as a suitor without checking with my father or me?'

'Your father designated me your guru. You're aware of the tradition, prince; a father, a mother or a guru can make the decision on a child's marriage. Do you want to break this law?'

A stunned Ram stood rooted to the spot, his eyes blazing with anger.

'Furthermore, if you refuse to attend the *swayamvar* despite your name being listed among the suitors, then you will be breaking the laws in *Ushna Smriti* and *Haarit Smriti*. Are you sure you want to do that?'

Ram did not utter a word. His body shook with fury. He had been cleverly trapped by Vishwamitra.

'Excuse me,' said Ram, abruptly, as he walked up the steps, lifted the roof door and climbed out. Lakshman followed his elder brother, banging the door shut behind him.

Vishwamitra laughed with satisfaction. 'He'll come around. He has no choice. The law is clear.'

Arishtanemi looked at the door sadly and then back at his guru, choosing silence.

Chapter 21

Ram walked down the stairway and reached the lower 'ground' level. He entered a public garden and sat on the first available bench, alive only to his inner turmoil. To the casual passer-by, his eyes seemed focused on the ground, his breathing slow and even, as though he was meditating deeply. But Lakshman knew his brother and his signs of anger. The deeper *Dada's* anger, the calmer he appeared. Lakshman felt the pain acutely, for his brother became distant and shut him out on such occasions.

'The hell with this, *Dada*!' Lakshman lashed out. 'Tell that pompous guru to take a hike and let's just leave.'

Ram did not react. Not a muscle twitched to suggest that he had even heard his brother's rant.

'*Dada*,' continued Lakshman, 'it's not as if you and I are particularly popular among the royal families in the Sapt Sindhu. Let Bharat *Dada* handle them. One of the few advantages of being disliked is that you don't need to fret over what others think about you.'

'I don't care what others think of me,' said Ram, his voice startlingly calm. 'But it is the law.'

'It's not your law. It's not our law. Forget it!'

Ram turned to look into the distance.

'*Dada*…' said Lakshman, placing his hand on Ram's shoulder.

Ram's body tensed in protest.

'*Dada*, whatever you decide, I am with you.'

His shoulder relaxed. Ram finally looked at his woebegone brother. He smiled. 'Let's take a walk into the city. I need to clear my head.'

—— 肽 ❡ ☼ ——

Beyond the Bees Quarter, the city of Mithila was relatively more organised, with well-laid out streets lined by luxurious buildings; luxurious in a manner of speaking, for it would be unfair to compare them to the grand architecture of Ayodhya. Dressed in the coarse, un-dyed garments of the common class, the brothers did not attract any attention.

Their aimless wandering led them into the main market area, built in a large, open square. It was lined by *pucca* stone-structured expensive shops, with temporary stalls occupying the centre, offering a low-cost option. The neatly numbered stalls were covered by colourful cloth awnings held up by upright bamboo poles. They were organised in a grid layout, marked by chalk lines with adequate lanes for people to walk around.

'*Dada*,' said Lakshman as he picked up a mango. He knew his brother loved the fruit. 'These must be among the early harvests of the season. It may not be the best, but it's still a mango!'

Ram smiled faintly. Lakshman immediately purchased two mangoes, handed one to Ram and set about devouring the other, biting and sucking the succulent pulp with gusto. It made Ram laugh.

Lakshman looked at him. 'What's the point of eating mangoes if you cannot make a mess of it?'

Ram set upon his own mango, joining his brother as he slurped noisily. Lakshman finished first and his brother stopped him in time from casually chucking the mango stone by the sidewalk. 'Lakshman…'

Lakshman pretended as if nothing was amiss and, equally casually, walked up to a garbage collection pit dug next to a stall and dropped the mango stone in the rightful place. Ram followed suit. As they turned around to retrace their steps to the apartment, they heard a loud commotion from farther ahead in the same lane. They quickened their pace as they walked towards the hubbub.

They heard a loud, belligerent voice. 'Princess Sita! Leave this boy alone!'

A firm feminine voice was heard in reply. 'I will not!'

Ram looked at Lakshman, surprised.

'Let's see what's going on,' said Lakshman.

Ram and Lakshman pushed forward through the crowd that had gathered in a flash. As they broke through the first line of the throng, they came upon an open space, probably the centre of the square. They stood at the rear of a corner stall, beyond which their eyes fell on a little boy's back, probably seven or eight years of age. He held a fruit in his hand, as he cowered behind a woman, also facing the other way. The woman confronted a large and visibly angry mob.

'That's Princess Sita?' asked Lakshman, his eyes widening as he turned to look at Ram. His brother's visage knocked the breath out of him. Time seemed to inexplicably slow down, as if Lakshman was witnessing a cosmic event.

Ram stood still as he looked intently, his face calm. Lakshman detected the flush on his brother's dark-skinned face; his heart had clearly picked up pace. Sita stood with her back towards them, but Ram could see that she was unusually tall for a Mithilan woman, almost as tall as he was. She looked like a warrior in the army of the Mother Goddess, with her lean and muscular physique. She was wheatish-complexioned; she wore a cream-coloured *dhoti* and a white single-cloth blouse. Her *angvastram* was draped over her right shoulder, with one end tucked into her *dhoti* and the other tied around her left hand. Ram noticed a small knife scabbard tied horizontally to the small of her back. It was empty. He had been told that Sita was a little older than he was—she was twenty-five years of age.

Ram felt a strange restlessness; he felt a strong urge to behold her face.

'Princess Sita!' screamed a man, possibly the leader of the mob. Their elaborate attire suggested that this crowd was made up of the well-to-do. 'Enough of protecting these scum from the Bees Quarter! Hand him over!'

'He will be punished by the law!' said Sita. 'Not by you!'

Ram smiled slightly.

'He is a thief! That's all we understand. We all know whom your laws favour. Hand him over!' The man inched closer, breaking away from the crowd. The air was rife with tension; nobody knew what would happen next. It could spiral out of control any moment. Crazed mobs can lend a dangerous courage to even the faint-hearted.

Sita slowly reached for her scabbard, where her knife should have been. Her hand tensed. Ram watched with keen interest: no sudden movements, not a twitch of nervous energy when she realised she carried no weapon.

Sita spoke evenly. 'The law does not make any distinction. The boy will be punished. But if you try to interfere, so will you.'

Ram was spellbound. *She's a follower of the law...*

Lakshman smiled. He had never thought he would find another as obsessed with the law as his brother.

'Enough already!' shouted the man. He looked at the mob and screamed as he swung his hand. 'She's just one! There are hundreds of us! Come on!'

'But she's a princess!' Someone from the back tried to reason weakly.

'No, she's not!' shouted the man. 'She is not King Janak's real daughter. She's adopted!'

Sita suddenly pushed the boy out of the way, stepped back and dislodged with her foot an upright bamboo stick that held the awning of a shop in place. It fell to the ground. She flicked the stick with her foot, catching it with her right hand in one fluid motion. She swung the stick expertly in her hand, twirling it around with such fearsome speed that it whipped up a loud, humming sound. The leader of the mob remained stationary, out of reach.

'*Dada*,' whispered Lakshman. 'We should step in.'

'She has it under control.'

Sita stopped swinging and held the stick to her side, one end tucked under her armpit, ready to strike. 'Go back quietly to your houses, nobody will get hurt. The boy will be punished according to the law; nothing more, nothing less.'

The mob leader pulled out a knife and swiftly moved forward. Sita swerved back as he swung the blade wildly. In the same movement, she steadied herself by going back one step and then down on one knee, swinging her stick with both her hands. The weapon hit the man behind his knee. Even before his knee buckled, she transferred her weight to her other foot and yanked the stick upwards, using his own legs as leverage as his feet went up in the air. His legs flew upwards and he fell hard, flat on his back. Sita instantly rose, held the stick high above her head with both her hands, and struck his chest hard; one brutal strike. Ram heard the sound of the rib cage cracking with the fierce blow.

Sita twirled the stick and held it out, one end tucked under her armpit again; her left hand stretched out, her feet spread wide, offering her the balance she needed to move to either side swiftly. 'Anyone else?'

The crowd took one step back. The swift and brutal downing of their leader seemed to have driven some sense into them. Sita forced the point home. 'Anyone else wants a cracked rib, free of charge?'

They began to move backwards, even as the people in the back melted away.

Sita summoned a man who stood to the right of Ram, pointing towards the one who lay prone on the ground. 'Kaustav! Round up a few men and take Vijay to the *ayuralay*. I will check on him later.'

Kaustav and his friends rushed forward. As she turned, Ram finally beheld her visage.

Had the entire universe garnered all its talents into creating a perfect feminine face — of delicate beauty and ferocious will — this would be it. Her round face was a shade lighter than the rest of her body, with high cheekbones and a sharp, small nose; her lips were neither thin nor full; her wide-set eyes were neither small nor large; strong brows arched in a perfect curve above creaseless eyelids, and a limpid fire shone in her eyes, enhanced right now by what she had unleashed. A faint birthmark on her right temple made real a face that to Ram was both flawless and magnificent. She had the look of the mountain people from the Himalayas; Ram had fond memories of them from his short visit to the valley of Kathmandu, when he was young. Her straight, jet-black hair was braided and tied into a neat bun. Her warrior's body carried the proud scars from battle wounds.

'*Dada…*' Lakshman's voice seemed to have travelled from a distant land. It was, quite simply, almost inaudible to him.

Ram stood as if he was carved from marble. Lakshman knew his brother so well; the more transfixed his face, the deeper the tumult of emotions within.

Lakshman touched Ram's shoulder. '*Dada…*'

Ram still could not respond. He was mesmerised. Lakshman turned his attention back to Sita.

She threw the stick away and caught hold of the boy-thief. 'Come on.'

'My Lady,' pleaded the boy. 'I'm sorry. This will be the last time. I'm really sorry.'

Sita tugged at the boy's hand and began to walk briskly towards Ram and Lakshman. Lakshman took hold of Ram's elbow and attempted to step aside. But Ram seemed to be in the grip of a higher power. His face was expressionless, his body still, his eyes almost unblinking, his breathing even and regular. The only movement was his *angvastram* fluttering in the breeze; exaggerated by his immobility.

Almost as if it was beyond his control, Ram bowed his head.

Lakshman held his breath as his mouth fell open. He had never thought he'd see this day; after all, which woman would inspire the admiration of a man such as his brother? That love would slam into a heart that had only known obedience to, and strict control of, his mind? That a man whose mission was to raise every person's head with pride and purpose would find comfort in bowing to another?

A line from an ancient poem came floating into his mind; one that his romantic heart had found ethereal. But he had never thought his staid elder brother would find meaning in that line before he did.

She has that something, like the thread in a crystal-bead necklace. She holds it all together.

Lakshman could see that his brother had found the thread that would hold the disparate beads of his life together.

Ram's heart, despite the fact that it had never been given free rein due to his immense self-control, was probably aware that it had just found its greatest ally. It had found Sita.

She came to a standstill, surprised by these two strangers blocking her path; one looked like a giant but loveable ruffian, and the other was too dignified for the coarse clothes he wore. Strangely, for some reason, he was bowing to her.

'Out of my way!' snapped Sita, as she pushed past Ram.

Ram stepped aside, but she had already whizzed past, dragging the boy-thief along.

Lakshman immediately stepped up and touched Ram on his back. '*Dada…*'

Ram hadn't turned to see Sita walking away. He stood mystified, almost as if his disciplined mind was trying to analyse what had just happened; what his heart had just done to him. He seemed surprised beyond measure; by himself.

'Umm, *Dada…*' said Lakshman, smiling broadly now.

'Hmm?'

'*Dada*, she's gone. I think you can raise your head now.'

Ram finally looked at Lakshman, a hint of a smile on his face.

'*Dada!*' Lakshman gave a loud laugh, stepped forward and embraced his brother. Ram patted him on his back. But his mind was preoccupied.

Lakshman stepped back and said, 'She'll make a great *bhabhi!*'

Ram frowned, refusing to acknowledge his brother's unbridled enthusiasm in referring to the princess as his *sister-in-law*.

'I guess we will be going to the *swayamvar* now,' said Lakshman, winking.

'Let's go back to our room for now,' said Ram, his expression calm again.

'Right!' said Lakshman, still laughing. 'Of course, we should behave maturely about this! Mature! Calm! Stoic! Controlled! Have I forgotten any word, *Dada*?!'

Ram tried to keep his face expressionless but it was obviously a bigger struggle than usual. He finally surrendered to his inner joy and his face lit up with a dazzling smile.

The brothers began to walk back to the Bees Quarter.

'We must tell Arishtanemi*ji* that you will, after all, be participating in the *swayamvar* willingly!' said Lakshman.

As Ram fell a few steps behind Lakshman, he allowed himself another full smile. His mind had probably begun to understand what had just happened to him. What his heart had done to him.

— 𑀓 🐟 ☼ —

'This is good news,' said Arishtanemi. 'I'm delighted that you have decided to obey the law.'

Ram maintained a calm demeanour. Lakshman couldn't seem to control his smile.

'Yes, of course, Arishtanemi*ji*,' said Lakshman. 'How can we disregard the law? Especially one that has been recorded in two *Smritis*!'

Arishtanemi frowned, not really understanding Lakshman's sudden about-turn. He shrugged and turned to address Ram. 'I will inform Guru*ji* right away that you are willing to participate in the *swayamvar*.'

— 𑀓 🐟 ☼ —

'*Dada!*' said Lakshman, rushing into their room.

It had been just five days since Ram had seen Sita. And there were less than two days to go for the *swayamvar*.

'What's the matter?' asked Ram, putting down the palm-leaf book he had been reading.

'Just come with me, *Dada*,' insisted Lakshman, as he grabbed Ram by the hand.

—— |大| 🐟 ☼ ——

'What is it, Lakshman?' asked Ram once again.

They were on top of the Bees Quarter, walking down the streets. They moved in the direction away from the city. This section of the Bees Quarter actually merged with the inner fort wall, making it a fantastic lookout point to see the fields up to the outer wall and beyond at the land outside the city. A massive crowd had gathered, many of them pointing and gesticulating wildly as they spoke to each other.

'Lakshman… Where are you taking me?'

He did not get an answer.

'Move aside,' said Lakshman harshly as he pushed his way through the throng, leading Ram by the hand. People got out of the way at the sight of the muscular giant, and soon the brothers were at the wall.

As soon as they reached the edge, Ram's attention was caught by what he saw. Beyond the second wall and the lake-moat, in the clearing ahead of the forest line, a small army seemed to be gathering with devastating precision and discipline. There were ten standard bearers at regular intervals, holding their flags high. Waves of soldiers emerged from the forest in neat rows and, within a few minutes, they were all in formation, approximately a thousand behind each standard.

Intriguingly, they had left a large area clear, right in the centre of their formation.

Ram noticed that the colour of the *dhotis* that the soldiers wore was the same as their standards. He estimated that there must be ten thousand soldiers. Not a very large number, but enough to cause serious trouble to a city like Mithila, which was not a garrison city.

'Which kingdom has sent this army?' asked Ram.

'It's apparently not an army,' remarked the man standing next to Lakshman. 'It's a bodyguard corps.'

Ram was about to pose another question to the man when they were all distracted by the reverberating sounds of conch shells being blown by the soldiers in the clearing. A moment later, even this sound was drowned out by one that Ram had not heard before. It almost seemed like a giant demon was slicing through the air with quick strokes from a gigantic sword.

Lakshman looked up, tracing the source of the sound. 'What the...'

The crowd watched in awe. It must be the legendary flying vehicle that was the proud possession of Lanka, the *Pushpak Vimaan*. It was a giant conical craft, made of some strange, unknown metal. Massive rotors attached to the top of the vehicle, right at its pointed end, were swinging with a powerful force in a right to left, circular motion. A few smaller rotors were attached close to the base, on all sides. The body of the craft had many portholes, each of which was covered with thick glass.

The vehicle made a noise that could overpower that of trumpeting elephants in hot pursuit. It appeared to intensify as it hovered above the trees for a bit. As it did so, small circular metal screens descended over the portholes, covering them completely, blocking any view of the insides of the

Vimaan. The crowd gaped in unison at this outlandish sight as they covered their ears. So did Lakshman. But Ram did not. He stared at the craft with a visceral anger welling up deep inside him. He knew whom it belonged to. He knew who was in there. The man responsible for having destroyed all possibilities of a happy childhood before Ram was even born. He stood amidst the throng as if he was alone. His eyes burned with fearsome intensity.

The sound of the rotors suddenly dipped as the craft began its descent. The *Pushpak Vimaan* landed perfectly in the clearing designated for it, in the centre of the formations of the Lankan soldiers. The Mithilans of the Bees Quarter spontaneously broke into applause. For the soldiers of Lanka though, they may not have existed at all. They stood absolutely straight, rooted to their positions, in a remarkable display of raw discipline.

A few minutes later, a section of the conical *Vimaan* swung open, revealing a perfectly concealed door. The door slid aside and a giant of a man filled the doorway. He stepped out and surveyed the ground before him. A Lankan officer ran up to him and gave him a crisp salute. They exchanged some quick words and the giant looked intently towards the wall, at the avid spectators. He abruptly turned around and walked back into the *Vimaan*. After a while, he appeared again, this time walking out, followed by another man.

The second man was distinctly shorter than the first, and yet taller than the average Mithilan; probably of the same height as Ram. But unlike Ram's lean muscular physique, this Lankan was of gigantic proportions. His swarthy skin, handlebar moustache, thick beard and pock-marked face lent him an intimidating air. He wore a violet *dhoti* and *angvastram*, a colour-dye that was among the most expensive in the Sapt

Sindhu. He wore a large headgear with two threatening six-inch curved horns stretching out from either side. He stooped a bit as he walked.

'Raavan...' whispered Lakshman.

Ram did not respond.

Lakshman looked at Ram. '*Dada...*'

Ram remained silent, looking intently at the king of Lanka in the distance.

'*Dada,*' said Lakshman. 'We should leave.'

Ram looked at Lakshman. There was fire in his eyes. He then turned back to look at the Lankans beyond the second wall of Mithila; to *the* Lankan beyond the second wall of Mithila.

Chapter 22

'Please don't leave,' pleaded Arishtanemi. 'Guru*ji* is as troubled as you are. We don't know how or why Raavan landed up here. But Guru*ji* thinks it's safer for the two of you to remain within the fort walls.'

Ram and Lakshman sat in their room in the Bees Quarter. Arishtanemi had returned with a plea from Vishwamitra to the princes of Ayodhya: *please do not leave*. Raavan had set up camp outside the walls of Mithila. He had not entered the city, though a few of his emissaries had. They had gone straight to the main palace to speak to King Janak and his younger brother King Kushadhwaj; the latter had newly arrived in the city to attend the *swayamvar*.

'Why should I bother about what Guru Vishwamitra thinks?' asked Lakshman aggressively. 'I only care about my elder brother! Nobody can guess what this demon from Lanka will do! We have to leave! *Now!*'

'Please think about this with a calm mind. How will you be safe all alone in the jungle? You are better off within the walls of the city. The Malayaputras are here for your defence.'

'We cannot just sit here, waiting for events to unfold. I am leaving with my brother. You Malayaputras can do whatever the hell you want to!'

'Prince Ram,' Arishtanemi turned to Ram, 'please, trust me. What I am advising is the best course of action. Do not withdraw from the *swayamvar*. Do not leave the city.'

Ram's external demeanour was calm as usual, and yet Arishtanemi sensed a different energy; the inner serenity, so typical of Ram, was missing.

Had Ram been truly honest with himself, he would admit that there were many who had hurt him, who he should have at least resented, if not hated, with equal ferocity. Raavan, after all, had simply done his job; he had won a battle that he had fought. However, the child that Ram had once been was incapable of such rationalisation. That lonely and hurt child had focused all his frustration and anger at the injustices that he had faced on the iconic, invisible demon who had wrought such a devastating change in his father, turning him into a bitter man who constantly put his eldest son down and neglected him. As a child, he had convinced himself that Raavan had triggered all his misfortunes; that if Raavan had not won that battle on that terrible day in Karachapa, Ram would not have suffered so.

The anger that Ram reserved for Raavan stemmed from that childhood memory — it was overwhelming and beyond reason.

— 𝕀𝕩𝕝 🐟 ☼ —

Arishtanemi had left for Vishwamitra's guest quarters, leaving Ram and Lakshman to themselves.

'*Dada*, trust me, let's just escape from here,' said Lakshman. 'There are ten thousand Lankans; we're only two. I'm telling you, if push comes to shove, even the Mithilans and Malayaputras will side with Raavan.'

Ram stared at the garden beyond, through the only window in the room.

'*Dada*,' said Lakshman, insistent. 'We need to make a run for it. I've been told there's a second gate at the other end of the city-wall. Nobody, except for the Malayaputras, knows who we are. We can escape quietly and return with the Ayodhya army. We will teach the damned Lankans a lesson, but for now, we need to run.'

Ram turned to Lakshman and spoke with eerie calm. 'We are the descendants of Ikshvaku, the descendants of Raghu. We will not run away.'

'*Dada*…'

He was interrupted by a knock on the door. He cast a quick look at Ram and drew his sword. Ram frowned. 'Lakshman, if someone wanted to assassinate us, he wouldn't knock. He would just barge in. There is no place to hide in here.'

Lakshman continued to stare at the door, unsure whether he should sheath his sword.

'Just open the door, Lakshman,' said Ram.

Lakshman crept up the stairs to the horizontal door on the roof. He held his sword to his side, ready to strike if the need so arose. There was another knock, more insistent this time. Lakshman pushed the door open to find Samichi, the police and protocol chief of Mithila, peering down at him. She was a short-haired, tall, dark-skinned and muscular woman, and her soldier's body bore scars of honour from battles well fought. She wore a blouse and *dhoti* made from the same green cloth. She had on leather armbands and a leather under-blouse; a sheathed long sword hung by her waist.

Lakshman gripped his sword tight. 'Namaste, Chief Samichi. To what do we owe this visit?' he asked gruffly.

Samichi grinned disarmingly. 'Put your sword back in the scabbard, young man.'

'Let me decide what I should or should not do. What is your business here?'

'The prime minister wants to meet your elder brother.'

Lakshman was taken aback. He turned to Ram, who signalled his brother to let them in. He immediately slipped his sword in its scabbard and backed up against the wall, making room for the party to enter. Samichi stepped in and descended the stairs, followed by Sita. As Sita stepped down through the door hole, she gestured behind her. 'Stay there, Urmila.'

Lakshman instinctively looked up to see Urmila, even as Ram stood up to receive the prime minister of Mithila. The two women climbed down swiftly but Lakshman remained rooted, entranced by the vision above. Urmila was shorter than her elder sister Sita, much shorter. She was also fairer; so fair that she was almost the colour of milk. She probably remained indoors most of the time, keeping away from the sun. Her round, baby face was dominated by her large eyes, which betrayed a sweet, childlike innocence. Unlike her warrior-like elder sister, Urmila was clearly a very delicate creature, aware of her beauty, yet childlike in her ways. Her hair was arranged in a bun with every strand neatly in place. The *kaajal* in her eyes accentuated their exquisiteness; the lips were enhanced with some beet extract. Her clothes were fashionable, yet demure: a bright pink blouse was complemented by a deep red *dhoti* which was longer than usual — it reached below her knees. A neatly pressed *angvastram* hung from her shoulders. Anklets and toe-rings drew attention to her lovely feet, while rings and bracelets decorated her delicate hands. Lakshman was mesmerised. The lady sensed it, smiled genially, and looked away with shy confusion.

Sita turned and saw Lakshman looking at Urmila. She had noticed something that Ram had missed.

'Shut the door, Lakshman,' said Ram.

Lakshman reluctantly did as ordered.

Ram turned towards Sita. 'How may I help you, princess?'

Sita smiled. 'Excuse me for a minute, prince.' She looked at Samichi. 'I'd like to speak to the prince alone.'

'Of course,' said Samichi, immediately climbing out of the room.

Ram was surprised by Sita's knowledge of their identity. He revealed nothing as he nodded at Lakshman, who turned to leave with alacrity. Ram and Sita were alone in no time.

Sita smiled and pointed towards a chair in the room. 'Please sit, Prince Ram.'

'I'm all right.'

Is it Guru Vishwamitra himself who revealed my identity to her? Why is he so hell-bent on this alliance?

'I insist,' said Sita, as she sat down herself.

Ram sat on a chair facing Sita. There was an awkward silence for some time before Sita spoke up. 'I believe you were tricked into coming here.'

Ram remained silent, but his eyes gave the answer away.

'Then why haven't you left?' asked Sita.

'Because it would be against the law.'

Sita smiled. 'And is it the law that will make you participate in the *swayamvar* day after tomorrow?'

Ram chose silence, for he would not lie.

'You are Ayodhya, the overlord of Sapt Sindhu. I am only Mithila, a small kingdom with little power. What purpose can possibly be served by this alliance?'

'Marriage has a higher purpose; it can be more than just a political alliance.'

Sita smiled enigmatically. Ram felt like he was being interviewed; this, strangely enough, did not stop him from noticing that an impertinent strand had slipped out of Sita's neatly braided hair. The gentle breeze wafting in from the window lifted the wisp of hair playfully. His attention shifted seamlessly to the perfect curve of her neck. He noticed his heart begin to race. He smiled to himself ruefully and tried to restore his inner calm as he admonished himself. *What is wrong with me? Why can't I control myself?!*

'Prince Ram?'

'Excuse me?' asked Ram, bringing his focus back to what she was saying.

'I asked, if marriage is not a political alliance, then what is it?'

'Well, to begin with, it is not a necessity; there should be no compulsion to get married. There's nothing worse than being married to the wrong person. You should only get married if you find someone you admire, who will help you understand and fulfil your life's purpose. And you, in turn, can help her fulfil her life's purpose. If you're able to find that one person, then marry her.'

Sita raised her eyebrows. 'Are you advocating just one wife? Not many? Most people think differently.'

'Even if *all* people think polygamy is right, it doesn't make it so.'

'But most men take many wives; especially the nobility.'

'I won't. You insult your wife by taking another.'

Sita drew back her head, raising her chin in contemplation; as though she was assessing him. Her eyes softened in admiration. A charged silence filled the room. As she gazed at him, her expression changed with sudden recognition.

'Wasn't it you at the market place the other day?' she asked.

'Yes.'

'Why didn't you step in to help me?'

'You had the situation under control.'

Sita smiled slightly.

It was Ram's turn to ask questions. 'What is Raavan doing here?'

'I don't know. But it makes the *swayamvar* more personal for me.'

Ram was shocked, but his expression remained impassive. 'Has he come to participate in your *swayamvar*?'

'So I have been told.'

'And?'

'And, I have come here.'

Ram waited for her to continue.

'How good are you with a bow and arrow?' asked Sita.

Ram allowed himself a faint smile.

Sita raised her eyebrows. 'That good?'

Sita arose from her chair, as did Ram. The prime minister of Mithila folded her hands into a namaste. 'May Lord Rudra continue to bless you, prince.'

Ram returned Sita's namaste. 'And may He bless you, princess.'

Ram's eyes fell on the bracelet made of Rudraaksh beads that Sita wore on her wrists; she was a fellow Lord Rudra devotee. His eyes involuntarily strayed from the beads to her perfectly formed, artistically long fingers. They could have belonged to a surgeon. The battle scar on her left hand suggested, though, that Sita's hands used tools other than scalpels.

'Prince Ram,' said Sita, 'I asked—'

'I'm sorry, can you repeat that?' asked Ram, refocusing on the here and now, on what Sita was saying.

'Can I meet with you and your brother in the private royal garden tomorrow?'

'Yes, of course.'

'Good,' said Sita, as she turned to leave. Then she stopped, as if remembering something. She reached into the pouch tied to her waistband and pulled out a red thread. 'It would be nice if you could wear this. It's for good luck. It is a representation of…'

But Ram's attention was seized by another thought; his mind wandering once again, drowning out what Sita was saying. He remembered a couplet; one he had heard at a wedding ceremony long ago.

Maangalyatantunaanena bhava jeevanahetuh may. A line from old Sanskrit, it translated into: *With this holy thread that I offer to you, please become the purpose of my life…*

'Prince Ram…' said Sita, loudly.

Ram suddenly straightened up as the wedding hymn playing in his mind went silent. 'I'm sorry. What?'

Sita smiled politely, 'I was saying…' She stopped just as suddenly. 'Never mind. I'll leave the thread here. Please wear it if it pleases you.'

Placing the thread on the table, Sita began to climb up the stairs. As she reached the door, she turned around for a last look. Ram was holding the thread in the palm of his right hand, gazing at it reverentially, as if it was the most sacred thing in the world.

— 大 🐟 ☼ —

The city of Mithila became increasingly more visually appealing as one moved beyond the main market to the enclaves of the upper classes. This was where Ram and Lakshman had decided to walk, late the following evening.

'It's pretty, isn't it, *Dada*?' remarked Lakshman, as he looked around in appreciation.

Ram had been noting the sudden change in Lakshman's attitude towards Mithila since the previous day. The road they were on was relatively broad but meandering, much like village roads. Trees and flower beds lined dividers made of stone and mortar, around three to four feet in height. Beyond the road edge were an array of trees, gardens and the stately mansions of the wealthy. Idols of various personal and family deities were placed above the boundary walls of the mansions. Incense sticks and fresh flowers were placed as offerings to the deities, indicating the spiritual inclinations of the citizens; Mithila was a bastion of the devout.

'Here we are,' pointed Lakshman.

Ram followed his brother into a narrow, circuitous lane on the right. The sidewalls being higher, it was difficult to see what lay beyond.

'Should we just jump over?' asked Lakshman, grinning mischievously.

Ram frowned at him and continued walking. A few metres ahead lay an ornate wrought-iron gate. Two soldiers stood at the entrance.

'We have come to meet the prime minister,' said Lakshman, handing over a ring that had been given to him by Samichi.

The guard examined the ring, was seemingly satisfied, and signalled to the other to help him open the gates.

Ram and Lakshman quickly walked into the resplendent garden. Unlike the royal gardens of Ayodhya, this one was less variegated; it only contained local trees, plants and flower beds. It was a garden whose beauty could be attributed more to the ministrations of talented gardeners than to the impressive infusion of funds. The layout was symmetrical and well-manicured. The thick green carpet of grass was thrown into visual relief by the profusion of flowers and trees of all shapes and colours. Nature expressed itself in ordered harmony.

'Prince Ram,' Samichi walked up to them from the shadows behind a tree. She bowed low with a respectful namaste.

'Namaste,' said Ram, as he folded his hands together.

Lakshman too returned Samichi's greeting and then handed the ring back to her. 'The guards recognise your mark.'

'As they should,' said the police chief, before turning to Ram. 'Princesses Sita and Urmila await you. Follow me, princes.'

Lakshman beamed with delight as he followed Ram and Samichi.

— 大 🐟 ☼ —

Ram and Lakshman were led into a clearing at the back of the garden; below their feet was plush grass, above them the open evening sky.

'Namaste, princess,' said Ram to Sita.

'Namaste, prince,' replied Sita, before turning to her sister. 'May I introduce my younger sister, Urmila?' Gesturing towards Ram and Lakshman, Sita continued, 'Urmila, meet Prince Ram and Prince Lakshman of Ayodhya.'

'I had occasion to meet her yesterday,' said Lakshman, grinning from ear to ear.

Urmila smiled politely at Lakshman, with her hands folded in a namaste, then turned towards Ram and greeted him.

'I would like to speak with the prince privately, once again,' said Sita.

'Of course,' said Samichi immediately. 'May I have a private word before that?'

Samichi took Sita aside and whispered in her ear. Then she cast a quick look at Ram before walking away, leading Urmila by the hand. Lakshman followed Urmila.

Ram felt as if his interview from yesterday would proceed from where they had left off. 'Why did you want to meet me, princess?'

Sita made sure that Samichi and the rest had indeed left. She was about to begin when her eyes fell on the red thread tied around Ram's right wrist. She smiled. 'Please give me a minute, prince.'

Sita went behind a tree, bent and picked up a very long package covered in cloth. She walked back to Ram. He frowned, intrigued. Sita pulled the cloth back to reveal an intricately carved, unusually long bow. An exquisite piece of weaponry, it was a composite bow with recurved ends, which must give it a very long range. Ram carefully examined the carvings on the inside face of the limbs, both above and below the grip of the bow. It was the image of a flame, representative of Agni, the God of Fire. The first hymn of the first chapter of the *Rig Veda* was dedicated to the deeply revered deity. However, the shape of this particular flame seemed familiar to Ram, in the way its edges leapt out.

Sita pulled a flat wooden base platform out of the cloth bag and placed it on the ground ceremonially. She looked up at Ram. 'This bow cannot be allowed to touch the ground.'

Ram frowned, wondering what made it so important. Sita placed the lower limb of the bow on the platform, steadying it with her foot. She used her right hand to pull down the other end with force. Judging by the strain on her shoulder and biceps, Ram knew it was a very strong bow with tremendous resistance. With her left hand, Sita pulled the bowstring up and quickly strung it. She let the upper limb extend up and relaxed as she let out a long breath. The mighty bow adjusted to the constraints of the potent bowstring. She held the bow with her left hand and pulled the bowstring with her fingers, letting it go with a loud twang.

Ram knew from the sound of the string that this bow was special. It was the strongest he had ever heard. 'Wow. That's a good bow.'

'It's the best.'

'Is it yours?'

'I cannot own a bow like this. I am only its caretaker, for now. When I die, someone else will be deputed to take care of it.'

Ram narrowed his eyes as he closely examined the image of the flames around the grip of the bow. 'These flames look a little like—'

Sita interrupted him. 'This bow once belonged to the one whom we both worship. It still belongs to him.'

Ram stared at the bow with a mixture of shock and awe, his suspicion confirmed.

Sita smiled. 'Yes, it is the *Pinaka*.'

The *Pinaka* was the legendary bow of the previous Mahadev, Lord Rudra, considered the strongest bow ever made. Legend held that it was a composite, a mix of many materials, which had been given a succession of specific treatments to arrest its degeneration. It was also believed that maintaining this bow was not an easy task. The grip, the limbs and the recurved ends needed regular lubrication with special oil. Sita was obviously up to the task, for the bow was as good as new.

'How did Mithila come into the possession of the *Pinaka*?' asked Ram, unable to take his eyes off the beautiful weapon.

'It's a long story,' said Sita, 'but I want you to practice with it. This is the bow which will be used for the *swayamvar* competition tomorrow.'

Ram took an involuntary step back. There were many ways in which a *swayamvar* was conducted, two of them being: either the bride could directly select her groom; or she could mandate a competition. The winner would marry the bride. But this was unorthodox, to say the least: for a groom to be given advance notice and help. In fact, it was against the rules.

Ram shook his head. 'It would be an honour to even touch the *Pinaka*, much less hold the bow that Lord Rudra himself graced with his touch. But I will only do so tomorrow. Not today.'

Sita frowned. 'I thought you intended to win my hand.'

'I do. But I will win it the right way. I will win according to the rules.'

Sita smiled, shaking her head as she experienced a peculiar sense of fear mixed with elation.

'Do you disagree?' asked Ram, seeming a bit disappointed.

'No, I don't. I'm just impressed. You are a special man, Prince Ram.'

Ram blushed. His heart, despite his mental admonishments, picked up pace once again.

'I look forward to seeing you fire an arrow tomorrow morning,' said Sita.

Chapter 23

The *swayamvar* was held in the Hall of *Dharma* instead of the royal court. This was simply because the royal court was not the biggest hall in Mithila. The main building in the palace complex, which housed the Hall of *Dharma*, had been donated by King Janak to the Mithila University. The hall hosted regular debates and discussions on various esoteric topics: the nature of *dharma*, karma's interaction with *dharma*, the nature of the divine, the purpose of the human journey... King Janak was a philosopher-king who focused all his kingdom's resources on matters that were spiritual and intellectual.

The Hall of *Dharma* was in a circular building, built of stone and mortar, with a massive dome; quite rare in India. The delicate elegance of the dome was believed to represent the feminine, while the typical temple spire represented the masculine. The Hall of *Dharma* embodied King Janak's approach to governance: an intellectual love of wisdom and respectful equality accorded to all points of view. The hall, therefore, was circular. All *rishis* sat as equals, without a moderating 'head', debating issues openly and without fear; freedom of expression at its zenith.

However, today was different. There were no manuscripts lying on low tables, or *rishis* moving to the centre in a disciplined sequence, to deliver speeches or debate their points. The Hall of *Dharma* was set to host a *swayamvar*.

Temporary three-tiered spectator stands stood near the entrance. At the other end, on a wooden platform, was placed the king's throne. A statue of the great King Mithi, the founder of Mithila, stood on a raised pedestal behind the throne. Two thrones, only marginally less grand, were placed to the left and right of the king's throne. A circle of comfortable seats lined the middle section of the great hall, where kings and princes, the potential suitors, would sit.

The spectator stands were already packed when Ram and Lakshman were led in by Arishtanemi. Most contestants too had taken their seats. Not many recognised the two princes of Ayodhya, dressed as they were as hermits. A guard gestured for them to move towards the base platform of a three-tiered stand, occupied by the nobility and rich merchants of Mithila. Arishtanemi informed the guard that he accompanied a competitor. The guard was surprised but he did recognise Arishtanemi, the lieutenant of the great Vishwamitra, and stepped aside to let them proceed. After all, it would not be unusual for the devout King Janak to invite even Brahmin *rishis*, not just Kshatriya kings, for his daughter's *swayamvar*.

The walls of the Hall of *Dharma* were decorated by portraits of the greatest *rishis* and *rishikas* of times past: Maharishi Satyakam, Maharishi Yajnavalkya, Maharishika Gargi, and Maharishika Maitreyi, among others. Ram mused: *How unworthy are we, the descendants of these great ancestors. Maharishikas Gargi and Maitreyi were rishikas, and today there are fools who claim that women are not to be allowed to study the scriptures or to write new ones. Maharishi Satyakam was the son of a Shudra single mother. His profound knowledge and wisdom is recorded in our greatest Upanishads; and today there are bigots who claim that the Shudra-born cannot become rishis.*

Ram bowed his head and brought his hands together, paying obeisance to the great sages of yore. *A person becomes a Brahmin by karma, not by birth.*

'*Dada,*' said Lakshman, touching Ram's back.

Ram followed Arishtanemi to the allotted seat.

He seated himself as Lakshman and Arishtanemi stood behind him. All eyes turned to them. The contestants wondered who these simple mendicants were, who hoped to compete with them for Princess Sita's hand. A few, though, recognised the princes of Ayodhya. A conspiratorial buzz was heard from a section of the contestants.

'Ayodhya…'

'Why does Ayodhya want an alliance with Mithila?'

Ram, however, was oblivious to the stares and whispers of the assembly. He had eyes only for the centre of the hall; placed ceremonially on a table top was the bow. Next to the table, at ground level, was a large copper-plated basin.

Ram's eyes first lingered on the *Pinaka*. It was unstrung. An array of arrows was placed by the side of the bow.

Competitors were first required to pick up the bow and string it, which itself was no mean task. But it was then that the challenge truly began. The contestant would move to the copper-plated basin. It was filled with water, with additional drops trickling in steadily from the rim of the basin, attached to which was a thin tube. Excess water was drained out of the basin by another thin tube, attached to the other side. This created subtle ripples within the bowl, which spread out from the centre towards the edge. Agonisingly, the drops of water were released at irregular intervals, making the ripples, in turn, unpredictable.

A hilsa fish was nailed to a wheel, fixed to an axle that was suspended from the top of the dome, a hundred metres above the ground. The wheel, thankfully, revolved at a constant speed. The contestants were required to look at the reflection of the fish in the unstill water below, disturbed by ripples generated at irregular intervals, and use the *Pinaka* bow to fire an arrow into the eye of the fish, fixed on the revolving wheel high above them. The first to succeed would win the hand of the bride.

'This is too simple for you, *Dada*,' said Lakshman, mischievously. 'Should I ask them to make the wheel revolve at irregular intervals, too? Or twist the feather-fletching on the arrow? What do you think?'

Ram looked up at Lakshman, narrowed his eyes and glared at his brother.

Lakshman grinned. 'Sorry, *Dada*.'

He stepped back as the king was announced.

'The Lord of the Mithi clan, the wisest of the wise, beloved of the *rishis*, King Janak!'

The court arose to welcome their host, Janak, the king of Mithila. He walked in from the far end of the hall. Interestingly, in a deviation from tradition, he followed Vishwamitra, who was in the lead. Behind Janak was his younger brother, Kushadhwaj, the king of Sankashya. Even more interestingly, Janak requested Vishwamitra to occupy the throne of Mithila, as he moved towards the smaller throne to the right. Kushadhwaj walked towards the seat on the left of the great maharishi. A flurry of officials scuttled all over the place, for this was an unexpected breach of protocol.

A loud buzz ran through the hall at this unorthodox seating arrangement, but Ram was intrigued by something else. He turned towards Lakshman, seated behind him. His younger brother verbalised Ram's thought. 'Where is Raavan?'

The court crier banged his staff against the large bell at the entrance of the hall, signalling a call for silence.

Vishwamitra cleared his throat and spoke loudly. The superb acoustics of the Hall of *Dharma* carried his voice clearly to all those present. 'Welcome to this august gathering called by the wisest and most spiritual of rulers in India, King Janak.'

Janak smiled genially.

Vishwamitra continued. 'The princess of Mithila, Sita, has decided to make this a *gupt swayamvar*. She will not join us in the hall. The great kings and princes will, on her bidding, compete—'

The maharishi was interrupted by the ear-splitting sounds of numerous conch shells; surprising, for conch shells were usually melodious and pleasant. Everyone turned to the source of the sound: the entrance of the great hall. Fifteen tall, muscular warriors strode into the room bearing black flags, with the image of the head of a roaring lion emerging from a profusion of fiery flames. The warriors marched with splendid discipline. Behind them were two formidable men. One was a giant, even taller than Lakshman. He was corpulent but muscular, with a massive potbelly that jiggled with every step. His whole body was unusually hirsute — he looked more like a giant bear than human. Most troubling, for all those present, were the strange outgrowths on his ears and shoulders. He was a Naga. Ram recognised him as the first to have emerged from the *Pushpak Vimaan*.

Walking proudly beside him was Raavan, his head held high. He moved with a minor stoop; perhaps a sign of increasing age.

The two men were followed by fifteen more warriors, or more correctly, bodyguards.

Raavan's entourage moved to the centre and halted next to the bow of Lord Rudra. The lead bodyguard made a loud announcement. 'The king of kings, the emperor of emperors, the ruler of the three worlds, the beloved of the Gods, Lord Raavan!'

Raavan turned towards a minor king who sat closest to the *Pinaka*. He made a soft grunting sound and flicked his head to the right, a casual gesture which clearly communicated what he expected. The king immediately rose and scurried away, coming to a standstill behind another competitor. Raavan walked to the chair, but did not sit. He placed his right foot on the seat and rested his hand on his knee. His bodyguards, including the giant bear-man, fell in line behind him. Raavan finally cast a casual glance at Vishwamitra. 'Continue, great Malayaputra.'

Vishwamitra, the chief of the Malayaputras, was furious. He had never been treated so disrespectfully. 'Raavan…' he growled.

Raavan stared at Vishwamitra with lazy arrogance.

Vishwamitra managed to rein in his temper; he had an important task at hand. He would deal with Raavan later. 'Princess Sita has decreed the sequence in which the great kings and princes will compete.'

Raavan began to walk towards the *Pinaka* while Vishwamitra was still speaking. The chief of the Malayaputras completed his announcement just as Raavan was about to reach for the bow. 'The first man to compete is not you, Raavan. It is Ram, the prince of Ayodhya.'

Raavan's hand stopped a few inches from the bow. He looked at Vishwamitra, and then turned around to see who had responded to the sage. He saw a young man, dressed in the simple white clothes of a hermit. Behind him stood another young, though gigantic man, next to whom was Arishtanemi. Raavan glared first at Arishtanemi, and then at Ram. If looks could kill, Raavan would have certainly felled a few today. He turned towards Vishwamitra, Janak and Kushadhwaj, his fingers wrapped around the macabre, finger-bone pendant that hung around his neck. He growled in a loud and booming voice, 'I have been insulted!'

Ram noticed that the giant bear-man, who stood behind Raavan's chair, was shaking his head imperceptibly; seemingly rueing being there.

'Why was I invited at all if you planned to make unskilled boys compete ahead of me?!' Raavan's body shook with fury.

Janak looked at Kushadhwaj with irritation before turning to Raavan and interjecting weakly, 'These are the rules of the *swayamvar*, Great King of Lanka...'

A voice that sounded more like the rumble of thunder was finally heard; it was the giant bear-man. 'Enough of this nonsense!' He turned towards Raavan. '*Dada*, let's go.'

Raavan suddenly bent and picked up the *Pinaka*. Before anyone could react, he had strung it and nocked an arrow on the string. Everyone sat paralysed as Raavan pointed the arrow directly at Vishwamitra. Lakshman was forced to acknowledge the strength as well as the skill of this man.

The crowd gasped collectively in horror as Vishwamitra stood up, threw his *angvastram* aside, and banged his chest with his closed fist. 'Shoot, Raavan!'

Ram was stunned by the warrior-like behaviour of this *rishi*. Raw courage in a man of knowledge was a rarity. But then, Vishwamitra had been a warrior once.

The sage's voice resounded in the great hall. 'Come on! Shoot, if you have the guts!'

Raavan released the arrow. It slammed into the statue of Mithi behind Vishwamitra, breaking off the nose of the ancient king. Ram stared at Raavan; his fists were, uncharacteristically, clenched. This insult to the founder of the city was not challenged by a single Mithilan.

Raavan dismissed King Janak with a wave of his hand as he glared at King Kushadhwaj. He threw the bow on the table and began to walk towards the door, followed by his guards. In all this commotion, the giant bear-man stepped up to the table, unstrung the *Pinaka,* and reverentially brought it to his head as he held it with both hands; almost like he was apologising to the bow. He turned around and briskly walked out of the room, behind Raavan. Ram's eyes remained pinned on him till he left the room.

As the last of the Lankans exited, the people within the hall turned in unison from the doorway to those seated at the other end of the room: Vishwamitra, Janak and Kushadhwaj.

What are they going to do now?

Vishwamitra spoke as if nothing had happened. 'Let the competition begin.'

The people in the room sat still, as if they had turned to stone, en masse. Vishwamitra spoke once again, louder this time. 'Let the competition begin. Prince Ram, please step up.'

Ram rose from his chair and walked up to the *Pinaka.* He bowed with reverence, folded his hands together into a namaste, and softly repeated an ancient chant: '*Om Rudr ya Namah.*' *The universe bows to Lord Rudra. I bow to Lord Rudra.*

He raised his right wrist and touched both his eyes with the red thread tied around it. He felt a charge run through his body as he touched the bow. Was this his devotion towards Lord Rudra, or did the bow unselfishly transmit its accumulated power to the prince of Ayodhya? Those seeking only factual knowledge would analyse what happened. Those in love with wisdom would simply enjoy the moment. Ram savoured the moment as he touched the bow again. He then brought his head down and placed it on the bow; he asked to be blessed.

He breathed steadily as he lifted the bow with ease. Sita, hidden behind a latticed window next to Kushadhwaj, looked at Ram intently with bated breath.

Ram placed one arm of the bow on a wooden stand placed on the ground. His shoulders, back and arms strained visibly as he pulled down the upper limb of the *Pinaka*, simultaneously pulling up the bowstring. His body laboured at the task, but his face remained serene. He bent the upper limb farther with a slight increase in effort as he tied the bowstring. His muscles relaxed as he let go of the upper limb and held the bow at the grip. He brought the bowstring close to his ear and plucked; the twang was perfect.

He picked up an arrow and walked to the copper-plated basin with deliberate, unhurried footsteps. He went down on one knee, held the bow horizontally above his head and looked down at the water; at the reflection of the fish that moved in a circle above him. The rippling water in the basin danced as if to tantalise his mind. Ram focused on the image of the fish to the exclusion of all else. He nocked the arrow on the string of the bow and pulled slowly with his right hand, his back erect, the core muscles activated with ideal tension. His breathing was steady and rhythmic. As was his consciousness, so was the response from the universe. He handed himself over to a higher force as he pulled the string all the way back and released the arrow. It shot up, as did the vision of each person in the room. The unmistakable sound of a furiously speeding arrow crashing into wood reverberated in the great hall. It had pierced the right eye of the fish, and lodged itself into the wooden wheel. The wheel swirled rhythmically as the shaft of the arrow drew circles in the air. Ram's mind reclaimed its awareness of the surroundings as his eyes continued to study the rippling water; he smiled. Not because he had hit the target. He had, in fact, earned a sense of completion of his being, with that shot. From this moment on, he was no longer alone.

He whispered, in the confines of his mind, a tribute to the woman he admired; Lord Rudra had said the same words to Lady Mohini, the woman he loved, many many centuries ago.

I have become alive. You have made me alive.

Chapter 24

The wedding was a simple set of solemn rituals, observed in the afternoon of the day that Ram won the *swayamvar*. To Ram's surprise, Sita had suggested that Lakshman and Urmila get married in the same auspicious hour of the day. To Ram's further disbelief, Lakshman had enthusiastically agreed. It was decided that while both the couples would be married in Mithila — to allow Sita and Urmila to travel with Ram and Lakshman to Ayodhya — a set of grand ceremonies would be held in Ayodhya as well; ones befitting the scions of the clan of Raghu.

Sita and Ram were alone at last. They sat on floor cushions in the dining hall, their dinner placed on a low stool. It was late in the evening, the sixth hour of the third *prahar*. Despite the fact that their relationship had been sanctified by *dharma* a few hours earlier, there was an awkwardness that underlined their ignorance of each other's personalities.

'Umm,' said Ram, as he stared at his plate.

'Yes, Ram?' asked Sita. 'Is there a problem?'

'I'm sorry, but … the food…'

'Is it not to your liking?'

'No, no, it's good. It's very good. But…'

'Yes?'

'It needs a bit of salt.'

Sita immediately pushed her plate aside, rose and clapped her hands. An attendant came rushing in.

'Get some salt for the prince, please.' As the attendant turned, Sita ordered with emphasis, 'Quickly!'

The attendant broke into a run.

Ram cleaned his hand with a napkin as he waited for the salt. 'I'm sorry to trouble you.'

Sita frowned as she resumed her seat. 'I'm your wife, Ram. It's my duty to take care of you.'

Ram smiled. 'Umm, may I ask you something?'

'Of course.'

'Tell me something about your childhood.'

'You mean, before I was adopted? You do know that I was adopted, right?'

'Yes... I mean, you don't have to talk about it if it troubles you.'

Sita smiled. 'No, it doesn't trouble me, but I don't remember anything. I was too young when I was found by my adoptive parents.'

Ram nodded.

Sita answered the question that she thought was on his mind. 'So, if you ask me who my birth-parents are, the short answer is that I don't know. But the one I prefer is that I am a daughter of the earth.'

'Birth is completely unimportant. It is just a means of entry into this *world of action*, into this *karmabhoomi*. Karma is all that matters. And your karma is divine.'

Sita smiled. Ram was about to say something when the attendant came rushing in with the salt. Ram added some to his food and resumed eating as the attendant retreated from the room.

'You were saying something,' said Sita.

'Yes,' said Ram, 'I think that…'

Ram was interrupted again, this time by the doorkeeper announcing loudly, 'The chief of the Malayaputras, the *Saptrishi Uttradhikari*, the protector of the way of the Vishnus, Maharishi Vishwamitra.'

Sita frowned and looked at Ram. Ram shrugged, clearly conveying he did not know what this visit was about.

Ram and Sita rose as Vishwamitra entered the room, followed by Arishtanemi. Sita gestured to her attendant to get some washing bowls for Ram and herself.

'We have a problem,' said Vishwamitra, not feeling the need to exchange pleasantries.

'What happened, Guru*ji*?' asked Ram.

'Raavan is mobilising for an attack.'

Ram frowned. 'But he doesn't have an army. What's he going to do with ten thousand bodyguards? He can't hold a city of even Mithila's size with that number. All he'll achieve is getting his men killed in battle.'

'Raavan is not a logical man,' proffered Vishwamitra. 'His ego is hurt. He may lose his bodyguard corps, but he will wreak havoc on Mithila.'

Ram looked at Sita, who shook her head with irritation and addressed Vishwamitra. 'Who in Lord Rudra's name was that demon invited for the *swayamvar*? I know it was not my father.'

Vishwamitra took a deep breath as his eyes softened. 'That's water under the bridge, Sita. The question is, what are we going to do now?'

'What is your plan, Guru*ji*?'

'I have with me some important material that was mined at my *ashram* by the Ganga. I needed it to conduct a few science experiments at Agastyakootam. This was why I had visited my *ashram*.'

Agastyakootam was the capital of the Malayaputras, deep in the south of India, beyond the Narmada River. In fact, it was very close to Lanka itself.

'Science experiments?' asked Ram.

'Yes, experiments with the *daivi astras*.'

Sita drew a sharp breath for she knew the power and ferocity of the *divine weapons*. 'Guru*ji*, are you suggesting that we use *daivi astras*?'

Vishwamitra nodded in confirmation as Ram spoke up. 'But that will destroy Mithila as well.'

'No, it won't. This is not a traditional *daivi astra*. What I have is the *Asuraastra*.'

'Isn't that a biological weapon?' asked Ram, deeply troubled now.

'Yes. Poisonous gas and a blast wave from the *Asuraastra* will incapacitate the Lankans, paralysing them for days on end. We can easily imprison them in that state and end this problem.'

'Just paralyse, Guru*ji*?' asked Ram. 'I have learnt that, in large quantities, the *Asuraastra* can kill as well.'

Vishwamitra knew that only one man could have possibly taught this to Ram. None of the other *daivi astra* experts had ever met this young man. He was immediately irritated. 'Do you have any better ideas?'

Ram fell silent.

'But what about Lord Rudra's law?' asked Sita.

Lord Rudra, the previous Mahadev who was the Destroyer of Evil, had banned the unauthorised use of *daivi astras* many centuries ago. Practically everyone obeyed this diktat from the fearsome Lord Rudra. Those who broke the law he had decreed would be punished with banishment for fourteen years. Breaking the law for the second time would be punishable by death.

'I don't think that law applies to the use of the *Asuraastra*,' said Vishwamitra. 'It is not a weapon of mass destruction, just mass incapacitation.'

Sita narrowed her eyes. Clearly, she wasn't convinced. 'I disagree. A *daivi astra* is a *daivi astra*. We cannot use it without the authorisation of the Vayuputras, Lord Rudra's tribe. I am a Lord Rudra devotee. I will not break his law.'

'Do you want to surrender, then?'

'Of course not! We will fight!'

Vishwamitra laughed derisively. 'Fight, is it? And who, please explain, will fight Raavan's hordes? The namby-pamby intellectuals of Mithila? What is the plan? Debate the Lankans to death?'

'We have our police force,' said Sita quietly.

'They're not trained or equipped to fight the troops of Raavan.'

'We are not fighting his troops. We are fighting his bodyguard platoons. My police force is enough for them.'

'They are not. And you know that.'

'We will not use the *daivi astras*, Guru*ji*,' said Sita firmly, her face hardening.

Ram spoke up. 'Samichi's police force is not alone. Lakshman and I are here, and so are the Malayaputras. We're inside the fort, we have the double walls; we have the lake surrounding the city. We can hold Mithila. We can fight.'

Vishwamitra turned to Ram with a sneer. '*Nonsense!* We are vastly outnumbered. The double walls...' He snorted with disgust. 'It seems clever. But how long do you think it will take a warrior of Raavan's calibre to figure out a strategy that works around that obstacle?'

'We will not use the *daivi astras*, Guru*ji*,' said Sita, raising her voice. 'Now, if you will excuse me, I have a battle to prepare for.'

It was late at night; the fourth hour of the fourth *prahar*. Ram and Sita had been joined by Lakshman and Samichi on top of the Bees Quarter, close to the inner wall edge. The entire Bees Quarter complex had been evacuated as a precautionary step. The pontoon bridge that spanned the moat-lake had been destroyed.

Mithila had a force of four thousand policemen and policewomen, enough to maintain law and order for the hundred thousand citizens of the small kingdom. Notwithstanding the strategic advantage of the double walls, would they be able to thwart an attack from the Lankan bodyguards of Raavan? They were outnumbered five to two.

Ram and Sita had abandoned any plans of securing the outer wall. They wanted Raavan and his soldiers to scale it and launch an assault on the inner walls; the Lankans would, then, be trapped between the two walls, which the Mithilan arrows would convert into a killing field. They expected a volley of arrows from the other side, in preparation for which the police had been asked to carry their wooden shields, normally used for crowd control within Mithila. Lakshman had taught them some basic manoeuvres with which they could protect themselves from the arrows.

'Where are the Malayaputras?' Lakshman asked Ram.

The Malayaputras had, much to Ram's surprise, not come to the battle-front. Ram whispered, 'I think it's just us.'

Lakshman shook his head and spat. 'Cowards.'

'Look!' said Samichi.

Sita and Lakshman looked in the direction that Samichi had pointed. Ram, on the other hand, was drawn to something else: a hint of nervousness in Samichi's voice. Unlike Sita, she appeared troubled. Perhaps she was not as brave as Sita believed her to be. Ram turned his attention to the enemy.

Torches lined the other side of the moat-lake that surrounded the outer wall of Mithila. Raavan's bodyguards had worked feverishly through the evening, chopping down trees from the forest and building rowboats to carry them across the lake.

Even as they watched, the Lankans began to push their boats into the moat-lake. The assault on Mithila was being launched.

'It's time,' said Sita.

'Yes,' said Ram. 'We have maybe another half hour before they hit our outer wall.'

— |大| 🐟 ☼ —

Conch shells resounded through the night, by now recognised as the signature sound of Raavan and his men. As they watched in the light of the flickering flames of torches, the Lankans propped giant ladders against the outer walls of Mithila.

'They are here,' said Ram. Messages were relayed quickly down the line to the Mithila police-soldiers. Ram expected a shower of arrows now from Raavan's archers. The Lankans would fire their arrows only as long as their soldiers were outside the outer wall. The shooting would stop the moment the Lankans climbed over. The archers would not risk hitting their own men.

A loud whoosh, like the sudden onrush of a gale, heralded the release of the arrows.

'Shields!' shouted Sita.

The Mithilans immediately raised their shields, ready for the Lankan arrows that were about to rain down on them. But Ram was perturbed. Something about the sound troubled him. It was much stronger than the sound of a thousand arrows being fired. It sounded like something much bigger. He was right.

Huge missiles rammed through the Mithilan defences with massive force. Desperate cries of agony mixed with sickening thuds as shields were ripped through and many in the Mithilan ranks were brought down in a flash.

'What is that?' screamed Lakshman, hiding behind his shield.

Ram's wooden shield snapped into two pieces as a missile tore through it like a knife through butter. It missed him by a hair's breadth. Ram looked at the fallen missile.

Spears!

Their wooden shields were a protection against arrows, not large spears.

How in Lord Rudra's name are they throwing spears over this distance? It's impossible!

The first volley was over and Ram knew they had but a few minutes of respite before the next. He looked around him.

'Lord Rudra, be merciful…'

The destruction was severe. At least a quarter of the Mithilans were either dead or severely injured, impaled on massive spears that had brutally ripped through their shields and bodies.

Ram looked at Sita as he commanded, 'Another volley will be fired any moment! Into the houses!'

'Into the houses!' shouted Sita.

'Into the houses!' repeated the lieutenants, as everybody ran towards the doors, lifted them and jumped in. It was one of the most disorganised retreats ever seen, but it was effective. In a few minutes, practically every surviving Mithilan police-soldier had jumped to safety within the houses. As the doors closed, the volley of spears resumed on the roofs of the Bees Quarter. A few stragglers were killed as the rest made it to safety; for now.

Lakshman did not say anything as he looked at Ram. But his eyes sent out a clear message. *This is a disaster.*

'What now?' Ram asked Sita. 'Raavan's soldiers must be scaling the outer walls. They will be upon us soon. There's no one to stop them.'

Sita was breathing hard, her eyes flitting like that of a cornered tigress, anger bursting through every pore. Samichi stood behind her princess, helplessly rubbing her forehead.

'Sita?' prompted Ram.

Sita's eyes suddenly opened wide. 'The windows!'

'What?' asked Samichi, surprised by her prime minister.

Sita immediately gathered her lieutenants around her. She ordered them to get the surviving Mithilans to break the wood-panel-sealed windows of the houses in the Bees Quarter; the ones that shared the inner wall, or opened into the narrow gaps between some of the houses; like the one they were in. Their window overlooked the ground between the two fort walls. Arrows would be fired at the charging Lankans, after all.

'Brilliant!' shouted Lakshman, as he rushed to a barricaded window. He pulled back his arm, flexed his muscles, and punched hard at the wood, smashing the barricade with one mighty blow.

All the houses in this section of the Bees Quarter were internally connected through corridors. The message travelled rapidly. Within moments, the Mithilans smashed open the sealed windows and fired arrows at the Lankans, caught between the outer and inner wall. The Lankans had expected no resistance. They were effectively caught off-guard and arrows shredded through their lines. The losses were heavy. The Mithilans fired arrows without respite, killing as many of the Lankans as they could, slowing the charge dramatically.

Suddenly, the conch shells sounded; but this time, they played a different tune. The Lankans immediately turned and ran, retreating as rapidly as they had arrived.

A loud cheer went up from the Mithilan quarters. They had beaten back the first attack.

Ram, Sita and Lakshman stood on the roof of the Bees Quarter as dawn broke through. The gentle rays of the sun threw into poignant contrast the harsh devastation of the Lankan spears. The damage was heart-rending.

Sita stared at the mutilated bodies of the Mithilans strewn all around her: heads hanging by a sinew to bodies, some with their guts spilled out, many simply impaled on spears, having bled to death. 'At least a thousand of my soldiers…'

'We too have hit them hard, *Bhabhi*,' said Lakshman to his *sister-in-law*. 'There are at least a thousand dead Lankans lying between the inner and the outer wall.'

Sita looked at Lakshman, her usually limpid eyes now brimming with tears. 'Yes, but they have nine thousand left. We have only three thousand.'

Ram surveyed the Lankan camp on the other side of the moat-lake. Hospital-tents had been set up to tend to the injured. Many Lankans, though, were furiously at work: hacking trees and pushing the forest line farther with mathematical precision. Clearly they did not intend to retreat.

'They will be better prepared next time,' said Ram. 'If they manage to scale the inner wall ... it's over.'

Sita placed her hand on Ram's shoulder and sighed as she stared at the ground. Ram found himself being momentarily distracted by her nearness. He looked at Sita's hand on his shoulder, then closed his eyes. He had to focus, teach his mind to re-learn the art of mastering his emotions.

Sita turned around and looked towards her city. Her eyes rested on the steeple of the massive temple dedicated to Lord Rudra, which loomed beyond the garden of the Bees Quarter. Fierce determination blazed from her eyes, resolve pouring steel into her veins. 'It's not over yet. I'll call upon the citizens to join me. Even if my people stand here with kitchen knives, we will outnumber the Lankan scum ten to one. We can fight them.'

Ram could not bring himself to share her confidence.

Sita nodded, like she had made up her mind, and rushed away, signalling other Mithilans to follow her.

Chapter 25

'Where have you been, Guru*ji*?' asked Ram, in a polite voice that belied the fury that defined his stony face and rigid body.

Vishwamitra had finally arrived in the fifth hour of the first *prahar*. The early morning light sharply outlined the frenetic activity in the Lankan camp. Sita was still trying to rally a citizen-army. Arishtanemi stood at a distance, strangely choosing to remain out of earshot.

'Where were the Malayaputra cowards, actually?' growled Lakshman, who did not feel the need for any attempt at politeness.

Vishwamitra cast Lakshman a withering look before addressing Ram. 'Someone has to be the adult here and do what must be done.'

Ram frowned.

'Come with me,' said Vishwamitra.

— |大| 🐟 ☼ —

In a hidden section of the roof of the Bees Quarter, far from the scene of the Lankan attack, Ram finally confronted what the Malayaputras had been busy with all night: the *Asuraastra*.

A simple weapon to configure, it had still taken a long time to set up. Vishwamitra and his Malayaputras had worked through the night, in minimal light. The missile and its launch stand were finally assembled and ready. The stand was a little taller than Lakshman and was made of wood. The outer body of the missile was made of lead. Its components, along with the core material that had been mined at the Ganga *ashram*, had been brought along by Vishwamitra and his party to Mithila. The core material was now loaded in the detonation chamber.

The missile was ready but Ram was unsure.

He looked across the outer wall.

The Lankans were hard at work, clearing the forest. They were building something.

'What are those people doing at the far end of the forest line?' asked Lakshman.

'Look closely,' said Vishwamitra.

A group of Lankans were working with planks fashioned from the trees that had been cut. At first Lakshman thought they were building boats, but a careful examination proved him wrong. They were linking these planks into giant rectangular shields with sturdy handles on the sides as well as at the base end. Each shield was capable of protecting twenty men, if they were lined up two abreast.

'Tortoise shields,' said Ram.

'Yes,' said Vishwamitra. 'They will return once they build enough of these. They will break the outer wall without any resistance from us; why scale it? They will move towards our inner wall, protected by their tortoise shields. Successive waves of attacks will breach our walls. You know what will be done to the city. Even the rats will not be spared.'

Ram stood quietly. He knew that Vishwamitra was right. They could see that fifteen or twenty of these massive shields were already ready. The Lankans had worked at a prodigious pace. An attack was imminent, probably as early as tonight. Mithila would certainly not be ready.

'You need to understand that firing the *Asuraastra* is the only solution available,' said Vishwamitra. 'Fire it right now, when they're still not ready, and are farthest away from the city. Once they launch the attack and breach the outer wall, we will not be able to do even this, without risking Mithila; the detonation would be too close.'

Ram stared at the Lankans.

This is the only way!

'Why don't *you* fire the weapon, Guru*ji*?' asked Lakshman, sarcasm dripping from his voice.

'I am a Malayaputra; the leader of the Malayaputras,' said Vishwamitra. 'The Vayuputras and the Malayaputras work in partnership, just as the Vishnus and the Mahadevs did over millennia. I cannot break the Vayuputra law.'

'But my brother choosing to do so is okay?'

'You can also choose to die. That option is always available,' Vishwamitra said caustically. Then he turned and spoke to Ram directly, 'So, what will it be, Ram?'

Ram turned around and looked in the direction of the Mithila palace, where Sita was probably trying desperately to convince her reluctant citizens to fight.

Vishwamitra stepped close to the prince of Ayodhya. 'Ram, Raavan will probably torture and kill every single person in this city. The lives of a hundred thousand Mithilans are at stake. Your wife's life is at stake. Will you, as a husband, protect your wife or not? Will you take a sin upon your soul for the good of others? What does your *dharma* say?'

I will do it for Sita.

'We will warn them first,' said Ram. 'Give them a chance to retreat. I have been told that even the Asuras followed this protocol before firing any *daivi astra.*'

'Fine.'

'And if they don't heed our warning,' said Ram, his fingers wrapping themselves around his Rudraaksh pendant, as if for strength, 'then I will fire the *Asuraastra.*'

Vishwamitra smiled with satisfaction, as though Ram's compliance was a trophy he had just earned.

The giant bear-man moved among the men, checking the tortoise shields. He heard the arrow a second before it slammed into the plank of wood close to his feet. He looked up in surprise.

Who in Mithila can fire an arrow that could travel this distance with such unerring accuracy?

He stared at the walls. All he could make out were two very tall men standing close to the inner wall, and a third, a trifle shorter. The third man held a bow; he seemed to be staring directly at him.

The bear-man immediately stepped forward to examine the arrow that had buried itself into the tortoise shield. It had a piece of parchment tied around its shaft. He yanked it out and untied the note.

'You actually believe they will do this, Kumbhakarna?' asked Raavan, snorting with disgust as he threw the note away.

'*Dada*,' said the bear-man, his voice booming even at its lowest amplitude, due to his massive vocal chords. 'If they fire an *Asuraastra*, it could be—'

'They don't have an *Asuraastra*,' interrupted Raavan. 'They're bluffing.'

'But *Dada*, the Malayaputras do have—'

'Vishwamitra is bluffing, Kumbhakarna!'

Kumbhakarna fell silent.

— 𑀧 🐟 ☼ —

'They haven't retreated an inch,' said Vishwamitra, with urgency. 'We need to fire the weapon.'

By the end of the third hour of the second *prahar*, the sun had risen high enough to afford good visibility. Three hours earlier, Ram had shot the warning message to the Lankans. It had clearly made no impact.

The Malayaputras had already rolled the missile tower to the section of the rooftop that faced the main body of the Lankan troops.

'We gave them a warning of one hour,' continued Vishwamitra. 'We have waited for three. They probably think we are bluffing by now.'

Lakshman looked at Vishwamitra. 'Don't you think we should check with Sita *Bhabhi*, first? She had clearly said that—'

Vishwamitra suddenly interrupted Lakshman. 'Look!'

Lakshman and Ram immediately turned in the direction Vishwamitra had pointed.

'Are they boarding their boats?' asked Ram.

'They could be testing them,' said Lakshman, hoping against hope. 'In which case, we still have some time.'

'Do you think we should take that chance, Ram?' asked Vishwamitra.

Ram did not move a muscle.

'We need to fire now!' said Vishwamitra, forcefully.

Ram lifted his bow from his shoulders, brought it close to his ear, and plucked the bowstring. *Perfect.*

'Bravo!' said Vishwamitra.

Lakshman glared at the maharishi. He touched his brother's shoulder. '*Dada…*'

Ram turned around and began walking away. Everyone followed him. Most *daivi astras* were fired from a distance by shooting a flaming arrow into a target on the launch pad. This protected the people igniting the weapon from getting incinerated in the initial launch explosion of the missile. Only a skilled archer could fire an arrow from a great distance and hit a target that was no larger than a fruit.

Vishwamitra halted Ram when they reached a distance of over five hundred metres from the *Asuraastra* stand. 'That's enough, Prince of Ayodhya.'

Arishtanemi handed him an arrow. Ram sniffed its tip; it had been coated with a combustible paste. He examined the fletching and was momentarily surprised. Arishtanemi had, clearly, used one of Ram's own arrows. He didn't stop to think too deeply if Arishtanemi had learnt Ram's secret of the spinning arrow. This was not the time. He nodded to Arishtanemi and faced the missile launch tower.

'*Dada…*' murmured Lakshman. He was visibly distressed at what he knew would take an immense toll on his law-abiding brother.

'Step back, Lakshman,' said Ram, as he flexed forward to stretch his back. Lakshman, Vishwamitra and Arishtanemi moved away. Ram slowed down his breathing without forcing the process; it reduced his heart rate in tandem. He stared at the missile launch tower as his mind drowned out the sounds around him. He squeezed his eyes as the rhythm of time slowed down, as if to keep pace with his heart beats; everything around him seemed to shift into slow motion. A crow flew over the *Asuraastra* tower, flapping its wings as it attempted to fly higher. Ram followed the movement of the crow's wings. It seemed to require less effort for the bird to gain height; it had wind beneath its wings.

Ram's mind processed this new information: the wind was blowing leftwards close to the tower. He flicked his thumb on the arrow tip and the flames burst through. He shifted his hand to hold the arrow by its fletching. He nocked it on the bowstring, allowing the shaft to rest between his left thumb and forefinger as his hand gripped the bow firmly. Ram tipped the bow slightly upwards, factoring in the parabolic movement that the arrow would need. Arishtanemi knew this was unorthodox; the angle of the arrow was a lot lower than he would have kept. But he was also aware of Ram's immense talent with the bow and arrow; and, of course, of the brilliant design of the arrow fletching. He did not say a word.

Ram took aim and focused on the target; it was a pineapple-sized red square, over five hundred metres away. The waving windsock next to the target was within his concentration zone; all else faded into nothingness. The sock had been pointing left, but it suddenly drooped completely. The wind had stopped.

Ram pulled the string back in that instant, but held steady. His forearm was at a slight angle upwards from the ground, his elbow aligned with the arrow, the weight of the bow transferred to the back muscle. His forearm was rigid, the bowstring touching his lips. The bow was stretched to its maximum capacity, the flaming arrowhead now touching his left hand. The windsock remained slumped. Ram released the arrow, flicking the fletching as he did, making the arrow spin rapidly as it sped forward. The spin made it face less wind resistance. Arishtanemi savoured the archery skill on display; it was almost poetic. This was why Ram could fire the arrow at a lower height despite the distance. The parabola was sharper as the arrow moved at a faster pace, the spin maintaining its fearsome speed as it tore through the air.

Kumbhakarna saw the flaming arrow being released by the archer. His instincts kicked in as he turned around, screaming loudly. '*Dada*!'

He charged towards his brother; Raavan stood at the massive door of the *Pushpak Vimaan*.

The arrow slammed into the small red square on the *Asuraastra* tower, pushing it backwards instantly. The fire from the arrow was captured in a receptacle behind the red square, and then it spread rapidly into the fuel chamber that powered the missile. In a flash, the initial launch explosions of the *Asuraastra* were heard. A few seconds later, heavy flames gathered near the base of the missile and then rose, steadily picking up pace.

Kumbhakarna threw his weight on his brother, who went flying backwards into the *Pushpak Vimaan*.

The *Asuraastra* flew in a mighty arc, covering the distance across the walls of Mithila in a few short seconds. None on the roof of the Mithila Bees Quarter could tear their eyes away from the spectacle. As the missile flew high above the moat-lake, there was a small, almost inaudible explosion, like that of a fire cracker meant for a child.

Lakshman's awe was quickly replaced by disappointment. He frowned. 'That's it? Is that the famed *Asuraastra*?'

Vishwamitra answered laconically. 'Cover your ears.'

Kumbhakarna, meanwhile, rose from the floor of the *Pushpak Vimaan* even as Raavan lay sprawled inside. He rushed to the door and hit the metallic button on the sidewall with his full body weight. The door of the *Pushpak Vimaan* began to slide as the bear-man watched, straining his muscles as if to lend it speed.

The *Asuraastra* hovered above the Lankans and exploded with an ear-shattering boom that shook the very walls of Mithila. Many Lankan soldiers felt their eardrums burst, sucking the air from their mouths. But this was only a prelude to the devastation that would follow.

Even as an eerie silence followed the explosion, the spectators on the Mithila rooftop saw a bright green flash of light emerge from where the missile had splintered. It burst with furious intensity as it hit the Lankans below like a flash of lightning. They stayed rooted, stunned into a temporary paralytic immobility. Fragments of the exploded missile showered on them mercilessly.

Kumbhakarna saw the flash of green light as the door of the *Pushpak Vimaan* slid shut. Even as the door sealed and locked automatically, saving those inside the flying vehicle from any further damage by the *Asuraastra*, Kumbhakarna collapsed, unconscious. Raavan rushed to his younger brother, screaming loudly.

'By the great Lord Rudra,' whispered Lakshman, cold fear having gripped his heart. He looked at his brother, similarly staggered by what he was witnessing.

'It's not over,' warned Vishwamitra.

A dreadful hissing sound became suddenly audible, like the battle-cry of a gigantic snake. Simultaneously, the fragments of the *Asuraastra* missile that had fallen to the ground emitted demonic clouds of green gas, which spread like a shroud over the stupefied Lankans.

'What is that?' asked Ram.

'That gas,' said Vishwamitra, 'is the *Asuraastra*.'

The deathly, thick gas gently enveloped the Lankans. It would put them in a coma that would last for days, if not weeks. It would possibly kill some of them. But there were no screams, no cries for mercy. None made an attempt to escape. They simply lay on the ground, motionless, waiting for the fiendish *Asuraastra* to push them into oblivion. The only sound in the otherwise grim silence was the hiss...

Ram touched his Rudraaksh pendant, his heart benumbed.

An agonising fifteen minutes later, Vishwamitra turned to Ram. 'It's done.'

Sita bounded up the stairway of the Bees Quarter, three steps at a time. She had been passionately conversing with the citizens of Mithila in the market square when she heard the explosion and saw the sudden flash in the sky. She had immediately known that the *Asuraastra* had been fired. She knew she had to rush back.

She first encountered Arishtanemi and the Malayaputras, standing in a huddle, away from Vishwamitra, Ram and Lakshman. A grim-faced Samichi followed Sita.

'Who shot it?' demanded Sita.

Arishtanemi just stepped aside, and Ram came into Sita's view, the only one holding a bow.

Sita cursed loudly as she ran towards her husband; she knew that he must be shattered. Ram, with his moral clarity and obsession with the law, would have been hurting inside at the sin he had been forced to commit. Forced by his sense of duty towards his wife and her people.

Vishwamitra smiled as he saw her approach. 'Sita, it is all taken care of! Raavan's forces are destroyed. Mithila is safe.'

Sita glared at Vishwamitra, too furious to say anything. She ran right up to her husband and embraced him. A shocked Ram dropped his bow. He had never been embraced by Sita. He knew that she was trying to comfort him. Yet, as he held his hands to the side, his heartbeat started picking up. The emotional overload drained him of energy as he felt a solitary tear trickle down his face.

Sita pulled her head back as she held Ram and looked deep into his empty eyes. Her face was creased with concern. 'I am with you, Ram.'

Ram remained silent. Strangely, a long-forgotten image entered his mind: of the *arya* concept of Emperor Prithu; Prithvi, the earth, had been named after him. Prithu had spoken of the ideal human archetype of the *aryaputra*, a 'gentleman', and the *aryaputri*, a 'lady', a prototypical human partnership of two strong individuals, who didn't compete for exact equality but were complementary, completing each other. Two souls that were dependent on each other, giving each other purpose; two halves of a whole.

Ram felt like an *aryaputra*, being held, being supported, by his lady.

Sita continued to hold Ram in a tight embrace. 'I am with you, Ram. We will handle this together.'

Ram closed his eyes. He wrapped his arms around his wife. He rested his head on her shoulder. *Paradise.*

Sita looked over her husband's shoulder and glared at Vishwamitra. It was a fearsome look, like the wrathful fury of the Mother Goddess.

Vishwamitra glared right back, unrepentant.

A loud sound disturbed them all. They looked beyond the walls of Mithila. Raavan's *Pushpak Vimaan* was sputtering to life. Its giant rotor blades had begun to spin. Within moments they picked up speed and the flying vehicle rose from the earth, hovering just a few feet above the ground. Then, with a great burst of sound and energy, it soared into the sky; away from Mithila, and the devastation of the *Asuraastra*.

Chapter 26

Sita cast an eye over her husband as he rode beside her. Lakshman and Urmila rode behind them. Lakshman was talking non-stop with his wife as she gazed at him earnestly. Urmila's thumb kept playing with the massive diamond ring on her left forefinger; an expensive gift from her husband. Behind them were a hundred Mithilan soldiers. Another hundred soldiers rode ahead of Ram and Sita. The convoy was on its way to Sankashya, from where it would sail to Ayodhya.

Ram, Sita, Lakshman and Urmila had set off from Mithila two weeks after the *Asuraastra* laid waste the Lankan camp. King Janak and his brother, King Kushadhwaj, had authorised the imprisonment of the Lankan prisoners-of-war left behind by Raavan. Vishwamitra and his Malayaputras left for their own capital, Agastyakootam, taking the Lankan prisoners with them. The sage intended to negotiate with Raavan on Mithila's behalf, guaranteeing the kingdom's safety in return for the release of the prisoners-of-war. It was a difficult decision for Sita to leave her friend Samichi behind, but the police force of Mithila could not afford a change in leadership at this vulnerable moment of time.

'Ram...'

Ram turned to his wife with a smile as he pulled his horse close to hers. 'Yes?'

'Are you sure about this?'

Ram nodded. There was no doubt in his mind.

'But you are the first in a generation to defeat Raavan. And, it wasn't really a *daivi astra*. If you—'

Ram frowned. 'That's a technicality. And you know it.'

Sita took a deep breath and continued. 'Sometimes, to create a perfect world, a leader has to do what is necessary at the time; even if it may not appear to be the "right" thing to do in the short term. In the long run, a leader who has the capacity to uplift the masses must not deny himself that opportunity. He has a duty to not make himself unavailable. A true leader will even take a sin upon his soul for the good of his people.'

Ram looked at Sita. He seemed disappointed. 'I have done that already, haven't I? The question is, should I be punished for it or not? Should I do penance for it? If I expect my people to follow the law, so must I. A leader is not just one who leads. He must also be a role model. He must practise what he preaches, Sita.'

Sita smiled. 'Well, Lord Rudra had said: "A leader is not just one who gives his people what they want. He must also be the one who teaches his people to be better than they imagined themselves to be".'

Ram smiled too. 'And I'm sure you will tell me Lady Mohini's response to this as well.'

Sita laughed. 'Yes. Lady Mohini said that people have their limitations. A leader should not expect more from them than what they are capable of. If you stretch them beyond their capacity, they will break.'

Ram shook his head. He did not really agree with the great Lady Mohini, respected by many as a Vishnu; though many others believed that she should not be called a Vishnu. Ram expected people to rise above their limitations and better themselves; for only then is an ideal society possible. But he didn't voice his disagreement aloud.

'Are you sure? Fourteen years outside the boundaries of the Sapt Sindhu?' Sita looked at Ram seriously, returning to the original discussion.

Ram nodded. He had already made his decision. He would go to Ayodhya and seek permission from his father to go on his self-imposed exile. 'I broke Lord Rudra's law. And this is his stated punishment. It doesn't matter whether the Vayuputras pass the order to punish me or not. It doesn't matter whether my people support me or not. I must serve my sentence.'

Sita leaned towards him and whispered, 'We ... not I.'

Ram frowned.

Sita reached out and placed her palm on Ram's hand. 'You share my fate and I share yours. That is what a true marriage is.' She entwined her fingers through his. 'Ram, I am your wife. We will always be together; in good times and bad; through thick and thin.'

Ram squeezed her hand as he straightened his back. His horse snorted and quickened its pace. Ram pulled back the reins gently, keeping his horse in step with his wife's steed.

'I'm not sure this will work,' said Ram.

The newly-wed couples, Ram-Sita and Lakshman-Urmila, were on the royal ship of Ayodhya, sailing up the Sarayu, on their way home. They would probably reach Ayodhya within a week.

Ram and Sita sat on the deck discussing what an ideal society meant, and the manner in which a perfect empire must be governed. For Ram, an ideal state was one which treated everyone as equal before the law.

Sita had thought long and hard about the meaning of equality. She felt that just promoting equality before the law would not solve society's problems. She believed that true equality existed only at the level of the soul. But in this material world, everyone was, in fact, not equal. No two created entities were exactly the same. Among humans, some were better at knowledge, others at warfare, some at trading and others offered their manual skills and hard work. However, the problem, according to Sita, was that in the present society, a person's path in life was determined by his birth, not by his karma. She believed that a society would be perfect only if people were free to do what they actually wanted to, based on their karma, rather than following the diktats of the caste they were born into.

And where did these diktats come from? They came from parents, who forced their values and ways on their children. Brahmin parents would encourage and push their child towards the pursuit of knowledge. The child, on the other hand, may have a passion for trade. These mismatches led to unhappiness and chaos within society. Furthermore, the society itself suffered as its people were forced to work at jobs they didn't want to do. The worst end of this stick was reserved for the poor Shudras. Many of them could have been capable Brahmins, Kshatriyas or Vaishyas, but the rigid and unfair birth-based caste system forced them to remain skill-workers. In an earlier era, the caste system had been flexible. The best example of that was from many centuries ago: Maharishi Shakti, now known as Ved Vyas, a title used through successive ages for those who compiled, edited or differentiated the Vedas. He was born a Shudra, but his karma turned him into not just a Brahmin, but a *rishi*. A *rishi* was the highest status, below Godhood, that any person could achieve. However, today, due to the rigid birth-based caste system, a Maharishi Shakti emerging from among the Shudras was almost impossible.

'You may think this is unworkable; you may even consider it harsh. I concede your point that all should be equal before the law and equally deserving of respect. But just that is not enough. We need to be harsh to destroy this birth-based caste system,' said Sita. 'It has weakened our *dharma* and our country. It must be destroyed for the good of India. If we don't destroy the caste system as it exists today, we will open ourselves to attacks from foreigners. They will use our divisions to conquer us.'

Sita's solution, which indeed seemed harsh to Ram, would be complicated to implement. She proposed that all the children of a kingdom must be compulsorily adopted by the state at the time of birth. The birth-parents would have to surrender their children to the kingdom. The kingdom would raise these children, educate and hone the natural skills that they were born with. At the age of fifteen, they would appear for an examination that would test them on their physical, psychological and mental skills. Based on the result, appropriate castes would be allocated to the children. Subsequent training would further polish their natural talent, after which the children would be put up for adoption by citizens from the same caste as the ones assigned to the adolescents through the examination process. The children would never know their birth-parents, only their caste-parents.

'I agree that this system would be exceedingly fair,' conceded Ram. 'But I can't imagine parents willingly giving up their birth-children to the kingdom permanently, making the decision never to meet them again, or even know them. Is it even natural?'

'Humans moved away from the "natural way" when we began to wear clothes, cook our food and embraced cultural norms over instinctive urges. This is what civilisation does. Among the "civilised", right and wrong is determined by cultural conventions and rules. There were times when polygamy was considered abhorrent, and other times when it was considered a solution when there was a shortage of men due to war. And now, for all you know, you may succeed in bringing monogamy back in fashion!'

Ram laughed. 'I'm not trying to start a trend. I don't want to marry another woman because I will be insulting you by doing so.'

Sita smiled as she pushed her long, straight hair away from her face as it dried in the breeze. 'But polygamy is unfair only according to you; others may disagree. Remember, justice in terms of "right" or "wrong" is a man-made concept. It is entirely up to us to define justice in new terms of what is fair or unfair. It will be for the greater good.'

'Hmm, but it will be very difficult to implement, Sita.'

'No more difficult than getting the people of India to actually respect laws!' laughed Sita, for she knew that was Ram's pet obsession.

Ram laughed loudly. '*Touché!*'

Sita moved close to Ram and held his hand. Ram bent forward and kissed her, a slow, gentle kiss that filled their souls with deep happiness. Ram held his wife as they observed the Sarayu waters flowing by and the green riverbanks in the distance.

'We didn't finish that Somras conversation... What were

you thinking?' asked Sita.

'I think it should either be made available to all or to none. It's not fair that a few chosen ones from the nobility get to live so much longer, and be healthier, than most others.'

'But how would you ever be able to produce enough Somras for everyone?'

'Guru Vashishta has invented a technology that can mass-produce it. If I rule Ayodhya—'

'When,' interrupted Sita.

'Sorry?'

'*When* you rule Ayodhya,' said Sita. 'Not "if". It will happen, even if it is fourteen years from now.'

Ram smiled. 'All right, *when* I rule Ayodhya, I intend to build this factory that Guru Vashishta has designed. We will offer the Somras to all.'

'If you are going to create an entirely new way of life, then you must have a new name for it as well. Why carry the karma of the old?'

'Something tells me you have thought of a name already!'

'A land of pure life.'

'That's the name?'

'No. That is simply what the name will mean.'

'So, what will be the new name of my kingdom?'

Sita smiled. 'It will be Meluha.'

—— 大 ▮ ☼ ——

'Are you insane?' shouted Dashrath.

The emperor was in his new private office in Kaushalya's palace. Ram had just informed Dashrath about his decision to banish himself from the Sapt Sindhu to atone for the sin of firing a *daivi astra* without the permission of the Vayuputras; a decision that had not gone down too well with Dashrath, to say the least.

A worried Kaushalya hurried to her husband and tried to get him to remain seated. His health had been deteriorating rapidly of late. 'Please calm down, Your Majesty.'

Kaushalya, still unsure of the influence that Kaikeyi exercised over Dashrath, had remained careful in her dealings with her husband. She wasn't sure how long she would remain Dashrath's favourite queen. To her, he was still 'His Majesty'. But this kid-glove treatment only agitated Dashrath further.

'In Lord Parshu Ram's name, Kaushalya, stop mollycoddling me and knock some sense into your son,' screamed Dashrath. 'What do you think will happen if he is gone for fourteen years? Do you think the nobles will just wait around patiently for his return?'

'Ram,' said Kaushalya. 'Your father is right. Nobody has asked for you to be punished. The Vayuputras have not made any demands.'

'They will,' said Ram in a steady voice. 'It's only a matter of time.'

'But we don't have to listen to them. We do not follow their laws!'

'If I expect others to follow the law, then so should I.'

'Are you trying to be suicidal, Ram?' asked Dashrath, his face flushed, his hands trembling in anger.

'I am only following the law, Father.'

'Can't you see what my health is like? I will be gone soon. If you are not here, Bharat will become king. And, if you are out of the Sapt Sindhu for fourteen years, by the time you return Bharat will have consolidated his rule. You will not even get a village to govern.'

'Firstly, Father, if you pronounce Bharat crown prince when I am gone, then it is his right to become king. And I think Bharat will make a good ruler. Ayodhya will not suffer. But if you continue with me as the crown prince even while I'm in exile, I am sure that Bharat will give back the throne to me when I return. I trust him completely.'

Dashrath laughed harshly. 'You actually think it will be Bharat ruling Ayodhya once you're gone? *No!* It will be his mother. And Kaikeyi will have you killed in exile, son.'

'I will not allow myself to be killed, Father. But if I am killed, maybe that is what fate has in store for me.'

Dashrath banged his fist on his head, his frustration ringing loudly through the angry grunt he let out.

'Father, my mind is made up,' said Ram with finality. 'But if I leave without your permission, it will be an insult to you; and an insult to Ayodhya. How can a crown prince disobey the king's orders? That's why I am asking you to please banish me.'

Dashrath turned to Kaushalya, throwing up his hands in frustration.

'This is going to happen, Father, whether you like it or not,' said Ram. 'Your banishing me will keep Ayodhya's honour intact. So, please do it.'

Dashrath's shoulders drooped in resignation. 'At least agree with my other suggestion.'

Ram stood resolute, but with an apologetic expression on his face. *No.*

'But Ram, if you marry a princess from a powerful kingdom, then you will have a strong ally when you return to claim your inheritance. Kekaya will never side with you. Ashwapati is Kaikeyi's father after all. But if you marry a princess from another powerful kingdom, then—'

'My apologies for interrupting you, Father. But I have always maintained that I will marry only one woman. And I have. I will not insult her by marrying another.'

Dashrath stared at him helplessly.

Ram felt he needed to clarify further. 'And if my wife dies, I will mourn her for the rest of my life. But I will never ever marry again.'

Kaushalya finally lost her temper. 'What do you mean by that, Ram? Are you trying to imply that your own father will get your wife killed?'

'I didn't say that, Mother,' said Ram, calmly.

'Ram, please understand,' pleaded Dashrath, desperately trying to keep his temper in check. 'She is the princess of Mithila, a minor kingdom. She will not prove to be of any use in the struggle you will face ahead.'

Ram stiffened, but kept his voice polite. 'She is my wife, Father. Please speak of her with respect.'

'She is a lovely girl, Ram,' said Dashrath. 'I have been observing her for the last few days. She is a good wife. She will keep you happy. And you can remain married to her. But if you marry another princess, then—'

'Forgive me, Father. But no.'

'Dammit!' screamed Dashrath. 'Get out of here before I burst a blood vessel!'

'Yes, Father,' said Ram, and calmly turned to leave.

'And you are not leaving this city without my order!' yelled Dashrath at Ram's retreating form.

Ram looked back, his face inscrutable. With deliberate movements, he bowed his head, folded his hands into a namaste, and said, 'May all the Gods of our great land continue to bless you, Father.' And then, with equal lack of haste, he turned and walked out.

Dashrath glared at Kaushalya, rage pouring out of his eyes. His wife cowered with an apologetic expression on her face, as though she had somehow failed him in this show of will by Ram.

Chapter 27

On returning to his section of the palace, Ram was told that his wife was out, visiting the royal garden. He decided to join her, and found her in conversation with Bharat. Just like everyone else, his brother had initially been shocked when he heard about Ram's marriage to an adopted princess from a small kingdom. However, within a short span of time, Bharat had grown to respect Sita, her intelligence and strength of character. The two had spent a lot of time with each other, finding a deep sense of appreciation for the qualities they discovered in the other.

'…Which is why I think freedom is the most important attribute of life, *Bhabhi*,' said Bharat.

'More important than the law?' asked Sita.

'Yes. I believe there should be as few laws as possible; enough just to provide a framework within which human creativity can express itself in all its glory. Freedom is the natural way of life.'

Sita laughed softly. 'And what does your elder brother have to say about your views?'

Ram walked up to them from behind and placed his hands on his wife's shoulders. 'His elder brother thinks that Bharat is a dangerous influence!'

Bharat burst out laughing as he rose to embrace his brother. '*Dada*…'

'Should I be thanking you for entertaining your *bhabhi* with your libertarian views?!'

Bharat smiled as he shrugged. 'At least I won't convert the citizens of Ayodhya into a bunch of bores!'

Ram laughed and said, tongue in cheek, 'That's good then!'

Bharat's expression instantly transformed and became sombre. 'Father is not going to let you go, *Dada*. Even *you* know that. You're not going anywhere.'

'Father doesn't have a choice. And neither do you. You will rule Ayodhya. And you will rule it well.'

'I will not ascend the throne this way,' said Bharat, shaking his head. 'No, I will not.'

Ram knew that there was nothing he could say that would ease Bharat's pain.

'*Dada*, why are you insisting on this?' asked Bharat.

'It's the law, Bharat,' said Ram. 'I fired a *daivi astra*.'

'The hell with the law, *Dada*! Do you actually think your leaving will be in the best interests of Ayodhya? Imagine what the two of us can achieve together; your emphasis on rules and mine on freedom and creativity. Do you think either you or I can be as effective alone?'

Ram shook his head. 'I'll be back in fourteen years, Bharat. Even you just conceded that rules have a significant place in a society. How can I convince others to follow the law if I don't do so myself? The law must apply equally and fairly to every single person. It is as simple as that.' Then Ram stared directly into Bharat's eyes. 'Even if it helps a heinous criminal escape death, the law should not be broken.'

Bharat stared right back, his expression inscrutable.

Sita, sensing that the brothers were talking about something else and that things were getting decidedly uncomfortable, rose from the bench and said to Ram, 'You have a meeting with General Mrigasya.'

'I don't mean to be rude, but are you sure that your wife should be here?' asked Mrigasya, the general of the Ayodhyan army.

Ram and Sita had received the general in their private office.

'There are no secrets between us,' said Ram. 'In any case, I would tell her what has been discussed. She may as well hear it directly from you.'

Mrigasya cast an enigmatic look at Sita, and let out a long breath before addressing Ram. 'You can be emperor right away.'

The king of Ayodhya automatically became the emperor of the Sapt Sindhu; this had been the privilege of the Suryavanshi clan that ruled Kosala, since the days of Raghu. Mrigasya was offering to smoothen the path for Ram to ascend the throne of Ayodhya.

Sita was stunned, but kept her face deadpan. Ram frowned.

Mrigasya misunderstood what was going through Ram's mind. He assumed that Ram was wondering why the general would help him, when one of his officials had been penalised on the orders of the prince, for what Mrigasya thought was a minor crime of land-grabbing.

'I am willing to forget what you did to me,' said Mrigasya, 'if you are willing to remember what I am doing for you right now.'

Ram remained silent.

'Look, Prince Ram,' continued Mrigasya, 'the people love you for your police reforms. There is the matter of Dhenuka, for which you became unpopular for a while, but that has been forgotten in the glow of your victory over Raavan in Mithila. In fact, you may not know this, but you have become popular among the common people across India, not just Kosala. Nobody is hated more in the Sapt Sindhu than Raavan, and you defeated him. I can bring the nobles of Ayodhya to your side. Most of the major kingdoms in the Sapt Sindhu will swing towards the eventual winner. The only one we need to worry about is Kekaya and the kingdoms under its influence. But even those kingdoms, the descendants of King Anu, have differences among themselves that we could easily exploit. In short, what I'm telling you is that the throne is yours for the taking.'

'What about the law?' asked Ram.

Mrigasya looked baffled, like someone had spoken in an unknown language. 'The law?'

'I have fired the *Asuraastra* and I have to serve my sentence.'

Mrigasya laughed. 'Who will dare punish the future emperor of the Sapt Sindhu?'

'Maybe the present emperor of the Sapt Sindhu?'

'Emperor Dashrath wants you to ascend the throne. Trust me. He will not send you off on some ludicrous exile.'

Ram's expression did not change but Sita could sense that her husband was getting deeply irritated as he closed his eyes.

'Prince?' asked Mrigasya.

Ram ran his hand across his face. His fingers rested on his chin as he opened his eyes and stared into Mrigasya's; he whispered, 'My father is an honourable man. He is a descendant of Ikshvaku. He will do the honourable thing; as will I.'

'Prince, I don't think you understand—'

Ram interrupted Mrigasya. 'I don't think *you* understand, General Mrigasya. I am a descendant of Ikshvaku. I am a descendant of Raghu. My family would rather die than bring disrepute to our clan's honour.'

'Those are mere words…'

'No. It is a code; a code that we live by.'

Mrigasya leaned forward, adopting a manner as if he was speaking to a child not familiar with the ways of the world. 'Listen to me, Prince Ram. I have seen a lot more of this world than you have. Honour is for the textbooks. In the real world…'

'I think we are done, General,' said Ram, rising with a polite namaste.

—— 岽 ⬯ ☼ ——

'What?' asked Kaikeyi. 'Are you sure?'

Manthara had rushed to Kaikeyi's chamber, secure in the knowledge that neither Dashrath nor any of his personal staff would be present. Kaikeyi's staff was not a concern; originally from her parental home in Kekaya, they were fiercely loyal to her. Seating herself beside the queen, she nevertheless exercised abundant caution and commanded the queen's maids to leave the room, ordering them to shut the door on their way out.

'I wouldn't be here if I wasn't sure,' said Manthara, as she shifted in her chair to ease the discomfort to her back. The royal furniture was a travesty compared to the well-designed, ergonomic furniture in Manthara's opulent home. 'Money opens all mouths; everyone has a price. The emperor is all set to announce in court tomorrow that Ram will be king in his stead, and that he will take *Vanvaas* in the forests. *Vanvaas* with all his queens, I might add. You too may have to live in some jungle hut, from now on.'

Kaikeyi scowled at her, as she gritted her teeth.

'Gritting your teeth will only wear out the enamel,' said Manthara. 'If you think you should do something more practical, then today is the day. The time is right now. You will never get an opportunity like this again.'

Kaikeyi was annoyed at Manthara's tone; her demeanour had changed from the day she had given her that money to carry out her vengeance. But she needed the powerful trader for now, so she exercised restraint. 'What do you suggest?'

'You once mentioned the promise that Dashrath made to you after you saved him at the Battle of Karachapa.'

Kaikeyi leaned back in her chair as she remembered the long-forgotten promise, a debt she never really believed she would need to collect. She had saved his life in that disastrous battle with Raavan, losing a finger and getting seriously injured herself. When Dashrath had regained consciousness, he had, in his gratitude, made an open-ended promise to Kaikeyi that he would honour any two wishes she made, anytime in life. 'The two boons! I can ask for anything!'

'And he has to honour it. *Raghukul reet sadaa chali aayi, praan jaaye par vachan naa jaaye.*'

Manthara had recited the motto of the Suryavanshi clan that ruled Ayodhya; or at least, what had been their motto since the days of the great Emperor Raghu. It translated as: The clan of Raghu has always followed a tradition; they would much rather die than dishonour their word.

'He cannot say no…' whispered Kaikeyi, a glint in her eye.

Manthara nodded.

'Ram should be banished for fourteen years,' said Kaikeyi. 'I'll tell him to say publicly that he is doing so to punish him according to the rules of Lord Rudra.'

'Very wise. That will make the public accept it. Ram is popular with the people now, but nobody will want to break Lord Rudra's rule.'

'And he has to declare Bharat the crown prince.'

'Perfect! Two boons; the solution to all problems.'

'Yes…'

——— |⼤| 🐟 ☼ ———

As she rode over the bridge that spanned the Grand Canal, Sita looked around to check that she was not being followed. She had covered her face and upper body with a long *angvastram*, as if protecting herself from the cold, late evening breeze.

The road stretched into the distance, heading east towards lands that Kosala controlled directly. A few metres ahead, she looked back again, and steered the reins to the left, off the road. She rode into the jungle and immediately made a clicking sound, making her horse break into a swift gallop. She had to cover an hour's distance in just half the time.

——— |⼤| 🐟 ☼ ———

'But what will your husband say?' asked the Naga.

Sita stood in a small clearing in the jungle, her hand on the hilt of her knife, encased within a small scabbard; a precaution against wild animals.

She did not need any protection from the man she had just met, though. He was a Malayaputra, and she trusted him like an elder brother. The Naga had a hard and bony mouth, extending out of his face like a beak. His head was bare but his face was covered with fine downy hair. He looked like a man with the face of a vulture.

'Jatayu*ji*,' said Sita, respectfully, 'my husband is not just unusual, he's the kind of man who comes along once in a millennium. Sadly, he doesn't realise how important he is. As far as he is concerned, he simply thinks he's doing the right thing by asking to be exiled. But in doing so, he is also putting himself in serious danger. The moment we cross the Narmada, I suspect we will face repeated attacks. They will try every trick in the book to kill him off.'

'You have tied a *rakhi* on my hand, my sister,' said Jatayu. 'Nothing will happen to you or the one you love, for as long as I am alive.'

Sita smiled.

'But you should tell your husband about me, about what you are asking me to do. I don't know if he dislikes the Malayaputras. But if he does, it would not be completely unfair. He may harbour some ill-will about what happened at Mithila.'

'Let me worry about how to handle my husband.'

'Are you sure?'

'I know him quite well by now. He won't understand at present that we might need some protection in the forest; maybe later. For now, I just need your soldiers to keep a constant but discreet watch on our positions and prevent any attacks.'

Jatayu thought he heard a sound. He pulled out his knife and stared into the darkness beyond the trees. A few seconds later he relaxed and turned his attention back to Sita.

'It's nothing,' said Sita.

'Why is your husband insisting on being punished?' asked Jatayu. 'It can be argued against. The *Asuraastra* is not really a weapon of mass destruction. He can get away on a technicality, if he chooses to.'

'He is insisting on being punished because that is the law.'

'He can't be so…' Jatayu didn't complete his statement. But it was obvious what he wanted to say.

'People see my husband as a naive and blind follower of the law. But a day will come when the entire world will see him as one of the greatest leaders ever. It is my duty to protect him and keep him alive till then.'

Jatayu smiled.

Sita was embarrassed by her next request, as it seemed selfish. But she had to be sure. 'And the…'

'The Somras will be arranged. I agree that you and your husband will need it, especially if you have to be strong enough to complete your mission when you return fourteen years later.'

'But won't you face difficulties in getting the Somras out? What about…'

Jatayu laughed. 'Let me worry about that.'

Sita had heard all that she needed to. She knew that Jatayu would come through.

'Goodbye. Go with Lord Parshu Ram, my brother.'

'Go with Lord Rudra, my sister.'

Jatayu lingered for a bit after Sita mounted her horse and rode away. Once sure that she was gone, he touched the ground she had been standing on, picked up some of the dust that had been touched by her sandals, and then brought it reverentially to his forehead; a mark of respect for a great leader.

— 𑀓 🐟 ☀ —

'*Chhoti Maa* is in the *kopa bhavan*!' exclaimed a surprised Ram, referring to his stepmother, Kaikeyi.

'Yes,' said Vashishta.

Ram had earlier been informed that his father would announce the ascension of the prince to the throne the next day. He had determined his next course of action. He was planning to abdicate the throne and install Bharat as king instead. He would then leave for the forest. But Ram had misgivings about this plan as it would, in effect, mean publicly dishonouring his father's wishes.

Therefore, when Vashishta came in and told Ram about his stepmother's move, his first reaction was not negative.

Kaikeyi had lodged herself in the *kopa bhavan*, the *house of anger*. This was an institutionalised chamber created in royal palaces many centuries ago, once polygamy became a common practice among the royalty. Having multiple wives, a king was naturally unable to spend enough time with all of them. A *kopa bhavan* was the assigned chamber a wife would go to if angry or upset with her husband. This would be a signal for the king that the queen needed redressal for a complaint. It was believed to be inauspicious for a husband to allow his wife to stay overnight in the *kopa bhavan*.

Dashrath had no choice but to visit his aggrieved spouse.

'Even if her influence has reduced, if there's one person who can force my father to change his mind, it would be *Chhoti Maa*,' said Ram.

'It looks like your wish will come true after all.'

'Yes. And, if ordered so, Sita and I will leave immediately.'

Vashishta frowned. 'Isn't Lakshman going with you?'

'He wants to, but I don't think that's necessary. He needs to stay here, with his wife, Urmila. She is delicate. We should not impose a harsh forest-life on her.'

Vashishta nodded in agreement. Then he leaned over and spoke earnestly. 'I will spend the next fourteen years preparing the ground for you.'

Ram smiled at his guru.

'Remember your destiny. You will be the next Vishnu, regardless of what anyone else says. You have to rewrite the future of our nation. I will work towards that goal and make sure that we are ready for you when you return. But you have to ensure that you remain alive.'

'I will certainly try my best.'

Chapter 28

Dashrath stepped out of the palanquin with assistance and hobbled into the *kopa bhavan*. He seemed to have aged a decade; the stress of the last few days had been immense. He sat on his usual rocking chair and dismissed the attendant with a wave of his hand.

He raised his eyes and observed his wife; Kaikeyi had not acknowledged his entry into the room. She sat on a divan, her hair undone, unkempt. Not a speck of jewellery on her person, her *angvastram* lay on the ground. She wore a white *dhoti* and blouse, and sat with an appearance of calm that belied the fury that raged within; he knew her well; he also knew what was going to happen and that he couldn't say no.

'Speak,' said Dashrath.

Kaikeyi looked at him with sorrow-filled eyes. 'You may not love me anymore, Dashrath, but I still love you.'

'Oh, I know you love me. But you love yourself more.'

Kaikeyi stiffened. 'And are you any different? Are you going to teach me about selflessness? Seriously?'

Dashrath smiled ruefully. '*Touché.*'

Kaikeyi seethed with the anger of a woman scorned.

'You were always the smartest of all my wives. I enjoyed my verbal battles with you the way I enjoyed duelling with a warrior.

I miss those sharp, acerbic words that could even draw blood.'

'I can bleed you with a sword, too.'

Dashrath laughed. 'I know.'

Kaikeyi leaned back on the divan, trying to slow down her breathing, trying to control herself. But the hurt still showed through. 'I dedicated my life to you. I nearly died for you. I disfigured myself in saving your life. I never ever humiliated you in public, unlike your precious Ram.'

'Ram has never—'

Kaikeyi interrupted Dashrath. 'He has, now! You know that he will not follow your order tomorrow. He will dishonour you. And Bharat would never—'

It was Dashrath's turn to interrupt. 'I am not choosing between Bharat and Ram. You know they have no problems with each other.'

Kaikeyi leaned forward and hissed, 'This is not about Ram and Bharat. This is about Ram and me. You have to choose between Ram and me. What has he ever done for you? He saved your life once. That's it. I have saved your life every day, for the last so many years! Do my sacrifices count for nothing?'

Dashrath refused to succumb to her emotional blackmail.

Kaikeyi laughed contemptuously. 'Of course! When you don't have any counter argument, all you do is clam up!'

'I do have an answer, but you will not like it.'

Kaikeyi laughed harshly. 'All my life, I have tolerated things that I don't like. I submit to the insults of my father. I tolerate your selfishness. I live with my son's disdain for me. I can tolerate a few words. Tell me!'

'Ram offers me immortality.'

Kaikeyi was confused. And it showed on her face. She had always managed to get large quantities of Somras for Dashrath, repeatedly haranguing Raj Guru Vashishta for the legendary drink of the Gods. It dramatically increased the life-spans of those who consumed it. For some reason, it had not worked its wonders on Dashrath.

Dashrath explained. 'Not immortality for my body. The last few days have made me fully aware of my mortality. I'm talking about immortality for my name. I know that I have wasted my life and my potential. People compare me to my great ancestors and find me wanting. But Ram... He will go down in history as one of the greatest ever. And he will redeem my name. I will be remembered as Ram's father for all time to come. Ram's greatness will rub off on me. He has already defeated Raavan!'

Kaikeyi burst out laughing. 'That was pure luck, you fool. It was sheer chance that Guru Vishwamitra happened to be there with the *Asuraastra*!'

'Yes, he got lucky. That means the Gods favour him.'

Kaikeyi cast him a dark look. This was getting nowhere. 'The hell with this. Let's get this over with. You know you cannot refuse me.'

Dashrath sat back and smiled sadly. 'Just when I was beginning to enjoy our conversation...'

'I want my two boons.'

'Both of them?' asked Dashrath, surprised. He had expected only one of them to be called.

'I want Ram banished from the Sapt Sindhu for fourteen years. You can announce at court that this is because he broke Lord Rudra's law. You will be praised for it. Even the Vayuputras will applaud you.'

'Yes, I know how concerned you are about my prestige!' said Dashrath caustically.

'You cannot say no!'

Dashrath sighed. 'And the second?'

'You will declare Bharat the crown prince tomorrow.'

Dashrath was shocked. This was unexpected. The implication was obvious. He growled softly, 'If Ram is killed in exile, people will lynch you.'

Kaikeyi was aghast. She shouted, 'Do you really think I could shed royal blood? The blood of Raghu?'

'Yes, I think you could. But I know that Bharat won't. I will warn him about you.'

'You do what you want. Just honour my two boons.'

Dashrath stared at Kaikeyi with anger. He suddenly looked towards the door. 'Guards!'

Four guards rushed in with Dashrath's attendant.

'Order my palanquin,' said Dashrath, brusquely.

'Yes, Your Highness,' said his attendant, as they all scurried out.

As soon as they were alone, Dashrath said. 'You can leave the *kopa bhavan*. You will get your two boons. But I am warning you, if you do anything to Ram, I will…'

'I will not do anything to your precious Ram!' screamed Kaikeyi.

— 大 🐟 ☀ —

The royal court assembled in the massive Great Hall of the Unconquerable in the second hour of the second *prahar*. Dashrath sat on his throne, visibly tired and unhappy, but dignified. Not one of the queens was present. Vashishta, the raj guru, sat on the throne to the right of the emperor. The court was packed with not just the nobility, but also as many of the common people as could be accommodated in the hall.

Except for a few, most were unaware of what was to transpire that morning. They simply couldn't understand why Ram should be punished for defeating Raavan. In fact, the crown prince deserved to be commended for restoring Ayodhya's glory and washing away the taint on his birth.

'Silence!' announced the court crier.

Dashrath sat with heartbreaking majesty upon the throne, as if seeking honour from his son. Ram stood in the middle of the great hall, directly in his line of sight. The emperor coughed softly as his eyes fell on the lion-shaped armrest. He tightened his hold around it as he felt an overpowering temptation to change his mind. Realising the futility of the sentiment, he closed his eyes in resignation.

How do you save someone who thinks that doing so is an act of dishonour?

Dashrath looked straight into the eyes of his insanely virtuous son. 'The law of Lord Rudra has been broken. Some good did come of it, for Raavan's bodyguard corps was destroyed. By all accounts, he is licking his wounds in Lanka!'

The audience broke into a loud cheer. Everybody hated Raavan; almost everybody.

'Mithila, the kingdom of our Princess Sita, the wife of my beloved son Ram, was saved from annihilation.'

The crowd cheered once again, but it was more muted this time. Very few knew Sita, and most did not understand why their crown prince had forged an alliance with a deeply spiritual but powerless kingdom.

Dashrath's voice shook as he continued. 'But the law has been broken. And Lord Rudra's word has to be honoured. His tribe, the Vayuputras, have not yet asked for Ram to be punished. But that will not stop the Raghuvanshis from doing the right thing.'

A hushed silence descended on the hall. The people felt a dread as they steeled themselves to hear what they now feared their king would say to them.

'Ram has accepted the punishment that must be his. He will leave Ayodhya, for I banish him from the Sapt Sindhu for fourteen years. He will return to us after cleansing himself with the fire of penance. He is a true follower of Lord Rudra. Honour him!'

A loud cry rent the air: of dismay from the commoners and shock from the nobility.

Dashrath raised his hands and the crowds fell silent. 'My other beloved son, Bharat, will now be the crown prince of Ayodhya, the kingdom of Kosala and the Sapt Sindhu Empire.'

Silence. The mood in the hall had turned sombre.

Ram held his hands together in a formal namaste as he spoke in a loud and clear voice. 'Father, even the Gods in the sky marvel at your wisdom and justice today!'

Many among the common folk were openly crying now.

'The golden spirit of the greatest Suryavanshi, Ikshvaku himself, lives strong in you, my father!' said Ram loudly. 'Sita and I will leave Ayodhya within a day.'

In the far corner of the hall, standing unobtrusively behind a pillar, was a tall, unusually fair-skinned man. He wore a white *dhoti* and *angvastram*; he seemed visibly uncomfortable in the *dhoti,* though — perhaps it wasn't his normal attire. His most distinguishing features were his hooked nose, beaded full beard, and drooping moustache. His wizened face creased into a smile as he heard Ram's words.

Guru Vashishta has chosen well.

'I must say that I am surprised by the emperor,' said the fair-skinned man with the hooked nose, adjusting his uncomfortable *dhoti*.

He sat with Vashishta in the raj guru's private chamber.

'Do not forget where the real credit lies,' said Vashishta.

'I think that's obvious. I must say you have chosen well.'

'And will you play your role?'

The fair-skinned man sighed. 'You know we cannot get involved too deeply, Guru*ji*. It is not our decision to make.'

'But…'

'But we will do all that we can. That is our promise. And you know that we don't break our promises.'

Vashishta nodded. 'Thank you, my friend. That is all I ask. Glory to Lord Rudra.'

'Glory to Lord Parshu Ram.'

— |쉿| ⬮ ☼ —

Bharat walked into Ram and Sita's sitting room even as he was being announced. They had already changed into the garb of hermits, made from rough cotton and bark. It made Bharat wince.

'We have to dress the way forest people do, Bharat,' said Sita.

Tears sprang into his eyes. He looked at Ram as he shook his head. '*Dada*, I don't know whether to applaud you or try and knock some sense into you.'

'You needn't do either,' said Ram, smiling. 'Just embrace me and wish me goodbye.'

Bharat rushed towards his brother and gathered him in his arms as a torrent of tears ran down his face. Ram held him tight.

As Bharat stepped back, Ram said, 'Don't worry. Sweet are the fruits of adversity. I will return with more sense knocked into me, I assure you.'

Bharat laughed softly. 'One of these days, I'll stop speaking to you for the fear of being understood.'

Ram laughed as well. 'Rule well, my brother.'

There were some who believed that Bharat's emphasis on liberty was more suited to the temperament of Ayodhya citizens, indeed the people of the Sapt Sindhu.

'I won't lie that I did not want it,' said Bharat. 'But not this way ... not this way...'

Ram put his hands on Bharat's strong muscular shoulders. 'You will rule well. I know that. Make our ancestors proud.'

'I don't care what our ancestors think.'

'Then make *me* proud,' said Ram.

Bharat's face fell, along with a fresh stream of tears. He embraced his brother again and they held each other for a long time. Ram overcame his natural reserve as he held on to Bharat. He knew his brother needed this.

'Enough,' said Bharat, pulling back, wiping his tears and shaking his head. He turned to Sita. 'Take care of my brother, *Bhabhi.* He does not know how unethical this world is.'

Sita smiled. 'He knows. But he still tries to change things.'

Bharat sighed. Then he turned towards Ram as an idea struck him. 'Give me your slippers, *Dada.*'

Ram frowned as he looked down at his simple hermit slippers.

'Not these,' said Bharat. 'Your royal slippers.'

'Why?'

'Just give them to me, *Dada.*'

Ram walked to the side of the bed, where his recently discarded royal garments lay. On the floor was a pair of gold-coloured slippers, with exquisite silver and brown embroidery. Ram picked them up and handed them to Bharat.

'What are you going to do with these?' asked Ram.

'When the time comes, I will place these rather than myself on the throne,' said Bharat.

Ram and Sita immediately understood the implication. With this one gesture, Bharat would effectively declare that Ram was the king of Ayodhya and that he, Bharat, was only a caretaker in his elder brother's absence. Any attempts to murder the king of Ayodhya would invite the wrath of the mighty empire of the Sapt Sindhu. This was mandated by the treaties between the various kingdoms of the Sapt Sindhu. Added to the cold reality of treaty obligations was the superstition that it was bad karma to kill kings and crown princes, except in battle or open combat. It would offer a powerful shield of protection to Ram, though it would severely undercut Bharat's own authority and power.

Ram embraced his Bharat again. 'My brother…'

—— 灯 🐟 ☀ ——

'Lakshman?' said Sita. 'I thought I'd told you…'

Lakshman had just entered Ram and Sita's sitting room. He wore the same attire that his elder brother and sister-in-law did: one of a forest hermit.

Lakshman dared Sita with determination blazing in his eyes. 'I'm coming, *Bhabhi*.'

'Lakshman…' pleaded Ram.

'You will not survive without me, *Dada*,' said Lakshman. 'I'm not letting you go without me.'

Ram laughed. 'It's touching to see the faith my family has in me. No one seems to trust me to be able to keep myself alive.'

Lakshman laughed too, but turned serious in a flash. 'You're free to laugh or cry about it, *Dada*. But I am coming with you.'

— |大| 🏺 ☼ —

An excited Urmila greeted Lakshman as he entered his private chamber. She was dressed in simple, yet fashionable attire. Her *dhoti* and blouse were dyed in the common colour brown, but an elegant gold border ran along its edges. She wore simple, modest gold jewellery, unlike what she normally favoured.

'Come, my darling,' said Urmila, smiling with childlike enthusiasm. 'You must see this. I have single-handedly supervised the packing and most of it is done already.'

'Packing?' asked a surprised Lakshman, with a fond smile.

'Yes,' said Urmila, taking his hand and pulling him into the wardrobe room. Two massive trunks made of teak were placed in the centre. Urmila quickly opened both. 'This one has my clothes and that one has yours.'

Lakshman stood nonplussed, not knowing how to react to his innocent Urmila.

She pulled him into their bed chamber, where lay another trunk, packed and ready. It was full of utensils. A small container in one corner caught her attention. Urmila opened it to reveal small packets of spices. 'See, the way I understand it, we should be able to get meat and vegetables easily in the jungle. But spices and utensils will be difficult. So…'

Lakshman stared at her, bemused and a trifle dismayed.

Urmila moved towards him and embraced her husband, smiling fondly. 'I will cook the most divine meals for you. And for Sita *Didi* and Ram *Jijaji* also, of course. We will return fat and healthy from our fourteen-year holiday!'

Lakshman returned his wife's embrace gently; her head reached his muscular barrel-chest. *Holiday?*

He looked down at his excited wife, who was obviously trying very hard to make the best of what was a bewildering situation for her. *She has been a princess all her life. She assumed that she would be living in an even more luxurious palace in Ayodhya. She is not a bad soul. She just wants to be a good wife. But is it right of me, her husband, to agree to her following me into the jungle, even if she wants to do so? Isn't it my duty to protect her, just like it is my duty to protect my Ram* Dada?

She will not last a day in the jungle. She won't.

A heavy weight settled on Lakshman's heart as it became obvious what he had to do. But he knew he must do so gently so it would not break his Urmila's tender heart.

Keeping one arm around her, he raised her chin with his other hand. Urmila gazed at him lovingly with her childlike innocence. He spoke tenderly, 'I'm worried, Urmila.'

'Don't be. We'll handle it together. The forest will be...'

'It's not about the forest. I'm worried about what will happen here, in the palace.'

Urmila arched her spine and threw her head back so she could get a better look at her extremely tall husband. 'In the palace?'

'Yes! Father's not keeping too well. *Chhoti Maa* Kaikeyi will be controlling everything now. And, frankly, I don't think Bharat *Dada* can stand up to her. My mother will at least have Shatrughan to look after her. But who will look after *Badi Maa* Kaushalya? What will happen to her?'

Urmila nodded. 'True...'

'And if *Chhoti Maa* Kaikeyi can do this to Ram *Dada*, can you imagine what she will do to *Badi Maa*?'

Urmila's open face was guileless.

'Someone has to protect *Badi Maa*,' Lakshman repeated, as if to drive home his point.

'Yes, that's true, but there are so many people in the palace. Hasn't Ram *Dada* made any arrangements?' asked Urmila.

Lakshman smiled sadly. 'Ram *Dada* is not the most practical of men. He thinks everyone in the world is as ethical as he is. Why do you think I'm going with him? I need to protect him.'

Urmila's face fell as she finally understood what Lakshman was trying to say. 'I'm not living here without you, Lakshman.'

He pulled his wife close. 'It will be for a short time, Urmila.'

'*Fourteen years?* No, I'm not…' Urmila burst into helpless tears as she hugged him tight.

Lakshman eased his hold as he gently raised her chin again. He wiped away her tears. 'You are a Raghuvanshi now. We hold duty above love; we uphold honour, even at the cost of happiness. This is not a matter of choice, Urmila.'

'Don't do this, Lakshman. Please. I love you. Don't leave me.'

'I love you too, Urmila. And I cannot force you to do anything you don't want to do. I am only requesting you. But before you give me your answer, I want you to think of Kaushalya *Maa*. Think of the love she has showered upon you over the last few days. Didn't you tell me that after a long time, you felt as if you had a mother again, in Kaushalya *Maa*? Doesn't she deserve something in return?'

Urmila burst out crying and embraced Lakshman tightly again.

— 𝍦 🐟 ☀ —

A cool evening breeze blew through the palace at the fifth hour of the third *prahar*, as Sita walked towards Lakshman and Urmila's private chambers. The guards immediately stood at attention. As they turned to announce her, they were halted by a pensive Lakshman emerging from the chambers. Sita felt a lump in her throat as she looked at his face.

'I'll sort this out,' said Sita sternly, as she attempted to walk past him and enter her sister's chambers.

Lakshman stopped her, holding her hand with a pleading expression in his eyes. 'No, *Bhabhi.*'

Sita looked at her giant brother-in-law, who suddenly seemed so vulnerable and alone.

'Lakshman, my sister listens to me. Trust me—'

'No, *Bhabhi*,' interrupted Lakshman, shaking his head. 'Forest life will not be easy. We will face death every day. You know that. You are tough, you can survive. But she is…' Tears welled up in his eyes. 'She wanted to come, *Bhabhi*, but I don't think she should. I convinced her not to… This is for the best.'

'Lakshman…'

'This is for the best, *Bhabhi*,' repeated Lakshman, almost as though he was convincing himself. 'This is for the best.'

Chapter 29

It had been an eventful six months since Ram, Lakshman and Sita had left Ayodhya. Word that Dashrath had passed away had made Ram repeatedly curse his fate for not being able to perform the duties of an eldest son and conduct the funeral rites of his father. It broke Ram's heart that he had discovered his father so late in his life. Returning to Ayodhya was not possible, but he had performed a *yagna* in the forests for the journey his father's soul had undertaken. Bharat had remained true to his word. He had placed Ram's slippers on the throne of Ayodhya, and had begun governing the empire as his brother's regent. It could be said that Ram was appointed emperor in absentia. It was an unorthodox move but Bharat's liberal and decentralising style of governance made the decision palatable to the kingdoms within the Sapt Sindhu.

Ram, Lakshman and Sita had travelled south, primarily walking by the banks of rivers, moving inland only when necessary. They had finally reached the borders of the Sapt Sindhu, near the kingdom of South Kosala, ruled by Ram's maternal grandfather.

Ram went down on both knees and touched the ground with his forehead; this was the land that had nurtured his mother. As he straightened, he looked at his wife and smiled, as if he knew her secret.

'What?' asked Sita.

'There are people who have been shadowing us for weeks,' said Ram. 'When do you plan to tell me who they are?'

Sita shrugged delicately and turned to the forest line in the distance, where she knew Jatayu and his soldiers walked stealthily. They had remained out of sight, though close enough to quickly move in if the need arose. Evidently, they were not as discreet as she would have liked them to be; more likely, she had underestimated her husband's abilities and keen awareness of his surroundings. 'I will tell you,' said Sita, with a broad smile, 'when the time is right. For now, know that they are here for our protection.'

Ram gave her a piercing look, but let it go for now.

'Lord Manu banned the crossing of the Narmada,' said Lakshman. 'If we cross, then we cannot return, according to the law.'

'There is a way,' said Sita. 'If we travel south along *Maa* Kaushalya's father's kingdom, we may not have to "cross" the Narmada. The entire kingdom of South Kosala lies to the east of the origin of the Narmada River. And the river itself flows west. If we simply keep travelling south, we will reach the *Dandakaranya* without "crossing" the Narmada. So, we would not be violating Lord Manu's ban, right?'

'That's a technicality, *Bhabhi*, and you know it. It may work for you and me, but it won't for Ram *Dada*.'

'Hmm, should we travel east and leave the Sapt Sindhu by boat then?' asked Ram.

'We can't do that,' said Sita. 'The seas are ruled by Raavan. He has dotted the Indian peninsula with port-forts. It is common knowledge that he dominates the western coast, but the fact is, he has outposts on the eastern coast as well. That rules out the sea routes. But Raavan doesn't hold sway in the hinterland. We will be safe south of the Narmada, in the forests of Dandak.'

'But *Bhabhi*,' argued Lakshman, 'Lord Manu's laws clearly state—'

'Which Lord Manu?'

Lakshman was shocked. *Didn't Bhabhi know who Lord Manu was?* 'The founder of the Vedic way of life, *Bhabhi*. Everyone knows…'

Sita smiled indulgently. 'There have been many Manus, Lakshman, not just one. Each age has its own Manu. So when you speak of the laws of Manu, you will have to also specify which Lord Manu.'

'I didn't know this…' said Lakshman.

Sita shook her head, as she teased the men affectionately. 'Did you boys learn anything at all in your *gurukul*? You know very little.'

'I knew that,' Ram protested. 'Lakshman never paid attention in class. Don't lump me with him.'

'Shatrughan was the one who knew everything, *Dada*,' said Lakshman. 'All of us depended on him.'

'You more than the others,' joked Ram, as he stretched his back.

Lakshman laughed as Ram turned to Sita. 'Okay, I concede your point. But it was the Manu of our age who decreed that we cannot cross the Narmada. And, that if we do, we cannot return. So…'

'It wasn't a law. It was an agreement.'

'An agreement?' asked Ram and Lakshman together, surprised.

Sita continued. 'I'm sure you're aware that Lord Manu was a prince from the kingdom of Sangamtamil, deep in the south of India. He led many of his own people, and those of

Dwarka, up north into the Sapt Sindhu, when their own lands were swallowed by the rising sea.'

'Yes, I'm aware of that,' said Ram.

'But all the people from these two lands did not leave with Lord Manu. The majority remained behind in Sangamtamil and Dwarka. Lord Manu had radical ideas about how a society should be organised, which many did not agree with. He had his share of enemies. He was allowed to leave with his followers, from both Sangamtamil and Dwarka, on the condition that he would never venture back. In those days, Narmada formed the upper boundary of Dwarka, with Sangamtamil of course being in the deep south. In effect, they promised to leave each other in peace and part ways. The Narmada was to be the natural boundary under the agreement. It was not a law, but an agreement.'

'But if we are his descendants, then we need to honour the agreement that he made,' said Ram.

'Valid point,' said Sita. 'But tell me, what does an agreement require at the very least?'

'It needs two parties to agree on something.'

'And, if one of the parties doesn't exist anymore, is the agreement still valid?'

Ram and Lakshman were stumped.

'Many parts of Sangamtamil were already submerged by the time Lord Manu left. The rest went underwater soon after. The seas rose rapidly. Dwarka survived for longer. Progressively though, as the seas rose, the large land mass of Dwarka that had been attached to India was reduced to a long, lonely island.'

'Dwaravati?' asked Ram, incredulously.

Dwaravati had been a long, narrow island off the coast of western India, running north to south for nearly five hundred kilometres. The island was swallowed by the sea over three thousand years ago. The survivors from Dwaravati dispersed all over the mainland, and frankly, no one took their claims of being the descendants of the original Dwarkans seriously. This was mainly because the Yadavs, belonging to a powerful kingdom based near the banks of the Yamuna, stridently claimed that they were the sole direct descendants of the Dwarkans. The truth was that the intermingling among the different tribes across India had been so widespread, everybody could claim descent from both the Sangamtamils and the Dwarkans.

Sita nodded. 'The island of Dwaravati was home to the true survivors of Dwarka. Today, they exist among us all.'

'Wow.'

'So the pure descendants of the Sangamtamils and Dwarkans are long gone. The only ones around are us, their common descendants. How will we breach an agreement we made with ourselves? There's no other party anymore!'

The logic was irrefutable.

'So, *Bhabhi*,' said Lakshman, 'should we be heading south and staying in the forests of Dandak?'

'Well, yes. It is the safest place for us.'

—— 𝕀𝕏𝕀 ● ☼ ——

Ram, Lakshman and Sita stood on the southern banks of the Narmada River. Ram went down on one knee and reverentially picked up a fistful of soil. He smeared it across his forehead in three horizontal lines, like the followers of Lord Rudra did with the holy ashes consecrated by the Gods. He whispered, 'May the land of our ancestors ... the soil that was witness to great karma ... bless us.'

Sita and Lakshman followed Ram's example as they smeared a *tilak* across their foreheads.

Sita smiled at Ram. 'You do know what Lord Brahma said about this land, right?'

Ram nodded. 'Yes; more often than not, whenever India faces an existential crisis, our regeneration emerges from the Indian peninsula, from the land that is to the south of the Narmada.'

'Do you know why he said that?'

Ram shook his head.

'Our scriptures tell us that the south is the direction of death, right?'

'Yes.'

'Death is believed to be inauspicious in some foreign lands to the west of us; to them it signifies the end of everything. But nothing ever really dies. No material can ever truly escape the universe. It just changes form. In that sense, death is actually also the beginning of regeneration; the old form dies and a new form is born. If the south is the direction of death, then it is also the direction of regeneration.'

Ram was intrigued by this thought. 'The Sapt Sindhu is our *karmabhoomi*, the *land of our karma*. And the land to the south of the Narmada is our *pitrbhoomi*, the *land of our ancestors*. This is the land of our regeneration.'

'And, one day, we will return from the south to drive the regeneration of India.' Saying so, Sita held out two cups made of dried clay. They contained a bubbly milk-white liquid. She handed one to Lakshman and the other to Ram.

'What is it, *Bhabhi*?' asked Lakshman.

'It's for your regeneration,' said Sita. 'Drink it.'

Lakshman took a sip and grimaced. 'Yuck!'

'Just drink it, Lakshman,' ordered Sita.

He held his nose as he drained the liquid. He walked to the river and rinsed his mouth as well as the cup.

Ram looked at Sita. 'I know what this is. Where did you get it from?'

'From the people who protect us.'

'Sita…'

'You are important to India, Ram. You have to remain healthy. You have to stay alive. We have a lot to do when we return, fourteen years from now. You cannot be allowed to age. Please drink it.'

'Sita,' laughed Ram, 'one cup of Somras is not going to achieve much. We need to drink it regularly for years for it to be effective. And you know how difficult it is to procure Somras. There will never be enough.'

'Leave that to me.'

'I'm not drinking it without you. What's the point of my long life, if I don't have you to share it with?'

Sita smiled. 'I have already had mine, Ram. I had to, as one normally falls ill the first time one drinks the Somras.'

'Is that why you were ill last week?'

'Yes. If all three of us were to fall ill at the same time, it would be difficult to manage, right? You looked after me when I was unwell. And I will take care of Lakshman and you now.'

'I wonder why the Somras makes one fall ill the first time.'

Sita shrugged. 'I don't know. That is a question for Lord Brahma and the *Saptrishis*. But don't worry about the illness; I have enough medicines in my bag.'

———— |太| 🐟 ☼ ————

Sita and Ram were both poised on one knee, staring intently at the wild boar. Ram held his bow with the arrow nocked, ready to fire.

'Sita,' whispered Ram, 'I have the animal in perfect sight. I can finish it immediately. Are you sure you want to do this?'

'Yes,' whispered Sita. 'Bows and arrows are your thing. Swords and spears are mine. I need the practice.'

Ram, Sita and Lakshman had been in exile for eighteen months now. Sita had finally introduced Jatayu to Ram some months back. Trusting Sita, Ram had accepted the Malayaputra and his fifteen soldiers as members of his team. Together they were one short of twenty now; more defendable than a group of three. Ram understood this, as well as the importance of allies in the situation they were in. But he remained wary of the Malayaputras.

Admittedly, Jatayu had given him no reason to be suspicious, but Ram could not ignore the fact that he and his people were followers of Guru Vishwamitra. Ram shared his guru Vashishta's misgivings about the chief of the Malayaputras; he baulked at the ease with which Vishwamitra had been willing to use the *Asuraastra*, with little regard for the law.

The members of the party had settled into established routines as they moved deeper into the forests of Dandak. Still not having found a suitable enough permanent camp, they usually stayed in one place for around two to three weeks before moving on. Standard perimeter and security formations had been agreed upon. Cooking and cleaning duties were shared by rotation, as was the task of hunting. But since not everyone in the camp ate meat, hunting wasn't something that was required often.

'These beasts are dangerous when they charge,' warned Ram, looking at Sita with concern.

Sita smiled at her husband's protectiveness as she drew her sword. 'Which is why I want you to stay behind me once you fire the arrow,' she teased.

Ram smiled in return. He focused his attention on the wild boar as he took aim. He pulled the bowstring back and released the arrow. The missile flew in a neat arc, brushed past its head and landed to its left. The animal jerked its head in the direction of the intruders who had dared to disturb its peace. It grunted aggressively but did not move.

'Once more,' said Sita as she slowly rose, her knees slightly bent, her feet spread wide, the sword held to the side.

Ram quickly nocked another arrow and fired. It whizzed past the boar's ear and buried itself into the ground.

Another belligerent grunt was accompanied by a stomping of its feet, this time. It lowered its head threateningly as it stared in the direction that the arrow had come from. Its curved tusks projected from below the snout, like two long knives, ready to strike.

'Now, get behind me,' whispered Sita.

Ram dropped his bow, quickly slipped a few feet behind her, and drew his sword as well; he wouldn't lose a second if she needed his help.

Sita screamed loudly as she jumped into view. The beast immediately took up the challenge that was thrown. It charged towards her with fearsome speed, its head low, its tusks jutting out like menacing swords. Sita stood her ground, breathing steadily as the wild boar speedily moved towards her. At the last second, when it appeared that it was upon her and would gore her to death, Sita took a few quick steps and leapt high into the air; an exquisite leap with which she flew horizontally above the charging boar. As she did, she struck her sword vertically down, stabbing the animal's neck. Her suspended body-weight made the blade sink deep into the neck, shattering the cervical vertebrae. She superbly leveraged the sword hilt to flip forward and land on her feet, just as the boar collapsed, dead, in front of Ram.

Ram's eyes widened with wonder. Sita strode back to the boar, breathing hard. 'The sword needs to simply break the neck and the animal dies instantly. No pain.'

'Clearly,' said Ram, sheathing his sword.

Sita bent down, touched the boar's head, and whispered, 'Forgive me for killing you, O noble beast. May your soul find purpose again, while your body sustains my soul.'

Ram held the hilt of Sita's sword in a firm grip and attempted to prise the blade out of the beast's body. It was stuck. He looked at Sita. 'It has gone in deep!'

Sita smiled. 'Let me retrieve your arrows while you pull it out.'

Ram began the delicate operation of extracting Sita's sword from the boar's neck. He needed to make sure that the blade didn't get damaged by rubbing against the hard bone. After extricating it he sat on his haunches and wiped it clean with some leaves; he checked the edges; they remained sharp; there was no damage. He looked up to see Sita approaching him from the distance, with the arrows that he had fired in the beginning. He pointed at her sword and raised his thumb, signalling that it was still in fine fettle. Sita smiled. She was still some distance away from him.

'My Lady!'

A loud shout rang through the jungle. Ram's eyes flew towards Makrant, a Malayaputra, as he raced towards Sita. Ram looked in the direction that the man was pointing. His heart jumped into his mouth as he saw two wild boars emerge from the thick of the woods, charging straight at Sita. Her sword was with him. All she had was her knife. Ram sprang to his feet and sprinted towards his wife. 'Sita!'

Alerted by the panic in his voice, Sita whirled around. The boars were almost upon her. She drew her knife and faced the animals. It would have been suicidal to make a dash for it, away from them; she could not outrun them; better to look them in the eye. Sita stood steady, took quick deep breaths and waited.

'My Lady!' shouted Makrant, as he leapt in front of Sita just in time, swinging his sword as he successfully deflected the first attack. The first boar swerved away but the second charged in, even as Makrant struggled to regain his balance. Its tusk pierced his upper thigh.

'Sita!' screamed Ram, as he threw her sword to her, drawing his own as he rushed towards Makrant.

Sita caught the sword deftly and turned to the first beast, which had turned around now and was charging down at her again. Makrant, impaled momentarily on the other boar's tusk, had been flung into the air by its fearsome momentum. But the weight of his body had thrown the boar off balance as well, making him tip to the right, exposing its underbelly. Ram chose that moment to stab it viciously. The blade sank into the beast's chest, right through to its heart. It collapsed to the ground, dead.

Meanwhile, the first boar swung its head fiercely as it closed in on Sita. She jumped up high, tucking her feet up, neatly avoiding the boar. On her way down, she swung her sword, partially decapitating the beast. It wasn't clean, but was enough to incapacitate the animal; it fell to the ground. Sita yanked her sword out as she landed. She went down on one knee and struck hard again, beheading the beast completely, putting it out of its misery.

She turned around to see that Ram was rushing towards her, his sword held to the side.

'I'm all right!' she reassured him.

He nodded and headed towards Makrant as Sita also ran to the injured Malayaputra. Ram hastily tied the soldier's *angvastram* around the injury, barely staunching the blood that continued to gush out. He quickly came to his feet and picked up Makrant.

'We have to get back to the camp right away!' Ram said.

— |大| 🐟 ☼ —

The wild boar's tusk had cut through his upper quadriceps, piercing the femoral artery. Fortunately, the tusk had come into contact with the hard pelvic bone, flinging him off as the beast's jangled nerves made it shake its head on impact. This had probably saved his life, for if the tusk had pushed through and penetrated deeper, it would have ruptured his intestines. The resultant infection would have been impossible to treat in the jungle; it would have meant certain death. The man had lost a lot of blood, though, and was not yet out of danger.

Ram, mindful that Makrant had unselfishly risked his life to save his wife, worked tirelessly to nurse the soldier back to health, ably assisted by Sita. For Ram, it was the most natural thing to do. But it surprised the Malayaputras to see a Sapt Sindhu royal willingly doing work that was not, customarily, his domain.

'He is a good man,' said Jatayu.

Jatayu and two Malayaputra soldiers were outside the camp's main tent, cooking the evening meal.

'I'm surprised that, despite being a prince, he is willing to do the work that mere soldiers and medical assistants should be doing,' said one of the Malayaputras, stirring the contents of a pot on a low flame.

'I have always found him impressive,' said the other soldier, chopping some herbs on a wooden block. 'He has absolutely no airs, unlike the other royal Sapt Sindhu brats.'

'Hmm,' said Jatayu. 'I have also heard how he effectively saved Makrant's life by acting quickly. If he had not killed the boar immediately, it could have gored Makrant again, possibly killing him, apart from harming Lady Sita as well.'

'He's always been a great warrior. We have seen and heard enough instances of that,' said the second soldier. 'But he is also a good man.'

'Yes, he treats his wife well. He is calm and clear-headed. He leads well. He is a good warrior. But most importantly, it is clear that he has a heart of gold,' said the first Malayaputra soldier, full of praise. 'I think Guru Vashishta probably chose well.'

Jatayu glared at the soldier, almost daring him to say another word. The poor man knew that he had gone too far. He immediately fell silent as he shifted his attention to the task of stirring the pot.

Jatayu understood that he could not afford any doubts among his men regarding this issue. Their loyalty was to lie exclusively with the Malayaputra goal. 'No matter how trustworthy Prince Ram may appear, always remember, we are the followers of Guru Vishwamitra. We have to do what he has ordered us to do. He is our chief and he knows best.'

The two Malayaputra soldiers nodded.

'Of course, we can trust him,' said Jatayu. 'And it is good that he also appears to trust us now. But do not forget where our loyalties lie. Is that clear?'

'Yes, Captain,' said both the soldiers simultaneously.

—— 大 ● ☀ ——

Six years had lapsed since Ram, Sita and Lakshman had left Ayodhya.

The band of nineteen had finally settled along the western banks of the early course of the mighty Godavari River, at *Panchavati,* or the *place with five banyan trees.* The river provided natural protection to the small, rustic, yet comfortable camp. The main mud hut at the centre of the camp had two rooms—one for Ram and Sita, and the other for Lakshman—and an open clearing for exercise and assembly. A rudimentary alarm system had been set around the far perimeter as warning against wild animals.

The perimeter of this camp was made of two circular fences. The one on the outside was covered with poisonous creepers to keep animals out. The fence on the inside comprised nagavalli creepers, rigged with an alarm system consisting of a continuous string that ran all the way to a very large wooden cage, filled with birds. The birds were well looked after, and replaced every month with new ones that were caught, as the old ones were released. If anyone made it past the outer fence and attempted to enter the nagavalli hedge, the alarm system would trigger the opening of the birdcage roof. The noisy flutter of the escaping birds would offer a few precious minutes of warning to the inmates of the camp.

Another cluster of huts to the east housed Jatayu and his band of soldiers. Despite Ram's trust in Jatayu, Lakshman remained suspicious of the Malayaputra. Like most Indians, he held strong superstitions about the Nagas. He simply could not bring himself to trust the 'vulture-man', the name Lakshman had given to Jatayu behind his back.

They had faced dangers, no doubt, in these six years, but these had not been due to any human intervention. The occasional scars served as reminders of their adventures in the jungle, but the Somras had ensured that they looked and felt as young as the day they had left Ayodhya. Exposure to the harsh sun had darkened their skin. Ram had always been dark-skinned, but even the fair-skinned Sita and Lakshman had acquired a dusky appearance. Ram and Lakshman had grown beards and moustaches, making them look like warrior-sages.

Life had fallen into a predictable pattern. Ram and Sita liked to go to the Godavari River in the early morning hours, to bathe and spend some private time together. It was their favourite time of the day.

This was one such day. They washed their hair in the clear waters of the Godavari, and then sat on the banks of the river, indulging themselves with conversation over an array of fresh berries, as they dried their hair in the early morning breeze. Ram combed Sita's hair and braided it. Sita then moved behind her husband and ran her fingers through his half-dry hair, untangling the strands.

'Ouch!' protested Ram, as his head was jerked back.

'Sorry,' said Sita.

Ram smiled.

'What are you thinking?' asked Sita, as she gingerly untangled another knot.

'Well, they say the jungles are dangerous and it is the cities where you find comfort and security. It has been exactly the other way round for me. I have never been more relaxed and happy in my life than in the *Dandakaranya*.'

Sita murmured in agreement.

Ram turned his head to look at his wife. 'I know that you suffered, too, in the world of the "civilised"…'

'Yeah, well,' said Sita, shrugging. 'They say it takes immense pressure to create diamonds.'

Ram laughed softly. 'You know, Guru Vashishta had said to me, when I was a child, that compassion is sometimes an overrated virtue. He told me the story of the butterfly emerging from the hard pupa. Its life begins as an "ugly" caterpillar. When the time is right, it forms a pupa and retreats behind its hard walls. Within its shell, it transforms into a butterfly, unseen, unheard. When ready, it uses its tiny, sharp claws at the base of its forewings to crack a small opening in the hard, protective outer shell. It squeezes through this tiny opening and struggles to make its way out. This is a difficult, painful and prolonged process. Misguided compassion may make us want to enlarge the hole in the pupa, imagining that it would ease the butterfly's task. But that struggle is necessary; as the butterfly squeezes its body out of the tiny hole, it secretes fluids within its swollen body. This fluid goes to its wings, strengthening them; once they've emerged, as the fluid dries, the delicate creatures are able to take flight. Making the hole bigger to "help" the butterfly and ease its struggle will only debilitate it. Without the struggle, its wings would never gain strength. It would never fly.'

Sita nodded and smiled. 'I was told a different story. Of small birds being pushed out of their nests by their parents so that they are forced to fly. But yes, the point was the same.'

Ram smiled. 'Well, wife! This struggle has made us stronger.'

Sita picked up the wooden comb and began running it through Ram's hair.

'Who told you about the little birds? Your guru?' asked Ram.

Since Ram was looking ahead, he didn't see the split-second of hesitation that flitted across her face. 'I've learnt from many people, Ram. But none was as great as your guru, Vashishta*ji*.'

Ram smiled. 'I was lucky to have him as my guru.'

'Yes, you were. He has trained you well. You will be a good Vishnu.'

Ram felt a flush of embarrassment. While he was certainly willing to shoulder any responsibility for the sake of his people, the great title that Vashishta felt certain Ram would achieve left him humbled. He doubted his capability, and wondered if he was even ready for it. He had shared these doubts with his wife.

'You will be ready,' said Sita, smiling, almost reading her husband's mind. 'Trust me. You don't know how rare a person you are.'

Ram turned to Sita and touched her cheek gently as he looked deep into her eyes. He smiled faintly as he turned his attention back to the river. She tied a knot on top of his head, the way he always liked it, then wrapped threaded beads around the knot to hold it in place. 'Done!'

Chapter 30

Ram and Sita had returned from a hunt with the body of a deer tied to a long wooden pole. They balanced the pole on their shoulders. Lakshman had stayed behind, it being his turn to cook. They had lived outside the Sapt Sindhu for thirteen years now.

'Just one more year, Ram,' said Sita, as the pair walked into the compound of their camp.

'Yes,' said Ram. They set down the pole. 'That's when our real battle begins.'

Lakshman walked up as he unsheathed a long knife from the scabbard tied horizontally across the small of his back. 'The two of you can begin your philosophy and strategy discussions while I attend to some womanly chores!'

Sita gently tapped Lakshman on his cheek. 'Men are also counted among the best chefs in India, so what's so womanly about cooking? Everyone should be able to cook!'

Lakshman bowed theatrically, laughing. 'Yeesssss, *Bhabhi*!'

Ram and Sita laughed as well.

—— 𑀦 𑀲 ☼ ——

'The sky is beautiful this evening, isn't it?' remarked Sita, admiring the handiwork of *Dhyauspita*, the *Sky Father*. Ram and Sita lay on the floor outside the main hut.

It was the fifth hour of the third *prahar*. The chariot of *Surya*, the Sun God, had left a trail of vivid colours behind as he blazed though the sky. A cool evening breeze blew in from the west, giving respite at the end of an unseasonal, oppressively hot day. The monsoon months had ended, heralding the beginning of winter.

'Yes,' smiled Ram, as he reached for her hand, pulled it close to his lips and kissed her fingers, gently.

Sita turned towards Ram and smiled. 'What's on your mind, husband?'

'Very husbandly things, wife…'

A loud clearing of the throat was heard. Sita and Ram looked up to find an amused Lakshman standing before them. They stared at him with mock irritation.

'What?' shrugged Lakshman. 'You're blocking the entry into the hut. I need my sword. I have to go for a practice session with Atulya.'

Ram shifted to the right and made room for Lakshman. Lakshman walked in. 'I'll be gone soon…'

No sooner had he stepped into the hut than he stopped in his tracks. The flock of birds in the cage linked to the alarm had suddenly fluttered noisily. Lakshman whirled around as Ram and Sita sprang to their feet.

'What was that?' asked Lakshman.

Ram's instincts told him that the intruders were not animals.

'Weapons,' ordered Ram calmly.

Sita and Lakshman tied their sword scabbards around their waist. Lakshman handed Ram his bow, before picking up his own. The brothers quickly strung their bows. Jatayu and his men rushed in, armed and ready, just as Ram and Lakshman tied quivers full of arrows to their backs. Sita picked up a long spear, as Ram tied his sword scabbard to his waist. They already wore a smaller knife scabbard, tied horizontally across the small of their backs; a weapon they kept on their person at all times.

'Who could they be?' asked Jatayu.

'I don't know,' said Ram.

'Lakshman's Wall?' asked Sita.

Lakshman's Wall was an ingenious defensive feature designed by him to the east of the main hut. It was five feet in height; it covered three sides of a small square completely, leaving the inner side facing the main hut partially open; like a cubicle. The entire structure gave the impression that it was an enclosed kitchen. In actual fact, the cubicle was bare, providing adequate mobility to warriors — though they would have to be on their knees — unseen by enemies on the other side of the wall. A small *tandoor*, a *cooking platform*, emerged on the outside from the south-facing wall. Half the enclosure was roof-covered, completing the camouflage of a cooking area; it afforded protection from enemy arrows. The south, east and north-facing walls were drilled with well-spaced holes. These holes were narrow on the inner side and broad on the outer side, giving the impression of ventilation required for cooking. Their actual purpose was to give those on the inside a good view of the approaching enemy, while preventing those on the outside from looking in. The holes could also be used to fire arrows.

Made from mud, it was not strong enough to withstand a sustained assault by a large force. Having said that, it was good enough for defence against small bands sent on assassination bids, which is what Lakshman suspected they would face. Designed by Lakshman, it had been built by everyone in the camp; Makrant had named it 'Lakshman's Wall'.

'Yes,' said Ram.

Everyone rushed to the wall and crouched low, keeping their weapons ready; they waited.

Lakshman hunched over and peeped through a hole in the south-facing wall. As he strained his eye, he detected a small band of ten people marching into the camp premises, led by a man and a woman.

The man in the lead was of average height and unusually fair-skinned. His reed-thin physique was that of a runner; this man was no warrior. Despite his frail shoulders and thin arms, he walked as if he had boils in his armpits, pretending to accommodate impressive biceps. Like most Indian men, he had long, jet black hair that was tied in a knot at the back of his head. His full beard was neatly-trimmed, interestingly coloured a deep brown. He wore a classic brown *dhoti* and an *angvastram* that was a shade lighter. His jewellery was rich but understated: pearl ear studs and a thin, copper bracelet. He looked dishevelled right now, as though he had been on the road for too long, without a change of clothes.

The woman beside him faintly resembled the man, but was bewitching; she was possibly his sister. Almost as short as Urmila, her skin was as white as snow; it should have made her look pale and sickly, instead, she was distractingly beautiful. Her sharp, slightly upturned nose and high cheekbones made her look like a Parihan. Unlike them, though, her hair was blonde, a most unusual colour; every strand of it was in place. Her eyes were magnetic. Perhaps she was the child of *Hiranyaloman Mlechchas; fair-skinned, light-eyed and light-haired foreigners who lived half a world away towards the north-west;* their violent ways and incomprehensible speech had led to the Indians calling them barbarians. But this lady was no barbarian. Quite the contrary, she was elegant, slim and petite, except for breasts that were disproportionately large for her body. She wore a classic, expensively-dyed purple *dhoti,* which shone like the waters of the Sarayu. Perhaps it was the legendary silk cloth from the east, one that only the richest could afford. The *dhoti* was tied fashionably low, exposing her flat tummy and slim, curvaceous waist. Her blouse, also made of silk, was a tiny sliver of cloth, affording a generous view of her cleavage. Her *angvastram* had deliberately been left hanging loose from a shoulder, instead of across the body. Extravagant jewellery completed the picture of excess. The only incongruity was the knife scabbard tied to her waist. She was a vision to behold.

Ram cast a quick glance at Sita. 'Who are they?'

Sita shrugged.

'Lankans,' whispered Jatayu.

Ram turned to Jatayu, crouching a few feet away. 'Are you sure?'

'Yes. The man is Raavan's younger half-brother Vibhishan, and the woman is his half-sister Shurpanakha.'

'What are they doing here?' asked Sita.

Atulya had been observing the approaching party through a hole in the wall. He turned towards Ram. 'I don't think they have come to make war. Look...' He gestured towards the hole.

Everyone looked through the peepholes. A soldier next to Vibhishan held aloft a white flag, the colour of peace. They obviously wanted to parley. The mystery was: what did they want to talk about?

'Why the hell would Raavan want to speak with us?' asked Lakshman, ever suspicious.

'According to my sources, Vibhishan and Shurpanakha don't always see eye to eye with Raavan,' said Jatayu. 'We shouldn't assume that Raavan has sent them.'

Atulya cut in. 'Apologies for disagreeing with you, Jatayu*ji*. But I cannot imagine Prince Vibhishan or Princess Shurpanakha having the courage to do something like this on their own. We must assume that they have been sent by Lord Raavan.'

'Time to stop wondering and start asking some questions,' said Lakshman. '*Dada?*'

Ram looked through the hole again, and then turned towards his people. 'We will all step out together. It will stop them from attempting something stupid.'

'That is wise,' said Jatayu.

'Come on,' said Ram, as he stepped out from behind the protective wall with his right hand raised, signifying that he meant no harm. Everyone else followed Ram's example and trooped out to meet the half-siblings of Raavan.

Vibhishan nervously stopped in his tracks the moment his eyes fell on Ram, Sita, Lakshman, and their soldiers. He looked sideways at his sister, as if uncertain as to the next course of action. But Shurpanakha had eyes only for Ram. She stared at him, unashamedly. A look of recognition flashed across a surprised Vibhishan's face when he saw Jatayu.

Ram, Lakshman and Sita walked in the lead, with Jatayu and his soldiers following close behind. As the forest-dwellers reached the Lankans, Vibhishan straightened his back, puffed up his chest, and spoke with an air of self-importance. 'We come in peace, King of Ayodhya.'

'We want peace as well,' said Ram, lowering his right hand. His people did the same. He made no comment on the 'King of Ayodhya' greeting. 'What brings you here, Prince of Lanka?'

Vibhishan preened at being recognised. 'It seems Sapt Sindhuans are not as ignorant of the world as many of us like to imagine.'

Ram smiled politely. Meanwhile, Shurpanakha pulled out a small violet kerchief and covered her nose delicately.

'Well, even I respect and understand the ways of the Sapt Sindhuans,' said Vibhishan.

Sita watched Shurpanakha, hawk-eyed, as the lady continued to stare at her husband unabashedly. Up close, it was clear that the magic of Shurpanakha's eyes lay in their startling colour: bright blue. She almost certainly had some *Hiranyaloman Mlechcha* blood. Practically nobody, east of Egypt, had blue eyes. She was bathed in fragrant perfume that overpowered the rustic, animal smell of the Panchavati camp; at least for those in her vicinity. Not overpowering enough for her, evidently. She continued to hold the stench of her surroundings at bay, with the kerchief pressed against her nose.

'Would you like to come inside, to our humble abode?' asked Ram, gesturing towards the hut.

'No, thank you, Your Highness,' said Vibhishan. 'I'm comfortable here.'

Jatayu's presence had thrown him off-guard. Vibhishan was unwilling to encounter other surprises that may lay in store for them, within the closed confines of the hut, before they had come to some negotiated terms. He *was* the brother of the enemy of the Sapt Sindhu, after all. It was safer here, out in the open; for now.

'All right then,' said Ram. 'To what do we owe the honour of a visit from the prince of golden Lanka?'

Shurpanakha spoke in a husky, alluring voice. 'Handsome one, we come to seek refuge.'

'I'm not sure I understand,' said Ram, momentarily flummoxed by the allusion to his good looks by a woman he did not know. 'I don't think we are capable of helping the relatives of…'

'Who else can we go to, O Great One?' asked Vibhishan. 'We will never be accepted in the Sapt Sindhu because we are Raavan's siblings. But we also know that there are many in the Sapt Sindhu who will not deny you. My sister and I have suffered Raavan's brutal oppression for too long. We needed to escape.'

Ram remained silent, contemplative.

'King of Ayodhya,' continued Vibhishan, 'I may be from Lanka but I am, in fact, like one of your own. I honour your ways, follow your path. I'm not like the other Lankans, blinded by Raavan's immense wealth into following his demonic path. And Shurpanakha is just like me. Don't you think you have a duty towards us, too?'

Sita cut in. 'An ancient poet once remarked, "When the axe entered the forest, the trees said to each other: do not worry, the handle in that axe is one of us".'

Shurpanakha sniggered. 'So the great descendant of Raghu lets his wife make decisions for him, is it?'

Vibhishan touched Shurpanakha's hand lightly and she fell silent. 'Queen Sita,' said Vibhishan, 'you will notice that only the handles have come here. The axe-head is in Lanka. We are truly like you. Please help us.'

Shurpanakha turned to Jatayu. It had not escaped her notice that, as usual, every man was gaping intently at her; every man, that is, except Ram and Lakshman. 'Great Malayaputra, don't you think it is in your interest to give us refuge? We could tell you more about Lanka than you already know. There will be more gold in it for you.'

Jatayu stiffened. 'We are the followers of Lord Parshu Ram! We are not interested in gold.'

'Right...' said Shurpanakha, sarcastically.

Vibhishan appealed to Lakshman. 'Wise Lakshman, please convince your brother. I'm sure you will agree with me when I say that we can be of use to you in your fight when you get back.'

'I could agree with you, Prince of Lanka,' said Lakshman, smiling, 'but then we would both be wrong.'

Vibhishan looked down and sighed.

'Prince Vibhishan,' said Ram, 'I am truly sorry but—'

Vibhishan interrupted Ram. 'Son of Dashrath, remember the battle of Mithila. My brother Raavan is your enemy. He is my enemy as well. Shouldn't that make you my friend?'

Ram kept quiet.

'Great King, we have put our lives at risk by escaping from Lanka. Can't you let us be your guests for a while? We will leave in a few days. Remember what the *Taitreya Upanishad* says: *"Athithi Devo Bhava"*. Even the many *Smritis* say that the strong should protect the weak. All we are asking for is shelter for a few days. Please.'

Sita looked at Ram. A law had been invoked. She knew what was going to happen next. She knew Ram would not turn them away now.

'Just a few days,' pleaded Vibhishan. 'Please.'

Ram touched Vibhishan's shoulder. 'You can stay here for a few days; rest for a while, and then continue on your journey.'

Vibhishan folded his hands together into a namaste and said, 'Glory to the great clan of Raghu.'

—— |大| 🐟 ☼ ——

'I think that spoilt princess fancies you,' said Sita.

Ram and Sita sat alone in their room in the second hour of the fourth *prahar*, having just finished their evening meal. Shurpanakha had complained bitterly about the food that Sita had cooked that day. Sita had told her to remain hungry if the food was not to her liking.

Ram shook his head, his eyes clearly conveying he thought this was silly. 'How can she, Sita? She knows I'm married. Why should she find me attractive?'

Sita lay down next to her husband on the bed of hay. 'You should know that you are more attractive than you realise.'

Ram frowned and laughed. 'Nonsense.'

Sita laughed as well and put her arms around him.

The guests had been staying in Panchavati with the forest-dwellers for a week now. They had not been troublesome at all, except for the Lankan princess. However, Lakshman and Jatayu remained suspicious of the Lankans. They had disarmed the visitors on the first day itself, and locked up their weapons in the camp armoury. They also maintained a strict but discreet and staggered twenty-four-hour vigil, keeping a constant watch on the guests.

Having stayed awake the previous night with his sword and warning conch shell ready by his side, a tired Lakshman had slept through the morning. He awoke in the afternoon to observe unusual activity in the camp.

As he stepped out of the hut, he came upon Jatayu and the Malayaputras emerging from the armoury with the Lankan weapons. Vibhishan and his party were ready to leave. Having collected their weaponry, they waited for Shurpanakha, who had gone to the Godavari to bathe and get ready. She had requested Sita to accompany her, for help with her clothes and hair. Sita was happy to finally be rid of the troublesome diva whose demands in this simple jungle camp were never-ending. She had readily agreed to this last request.

'Thank you for all your help, Prince Ram,' said Vibhishan.

'It was our pleasure.'

'And may I request you and your followers to not reveal to anyone where we are headed?'

'Of course.'

'Thank you,' said Vibhishan, folding his hands into a namaste.

Ram looked towards the dense forest line, beyond which lay the Godavari. He expected his wife Sita and Vibhishan's sister Shurpanakha to emerge from that direction any moment now.

Instead, a loud female scream emanated from the forest. Ram and Lakshman cast a quick glance at each other and then moved rapidly in the direction of the sound. They came to a standstill as Sita emerged from the woods, tall, regal but dripping wet and furious. She dragged a struggling Shurpanakha mercilessly by her arm. The Lankan princess' hands had been securely tied.

Lakshman immediately drew his sword, as did everyone else present. The younger prince of Ayodhya was the first to find his voice. Looking at Vibhishan accusingly, he demanded, 'What the hell is going on?'

Vibhishan couldn't take his eyes off the two women. He seemed genuinely shocked for a moment, but quickly gathered his wits and replied. 'What is your sister-in-law doing to my sister? She is the one who has clearly attacked Shurpanakha.'

'Stop this drama!' shouted Lakshman. '*Bhabhi* would not do this unless your sister attacked her first.'

Sita walked into the circle of people and let go of Shurpanakha. The Lankan princess was clearly livid and out of control. Vibhishan immediately rushed to his sister, drew a knife and cut the ropes that bound her. He whispered something into her ear. Lakshman couldn't be sure what Vibhishan said, but it sounded like 'Quiet'.

Sita turned to Ram and gestured towards Shurpanakha, as she held out some herbs in the palm of her hand. 'That pipsqueak Lankan stuffed this in my mouth as she pushed me into the river!'

Ram recognised the herbs. It was normally used to make people unconscious before conducting surgeries. He looked at Vibhishan, his piercing eyes red with anger. 'What is going on?'

Vibhishan stood up immediately, his manner placatory. 'There has obviously been some misunderstanding. My sister would never do something like that.'

'Are you suggesting that I imagined her pushing me into the water?' asked Sita, aggressively.

Vibhishan stared at Shurpanakha, who had also stood up by now. He seemed to be pleading with her to stay quiet. But the message was clearly lost on the intended recipient.

'That is a lie!' screeched Shurpanakha. 'I didn't do anything like that!'

'Are you calling me a liar?' growled Sita.

What happened next was so sudden that very few had the time to react. With frightening speed, Shurpanakha reached to her side and drew her knife. Lakshman, who was standing to the left of Sita, saw the quick movement and rushed forward, screaming, '*Bhabhi!*'

Sita quickly moved in the opposite direction to avoid the strike. In that split second, Lakshman lunged forward and banged into a charging Shurpanakha, seizing both her arms and pushing her back with all his force. The elfin princess of Lanka went flying backwards, her own hand, which held the knife, striking her face as she crashed into the Lankan soldiers who stood transfixed behind her. The knife struck her face horizontally, cutting deep into her nose. It fell from her hand as she lay sprawled on the ground, the shock having numbed any sensation of pain. As blood gushed out alarmingly, her conscious mind asserted control and the horror of it all reverberated through her being. She touched her face and looked at her blood-stained hands. She knew she would be left with deep scars on her face. And that painful surgeries would be required to remove them.

She screeched with savage hate and lunged forward again, this time going for Lakshman. Vibhishan rushed to her and caught hold of his maddened sister.

'Kill them!' screamed Shurpanakha in agony. 'Kill them all!'

'Wait!' pleaded Vibhishan, stricken with visceral fear. He knew they were outnumbered. He didn't want to die. And he feared something even worse than death. 'Wait!'

Ram held up his left hand, his fist closed tight, signalling his people to stop but be on guard. 'Leave now, prince. Or there will be hell to pay.'

'Forget what we were told!' screeched Shurpanakha. 'Kill them all!'

Ram spoke to a clearly stunned Vibhishan, who held on to a struggling Shurpanakha for all he was worth. 'Leave now, Prince Vibhishan.'

'Retreat,' whispered Vibhishan.

His soldiers began stepping back, their swords still pointed in the direction of the forest-dwellers.

'Kill them, you coward!' Shurpanakha lashed out at her brother. 'I am your sister! Avenge me!'

Vibhishan dragged a flailing Shurpanakha, his eye on Ram, mindful of any sudden movement.

'Kill them!' shouted Shurpanakha.

Vibhishan continued to pull his protesting sister away as the Lankans left the camp and escaped from Panchavati.

Ram, Lakshman and Sita stood rooted to their spot. What had happened was an unmitigated disaster.

'We cannot stay here anymore,' Jatayu stated the obvious. 'We don't have a choice. We need to flee, *now*.'

Ram looked at Jatayu.

'We have shed Lankan royal blood, even if it is that of the royal rebels,' said Jatayu. 'According to their customary law, Raavan has no choice but to respond. It would be the same among many Sapt Sindhu royals as well, isn't it? Raavan will come. Have no doubt about that. Vibhishan is a coward, but Raavan and Kumbhakarna aren't. They will come with thousands of soldiers. This will be worse than Mithila. There it was a battle between soldiers; a part and parcel of war; they understood that. But here it is personal. His sister, a member of his family, has been attacked. Blood was shed. His honour will demand retribution.'

Lakshman stiffened. 'But I didn't attack her. She—'

'That's not how Raavan will see it,' interrupted Jatayu. 'He will not quibble with you over the details, Prince Lakshman. We need to run. Right now.'

— 衤 🐟 ☼ —

Around thirty warriors sat together in a small clearing in the forest, briskly shovelling food into their mouths. They appeared to be in a tearing hurry. All of them were dressed alike: a long brownish-black cloak covered their bodies, held together across the waist by a thick cord. The cloaks could not conceal the fact that each carried a sword. The men were all unnaturally fair-skinned, an unusual sight in the hot plains of India. Their hooked noses, neatly beaded full beards, sharp foreheads, lengthy locks emerging from under square white hats, and drooping moustaches made it clear who these people were: Parihans.

Pariha was a fabled land beyond the western borders of India. It was the land that was home to the previous Mahadev, Lord Rudra.

The most intriguing member of this motley group was its leader, clearly a Naga. He too was fair-skinned, just like the Parihans. But in every other respect, he stood apart from them. He was not dressed like them. He was, in fact, dressed like an Indian: in a *dhoti* and *angvastram*, both dyed saffron. An outgrowth jutted out from his lower back, almost like a tail. It flapped in constant rhythm, as though it had a mind of its own. The hirsute Naga leader of the Parihans was very tall. His massive build and sturdy musculature gave him an awe-inspiring presence and a godly aura. He could probably break an unfortunate's back with his bare hands. Unlike most Nagas, he did not cover his face with a mask or his body with a hooded robe.

'We have to move quickly,' said the leader.

His nose was flat, pressed against his face. His beard and facial hair surrounded the periphery of his face, encircling it with neat precision. Strangely though, the area above and below his mouth was silken smooth and hairless; it had a puffed appearance and was light pink in colour. His lips were a thin, barely noticeable line. Thick eyebrows drew a sharp curve above captivating eyes that radiated intelligence and a meditative calm; they also held a promise of brutal violence, if required. His furrowed brow gave him a naturally intellectual air. It almost seemed like the Almighty had taken the face of a monkey and placed it on a man's head.

'Yes, My Lord,' said a Parihan. 'If you could give us a few minutes more... The men have been marching continuously and some rest will...'

'There is no time for rest!' growled the leader. 'I have given my word to Guru Vashishta! Raavan cannot be allowed to reach them before we do! We need to find them now! Tell the men to hurry!'

The Parihan rushed off to carry out the orders. Another Parihan, who had finished his meal, walked up to the Naga. 'My Lord, the men need to know: Who is the primary person?'

The leader didn't hesitate even for a second. 'Both. They are both vital. Princess Sita is important to the Malayaputras, and Prince Ram is to us.'

'Yes, Lord Hanuman.'

— 🜉 🐟 ☼ —

They had been on the run for thirty days. Racing east through the *Dandakaranya*, they had moved a reasonable distance parallel to the Godavari, so that they couldn't be easily spotted or tracked. But they couldn't afford to stray too far from the tributary rivers or other water bodies, for the best chance of hunting animals would be lost.

Ram and Lakshman had just hunted a deer and were making their way back to the temporary camp through the dense jungle. They carried a long staff between them, Ram in front, carrying one end on his shoulder, and Lakshman behind, balancing the other. The deer's body dangled from the wooden pole.

Lakshman was arguing with Ram. 'But why do you think it's irrational to think Bharat *Dada* could...'

'Shhh,' said Ram, holding his hand up to silence Lakshman. 'Listen.'

Lakshman strained his ears. A chill ran down his spine. Ram turned towards Lakshman with terror writ large on his face. They had both heard it. *A forceful scream!* It was Sita. The distance made faint her frantic struggle. But it was clearly Sita. She was calling out to her husband.

Ram and Lakshman dropped the deer and dashed forward desperately. They were still some distance away from their temporary camp.

Sita's voice could be heard above the din of the disturbed birds.

'… Raaam!'

They were close enough now to hear the sounds of battle as metal clashed with metal.

Ram screamed as he ran frantically through the forest. 'Sitaaaa!'

Lakshman drew his sword, ready for battle.

'… Raaaam!'

'Leave her alone!' shouted Ram, cutting through the dense foliage, racing ahead.

'… Raaam!'

Ram gripped his bow tight. They were just a few minutes from their camp. 'Sitaaa!'

'… Raa…'

Sita's voice stopped mid-syllable. Trying not to imagine the worst, Ram kept running, his heart pounding desperately, his mind clouded with worry.

They heard the loud whump, whump of rotor blades. It was Raavan's legendary *Pushpak Vimaan*, his *flying vehicle*.

'Nooo!' screamed Ram, wrenching his bow forward as he ran. Tears were streaming down his face.

The brothers broke through to the clearing that was their temporary camp. It stood completely destroyed. There was blood everywhere.

'Sitaaa!'

Ram looked up and shot an arrow at the *Pushpak Vimaan*, which was rapidly ascending into the sky. It was a shot of impotent rage, for the flying vehicle was already soaring high above.

'Sitaaa!'

Lakshman frantically searched the camp. Bodies of dead soldiers were strewn all over. But there was no Sita.

'Pri... nce... Ram...'

Ram recognised that feeble voice. He rushed forward to find the bloodied and mutilated body of the Naga.

'Jatayu!'

The badly wounded Jatayu struggled to speak. 'He's...'

'What?'

'Raavan's... kidnapped... her.'

Ram looked up enraged at the speck moving rapidly away from them. He screamed in anger, 'SITAAAA!'

'Prince...'

Jatayu could feel life slipping away. Using his last reserves of will, he raised his body, reached his hand out and pulled Ram towards him.

With his dying breaths, Jatayu whispered, 'Get ... her back ... I ... failed... She's important ... Lady Sita ... must be saved ... Lady Sita ... must be saved ... Vishnu ... Lady Sita ...'

... to be continued

ALSO BY AMISH

The Shiva Trilogy

The Shiva Trilogy is the story of a simple man whose karma recast him as our Mahadev, the God of Gods.

1900 BC. In what modern Indians mistakenly call the Indus Valley Civilization. The inhabitants of that period call it Meluha — a near perfect empire created centuries earlier by Lord Ram. Her emperor, Daksha, sends emissaries across the world to ask different tribes to immigrate to Meluha. Among these tribes are the Gunas from Tibet, and their chief Shiva, is a mighty warrior. He moves to Meluha and in a curious occurrence that sees him alone of all his tribe unaffected by a high fever, Shiva's throat turns blue. Even more surprisingly, the highly advanced Meluhans announce him as the Neelkanth, their fabled mythic savior. One who will save the empire from her enemies, the Chandravanshis and the Nagas. And thus begins Shiva's journey.

Drawn suddenly to his destiny, by duty as well as by love, will Shiva lead the Meluhan vengeance and destroy Evil? What will be the real cost of battling Evil? And will he accept the title given to him, that of the 'God of Gods'?

The Shiva Trilogy — comprising *The Immortals of Meluha*, *The Secret of the Nagas*, and *The Oath of the Vayuputras* — has attracted a wide and devoted audience. Over two million copies of the books have been sold.

Visit www.authoramish.com to know more about the world of Amish's books.

Visit authoramish.com/promotions for special offers.

Other Titles by Amish
<u>Shiva Trilogy</u>

<u>Ram Chandra Series</u>